From New York T[...] *author* Thea Harri[...] *spellbinding Moonshadow trilogy…*

King Oberon reigned over his Dark Court in Lyonesse for centuries until an assassination attempt laid him low. Now he lies unconscious in his snow-bound palace while his Power battles the enchantment that threatens to end his life.

A skilled trauma surgeon and magic user, Dr. Kathryn Shaw reigns at the top of her profession in New York. Then comes a challenge she can't resist—she is asked to cure the incurable. Just getting close enough to try healing Oberon is a dangerous proposition. When she does reach him, he awakens too soon.

Roused from darkness by Kathryn's presence, Oberon confronts the beautiful stranger who claims she wants to save his life. But the enchantment has frozen his emotions. How can he learn to trust her when he can't feel anything?

Oberon's desire is icy, devoid of all tenderness. Not only must Kathryn match wits with him, she must also fight her reaction to his touch, because there is so much more at stake than her own endangered heart.

For the Dark Court faces its most deadly peril yet. Its ancient enemy Isabeau, Queen of the Light Court, is obsessed with its annihilation, and Oberon must be brought to remember his loyalty and affection for his people.

Because if he won't fight for them, Lyonesse itself may very well be destroyed…

Lionheart

Thea Harrison

Lionheart

Copyright © 2018 by Teddy Harrison LLC
ISBN 13: 978-1-947046-10-8
Print Edition

Cover design by Gene Mollica

Praise for Moonshadow

"*Moonshadow* is exactly what I expect of a Thea Harrison story, a stay-up-all-night read. Marvelous characters, lots of action and romance, and just the right touch of humor. This one goes on my keeper shelf. I loved this book."

~ Patricia Briggs—#1 *New York Times* bestselling author of the Mercy Thompson series

"*Moonshadow* hits all the right checkmarks on my must-have paranormal romance list: an Alpha hero, a heroine who kicks butt, worldbuilding that just keeps getting better, and a steamy plot that pulls me in from the first page!"

~ Carrie Ann Ryan—*NYT* Bestselling Author of *Wolf Betrayed*

"I loved this book. *Moonshadow* is Thea Harrison at her finest. I haven't been this excited since *Dragon Bound*!"

~ Kristen Callihan—*USA Today* bestselling author

"A brilliant new chapter in an enthralling saga! *Moonshadow* kicks off a new trilogy in Thea Harrison's fantastic *Elder Races* series. With a compelling heroine entering this world, this is a perfect place for readers to step into the ongoing story. The hero is intense, the heroine clever, and the sexual tension sizzling. Can't wait to find out what happens next!"

~ Jeffe Kennedy, Award Winning Author of *The Twelve Kingdoms* and *The Uncharted Realms*

"I'm already addicted to Thea Harrison's new world of Arthurian alpha warriors—especially after an American kick-ass heroine with serious magic powers teaches them a lesson about 21st century women!"

~ Eloisa James, *New York Times* bestselling author of *When Beauty Tamed the Beast*

"Scorching chemistry, perfect pacing & memorable characters sent me on a roller coaster ride of emotions! I want to live in the Moonshadow world."

~ Katie Reus, *New York Times* bestselling author of *Breaking Her Rules*

"*Moonshadow* is a beautiful book and exactly what I needed— hot romance, wild sex and a happy ending. Please don't miss anything written by Thea Harrison. She is a wonder."

~ Ann Aguirre, *New York Times* bestselling author

"Thrilling and deliciously sexy, *Moonshadow* is a smart, action-packed introduction to a new adventure in Harrison's complex and compelling Elder Races world. Intrigue goes hand-in-hand with an addictive romance that will please new and established readers alike. I can't wait to see what comes next."

~ Elizabeth Hunter, bestselling author of the Elemental Mysteries series

"A breathless, rollercoaster ride of a tale, complete with a fierce, capable heroine and a powerful hero worthy of her in every way. The bonds of love, trust, and friendship are stretched and sometimes snapped in a war of attrition that crosses time and worlds. Thea Harrison blows the doors off with some rollicking good storytelling in *Moonshadow*."

~ Grace Draven – *USA Today* bestselling author of *Radiance*

Chapter One

London, 1811

THE ATTACK HAPPENED at one of those bloody masques King Oberon and his Dark Court had once been so fond of hosting.

Those of the Elder Races—along with a select few humans chosen for their Power and political influence—traveled from around the world to attend Oberon's masques, and all England knew that whatever the weather, snow always fell in the Vauxhall Pleasure Gardens on the winter solstice.

The guests were treated to a lavish array of exotic foods and mulled wine, magic, and mystery, all served by attendants dressed in spotless, intricately embroidered white uniforms. Intrigues always occurred along with intimate conversations amid the entertainment. Illicit affairs were pursued in the shadows. Treaties were born and sometimes broken, and there was always the opportunity to forge new alliances.

But mostly the annual festival was Oberon's way of saying *fuck you* to his greatest enemy, Isabeau and her Light Court. The richness of the revelry, the contrived excess—it all said, we dance in spite of you. We thrive.

Until at one masque, Oberon stood watching a swirl of costumed dancers. As he cast a silent spell, large flakes of clear ice drifted down from a cloudless midnight sky as if the frozen stars themselves fell to earth.

The flakes reflected pagan color from nearby bonfires until the air glittered with brilliant gold and piercing light. All dancers came to a halt, and everyone stared upward in awe while fey music raced through the clearing at a hectic pace.

Laughter broke out along with applause, even among the most Powerful and jaded of the guests. Oberon smiled to see one pretty Vampyre reaching up with a slender white hand to catch a flake. She stared, eyes wide with wonder as the glittering ice melted in her fingers.

A sharp sting pierced Oberon's neck along with a sense of alien magic. It broke his concentration, and the weather spell fractured.

His reactions were swift and catlike, but even as he slapped one gloved hand over the spot and focused fiercely on it, the brief pain faded. He spun around, his gaze racing over the crowd.

It had been an attack. He had no doubt.

His gaze fell on one individual, a tall, handsome man in elegant evening attire, wearing a plain black domino. The man held a hollow reed between the fingers of one gloved hand.

His direct hazel gaze met Oberon's. "I have killed you on the orders of the Light Fae Queen, and I must say I am sorry for it."

Oberon's lips drew back in a snarl. A roar burst from his throat as he lunged forward to slaughter the transgressor. Even as he sprang forward, an intense wave of dizziness struck him down.

Sharp voices soared overhead like the raw screech of hunting hawks. He recognized Nikolas and Gawain even as he turned his focus inward again, searching for that deadly thread of alien magic.

There it was, the enemy that had invaded his body. The magic wriggled deeper, seeking to enter his bloodstream. Where it touched, coldness spread.

Panicked hands gripped his arms, and another, more feral voice intruded upon his awareness: Robin. "Sire, what happened?"

"Assassins," he managed to hiss.

He did not need to say more. His knights roared through the milling crowd, cutting short the festivities with drawn swords. Trusting them to do their jobs, he closed his eyes and concentrated everything on stopping the malicious spell from completing its work.

Time passed while he tried spell after spell to counteract the attack. The masque ended early, and everyone went home. Over the next few weeks his knights roamed the streets of London, hunting the Light Queen's Hound, Morgan le Fae, for that was who the assassin had been. They never located the sorcerer. He had simply vanished, apparently into thin air.

Oberon retreated to the country, then eventually

back to Lyonesse, where he continued to search for ways to eradicate the magic that attacked him from within. Some spells seemed to work, at least temporarily, and for a while the progress of the magic halted.

He gained a measure of respite

Weeks, months. Even years.

But each time, after a period of stasis, the bastard evil that invaded his body reawakened and burrowed deeper, always aiming for his heart.

It caused undeniable damage. He could feel himself changing. The closer the magic came to his heart, the colder he grew. Colder in his thinking, in his emotions. He grew crueler, more calculating.

Once he had taken lovers who had longed for his touch and chased him for another taste of the ecstasy he had given them. As he changed, he took conquests, and although the pleasure he brought them was extreme, they did not beg for his return when he left.

After a few more years, he and his court stopped hosting the annual masque, and the Elder Races found a new popular venue in the Wyr demesne located in New York.

Oberon could see his changes reflected in the growing reserve in the eyes of those he had once considered his intimates. His family. They began to withdraw, and he didn't care. His fight for survival was easier that way. He was growing to distrust them anyway.

The magic burrowed deeper until it pressed against his heart. Finally he acknowledged he had to try a last, desperate gamble to save his own life.

He gathered the senior members of his court together—Nikolas, Gawain, Annwyn, and the others. The puck Robin came too, to bear witness.

"The sorcerer's spell has almost won," Oberon said to them. "I'm losing control over my own magic. I must try to put myself into a deep sleep, for if I can stop my own heart from beating, his cursed spell might not gain victory. In the meantime, you must leave the palace while you can. I... no longer trust myself."

His cousin Annwyn clasped him in a tight hug, and he allowed it out of respect for the memory of how he had once loved her.

"We will never stop fighting," she told him, her green eyes fierce. "Not for you, and not for Lyonesse. Rest well, Oberon, and know that you will awaken again."

She would make a splendid queen for the Daoine Sidhe should he die. He almost killed her right then and there, but that act would have been anathema to the man he had once been, and he would not let the damned sorcerer's spell dictate the actions of the man he had become.

Stepping back from her embrace, he watched as they left.

The puck had lingered behind the others, his thin frame lost in shadow. When they were gone, he crept out.

Oberon said slowly, "Guard this place and watch

them."

Robin's eyes gleamed. "As you wish, sire."

But the question was, could he still trust the puck? He was among the people Oberon had loved and trusted once. He could no longer feel those emotions, but he still had the memory of them.

How could he trust his own instincts when he could no longer tell how the spell was affecting him?

In the end, much as he hated it, there was nothing left for him to do but let go. Retreating deep into the palace, he cast the stasis spell that would plunge him into darkness.

There, full of rage, he slept and dreamed of vengeance.

Chapter Two

New York, present day

WHEN THE LORD of the Wyr issued a summons to those he kept on retainer, one responded with as much immediacy as one could manage. While Dr. Kathryn Shaw was no exception to that rule, she also refused to walk out of surgery to accommodate his demands.

"Tell him I'm busy," she said tersely to the nurse who had delivered the message to the operating room over the intercom.

As she spoke, Kathryn eyed the mangled leg in front of her with a frown. The leg belonged to a twelve-year-old boy who had taken a bad fall while trespassing on a construction site. It was a tricky operation that needed a combination of both magic and physical surgery—which was the only kind of case that Kathryn took on anymore—but she had her favorite surgery team with her, everyone worked really well with each other, and the boy stood a good chance of a near total recovery if Kathryn got it right.

So she would get it right.

A few minutes later the dragon himself broke into her mind. *Kathryn, I need you at Cuelebre Tower,* Dragos said telepathically. *Get here as fast as you can.*

She paused, frustrated, and when the nurse beside her gave her an inquiring glance, she held up a gloved finger and shook her head.

Everyone else in the world had a telepathic range of ten or fifteen feet—everyone but Dragos. His telepathic range was over a hundred miles, and Kathryn had had cause to regret that more than once in her professional life.

She snapped, *And I said I was busy. Is anybody on fire? Are any of the sentinels near imminent death?*

No, Dragos growled.

Well, I'm in the middle of surgery, and as I've told you before, I don't care for telepathic interruptions when I'm operating.

The Wyr Lord was frustrated too. She could hear it in his voice. *Can't you hand the surgery to someone else on your team?*

She could, but she wouldn't. She told him, *You wouldn't want me to walk out if I were operating on you, would you?*

As she had, in fact, recently operated on him, that hypothetical was more than a little potent. While in a battle to rescue his kidnapped wife, Dragos had been shot several times and taken a few hits to the chest. One of the bullets had come close to penetrating the truly spectacular protective casing around his powerful heart.

By his pause, she suspected he was thinking of that

injury too. *No, of course not.*

Then don't expect me to do it to someone else, she said. *If you don't have a clear-cut medical emergency for me to respond to, then you pick up your damn phone and call or text—and if I say you have to wait, you have to wait. Is that clear?*

Well, get here directly after surgery.

Of course. But right now I've got a twelve-year-old boy's leg to save, so get out of my head—and stay out. She inhaled deeply to get rid of the stress, then turned her total attention back to the boy on her table.

Three hours and twenty-six minutes later, she finished and stepped back to let Angus close for her. Euphoria and relief flooded her tight body. Rotating her head to release the tension in her neck and shoulders, she stripped off her operating gown, gloves, and mask, and headed out.

It had been a good afternoon's work. Better than good. It had been great. She would have a better idea of the boy's prognosis after his body had fully absorbed the spells, but when she felt this good about a surgery, she was rarely wrong about it later. She was pretty sure he would regain full mobility.

But it was too soon to tell his anxious parents that. For now it was enough to simply tell them she was pleased that the surgery had gone very well. While she briefed them, she multitasked and drank a hot, bracing cup of coffee. After promising to check on his post-op recovery that evening, she was finally able to head up to the hospital roof.

As she climbed the stairs, she texted Dragos. Out of surgery. On my way. Be there in 20.

His response was almost immediate. How is the boy?

That last caused her to shake her head and snort. Just when she got to thinking the Wyr Lord was a total self-absorbed ass, he switched things up on her. She answered him rapidly. Doing well.

Excellent. Come to the meeting hall when you get here.

Understood.

Once she reached the rooftop, she shapeshifted into her Wyr form, a falcon, and launched into flight.

She loved flying over New York. The cold, keen autumn wind blew away the last of the hospital scents while the huge, glittering city sprawled beneath her. New York City had been home to Kathryn for many years. She knew its moods and seasons, and she'd watched the skyline evolve. Flying over Central Park was especially glorious since all the trees were displaying their fall foliage in brilliant canopies of crimson, yellow, and orange.

The eighty-story-tall Cuelebre Tower was an unmistakable landmark and as familiar to her as the back of her hand. Swooping down to the roof, she shapeshifted back into her human form and headed for the stairs.

What she really wanted to do was take a detour to the cafeteria and eat a large steak for dinner, but that would have to wait.

Now that she had the time to turn her attention to Dragos's summons, she was growing intrigued.

The last she had heard, Dragos and his mate Pia had been recuperating at home with their newborn son Niall while their eldest son Liam was home visiting from college.

Something had lured Dragos back to the city, at least briefly, and whatever it was had to be compelling enough to get him to interrupt his personal family time.

If Dragos had wanted to meet with Kathryn personally, he was just as likely to show up at her office at the hospital or direct her to his. If it involved a matter internal to the Wyr demesne, the meeting venue would most likely have been one of the conference rooms on the top two stories of the tower.

Being summoned to the meeting hall... That meant outsiders were involved somehow. The meeting hall was where the Cuelebres' annual Masque of the Gods was held. It was a massive space suitable for public occasions, with tall windows, the high ceilings decorated with crown molding and the marble floors gleaming and polished.

It also had protection spells woven into the reinforcing steel beams, the walls, the ceiling and floor in case anything untoward were to happen—and with the Elder Races involved, something untoward almost always happened.

Kathryn hadn't taken the time to change, so when she had shapeshifted back into her human form she still wore her standard surgery fare—blue scrubs, a white long-sleeved thermal shirt underneath, and tennis shoes, and she had confined her straight, fine brown hair in a no-nonsense ponytail. Though her scrubs had been fresh when she'd donned them earlier, now they were crumpled, but in any case, scrubs weren't exactly suitable attire for the meeting hall.

With an internal shrug, she set speculation aside and headed down to the hall, which was located just above the ground-floor shops and restaurants and just below the law offices of the Wyr demesne.

This time she took the elevator, and when she stepped out she saw two sentinels, Bayne and Quentin, standing guard at the meeting hall's large, ornately carved double doors.

Curiouser and curiouser, as Alice would have said during her adventure in Wonderland.

Approaching, she said, "Hey, guys."

Quentin gave her a genial nod. He was a handsome devil and quite insane, as he had mated with the harpy Aryal and appeared to be quite content with the result of his life choices. Despite his undeniable sex appeal, nobody, at least that Kathryn knew of, was tempted to try to coax Quentin into cheating.

Bayne's handsome looks were much rougher. His Wyr form was a gryphon the size of an SUV, and his human form seemed not that much smaller.

The corners of his gray eyes crinkled as he looked at her. "Hey, Kathryn."

Oh, she had a soft spot for Bayne. She had a very soft spot for him. They had dated off and on in a casual way, and part of her was sorry that they hadn't managed to generate between them whatever it was that catapulted the Wyr into mating.

Maybe they were both too dedicated to their jobs?

Whatever the reason, their relationship was enough that she felt entirely comfortable stopping beside him and switching to telepathy. *Any clues about what's going on before I walk in there?*

His smile deepened. *Not my place, babe. All I gotta say is, buckle up.*

Well, a girl had to try. She was tall for a woman, but not unusually so. The top of her head came to his chin, and she smiled up at him.

Let's grab a bite to eat afterward if you've got time.

I'd like that. She touched his arm. *I have to check on a patient this evening, but other than that, I'm free.*

Good deal. He switched back to verbal speech. "Ready to go inside?"

"I guess so." She gave the closed doors a leery glance.

Quentin opened one of the doors and held it for her.

The tension in the meeting hall struck like a blow as soon as she took her first step inside, and it wasn't just emotional tension. Power prickled through the air from magics raised but not unleashed.

Oooo-kay then. Squaring her shoulders, she strode toward the group that had congregated in the middle of the expansive floor. As she approached, she took in details.

There were three clusters, each one standing far enough away from the others to set itself apart.

The first cluster was a party of two, stationed squarely between the other groups. One of them was Dragos who stood with his arms crossed as he surveyed the others. He was large and lethal, with midnight black hair, bronze features, and gold eyes.

The Wyr gryphon Rune stood beside him. Kathryn hesitated, looking between the two males. Rune was almost as tall as Dragos but not nearly as broad. His golden hair and handsome features were a familiar sight, but at the same time also a strange one.

For centuries, Rune had acted as Dragos's First sentinel, and he was a significant force to be reckoned with in his own right… but he and Dragos had argued while Rune had been in the middle of mating with the Vampyre elder Carling Severan. The strain of that argument had broken the relationship.

Since that time, the men had gradually been repairing it, and when Carling had been kidnapped along with Dragos's mate Pia, they had been thrown into working together. Apparently the crisis had eradicated any strain that had lingered between them.

Kathryn smiled. It was good to see them together again and acting as a team, for however long that might last.

Her gaze traveled to the second cluster. It was also a

party of two. A handsome dark-haired man stood beside a woman. Their scents revealed immediately that they were both lycanthropes, and as soon as she laid eyes on them, Kathryn knew who they were.

The infamous sorcerer Morgan le Fae was in attendance along with his companion, popular musician Sidonie Martel. Kathryn had heard of the pair, but she hadn't met them yet. The grapevine in the Wyr demesne was lively and thriving, so she already knew Dragos had offered asylum to Morgan and a select band of lycanthropes that had immigrated with him.

In other circumstances, her gaze might have been tempted to linger on the pair, but the open hostility in the third cluster of people pulled at her attention.

The third group was also the largest. Four individuals stood in postures of leashed aggression, their expressions tight. One was a mixed-Fae female who was spotted like a cheetah, with russet hair streaked with white, and a strong, lean body.

The mixed-Fae woman stared at Morgan and his companion with undisguised hatred. A powerfully built mixed-Fae male stood beside her, while another male with menacing, intense good looks stood by a woman whom Kathryn recognized.

Immediately, she threw aside any further examination of the scene.

"Sophie!" she exclaimed, in equal parts surprise and delight.

Sophie Ross was a mostly human witch with long,

curly black hair, pale gray-blue eyes, and freckled skin. Earlier that year, Kathryn had met Sophie in LA and offered her the quixotic stipulations set out by Kathryn's late father, the Earl of Weston, in his will.

Sophie had been given the opportunity to stay for ninety days at one of Kathryn's historical family holdings in the UK. If, during Sophie's stay, she was able to break into the magic puzzle box of a house that the Shaw family had owned for many generations, she would inherit the property and an annual stipend that went along with it.

Sophie had not only managed to break into the house. She had also fallen in love with a prominent member of the Dark Court and gotten embroiled in the centuries-long struggle between Oberon's people and the Light Court.

If Sophie was here, that meant the dark, brooding male standing so protectively beside her must be Nikolas Sevigny, one of Oberon's senior knights. And that meant their companions were probably also from the Dark Court…

No wonder the tension in the hall was so high. For many centuries, Morgan le Fae had acted as an agent on behalf of Isabeau, Queen of the Light Court—and the Light Court and the Dark Court were mortal enemies.

Then in recent months, news ran like wildfire through the Elder Races: Morgan had not been working for the Light Fae Queen of his own free will. He had been enslaved by a geas.

That could possibly be how Morgan and various members of Oberon's Court could stand together under the same roof without immediately breaking into battle... but Kathryn could see the strain was vibrating through all of them. Even Sophie's bright smile of greeting was brief. They would have to catch up in private another time.

Now that Kathryn's sweep of the hall was complete, she focused her attention on Dragos again as she strode forward. Telepathically she said to him, *Surely you all haven't been standing here for almost four hours while I finished surgery?*

The Wyr Lord didn't appear to appreciate her small spark of humor. His gold gaze flashed with irritation. *I sent them to opposite parts of the building to wait it out. They've only been back in the hall for a few minutes. We've got to get this meeting over with before somebody snaps.*

Aloud, he said to the russet-haired female, "This is Dr. Kathryn Shaw, as I promised. Kathryn, this is Annwyn Mathonwy, King Oberon's cousin and general of the Lyonesse armed forces. Her escorts are Gawain Blackwater, Nikolas Sevigny, and Sophie Ross." He swiveled on one booted heel and indicated the other cluster. "And over here, we have Morgan le Fae and his fiancée, Sidonie Martel. I've summoned you all here at Annwyn's request."

"If I may," Morgan murmured. "My last name is Garanhir. I have no desire to be connected to the Fae in any way whatsoever."

"Of course," Dragos told him. "My apologies."

Oh… dear. With a sinking heart, Kathryn watched as Annwyn prowled toward her. Nobody wore any visible weapons, but Annwyn was a weapon all on her own. She moved like danger personified, in one racy, effortless flow.

"Dr. Shaw," Annwyn said shortly.

"General," Kathryn replied, taking the hand she was offered and shaking it. "It's an honor to make your acquaintance in person."

"When I approached you in the summer to ask for a consultation on my cousin's condition, you turned me down," Annwyn told her. "I'm here to ask you again, in person. Oberon remains in a deeply unconscious state. Meanwhile his Power continues to rage unchecked. Without his will to control it, it's damaging our city and land, causing floods and forcing evacuations. We need to break through to him somehow, or we may end up with no livable homeland left. Our physicians and mages have had no luck in either healing him or in halting what's happening. All they can confirm is that his affliction is magical in nature." Swiveling to face Morgan, her voice chilled as she said, "And that led me to ask for you."

Morgan had put his hands in his pockets. He looked more relaxed than the raised magics snapping in the air might otherwise indicate. When he spoke, his voice was deep and pleasant. "If you intend to confirm whether I had anything to do with Oberon's present condition, the answer is yes. I did."

Annwyn hissed, and across the room, both Gawain and Nikolas grabbed for their waists. It was an instinctive move, Kathryn thought, as they reached for weapons they hadn't been allowed to wear into the hall.

"Ease up, gentlemen," Rune said in an aside to them. "Remember, this is a parley that *you* asked for, not a battlefield."

"For what it's worth," Morgan added, "I had no choice—I acted on Isabeau's command, and I deeply regret what happened. If you'll allow, I'll do what I can to help."

"Do you expect your apology can wipe out hundreds of years of armed conflict or bring back the dead you killed?" Nikolas bit out. "Do you think *I'm sorry* helps their families cope with their losses?"

"No, of course not," Morgan said quietly.

"We'll never let you set foot on our land, much less risk your getting close to the King again. How do we know there really was a geas on you—or that it is truly broken? There's no trust for you anywhere in Lyonesse, and no safety either."

"Then I will have to do what I can to make amends from here." Morgan turned to face Annwyn and Kathryn. "I'm at your disposal. Please call on me for anything you need."

Kathryn held up her hands. "Hold on a minute. This conversation is moving much too fast." She looked at Annwyn. "When you asked me to consult on Oberon's condition, I told you no, and the reasons for that haven't changed. The time slippage between Earth and Lyonesse is too extreme. If I spent a few weeks in Lyonesse, it would mean taking months away from my practice and my duties here in the Wyr demesne—plus those few weeks would be no guarantee of anything. It would take that long just to get the opportunity to assess his condition for myself. Healing him could possibly take much longer, and in the end, I might not be able to do anything for him anyway."

Annwyn's lean jaw tightened as she listened. When she spoke, it was with a measured discipline piloted by an iron will. "That is why I wanted to talk with you in person. We understand what a substantial commitment this would take on your part, and we're willing to discuss any terms of compensation that would help alleviate the challenges associated with this assignment."

"Any terms of compensation," Dragos murmured. His eyelids dropped, hiding the expression in that calculating gold gaze while he rubbed his jaw with the back of one thumb.

Kathryn glared at him. She said telepathically, *I blame you for this mess.*

Sure, go ahead.

His tone was so clearly indifferent her exasperation deepened. *Dragos, I can't go. You have me on retainer. I also have my rotation at the hospital. I can't just drop those things because someone is stubborn enough to ask twice. Unfortunately, there are people all over the world who need healing, and I can't help everybody. No doctor can.*

Still rubbing his jaw, he raised sleek black eyebrows and tilted his head first one way, then the other. Maybe it was in acknowledgment to what she said. Maybe he was weighing some internal issue in his head. She had no clue, and no time to query it, because Annwyn was speaking again, her tone quiet and urgent.

"Dr. Shaw, I understand you have your life here, and it is busy, complicated, and important." Sharp green eyes speared her. "But this is a matter of truly immense consequence for an entire people. It's not just about my cousin's life, although that's important too—and it isn't just about Lyonesse. Our home is in danger. You're talking about an entire demesne that may be displaced and become refugees if we don't *fix* this. This is threatening to become an international crisis."

Kathryn made the mistake of staring into Annwyn's fierce gaze, and she found herself trapped. How could one man's magical Power endanger an entire land and people? Thoughtfully, she glanced at Dragos, then at Morgan. Those two males—they held enough Power. They could cause that kind of damage.

Annwyn paused, giving her time to think, then murmured, "We have researched doctors. You are the best at what you do."

Kathryn's lips tightened. Every surgeon had her fair share of ego, but that was laying it on a bit too thick. "I am *one of the best*. Just one. There are others you could ask."

"No one with your unique combination of

sensitivities and skills," the other woman insisted.

What did Annwyn mean by that? Frowning, Kathryn opened her mouth to ask, but Dragos spoke first. "How goes the war against Isabeau?"

Kathryn pursed her lips. Why had the dragon chosen to ask that now, of all times? Where had his calculating, wily mind gone in his mental deliberations?

Morgan rubbed his face and looked disgusted. Clearly he would rather be anywhere else than in the middle of a discussion about Isabeau. Annwyn's attention shifted, and she watched the sorcerer closely.

Nikolas was the one who chose to answer. "Isabeau has had major setbacks. From all reports, Morgan wounded her severely when he broke free of her control. He also sent a large portion of the Light Court society into disarray when he destroyed her summer palace and killed Modred. She's disappeared, and we haven't yet been able to locate her, but we feel it is only a matter of time, especially if we can rouse Oberon from his comatose state."

"I see," Dragos replied. Everyone in the hall paused, waiting for him to make a point, or say something further, but he remained silent.

He was maddening. Truly, he was.

For a moment Kathryn fantasized about putting her hands around his neck and squeezing. She knew she couldn't really hurt him, nor did she want to. But she did *oh so mightily* want to elicit a look of consternation from him in retaliation for all the times he had disconcerted her.

Then, as Annwyn swung around to face Kathryn again, Dragos said, "Isabeau is reputed to have quite a library of books on magic, or so I've heard." He looked at Morgan. "Did you ever see it?"

"No," Morgan said drily. "She does have an extensive library, but she would never trust me enough to let me near it."

"Give me a moment to consult with my physician, and kindly don't kill each other while we're at it." Striding over to Kathryn, Dragos held out a hand, silently urging her to walk with him.

She obliged and followed him to the other side of the hall. During the course of the small journey, realization dawned. She said telepathically, *You want Isabeau's library, don't you?*

The sidelong look he gave her gleamed. *Of course I do. If and when the Dark Court does defeat Isabeau, we can't have her library out there waiting to fall into the wrong hands, can we? It needs to fall into my hands.*

She bit back a smile. *Naturally.*

He cocked an eyebrow. *Naturally. So, I have just one question to ask—are you interested in doing this? Because if you are, I will back that decision, continue to pay you your retainer while you are gone, and negotiate with the Dark Court for the right to send a team after the library once they have finished dealing with Isabeau. If your answer is still no, there's no need to discuss this any further.*

She paused, narrowing her eyes at him. *That's a fair*

question, she said slowly. *Before, I didn't allow myself to consider it very seriously.*

Dragos snapped his fingers. *What's the name of that young doctor on your surgical team?*

Do you mean Angus?

Yes, that's him. Angus could take over your rotation at the hospital and pick up your other duties while you're gone. He could be on call for the sentinels if need be. He's qualified enough—he fills in for you already when you go on vacations. This would just be an extension of that.

She retorted, *Are you saying I'm not as indispensable as I'd like to think?*

Dragos said, *I'm saying I want to know what you want to do, and I'll support you either way—and I've got a way this can work for me if you do want to go. On a side note, there are things going on here in the New York demesne that you don't yet know, mainly stemming from personal decisions that Pia and I have recently made. You'll find out about that later, but my point is, here in the city things are going to be in flux anyway for the next year. If you want to make this trip, it can just become part of that flux.*

She hesitated, then smiled as she admitted, *Okay, to be honest, I think it sounds fascinating. It's a medical puzzle and an adventure all at once. I'm curious about the spell Morgan concocted, and I'm interested to know if I can reverse Oberon's condition. And I've been meaning to travel back to England to visit Sophie and the property she inherited when she met the terms of my father's will. So—yes, I would like to go.*

Good enough. Dragos put a hand at her back. *Now, let's*

go make them pay for the privilege of your time and effort.

Suddenly amused, she murmured, *They're in genuine distress. Try not to gouge them too much, will you?*

The corners of his mouth indented in a subtle smile. *Well, they did offer.*

Chapter Three

A FTER FINALIZING DETAILS of the agreement with Annwyn, Kathryn took a week to get her affairs in order. The time slippage between Lyonesse and Earth worked strongly in her favor as long as she remained in New York, so she took full advantage of it.

She also took the opportunity to meet extensively with Morgan, which was a fascinating experience all on its own as the sorcerer taught her the sophisticated details of his assassination spell and the various tactics he thought might work in reversing it.

Talking to him was mind-bending. As she told Bayne later, Morgan was friendly, brilliant, and toweringly talented—basically the Stephen Hawking of all things magical. Isabeau had been incredibly destructive, both to his spirit and to the world in general, when she had weaponized him.

At the hospital, she worked to transfer all her active patients over to Angus. She owned her Manhattan apartment outright, so she had her furniture swathed in dustcovers and arranged her finances so the taxes and utilities would be automatically paid for the duration of her absence.

To cover emergencies, she signed a power of attorney over to the Wyr demesne legal department. And she spent her evenings going out on the town with Bayne and other friends she wouldn't see for months of their time.

As they enjoyed their dates, Bayne was all too happy to fill her in on the other changes that were soon to hit the Wyr demesne in New York.

The biggest and most sweeping change was that Dragos, his mate Pia, and their baby son Niall had decided to relocate to his newly named Other land of Rhyacia. For years, Dragos had been experimenting there with technology and magic, but other than the fruits of his labor, the land was pristine, easily protected, and as big as Greenland. The Cuelebres' departure would leave a power vacuum in the Wyr demesne that Dragos was determined to fill one way or another.

"Wow. Just… wow," she said as she sat back from her dinner and worked to absorb the news.

"Yeah, it's pretty huge," Bayne said laconically. He didn't stop eating when she did. They were enjoying a late meal at one of his favorite restaurants, and he'd also had a bit more time to adjust to the upcoming changes. "But I get why they made the decision."

As she thought things over, she did too. "What's going to happen here?"

He shrugged. "Don't know yet. At first Dragos was certain Liam would choose to take over, but then Liam went to talk things over with his mom. Turns out, Pia had other ideas. Liam decided to take her advice and finish his year away at college. He's promised to make his decision by the end of his college stint. In the meantime, Rune has agreed to step in as regent until Liam's year is over. Rune and Carling are moving into Cuelebre Tower by the end of the month."

Sipping her wine, she watched Bayne's expression with fascination. "What happens if Liam chooses not to take over? Is… that even a possibility?"

Bayne had just taken a huge bite of prime rib, so he shrugged without answering right away. "Nobody knows," he said after swallowing. "Apparently after talking to his mom, he had a long list of very good questions that he asked his dad—like, for example, would Liam take over as CEO for Cuelebre Enterprises as well as assume the title of Lord of the Wyr demesne when Dragos leaves?"

She rubbed her mouth to hide a smile. Pia had achieved what Kathryn could only daydream of—she managed to disconcert her mate on what was to Kathryn a satisfyingly regular basis. "And what did Dragos say to that, do you know?"

He snorted, eyes gleaming with amusement. "Dragos is about to start a very expensive community-building initiative in Rhyacia. He was counting on drawing on the profits from the company to fund it over the next five or so years. Yet Cuelebre Enterprises and the Wyr demesne are inextricably linked."

"That's never been a problem with Dragos in charge of both," she said.

"Exactly. He could move funds around as he wished. But as Liam pointed out, if he takes over the Wyr demesne and Dragos continues to operate as CEO of the company, albeit long-distance, Liam will always be under his father's control to some extent. That would not only undermine his authority internationally as the new Lord of the Wyr here, but it would also hamstring his ability to take any quick action that involved a significant expenditure of resources."

She burst out laughing. "I wish I could have been a fly on the wall for that conversation."

He grinned. "Me too. One dragon negotiating with another—it was truly a first in Wyr history. The talk caught Dragos by surprise, and you know how he hates to give up control *and* hates to lose money."

"Lord, no, he doesn't."

"Anyway, nobody is quite sure how this is going to play out, but all the sentinels are pretty certain we're going to be entertained by the process. Will Dragos relinquish control over the company? Will Liam decide to take over, or will he choose to go his own independent way? And in the meantime, what will Rune and Carling choose to do?" In a mock TV announcer's voice, he said, "Stay tuned for the next installment of Days of Our Wyr Demesne."

She laughed harder. "I'm starting to think I might be glad to be gone for the transition period. I can just come back and find out what happens next without having to live through it."

He nodded. "Never a dull moment around here, that's for sure. We're going to miss you though."

We, not *I*. It was a small thing, but important and telling, she thought without passion or hurt. She didn't blame Bayne in the slightest—she said things like that too. But it was all symptomatic of that elusive, ephemeral condition that transpired to keep their relationship squarely in the friend zone.

BY THE TIME she arrived in Westmarch, the English village nearest the property Sophie had inherited, Kathryn was too excited for jet leg to affect her much. While she had traveled extensively on Earth, it had been years since she had taken a trip to an Other land.

Experiencing Lyonesse would be interesting in its own right. Added to that, she would get to help a lot of people who were suffering while she attempted to solve a medical mystery. In the meantime, she had already learned more valuable magic to add to her repertoire of skills. Life just didn't get much better than that. She refused to dwell on the possibility that Oberon might not be salvageable. They would learn the truth about that soon enough.

Once in the village, she turned in her rental car. As she finished the transaction, Sophie pulled up in a Range Rover. A handsome male, clearly not human, with long dark hair and the cynical good looks of a dissipated rock star rode shotgun beside her.

His gaze landed on Kathryn and sparked with interest. Even though the windows of the Range Rover were closed to the damp, chill autumn air, Kathryn's Wyr hearing was sensitive enough to pick up Sophie's words as she turned to fix her companion with a hard stare.

"You behave."

The male gave Sophie a slow, sweet smile. "I always behave in direct relation to my companion's desires."

Sophie burst out laughing. "Bah. You're incorrigible."

Raising an eyebrow, Kathryn suppressed a smile. Clearly he was Trouble looking for someplace to happen. It was only when they stepped out of the vehicle that she caught a glimpse of the weapons he wore underneath his autumn jacket, as well as the hard, sweeping glance he gave the scene.

Comprehension clicked into place. She had spent far too much time with the sentinels in New York to miss the unmistakable signs of a guard on duty.

Sophie approached with a bright smile, and Kathryn gladly gave her a hug. "Thank you for meeting me here."

"Of course, it's totally my pleasure!" Sophie replied. "It made complete sense, since you're not going to need a car here for months. I'm so happy to see you. Until the conflict with Isabeau is resolved, I promised Nik I wouldn't leave the property without protection, so this is Rowan Nyghtseren—he's playing bodyguard today.

Rowan, this is Dr. Kathryn Shaw." She added telepathically, *Fair warning—he's a scamp. He's good at respecting boundaries, but he might tickle them a bit.*

The part of Kathryn's brain that loved etymology and word puzzles chewed on Rowan's last name. Sophie had pronounced it as "Night-seren," and *seren* in Welsh meant "star." Rowan's last name meant, literally, "Nightstar."

With a name like that, he really should have been a rock star. She grinned. *I appreciate you telling me.*

Rowan, she noted with approval, didn't turn his attention to her until he was fully satisfied their surroundings were clear. Then his dissipated-rock-star gaze met hers as he took her hand gently between his. "A great pleasure to meet you, Dr. Shaw," he said. "Or may I call you Kathryn?"

"Nice to meet you too." She recovered her hand from his grasp. "And Dr. Shaw will do fine, thanks."

His eyes narrowed in calculation until Sophie smacked his chest with the back of her hand. "For God's sake, give it up and stow her luggage in the car."

Genuine affection warmed his face as he tilted an eyebrow at Sophie. "Anything for you, love."

As Rowan put her luggage in the Range Rover, Sophie turned back to her. "Annwyn wanted me to go over the type of warm clothes you brought with you," she said. "She's concerned you might have brought things that are more suitable to the city."

Kathryn smiled. "I suppose she doesn't have any clue

how bitterly cold temperatures can get in New York."

"Well no, she doesn't." Sophie made a face. "But she also has a point. I've been over to Lyonesse, and right now the cold over there… It's not normal, Kathryn. The weather is awful all the time, and plus the terrain is very rugged. A shop has opened up here in town that specifically caters to those who travel back and forth across the reopened passageway. Do you want to stop and have a look at what they've got before we leave?"

She took a moment to consider. Despite her ability to meld comfortably into an urban landscape, she was one of the Wyr who had never moved very far from her wild roots. She loved the wilderness and being out in the elements, and she'd packed a selection of clothing she'd bought from a wilderness outfitter. But was it suitable for "not normal" weather?

"It won't do any harm to take a look," she replied.

"Great! It's just a few blocks from here." With a click of her key fob, Sophie locked the Range Rover, and the three of them headed down the sidewalk.

Once inside the shop, Kathryn inspected everything with interest. When she had packed, she had tried to balance the need for her gear to be portable with basic layering techniques for cold weather: using a base layer to wick sweat away from the skin, a middle insulating layer to retain body heat, and then a shell layer to shield from the weather.

She had underwear, three sets of thermal silk shirts and wool sweaters to wear over them, two pairs of flannel-lined jeans, three pairs of wool socks, hiking boots, an insulated down jacket with a hood, a woolen scarf, and insulated gloves. She would be wearing some of her cargo and would hopefully be able to utilize a horse, but if it came down to it, she could carry the rest in a rather heavy pack on her back.

Now she considered what Sophie had said while she browsed the wares in the store. Like Kathryn, the Daoine Sidhe weren't human. They were a hardy mix of the Elder Races, yet conditions were so bad in Lyonesse they were facing the possibility of needing to flee.

When she came upon a shelf dedicated to packets of emergency hand and body warmers, she picked one up curiously.

Time and space had buckled when the Earth had formed, and the Other lands—connected to Earth through crossover passageways—were magic saturated, and many modern technologies either didn't work or were outright dangerous to try to use.

But as she read the instructions on the package, the emergency hand and body warmers were made of biodegradable chemical compounds that were air activated, which was a passive enough, nature-based technology that made them safe to use in an Other land. She threw several into her basket.

She was already quite comfortable with the things she had brought—her carefully curated physician's kit, choice of toiletries, small portable hand axe, and Swiss Army knife, and her tried-and-true flint fire-starter kit was over 150 years old.

But after a few more minutes of consideration, she also chose several bags of jerky along with several more of a high-fat, high-calorie trail mix. Getting enough calories was important in harsh weather, and Kathryn had an animal form with a high metabolism that ensured she burned through calories at an accelerated rate.

Then she added a Mylar emergency blanket, as it was small, extremely lightweight, and would hold ninety percent of her body heat if needed. The last thing she considered was a rack of fur-lined, floor-length, water-resistant cloaks. They were bulky and they would be heavy. They would be great for heat retention and lousy for carting around. As she chewed on her lip, Sophie walked over to join her.

Kathryn told her, "I already have a down-insulated hooded coat."

Sophie pulled one of the cloaks off the rack. "This will fit over anything else you wear, and it's better to have too much than too little. You don't know what you're going to run into, and honestly, I don't know that it would be too much. If you find it's more than you need and you get tired of lugging it around, you can abandon it if you have to, or you can always donate it to someone else."

"Good point." Unfortunately, with the addition of the cloak, she was sacrificing some of her gear's valuable portability. There was no way around it. She going to need another pack. She grabbed a weatherproof bag and then took all her selections to the counter, but before she could pay, Rowan smoothly stepped in to hand over a credit card to the shop attendant.

"Don't fuss," he said as she turned to argue with him. His previous calculated charm had disappeared for the moment, and he gave her a simple, warm smile. "You're on Dark Court business, and I have my orders."

It was hard to argue with that, so she didn't. "Thank you."

With that, their small shopping excursion was over, so they walked back to the Range Rover and drove to the property.

Kathryn had heard about the changes that had occurred on the old estate, but it was still a shock to see them in person. In the summer, the manor house had sustained major structural damage during a battle with Morgan when he had still been enslaved by Isabeau and acting as her Captain of the Hounds. Sophie had been a part of that conflict.

Since that time, she had sold her inheritance to the Daoine Sidhe for a sizable sum. Now the structure of the main house was shored up with visible reinforcements. The charming little gatekeeper's cottage that had once been near the road had been completely demolished, and several more buildings had been added to the five acres. Before, the property had been an overgrown, abandoned relic, but now the entire place buzzed with people and purpose.

When Sophie parked in front of a new cottage,

Rowan left with a final, lingering look at Kathryn. She shook her head at him, and he lifted wide shoulders in a regretful shrug.

As he disappeared, she said laughingly, "Wow."

"Right? He is so much trouble." Sophie opened the back of the Range Rover and began to pull out luggage and packages. "I live for the day when I get to see Rowan meet the woman who will knock him on his ass—in a good way, of course. I don't want him to get hurt. I just want him to know what it's like to really fall for someone, you know?"

Kathryn picked up luggage. "When he sets aside the bullshit, there seems to be a nice guy in there underneath."

"I think there is. At the very least, I don't think he means any real *harm*, although more than likely he probably causes it anyway. But Nik trusts him, and I trust Nik, so there you have it." Sophie led the way into the cottage, which was unlocked. "I'm betting Annwyn will show up as soon as she hears you've arrived, so let's make the most of what time we have. Would you like some tea?"

"I would love some."

"I'm becoming very Anglicized and never bother with coffee anymore." Sophie grinned. "Also, I made some beef-and-tomato sandwiches, and there's fresh-baked scones—I didn't bake those, so they're actually delicious—and clotted cream."

"That sounds amazing," she replied. "I'm famished."

She followed Sophie to the kitchen where they visited over the tea, sandwiches, and scones. It was good to see the witch so happy. It showed in the sparkle in her eyes and the healthy luster of her freckled skin.

When Kathryn had met her, Sophie had still been in recovery from a life-threatening injury. She'd been closed in, strung tight, and underweight. Now, despite the presence of armed guards everywhere, she was obviously at home and relaxed, and she laughed often.

Seeing the changes made Kathryn happy. She cast around for something to say that would encourage Sophie to talk about it. "You and Nikolas are happy?"

"You know, we are," Sophie said. She sounded surprised, and then she laughed. "He's not anything I would have imagined for myself, and we fight all the time. He has this old-world chauvinism that drives me nuts—and I know I drive him nuts, because I don't let him get away with it. He says I'm too contrary, and I say he's too dictatorial, but in spite of all that, we manage to make things work. I can't even tell you how."

There it was, the elusive, ephemeral thing, condition, whatever you wanted to call it. Bond. Nik and Sophie had it in abundance, and they weren't even Wyr, or at least Sophie wasn't. Since the Daoine Sidhe were a community of mixed-race Elder Races, Kathryn supposed it was possible that Nik might have some Wyr in his blood.

Humans had the capacity to bond too. To love. But if things didn't work out, it rarely killed them like it did the Wyr when they lost a mate. The Wyr might mate for life, but perhaps it was good that mating was a relatively rare experience.

Every Wyr was conditioned from an early age to avoid pining for something that most likely wouldn't happen. It was entirely possible to have a full, satisfying life filled with many different kinds of loves—friendships, affairs, even marriages.

Kathryn had never met a potential mate, but she enjoyed a full life while experiencing the friendships and affairs. Still, it was fascinating to watch from the sidelines when others went through the mating process.

Children were also rare to all the Elder Races, but even children could come to unmated Wyr, just as Kathryn had come into her father's life. Her mother had been Francis Shaw's mistress, and when she had become pregnant he had honored the relationship by marrying her. She had died in a carriage accident when Kathryn was still a baby. She had always been grateful to have at least one of her parents as she was growing up. Losing her father decades ago to a terrorist attack in London was an old ache that never quite went away.

Pulling out of her reverie, she sipped her tea. "I suppose it doesn't matter if you don't know how your relationship with Nik works, as long as it does. The most important thing is that you're both in it together."

"Yes." Sophie's smile was bright and broad. "We're all in."

A quick tap sounded on the back door. Giving

Kathryn a meaningful nod and grin, Sophie rose to answer it, and a moment later Annwyn stalked into the kitchen. She was one of those people who could make a room shrink just by the strength of her presence.

Her fierce green gaze landed on Kathryn. "You're here."

Kathryn had lived with people like Annwyn for many, many years, and she could recognize Annwyn's type from a mile away. The other woman was so purpose-driven she would steamroll right over you if you let her. Kathryn wasn't going to let her.

"Yes. I arrived this morning, met with my solicitor to take care of a few things, and hopped in a rental car right after that." She bit into a scone with pleasure. "It's good to take a break and eat. This is my first meal of the day."

"Please, join us," Sophie said to Annwyn. "Would you like a cup of tea? Perhaps a sandwich and a scone?"

Just as Kathryn had seen her do in the meeting hall a week ago, Annwyn paused, then drew herself in as if reaching for patience. "Yes, thank you."

Annwyn seated herself as Sophie got her a cup, a plate, and silverware. After a moment, Annwyn said in a measured tone, "While I know just how significant the time slippage is between Earth and Lyonesse, it's hard to internalize it emotionally. For so long I've lived with a sense of urgency, and it's difficult to relax when I know so many of the Daoine Sidhe are suffering."

Kathryn met Sophie's gaze for a moment. Then, as the younger woman turned to get the teakettle from the stove, Kathryn smiled at Annwyn. Gently, she said, "I am going to do everything I can for him, you know."

Annwyn studied her closely, then sat back in her chair. "I believe you will. When will you be ready to cross over?"

Framing that as a question, she could see, took major effort. Like Annwyn said, it was hard for her not to push. She considered how she wanted to answer.

Finally she said, "I slept on the flight, I took care of the last of my business affairs this morning, and I'm not here to sightsee. Visiting with Sophie was the one thing I wanted to do, and we've been doing that. I want to finish my meal, take a shower, and put on an appropriate outfit. After that, I'm all yours."

Annwyn straightened in her chair, and the fierceness roared back. "Excellent."

As they resumed their meal, Kathryn asked, "So, what comes next?"

"Once we cross over, we lose the luxury of the extra time we've had here on Earth," Annwyn said. "So I have struck a bargain with one of our people. He's... unusual. He's a nature sprite, and he has agreed to help. He's waiting for us now on the other side of the passageway. With his aid we can reach the city much more quickly than we could if we had to travel on our own. Half the city is underwater from flooding, and the other half is frozen. We had to evacuate the general population from there some time ago. I want to set up a base camp on high ground, and we'll work from there."

Her plan sounded sensible enough. Kathryn nodded. "Sounds good to me."

When she finished eating, Sophie showed her the bathroom and brought towels and a washcloth. Thanking her, Kathryn said, "May I store my luggage here until I get back?"

"Of course!" Sophie gestured to her clothes. "I'll wash your outfit and store that in your suitcase, too, so it's ready for you when you get back."

"Thank you."

She took the towels, and when she would have stepped into the bathroom, Sophie laid a hand on her arm. Telepathically, she said, *I know the nature sprite Annwyn was talking about.*

Kathryn looked at her curiously. *Yes?*

His name is Robin, Sophie told her. *We bonded over the summer, and I love him, but he's quite unpredictable. Isabeau held him captive and tortured him for a very long time, and I don't think he's healed yet.*

How unfortunate. Why did Sophie consider this important enough to tell Kathryn privately? She wasn't sure she liked the implications in that. *What does that mean, exactly?*

It means… The other woman bit her lip, clearly struggling for the right words. *It means he doesn't always make the right decisions, or at least he makes decisions based on criteria that you and I might not have.*

Kathryn knew all about very old, damaged creatures. Several had been patients of hers at one time or another.

She pursed her lips. *I see.*

I want you to understand. Sophie looked at her intently. *Robin's not BAD. At least—I don't think he's bad, but he's dangerous. I'm not clear why he would make a bargain with Annwyn when he has unresolved resentment for the rest of the Dark Court. It's possible I'm overthinking this. He probably did it because his first loyalty is to Oberon, but I just wanted you to know. You're walking into a situation that has a lot of history and nuances. Lots and lots of nuances.*

I appreciate that. Kathryn squeezed her hand. *It's much better to be armed with knowledge than not. Thank you.*

You're welcome. I feel better now. Sophie stepped back. *Enjoy your shower.*

Sophie had given her plenty of food for thought. Kathryn mulled over everything as she brushed her teeth, then luxuriated in a long, hot shower and soaped through her hair twice. She even took the time to shave her legs, because she had no idea when she might get another hot shower or the chance to do so again. She was extrapolating, but access to easy, copious amounts of hot water didn't sound very plausible once she crossed over.

The near future felt uncertain and exciting. She liked that. Often her job made her feel that way, but for all its challenges, it fell prey to routine. *I needed more adventure in my life,* she mouthed as she stood with her head under the shower, relishing the sensual way the warm water poured around her moving lips.

The Dark Court sounded like it had a lot of heavy

baggage. That meant it sounded like virtually every other Elder Races demesne in the world. Old creatures meant tangled grudges, ancient resentments, divided loyalties, and hidden motives. Just like home.

Chuckling, she stepped out of the shower, toweled off, and dried her hair thoroughly. Once she was dressed, she went into the living room to rearrange the items she would take with her into her two packs.

Her original pack would be the one she would grab in case of emergency, and she wanted to tuck some of the food packs in it. She would ditch the second one if she had to, because she couldn't hike long distances carrying both. But they both contained items that would be useful to have. Hopefully she wouldn't have to leave one behind.

Annwyn had left while Kathryn got ready. When she returned, she was dressed in heavy winter clothing too, and she had a sword strapped to her back. She eyed Kathryn's new outfit with approval. "I like jeans."

"You would really like these. They're made for cold weather." Lifting up her sweater, she turned down the waistband so Annwyn could see the flannel lining inside.

The other woman's expression lit with interest. "When we return to Earth, I must seek out a pair of those. Are you ready?"

She nodded. Giving Sophie a quick hug, she hefted up her two packs, settled one on each shoulder by a strap, and followed Annwyn to the manor house. They met Rowan and Gawain at the huge front doors.

The men were dressed in hardy winter clothing as well. Nodding to her in greeting, they lifted her packs away. She didn't protest. They had much more body mass than she did, as well as wider shoulders, and decades of running a challenging medical practice had taught her to conserve her energy until she had to expend it.

As they followed Annwyn inside, Kathryn stared around in fascination. For hundreds of years the peculiar magic of the house had kept it locked against all who would enter. Sophie was the first person to unlock this house's mysteries and step inside. From the drunken euphoria in her voice when she called with the news, Kathryn could imagine how she had felt.

If Kathryn had merely been visiting, she might have wanted to poke around the house, but it was clear from Annwyn's own emotional struggle that too many people were depending on Kathryn to do her job. It wouldn't be fair to abrade already strained nerves by lingering.

She needed to get to Oberon as quickly as possible to examine him. Then she needed to heal him if she could.

Failing that, she would need to break the bad news to the Daoine Sidhe as quickly as possible so they knew in what direction they needed to move in order to heal as a people. A lot was riding on Kathryn getting this right.

So she would get it right.

Chapter Four

TRAVELING THE PASSAGEWAY at the manor house was certainly the most idiosyncratic crossover Kathryn had ever experienced.

A very long time ago, Morgan le Fae—she must remember to call him Garanhir and not something that was so offensive to him—had broken the crossover passageway in an ancient battle between Isabeau's Light Court and the Daoine Sidhe. Then Kathryn's idiotic ancestor had the perfect lack of good sense to build the manor house on top of the broken land magic.

Sophie had figured out the correct path through the broken pieces that would still lead to Lyonesse. It had involved descending into an oubliette and digging a tunnel, which had since been widened and supported with timber beams.

As Kathryn emerged from the tunnel behind Gawain, intense cold slapped her face. Pausing outside the entrance, she took a deep breath and looked around.

It was night in Lyonesse, with lowering clouds and bitter winds. Wilderness slashed across an uneven horizon that was broken with rock. The only illumination came from flickering torchlights and campfires from the troops stationed on the spot.

No halogen lighting. No electricity. No cars, no planes, no asphalt. In response, her Wyr side, the wildest part of her, surged up in fierce joy.

She looked over the tents and the raw timber frames of what would soon be structures. Sophie had kept Kathryn updated on various details of her new life regularly, and according to her emails they had started building the shelters months ago.

But since a fortnight in Lyonesse would take six months or more of Earth time to pass, here they had just begun to build the housing that would be necessary to keep the troops and their mounts in safety.

She followed Annwyn to the largest campfire, content to study the scene with reined-in glee while the general conferred with the soldiers huddling close to the warmth.

Rowan touched her arm. "Would you like to step inside one of the tents? We could get a hot drink for you."

She hadn't even resorted to putting up her hood yet and shook her head. "I'm good, thanks."

"Okay, but don't hesitate to say if you get too cold."

"Will do."

Annwyn turned back to them, frowning. "Robin has refused to stay in the camp, but he must be close by. Rowan and Gawain, circle the clearing and call out for him." Her frustrated gaze met Kathryn's briefly. "He'll show up when he's ready to, I guess."

Kathryn nodded as she continued to peruse the area.

Annwyn switched to telepathy. *About Robin. Just so you know, he's a puck—a nature sprite, which means he's wilder than most.*

She noted the other woman made no mention of old resentments or tensions. Was Annwyn unaware of them, or was she simply giving the kind of warning she thought was suitable for a visitor to hear?

Over the years, Kathryn had talked to countless families of patients and had heard and seen it all—justifications, arguments, enablers, outright hostility, love, hate, hope, lies, despair. Who knew what the truth was in Annwyn's case—and who cared? Kathryn had one job: healing Oberon. Anything else was superfluous.

I appreciate you telling me, she replied, filing the conversation away in case it became useful to her mission.

The troops had started to widen a natural clearing, and raw tree trunks studded the ground along the tree line. Also, she noted, shelter for their cattle had come first. They had already erected one wall of what would be a proper stable, and a rough roof of sorts comprised of pine tree boughs had been piled on top of the building frame. Campfires were positioned at both ends of the partial shelter. In the reflected light, she could see the animals standing close together, draped in heavy blankets.

Horses and cows could tolerate pretty cold

temperatures—twenty degrees Fahrenheit or lower if they had to—so the fact that the Daoine Sidhe were emphasizing their safety indicated how bitter the temperatures must get at night.

As if Annwyn had read her mind, the other woman said, "Lyle tells me the bad weather has been coming in waves. I don't know what that means about Oberon's condition, if anything, other than he's still alive. We're in a lull right now."

Kathryn nodded again. "Hopefully they'll get the barn finished before the next wave hits. Then if worse comes to worst, they can shelter with the animals."

The other woman nodded. "That was their thinking. The cattle throw off a lot of heat. It's a bit smelly to bunk with the animals, but overall it's a good survival tactic."

As they chatted, Kathryn's gaze fell on the area designated as the woodpile. Several cords had already been cut and stacked neatly, and still more lay in haphazard piles around the trunks that were being used to split the wood.

In the darkest shadow behind the cord farthest from the fire, a pair of eyes watched her.

The eyes themselves were so deep in shadow they were almost as dark as the rest of the night. Someone with lesser eyesight wouldn't have seen it, but Kathryn's vision was unusual even among the Wyr. Because of her animal form, she could pick out small prey from very long distances and a rabbit from up to two miles away.

She said nothing about the presence behind the woodpile. Instead, she positioned herself to face it and looked back steadily.

I see you. She didn't say it, either aloud or telepathically. She didn't have to. She merely waited.

Her patience was soon rewarded.

There was a flicker of barely seen movement. Then a figure in the shape of a tall, thin teenage boy detached from the shadows and walked toward the campfire.

Any potential resemblance to youth ended as the creature grew closer. Kathryn inspected him with interest. He had spiky, nut-brown hair, a thin, wild face and ageless, feral eyes.

While everyone else was bundled against the cold, he wore pants, boots, and a woolen coat left carelessly open. He also wore a rather odd scarf, royal blue with gold buttons, but he wore no gloves on hands that had too many fingers, and when he smiled he had too many teeth as well, and they were sharp and white.

Whatever form he might choose to wear, those teeth revealed something useful about his real nature. Those were a predator's teeth.

"You must be Robin," she said as he drew near. "I'm Kathryn Shaw."

"I am indeed," Robin said. "And I am a host of other names besides. I'll be betting you have other names and titles too. But which is the truest?"

As the only heir to an English title, it so happened that Kathryn did have other names and titles, but the only relevant title she cared about was the one she had earned through her own sweat equity.

His question was probably nothing more than playfulness, but it still caught at her. Which one was the truest—falcon or doctor? She didn't know.

"Thankfully," she replied, "we can be more than one thing simultaneously."

Annwyn had turned away to talk to the spokesman from the local troops again, and she spun back around. "Robin! There you are. The troops are already mustering. We will be ready to ride shortly."

The puck ignored her, his attention focused on Kathryn. "My Sophie knows a Dr. Kathryn Shaw and loves her."

My Sophie—both affectionate and possessive. She smiled. "Yes, that's me. And *my* Sophie knows and loves a puck named Robin."

Flinging out one narrow hand, he bowed. "'Tis I, although I was not in this form when we met, nor was I capable of any speech at the time." As he straightened to his full height again, his smile had disappeared. "She saved my life, at much risk to hers."

"She's very brave," she said. "And generous. I just finished having tea, sandwiches, and scones with her. I know she would love to see you again, whenever that becomes possible."

The strange creature's expression shadowed, eyelids lowering. "Perhaps there will be time enough again for that one day." When he looked up again, his gaze pierced her. He said, "I will carry you."

It was an assent to a question that Kathryn had not realized had been asked. She wasn't quite sure how to respond, so she kept it simple. "Thank you."

At that he shapeshifted into a huge black stallion with fiery eyes and long, feathery black hair at the fetlocks that covered massive hooves. The transition was so abrupt and the stallion's presence so Powerful, Kathryn fell back a step before she could catch herself.

According to the others she had talked to, Robin was a great many things, but at the moment he was simply magnificent.

"I have two bags," she told him apologetically. It didn't seem right for this wonderful creature to be used as a beast of burden, but he had offered.

He shook his head impatiently. "They mean nothing. Put them on my back."

"All right." She already had straps she could use to connect her packs. While the twenty troops who would travel with them gathered with their mounts, she knelt and buckled the packs together, then slung them over the stallion's neck.

He stamped one great hoof and snapped, "I will not tolerate a saddle or bridle."

She looked into his ferocious eyes. "I would never dream of suggesting it."

"Then climb on."

When she started to, a hand on her arm stopped her. Annwyn said, "Robin can't teleport like the Djinn can, but when he chooses to, he can move very fast. Falling at such a speed would probably be fatal." She said to the puck, "Robin, please rethink the saddle and bridle just this once."

"No," Kathryn said. When they both turned to stare at her, she told them, "I won't fall. It will be okay."

"I don't want to take the time to argue with you," Annwyn said impatiently. "You know how much is at stake here."

Kathryn regarded her and said again, "I won't fall."

The other woman pulled a sour expression. "Prove me right, and if the fall doesn't kill you, I might."

Then one of her men called to her, and she pivoted on one foot to stalk away.

Kathryn looked at the puck. "Did I refrain from rolling my eyes at that?"

The stallion tilted his head as if he wasn't quite sure what he had heard.

She added, "I couldn't tell. I was too busy trying to control myself."

Stamping one hoof again, he snorted. It sounded quite like horsy laughter. He told her again, "Climb on."

Not all the other troops had mustered, so it seemed a bit too soon to subject him to her weight. Still, she was beginning to feel the cold, and sitting on his back would be warmer than letting her feet turn to blocks of ice, so she turned and strode away, then whirled and raced toward him. With a leap, she landed on his wide back.

From somewhere nearby, someone let out a low

whistle and slow clap. Suppressing a smile, she edged closer to the stallion's shoulders and arranged the weight of her two packs so that they fell on her knees on either side.

The stallion shook his head and arched his neck. "You may hold on to my mane."

"That would be helpful," she said gravely. Wanting to experiment with how much of a handhold would be comfortable, she gathered together a decent amount of the coarse raven hair and gripped it in one fist.

Without warning, the stallion leaped forward.

"Whoa!" she said sharply, more from surprise than anything else, and clamped down with her knees to maintain her seat. She caught a brief glimpse of Annwyn and other soldiers turning to stare, their faces filled with shock and dismay.

Annwyn roared, "*ROBI*—"

The wind snatched away the last of his name.

Powerful muscles surged underneath Kathryn, and the wind bit into her skin. The land plunged by so quickly, by the time she looked over her shoulder, the encampment at the crossover passageway had already disappeared.

What. The. Hell.

She didn't know what was going on, but she knew for certain this was not what Annwyn believed would happen. They were supposed to travel as a group, but for some reason, Robin had decided to forge ahead on his own and leave the others behind.

The bones in her face were beginning to ache, but she didn't want to risk letting go with one hand to pull her hood up. It might be impossible to sound calm while breathless, but she gave it a try. "Robin, I don't like this. We weren't supposed to leave them behind."

The puck said, "That was not what I promised."

There was a vicious note in his voice, and her heart sank. She had heard all too many tales of bargains made with ancient creatures that hadn't been worded carefully enough. "But it's what Annwyn believes. Turn around and go back. It's not too late to fix this."

This, whatever this was. This kidnapping?

He ignored her. Where was he planning on taking her?

She was tempted to wait to find out, but just as it wouldn't have been fair to explore the manor house while the others waited, it didn't seem fair to prolong whatever this was either.

Crouching low over the stallion's back, she shapeshifted, and as soon as her body had transformed into a falcon's, she launched. She thought of her packs regretfully as she flung upward, most especially her physician's bag and the fire-starter kit she'd had for so long, but sometimes you just had to let go.

As she gained in height, she looked back at the puck. The stallion plunged around in a circle, completely at a loss, just as Annwyn and the troops had been moments ago. Rearing, he screamed at her in wordless rage and frustration.

She almost laughed except he was too dangerous, and she didn't know what he would do next. For all she knew, he could shapeshift into a bird and follow her. From Sophie's stories, he had been a small dog, and then a monkey as well as the horse.

Besides, flying away into the night wasn't what she had come here to do either.

With an inward sigh, she wheeled on the wind and arrowed back to the puck. Landing some distance away, she shapeshifted back into her human form, put up her hood, and crossed her arms.

He had wheeled to face her and stood, head lowered, almost as if he were a bull and she a red flag.

"Why did you leave them behind?" she asked.

He said nothing. Every line in his body was furious and recalcitrant, as if he were a two-thousand-pound, stubborn child. Gods, what a thought.

Cautiously she walked forward. "If you don't talk to me, I will fly away and not come back. Is that what you want?"

"Of course not." He gnashed huge teeth at her.

"Did you ever have any intention of taking me to Oberon?"

His pause went on a little too long for her liking. "Yes. Eventually. Probably. Annwyn might have studied you. She might have decided you were safe to have around our king. But I haven't, and I don't listen to what Annwyn or anyone else in the Dark Court says."

Sophie had been right. There was a long-held

resentment, and possibly even jealousy, vibrating in those words.

In the meantime, the wind had grown even colder, and now both her cheeks and toes had gone numb. "I need my cloak, and it's in one of the packs on your back," she said. "Do you mind?"

He glowered. "No."

Warily she approached, but he held still while she dug in the right pack to pull the cloak out. Shaking it out, she draped it around her shoulders and pulled the hood over that of her coat. Heaviness settled around her, but it was without warmth.

She was going to have to use one of her body warmers. Digging into the pack again, she pulled out a packet. Once she opened that and tucked it inside her coat, it began to put out a welcome heat that sank through her layers of clothing. Wrapping her arms around her chest, she hugged it close.

After a few minutes' thought, she said, "I'm not on Annwyn's side."

He lifted his head to stare at her. "Whose side are you on?"

Nobody's side. Not Annwyn's. Not yours. She rejected each possible answer as it occurred to her, as she tried to figure out what he wanted to hear.

Then she told him the truth. "I'm on Oberon's side. That's always true whenever I take on a patient—I'm on their side, especially the children and those who can't speak for themselves. Not their families. Not the courts.

Theirs." She paused. "Your king is going to die unless something is done for him."

"Can you fix him?" Despite how he obviously wanted to keep his guard up, hope and need slipped into his voice.

"I don't know. I can assess his condition, and I can do what is best for him—I will do everything I possibly can, but there's no way I can know what that might be without examining him. And the truth is, I might not be able to do anything. Only one thing is certain, Robin. Your king is going to die unless something is done for him. Why didn't you want to bring Annwyn and the troops with us?"

He stamped at the snow desultorily. Other than tangling his mane and tail, the wind and the massive cold didn't seem to affect him at all. "I wanted to judge you for myself while *they* weren't around. If you were a threat, I would take care of you." He looked at her sidelong to see how she took his words.

He might be old, unpredictable, and dangerous, but he had nothing on a cantankerous, bullheaded dragon. She said gently, "You were looking after your king."

"He told me to guard his place and watch them. A long time ago, Isabeau took me and held me captive for years. I failed him once. I won't fail him again."

Holding back a sigh, she thought, in the meantime, while you play out your guilt-ridden power fantasies, he is going to die unless something is done for him.

She bit back saying that too. Instead, she asked,

"How long will it take them to reach the city on their own?"

He gave an equine equivalent of a scornful shrug. "Perhaps a fortnight?"

"Okay. You know what? I think you should pay attention to what your Sophie thinks, not what Annwyn says or does. Your Sophie would want you to take me to Oberon. You can shadow me all you like. You can ask whatever questions you need to ask, and you can watch any procedure I might need to do. And I can explain everything I need to do before I do it. How does that sound?"

"That's a bargain I'm willing to accept." He bared his teeth. "And I can be there to stop you if you try to harm him in any way."

Annwyn would be beyond furious of course, but Kathryn had told Robin the truth when she'd said she wasn't on Annwyn's side. She was on Oberon's side, and this was the fastest way she could get to see her patient for the first time.

"Of course." She shrugged. "That too."

SOMETIMES YOU COULD slog away at something for months or years and never seem to make any headway. A long project, a difficult situation, a challenging surgery. In a way, Kathryn's journey to get to Lyonesse was like that—there had been so many moving parts, it had seemed to take forever.

And then suddenly life speeds up. You make a breakthrough, end the project, complete the difficult situation, finish the surgery. For Kathryn, that came the closest of anything she did to the feeling of flying while she was on the ground.

Until now.

Land streaked by as the stallion raced at a breakneck pace. She caught glimpses of the ever-changing landscape—sometimes it seemed like Scotland and at other times like Spain. It was its own unique place. Now she wanted to stop and sightsee. She couldn't imagine when she would have the time. She would probably never get the chance.

At one point they raced along a seemingly endless shore while dark thunderclouds larger than cities towered overhead and the howling of the wind sounded like a live creature full of viciousness and teeth. Robin's speed was incredible. They were traveling faster than she could fly.

And she loved it.

Leaning forward, she shouted, "Go faster!"

There was the slightest hitch in his stride. She had surprised him. Then he tossed his head and bugled in response. Stretching his body out, his long, powerful legs a blur, he raced faster. In that moment she forgave him everything—his recalcitrance, duplicity, obstructiveness, everything.

Just before dawn, as a knifelike light began to silver the restless shore, they came upon a dark, ruined city so quickly she could only snatch at details. Like the bones of an immense creature, the shadowed columns, roads, archways, and buildings flashed by, leaving behind an impression of broken grace and beauty. Half of it lay underwater, and what was left was covered in gargantuan swaths of ice and frozen icicles. It was a gorgeous, tragic place.

Once he stepped into the city, Robin had to slow down until he walked, picking his way along ruined causeways and climbing sides of aqueducts. Neither spoke, the eerie, howling wind ever present. She thought about offering to get down to walk but staying clenched in the same position throughout the long hours of the night had made her stiffen, and she decided not to mention it if he didn't.

Soon they left the submerged part behind as the puck picked a route that led uphill, and something else began to intrude on her awareness. The crazy wind was getting to her. She shook her head, but the feeling persisted. Covering her ears with both gloved hands, she tried to concentrate.

A sense of danger slid icy fingers down her spine. There was a Power that resided here, and it felt dark, vengeful, and awake. Like a predator, it tracked their progress through the streets but chose not to attack, at least not yet. It felt like it was biding its time.

Twisting, she studied the empty streets around them and took in deep lungful of the briny air. She caught no scents other than land, stone, and sea.

Robin, she said telepathically. *Something is tracking us.*

Do you sense that?

Yes. He sounded strangely peaceful. *He knows we're here.*

Holy hells. For the first in what seemed like a very long time, she felt seriously shaken. That predatory, malevolent-feeling Power was *Oberon?*

I don't get it, she thought. When all the members of the Dark Court spoke about Oberon, it was with a combination of love, pain, and respect, as if he was some kind of missing goddamn hero. How could they love this? It felt like a monster contemplating a slaughter. Oh Shaw, what have you gotten yourself into now?

"Wow, do I feel welcome," she muttered.

The puck appeared to miss her tone of sarcasm completely. "You should. When Annwyn and the troops arrive, the storms will rage through the city until ice shards drive through glass, and midday will seem black as night. You will want to shelter in place when that happens."

Surprise took her over. "What's the difference between our arrival and theirs?"

"Me," Robin said simply. "Maybe because I was the last one he saw before he fell to his sleep. Maybe because he gave me orders that I'm supposed to follow. No one knows for sure."

Fell to his sleep.

The puck's odd wording snagged her attention. It sounded ominous, like falling to his death. "Well, I'm glad I took you up on your offer to bring me. I had no idea just getting to him was going to be so difficult. What would happen if we split up?"

"I suggest you do not leave my side."

Oh, no worries about that. She had no intention of doing so.

By the time they came up to the palace, it was almost anticlimactic. The structure was, she decided, very palace-y—a large sprawl of a stone building with crenellations along the top, turrets at each end, and rows of columns and arches along the front.

The design seemed almost Moorish and looked both attractive and defensible. A long scar along the ground that bordered the front of the building might once have been a functional moat. Now that area was nothing more than a slick-looking, frozen smear.

Many years of doing her job had taught her one thing: to grab any chance available to get her needs met while she could. As they approached the building, she dug into a pack and pulled out a piece of jerky to chew while she considered what came next.

"Would you take me directly to him?" she asked.

The surprise was back in his voice as he replied, "I thought we might rest? It has been a long journey for both of us."

"I know you're tired, and I am too," she told him. "But from everything I was told, Oberon is supposed to be unconscious, yet his Power feels aware, and it appears to be reacting to stimuli. I would rather introduce myself right away in case he might be aware enough to take it in."

"He is asleep." The flat, uncertain note in the puck's voice persisted.

She explained, "Comatose patients can be more aware than people think. Sometimes after they awaken, they report hearing voices and conversations that occurred around them while they were in their comas. I don't know that Oberon is in a coma exactly, but I'd like to see if we can tell whether he will accept my presence. I don't want to be attacked by some freak bout of weather while I'm trying to sleep."

"You make a good point," he said after a moment. "We will go to see him straightaway."

"Thank you."

They had reached the wide, icy palace steps. When Robin drew to a halt, she slid off his back and dragged her packs off. Stiffly she bent to unbuckle them while the puck shapeshifted. As she pulled them apart, one of his thin, strong hands came into view.

Wordlessly he took the lighter pack. He had born her weight plus both packs through the night, so she wasn't about to complain. Straightening, she shouldered the other one. Then she followed him into the palace.

The interior was grand and abandoned. Normally she would have pored over every detail with intense fascination. Now she had neither the time or the energy. Spacious hallways, wide stairwells, and corridors all went by in a blur.

The sense of being watched by the dark Power

intensified until the tiny hairs stood up on the back of her neck. Every Wyr sense she owned was screaming: *Danger. Run.*

But she did no such thing. She followed Robin down a wide, richly appointed corridor to a set of double doors made of a glossy, very dark wood. She almost expected Robin to pull out a key. Instead, he merely turned the knob and pushed the door open to a deeply shadowed room.

Oberon was in there. She knew it. She could feel it in the goose bumps raising on her arms and legs. This was the culmination of her long journey.

Here, the presence of the dark Power was almost unbearably intense. It felt like a thunderclap about to break against her skin. She half expected lightning to shear across the dark interior space.

Robin was looking at her as if he expected her to do something.

Setting down her pack, she sat down carefully on the floor at the edge of the doorway. Then, because she was who she was, she multitasked and pulled out a bag of the high-calorie, high-fat trail mix.

Shaking some into her hand, she popped it in her mouth. After chewing and swallowing, she said, "Your majesty, my name is Dr. Shaw, and I've traveled a very long way to meet you. I'm here to help you if I can, but I won't attempt to do anything against your will. If you understand what I'm saying, please give me a sign that you consent to an examination."

Then she paused. Nothing happened. Her wary gaze shifted sideways to Robin, who had squatted by her side. The puck stared at her intently. She tilted the bag toward him.

Slowly, his feral gaze never leaving her face, he reached into the bag and took a handful of the trail mix.

She turned her attention back to the shadowed room. "Sir, I have to ask you again, do I have your consent to examine you? Give me a sign, Oberon, or I'm going to go away. I was led to believe you were unconscious, but you've got too much raised Power to be completely unaware, and I'm not going to risk my life just to examine you. I'll make this simple—do you want to live, or do you want to die? Because you're headed for death just fine on your own, and you don't need me to be here for that."

She ate some more trail mix while she waited. Mmm, chocolate.

Nothing happened.

Disappointment made her shoulders sag. Okay then. Pushing to her feet, she said, "I'm going... Going..."

Just as she was about to say *gone*, the unbearable intensity in the Power shifted. It didn't go away, but as she carefully assessed the change, it no longer felt like it was going to ram like a spike down her throat.

Suddenly magic arced like lightning, and light flared in round witchlights positioned around a richly appointed bedroom. The figure of a large man lay on the bed. His shape was a dark, heavy shadow against the crimson-and-gold bedcover.

She was going to ignore the fact that she had almost jumped out of her skin. She and Robin stared at each other, eyes wide.

"All right," she whispered. "I'm going to take that as a consent to enter." Even as she spoke, an unusual case of anxiety attacked her. Stepping inside that room felt like walking into the open mouth of a giant.

"I will enter with you," Robin replied softly.

"Sure, okay," she muttered, unimpressed. Oberon liked Robin.

Pushing to her feet, she left her pack in the doorway and slowly walked inside.

Then lightning bolts hit her after all as several realizations struck at once.

He was a big, hard behemoth of a man. It was difficult to tell with him lying down, but she thought he might easily be the size of one of the gryphon sentinels, if not larger. He sprawled in a casual pose on the massive bed, as if he had just laid down for a nap.

She glanced at the rich but plain masculine furniture and the luxuriously thick rug underneath as her mind flashed through rapid calculations.

A fortnight in Lyonesse roughly equaled six months on Earth, and on Earth Oberon had been in a comatose state for two hundred years. So that would be four Lyonesse weeks for each Earth year, and four times two hundred meant he had been unconscious in Lyonesse for eight hundred weeks.

It was silly to think Lyonesse might have fifty-two weeks in a year just because Earth did, she thought, but for the sake of compiling a completely useless statistic, let's say there were. That meant Oberon had been in a vegetative state for almost fifteen and a half years.

The entire room, even Oberon, should be coated with a layer of dust, but everything was pristine. His muscles should have wasted, but they hadn't. He looked fit, vital, and his skin was deeply burnished as if he spent a lot of time out in the sun. He had a strong, mature face with a short-clipped beard, and thick, packed muscles wrapped around a long, masculine frame.

It was a hard face, a dangerous face, with an outrageously sensual mouth. The severe cold invaded even this room, but he wore nothing except a pair of black pants and boots. A sprinkle of dark hair dusted the broad muscles of his chest and arrowed down to disappear into the waistband of his pants.

Studying him outside the sterility of a hospital examination room felt inappropriately intimate. Every detail struck her like bullets and burrowed underneath her skin. She felt invaded just by looking at him.

But none of that delivered the sucker punch.

That blow came when she took in her first breath after stepping into the room. For the first time, she breathed in his scent and reeled.

Oberon was Wyr.

Chapter Five

HE DREAMED OF killing the bitch over and over again, caught in an endless loop.

Isabeau, Queen of the Light Court. Satan personified. She had a beauty like a rotten peach whose perfect, blush skin invited you to partake, but when you bit into the flesh, poisonous worms spilled into your mouth.

He didn't want her merely dead. He wanted her utterly crushed, completely destroyed, and then violently executed. He wanted her aware of her own destruction so when she sank into that final darkness, she would know she had lost everything she had ever cared about and everything she had ever wanted.

Just as he had.

His hands squeezing around her neck. His thumbs gouging out her eyes. His sword sliding into her body.

Somehow in his dreams, it was never really satisfying, never really enough. Never really *finished*. Somehow she always slipped away to come at him in another fashion.

And so he had to kill her again while kingdoms fell and life devolved into a single sick feeling in the gut, because everything was always in a crisis, and all that remained was rage.

Until a woman started speaking to him.

At first it was meaningless background noise to his death-filled dreams. But then it intruded, and life gained a definition that went beyond the sick sense of crisis in his gut.

Now there was a second thing.

There was the sound of her voice. Her, the woman. He had never met her before, but suddenly she came to be present, and when she spoke to him, the words were calm, bright, and crisp.

Sometimes there was silence and the killing dreams returned, but then the woman came back. If he had been awake, it would have driven him crazy.

Because she talked and talked and talked.

And talked.

Then he no longer dreamed about killing Isabeau. Sometimes he dreamed about figuring out ways to shut that talkative woman up.

Chapter Six

IT WAS DAY four in this frozen hellhole. Day four. And it was freaking freezing *everywhere*.

Nothing stayed warm. Since their arrival, she had tried a new bedroom every night and had stocked it beforehand with plenty of firewood. Each night she had built a blazing fire, but they all burned without warmth. She could run her fingers through the flames without getting her skin singed.

The only way she survived was by wrapping herself up in coat, cloak, and blankets and then tucking the Mylar emergency blanket around the entire bundle so that it captured ninety percent of the heat she managed to generate. She felt like a giant foil-wrapped burrito.

Water didn't boil. Food never warmed. There was plenty of food in the cavernous palace kitchen and pantries, but it was all frozen hard as rocks. For every swallow of water, she needed to suck on a piece of ice until it melted.

In order to eat, she either had to do the same thing, or carry frozen bits of food around in her pocket so her body heat would eventually help it to thaw. She had a hardy constitution, but all the challenges were frankly wearing.

The hand and body warmers were lifesavers. She used one a day and got ten glorious hours of help with combating the cold in the form of a single miraculous little packet. But she had only two left. Soon she was going to have to rely solely on her own body's resources.

And Robin was no help. First, there was no way in hell she would suggest sharing blankets and body heat when she barely trusted him enough to turn her back while they were together in the same room.

Second, she couldn't suggest sharing body heat anyway, because after shadowing her obsessively for two days and listening to her constantly explain every little thing to him—which meant she frequently had to offer background medical lectures so he understood what she was saying, including drawing sketches in lieu of PowerPoint slideshows—he disappeared without warning or explanation.

She had no idea if he was off running some errand that he considered vitally important or if something had happened and he had gotten himself into real trouble. He had simply vanished.

Kathryn wrote "4" on a piece of parchment paper and propped it in one corner of Oberon's room within easy sight.

Day four meant Annwyn and her troops would be arriving in about ten days. Then, according to Robin, Kathryn would need to shelter in place as they entered the city.

Unless Robin had changed his mind and had gone to fetch them? But that didn't sound likely, so she had to plan for other contingencies. Probably the best place to shelter would be with Oberon in his bedroom, because presumably his Power wouldn't have any self-destructive tendencies when it rampaged the city.

After she had finished her morning ritual of straightening her possessions that had gotten strewn all over Oberon's furniture, she braced herself and turned to face the man lying on the bed. Every time she looked at him, she felt the same gut punch as the first time she had laid eyes on him. At least now she knew to prepare for it.

Yes, he was Wyr. According to his scent, he was some kind of feline. He was a big damn cat.

On the night of their arrival, when she discovered what Oberon was, she had exclaimed, "How come nobody told me he was Wyr? I thought the Daoine Sidhe was a community of mixed breeds from the Elder Races!"

She had always liked the idea. It sounded warm and inclusive, with none of the walls that people erect to keep out their perceived "other," so she felt a little shock of betrayal to discover the truth.

Robin had given her a thoughtful look. "He was mixed Dark Fae and Wyr for a very long time. It was only after Morgan's attack that he threw everything he had into trying to shapeshift. He thought it might help dislodge the magic. After he finally changed into his Wyr form, it did seem to work—for a while. He appeared to be healed for another two years, until the spell awoke again."

Robin described the reality of what every half-Wyr faced. They couldn't completely access many of the health and physical attributes of the full Wyr until they were able to successfully shapeshift into their animal forms. Most who were part-Wyr never managed to achieve that transition.

She couldn't imagine how Oberon had managed to shapeshift on his own without the assistance of an older Wyr. It spoke of a towering will and determination to survive. When she had met with Morgan, the sorcerer had confessed he was astonished Oberon had survived so long. As scary as Oberon's Power felt, she had tremendous respect for his will to live.

But this situation was maddening. Even though he appeared to be perfectly warm, the cold was so bitter she had draped blankets over his lax form before leaving that first time.

The next morning, when she had walked into the bedroom, everything she had done to him had been reversed. He lay back in his original position, and the blankets were tucked back in the closet.

The room lay in deep shadow, only flaring with light when she and Robin stepped back inside. Her possessions were the only things left alone... possibly because they were new to Oberon's unconscious mind and he didn't know what to do with them?

Who the hell knew? She could say only one thing for certain. In all her many years as a doctor, this was the most unique situation she had ever been in. And she *hated* to admit that it wasn't going well.

Because she didn't just have Morgan's sophisticated assassination spell to fight. That would have been difficult enough on its own. She had to fight Oberon himself.

And she wasn't winning.

She had run out of the jerky and trail mix. In an effort to keep her caloric intake high, she had taken to eating butter and other fats from the kitchen pantries because they melted easily after being in contact with her body heat.

Still, she had grown tired all the time, and while the Wyr didn't suffer from colds like humans did, her lungs felt raw from constantly breathing in the dangerously frigid air.

Also, her throat was sore. She was suffering from voice strain from all the damn talking she'd done over the past several days. She could cast a pain-relieving spell on herself, but she didn't want to do permanent damage to her vocal cords, and the only thing that would help them was to rest her voice.

She had started out with explaining every little thing to Robin, but then she found that if she didn't keep talking to Oberon every damn moment while she scanned him or did anything else, his Power would gather in the room like a black, malevolent thundercloud. And black, malevolent thunderclouds never boded well for anybody.

The only way she made headway was when she talked nonstop while she tried the various spells and techniques she had worked out with Morgan. Oberon didn't fight her when she was talking to him. When he lay acquiescent, she could sense the icy needle pressing against his heart. It was so close to taking him, so close.

But after long, careful work, she had only managed to wiggle that needle back a millimeter, then another... just as long as she kept talking. As soon as she paused to take a breath, or her voice faltered, his Power snapped around him like a clenched fist and she couldn't get back inside his body without doing damage, either to him or to herself.

What she wouldn't give for a warm, cooked meal and something hot to drink. Broth, coffee, tea. Anything. A whiskey toddy with lemon and honey sounded like heaven.

In the meantime, the bastard just lay there on his bed and looked like he could sit up at any minute. Even though he was shirtless in the wretched, unnatural cold, he was warm to the touch. Other than the few precious remaining packets of body warmers that remained, he was the only heat source in the entire city.

He was warm to the touch.

When the idea hit, it was filled with such simple brilliance her shoulders sagged—partly from relief at the thought and partly for how far and quickly she had fallen away from any semblance of keeping appropriate boundaries between her and her patient.

But he was warm to the touch, and her stiff muscles and tired mind needed some real rest before she expended more energy on trying to wrestle another round of healing spells into him. So she did the practical thing. She went down the hall to her latest bedroom and retrieved her Mylar blanket.

She was already wearing her fur-lined cloak over her coat. With two people under the Mylar blanket, she thought the cloak would be more than enough covering. And she had already gone to the kitchen for provisions. She'd hacked some ice chips into a tankard, and gathered frozen nuts, dried fruit, a small tub of butter, and a wheel of cheese, both as solid as blocks of ice.

Back in Oberon's room, she set the tankard on the mattress next to his hip and carefully propped it up with the food. Then she lay down on his other side, shook her cloak over them both, food and all, and then over that she spread the Mylar blanket, talking hoarsely the whole time.

"Look, I don't like this any more than you do—or any more than you would if you were really cognizant of what a monumental pain in the ass you've been. But until I break through to you or…" Or conclude I can't do anything for you. Something in her chest tightened at the thought. "…or you stop creating such terrible winter conditions, we've got to do whatever it takes to make this work. Understood?"

He said nothing, did nothing. Most importantly, his Power did not coalesce menacingly, so she eased down beside his long, hard form and eased her head down on the pillow next to his.

Soon she was more than warm. She quickly grew too hot. Eureka. Unzipping her coat, she shrugged out of it and let it fall by the bed. Deep exhaustion followed the wonderful warmth as her tense muscles finally unknotted for the first time since crossing over.

As she lay back down beside him, she murmured drowsily, "That's all that's coming off, buddy, so relax, you're safe."

She was even halfway convinced she was safe, at least for the moment, but she wasn't comfortable with the situation, not by a long shot, and she tried her damnedest to keep from coming into direct contact with his bare skin.

Yet she couldn't help but notice he smelled pretty good for a guy who hadn't bathed in fifteen and a half years. All clean and über-male, even if he was some kind of damn cat.

He was actually shockingly sexy, when she thought about it.

Stop thinking about it.

"We're never going to speak of this again," she informed him before she fell asleep.

Mmm. Sometime later, she inhaled the scent of sexy male as she rubbed her cheek against her pillow, which was made up of smooth, bare skin wrapped around solid, heavy muscles.

Sexual images played through her mind. Soon they would really wake up and entwine together, she and... and...

...and...

Just exactly *who* had she taken to bed?

What the hell. She couldn't even think of his name, and here she was, wrapped around him like a creeping vine—and she never had sex with a total stranger.

Bolting to a sitting position, she stared around wildly.

Oh right. Gotcha. King. Bed. Witchlights burning in their globes, lighting every detail in the palatial room.

She couldn't really say there was malevolence to the presence in the room, but it was definitely full of dark, heavy Wyr alpha male. It felt like melted dark chocolate against her skin, and she wanted to bathe in it.

The thought disgusted her. For fuck's sake, Shaw. Pull yourself together.

Dragging her fingers through her hair, she said without looking at the unconscious man beside her, "I am so, so sorry. I did not mean to cling to you like some sort of limpet. That all happened in my sleep. I wasn't aware of doing it."

Her voice was no more than a croak as her abused throat strained to get the words out. Just bloody marvelous. Glancing over her shoulder, she finally assessed Oberon's still features. He looked so peaceful, yet at the same time his Power had raged out of control and had sent his people running away from this beautiful city.

Sighing heavily, she lay back down and turned on her side to face him, this time *not* touching him. The frigid air bit at her cheeks, and she couldn't lie, it was hard to think about leaving the warmth their bodies had created in this nest.

"I'm going to put my hand on you," she whispered. "And I want to scan the interior of your chest. We've done this a dozen times already. There's nothing to it except a little tingle of magic. I don't need to keep talking to you ad nauseam to get this done, Oberon. Let's give it a rest, okay?"

She laid her hand on the hard, broad plate of his chest. So far so good. Then she fell silent as she started to scan him—and his Power surged to knock her magic out of his body.

Damn it.

Four damn days. Now almost five damn days of trying every trick she knew and expending every ounce of magical energy she possessed, and she had only managed to move Morgan's magic needle a few millimeters away from Oberon's heart.

That was a long, long way from healing him entirely.

"I can't help you if you keep fighting me at every turn," she ground out.

And she couldn't keep healing him if she contracted laryngitis. They were going to lose both those precious millimeters she had gained, because the magic in that needle would never stop, not as long as it remained in his body. It would simply lay dormant until it had generated enough energy to resume its task.

His strong, blunt profile remained oblivious. Even his short, dark beard was well trimmed. Not bad for a guy who hadn't shaved for a decade and a half. And that strong, molded mouth... It was as shockingly sexy as the rest of him.

Later, she could never adequately explain why she did what she did. There was no excuse. It was inexcusable. If she had done it in New York and had been caught, she could have lost her license to practice medicine.

But she wasn't in New York. She was alone in this frigid, gorgeous, terrible place, and her heart swelled and ached for a man who was actively destroying his best hope at returning to life. For the goddamn hero who had fallen so long ago and for whom his people had fought so hard, because Kathryn was beginning to believe she would probably never get to meet him when he was conscious and aware.

Leaning forward, she pressed her lips to his. His mouth was so still, so warm and perfect. Her closed eyes filled with dampness as she lingered over the sensation of touching his lips with hers.

It felt like saying goodbye to a man she had never met and could barely acknowledge to herself that she had truly wanted to.

Then he moved.

He moved.

His still mouth became mobile, his lips hardening on hers. As she froze in shock, one large hand came up to cup the back of her neck while his long body shifted to align with hers.

She couldn't breathe, couldn't think. Her entire consciousness seized on the warmth of his mouth and the dexterous, hungry way he kissed her.

He growled quietly. The sound went down her spine, unzipping her. She had remained steady and strong through almost every difficult period in her life, but not this time. This time she trembled everywhere.

He couldn't have shocked her more if he had grabbed two defibrillator paddles and zapped her. Meanwhile his mouth conquered the shape of hers—conquered and demanded more. He pressed between her lips, and they parted without her conscious volition, allowing him entrance. When he probed deep inside her mouth, her body pulsed with desire that culminated in a sharp, almost unendurable ache between her legs.

Consumed with the riot going on inside, she was only half aware of his heavy weight settling over her. He ravaged her mouth, laying waste to her senses, and it was only when she felt the growing length of hardness pressing against her hip that a sliver of sanity managed to wedge itself into her brain.

He had an erection. And from what she could sense through the layers of their clothing, it was a good-sized one too.

Not bad for a guy who'd been out of action for fifteen years.

What is wrong with you, Shaw!

She had to stop this. Mmm. Holy gods, he really knew what to do with his mouth… They could stop in just a moment, couldn't they?

Penetrating her over and over again with his tongue, he cupped her breast in a large, powerful hand as he pushed his hips against hers in a slow, deliberate, sexy grind.

The sliver of sanity screamed at her. She couldn't wait until later—she had to stop this crazy behavior right now!

HONESTLY, THIS WOMAN. She was driving him mad. Blah blah blah blah blah. How could anybody talk so much?

There was only one good thing about it. The sound of her voice drove Isabeau from his mind, so he focused on her with equal parts irritation and relief.

Then a third thing insinuated itself into his awareness: something was wrong. The woman sounded ragged, her voice hoarse with exhaustion. You would have thought that would be enough to shut her up, but no, it did not.

Almost, he frowned.

Then her lips touched his.

And everything in his head lit up. Yes! This solved all

of it... The woman stopped talking, and the sensation of her warm, soft mouth covering his drove any thoughts of Isabeau scuttling far into the darkness where they belonged.

Pleasure cascaded through him, but her touch was light and gentle to the point of being chaste, and he wanted more. So much more.

He came fully awake to the sensation of raw hunger. Fixing his mouth on hers, he feasted on her like a man who had been starving for centuries. Warm, wet, and sensual, she kissed him back, and when he demanded more, she gave it.

A wealth of details shouted for attention. She smelled so goddamn good, like everything he had never known to dream about but suddenly discovered he needed more than life itself. Her hair was fine and silken—that meant she would be silken between her legs as well. The thought made him growl, and she trembled all over in response.

He had to taste her, touch her all over, fuck her. Nothing else existed... Admittedly, her clothes were very strange, he found as he palmed one breast... but nothing else, and no one else, existed in this moment...

"Stop!" she gasped.

Well, dammit. Now she was back to talking again. It couldn't detract from the delectably soft skin along her jaw and neck. He ran his lips along the delicate path where her carotid artery beat underneath the warm silken skin perfumed with the intoxicating scent of aroused female.

He couldn't wait to eat her up.

Something struck his shoulder. Her fist. She had hit him.

She struck him again, not lightly, then she clouted him over the head. *"Oberon, stop!"*

She dared to strike *him*? He bared his teeth at her in a snarl, and out of the corner of his eye he saw her draw back her fist. Unbelievably, she was going to do it again.

He hissed, "You do not strike the King!"

"You're not my king!" she shouted back.

He caught a glimpse of her fine-boned features surrounded by a cloud of the silken brown hair spread out on the pillow. Fire flashed in narrowed amber eyes. This time her fist came flying directly at his face, but his reflexes were faster than they had ever been, and he ducked sideways to avoid the blow that landed on his shoulder.

Outraged, he pulled back his own fist to strike back. That was when he discovered she was as fast as he was and quite strong. For one moment all his weight was poised on one elbow, and with a neat, whole-body heave, she shoved him over, hard.

As it transpired, they had been tussling close to the edge of the bed. Flipping over, he landed on his back. As the back of his head connected with the hard, frigid floor, full awareness slammed into him.

"Look," the woman croaked. "I am so, so sorry for this. There's been—I don't even know what to call it—a massive misunderstanding. I'm sure you'll understand everything once I explain everything…"

He barely heard her as memories cascaded through his mind. The attack at the masque. The poisonous spell that he could tell was even now still working through his body. Saying goodbye to his court and casting the stasis spell. The slow, raging collapse into darkness.

He surged upward with an outraged roar that shook the walls, and his anger propelled him into a shapeshift. Changing into a lion, he sprang at the woman. That stasis spell had been the only thing standing between him and certain death. He would disembowel the interloper for daring to disrupt it… for *sex*?

He got one glimpse of her mortified expression as he leaped, claws out and ready to strike. His front paws closed on thin air as her slender body melted away.

There was a rush of wings. He caught colors out of the corner of his eye—dark brown, black markings, and soft, mottled gray and white, as well as the slender, wicked length of a hooked beak and strong, hooked talons. The interloper was a full Wyr, a falcon.

Cupping his front paws, he twisted his massive body in midair to try to catch her as she flew past him, but she dipped her body so sharply the tips of her wings brushed against his whiskers.

Roaring again, he leaped and rebounded off the nearest wall, cracking plaster as he lunged for her again. He had speed and power in spades, but she was much smaller than he and could move like greased lightning.

She flapped around the room so chaotically it was maddening. Growling, he tried to follow, uncaring for how he knocked items over or how the strong, well-built furniture fractured under his weight. For one fraction of a moment he thought he had cornered her—but then she dodged successfully again.

This time he got the chance to look into the falcon's eyes as she passed by. She looked as furious as he felt, and as she streaked between his outstretched paws, she reached down to rake the claws of one foot along the tip of his lion's nose.

Sharp pain flared along the needlelike scratches. *Bloody hell.*

The cuts on his nose were insult upon injury. He couldn't be in more of a frenzy. Whirling, he watched as the falcon arrowed through the open doors and angled right to disappear down the corridor.

Silence fell in the aftermath of her departure. Then, with a yawning crack, his large, damaged four-poster bed collapsed in on itself.

Oberon stared at the shambles of what had once been a masculine, elegant room. In the tussle, they had managed to break every single one of the witchlights stationed along the walls.

Taking in a deep breath, he inhaled the woman's scent. It was everywhere in the ruined room. She had been in here more than once. The puck's scent also saturated the room. Had Robin allowed this, or had she vanquished him in some kind of battle?

Other details sank in. Various implements lay scattered on the floor. He recognized a scalpel, vials, and other strange items he couldn't identify, and also a metal box that looked like it would fit into the palm of his hand. There were also broken pencils, and a number of papers littered the broken furniture.

On one of the trampled pages, a sketch of an oddly shaped oval item was clearly visible. It was labeled in English, OBERON'S HEART. An arrow pointed to a spot on the edge of the oval. That part was labeled MORGAN'S MAGIC NEEDLE.

The interloper had studied him. She knew what was going on inside his body, probably better than he did. What had she hoped to gain when she had kissed him? As he'd awakened, he'd had only one thing in mind—sex.

Had she planned on using him to try to get pregnant? The King's heir would have an unparalleled advantage in Lyonesse. He growled at the thought even as he realized that food had also been strewn everywhere.

Pieces of dried fruit lay sprinkled over the trampled crimson-and-gold bedspread like confetti, and there was the sharp, aromatic scent of cheese. Curious, he pawed at a small, overturned tub. As he flipped it over, one of his claws sank into soft butter.

He licked it off as he took in other details. Amid the rubble was a fur-lined cloak and a strange piece of clothing that looked like a formfitting blue coat, and another odd, lightweight sheet of something that looked like metal but was pliable and made of a foreign substance he had never seen before.

The interloper had planned a ravishment, and she had brought... *snacks?*

As he stared around in sharp incredulity, his first surge of bestial rage settled into something calmer, colder, and far more deadly.

Soundlessly, the lion padded into the wide, empty corridor, his focus coalescing into a single purpose. He had prey to hunt and many questions to ask before he decided how he was going to kill her.

Chapter Seven

T HE FALCON'S ELUSIVE scent lingered maddeningly in the corridor outside his bedroom. He followed it through the abandoned palace until he reached the Garden Hall, a great room lined with floor-to-ceiling windows along the outside wall that overlooked what had once been an extensive garden.

Now, as he glanced out the windows, there was nothing to be seen but ice and snow-covered branches of trees, and mounds where well-tended shrubbery had once been. The great room had marble floors that were currently as cold as ice, cracked white molding along the top edges of the walls, a mellow gold paint that had grown faded and blotched with water stains, and vaulted ceilings with arched nooks overhead that were filled with white alabaster statues.

Outside, heavy, dark clouds hung low in the sky, and the grayness of the day leached all color from what Oberon's memories told him had once been a bright, airy, and cheerful space.

Overhead, in the shadow of one graceful alabaster statue, the ruffled shape of a bird huddled. Her previous sleek shape had disappeared. She had fluffed out all her feathers and looked fat as a disgruntled partridge, small head sunk down between her wings.

It was comical enough to almost make him smile, except his rage still burned too cold to allow humor to set in.

As he prowled around the empty expanse, the fat partridge shrank back deeper into the shadows, but it was too late. He had already spotted her.

Restlessly, he sniffed along the floor and the edges of the great arched doorways, but there were no other fresh scents. The place smelled of winter, dry rot, and happier events that had occurred long ago. He and the Wyr female were the only two living creatures he could sense anywhere on the palace grounds.

She had chosen her perch wisely. In his lion form he had a huge spring in his leap, but the alcove where she huddled was still beyond his physical reach. As long as she remained there, he would have to consider his repertoire of magic when he was ready to launch a strike against her.

While he waited to see if she would speak, he considered the various possibilities. As he seemed to recall, she'd certainly had no problem with talking before he had fully awakened.

The silence drew out between them, and he grew irritated. The light scratches on his nose had already healed, but he wanted to paw at her, his own claws out, and draw blood like she had drawn his.

Silkily, he asked, *Cat got your tongue?*

If anything, her feathers ruffled further, and that small graceful head all but disappeared.

Very funny. Her grumpy mental voice sounded much better than her physical voice did. *Okay, I apologize. I am so very sorry for what happened—*

An apology wasn't what he wanted. Whirling to face the shadowed alcove where she perched, he snarled wordlessly. The bestial sound vibrated in the huge nearby windows, and her words snapped off as if he had sliced through them with a sword.

Come down here and face me properly, or are you too much of a coward to do so? He threw out the challenge carelessly. He had no real expectation she would comply. If they stood face-to-face and she was grounded from flight, he had no doubt he could easily destroy her.

And she certainly didn't seem to be motivated to continue the confrontation on the ground. Instead, she told him in a steady, crisp voice, *Oberon, you're going to die unless you consent to medical treatment.*

That voice. That sounded exactly like the voice that had wound through his dreams, interrupting his nightmares of Isabeau. He snapped, *I did not give you permission to address me by my name.*

She retorted, *I don't really give a shit.*

Cold fury blinded him. He flung himself at the wall just below the alcove where she sheltered. In his Wyr form, he weighed close to ninety stone, and as his body slammed into the wall, it shuddered. Cracks broke in the plaster, radiating out in a sunburst pattern.

Is that supposed to frighten me? she said coldly. *Because I assure you, it does not. Your temper tantrum doesn't change the facts. You're going to die unless you consent to receive medical treatment.*

Big as he was, too much rage filled his body for him to stand still. He paced the length of the Garden Hall and swung back around to prowl back toward her. He growled, *How is it any business of yours whether I live or die, woman?*

It's my business because I came here to heal you if I could, she told him. *My name is Dr. Kathryn Shaw, and I left a busy, full life behind in America to travel thousands of miles—across an ocean and two countries—just to see if I could help you. So far, this trip has been nothing but a disaster, but I am still here and willing for that to change if you are.*

He coughed out an incredulous laugh. *Do you really think I would consent for you to get anywhere near me again? You invaded my private space—you disrupted the stasis spell that was keeping me alive... You...*

His words trailed away as he recalled the soft, gentle way her lips had pressed to his. It hadn't really been an erotic gesture all on its own.

Not until he had kissed her back.

He shook his head sharply as if to dislodge the thought. What difference did any of that make now?

What I actually did, the falcon snapped, each word more crisply defined than ever, *was move that magic needle away from your heart by two millimeters. Did that have something to do with waking you up? I don't know. I wasn't here when you put yourself under your stasis spell. But I do know this: you still carry the assassination spell inside you, so the only thing I've gained you is a little more time.*

Now he really felt trapped as he paced the hall. Thanks to that infernal spell, he'd been going in circles for years. *If what you say is true,* he growled, *how long have I got?*

I don't know. It depends on how activated the assassination spell is. Maybe weeks? Maybe a few months? He could almost hear the shrug in her mental voice. *The only thing I know for certain is that you are going to die if you don't consent to more medical treatment.*

Or that's what you want me to believe! he snapped, even as he turned his awareness inward, seeking out the source of the poison in his body.

I don't care what you believe. The indifference in her voice was total.

There it was, his nemesis—exactly where she had said it was. It was a touch farther away from where it had been when he had put himself into stasis. The woman had been telling the truth, at least about that much. He recalled the vials, the scalpel, and the other odd things strewn about his room.

His cold fury abated, at least to a certain extent so he could think properly. Stretching out on the floor, he reclined while never letting his gaze stray from the shadowed part of the alcove where she perched.

Say I believe you about the assassination spell, he said

slowly. *What about the other things?*

There was a tiny rustle of feathers as she shifted. *What other things?*

She was beginning to sound tired. His lack of caring was monumental.

Laying his head between his paws, he said, *I can tell the spell has shifted a small amount away from my heart, which verifies what you have said. Also, there are implements and vials in the room that look like they could belong to a physician's bag. For now, I will accept that part of your story. But there are other things—odd items, clothing, drawings, and food. Butter? Cheese? There is also the scent of an old companion, but he has yet to show himself. Where is he? If you are a doctor intent on healing me, what's in it for you? Why did you kiss me?* He paused, eyes narrowed. *If you are as blameless as you claim, you will stop hiding in that niche, come down here, and present yourself properly.*

I agreed to try to heal you, she said. *I didn't agree to put myself in danger or make myself vulnerable to attack.*

He would find a way to trap her. He had a hunter's patience, and he was in no doubt of that. For now, he wanted to look on her human face again, and to hear her physically speak so he could better assess whether she was telling the truth.

And if she wasn't?

He hadn't eaten for a very long time, and he was in the mood to find out what a falcon tasted like.

✧   ✧   ✧

KATHRYN MIGHT NOT sound like it, but she was more

rattled than she could ever remember being.

Because Oberon in his Wyr form was frankly terrifying. Back in his bedroom, when he had shapeshifted into his animal form, it had catapulted her even more deeply into shock—and she'd been pretty far gone by that point already.

He was not just a big damn cat. He was the biggest white lion she had ever seen, easily the size of two tigers combined. How big was that... maybe twelve hundred pounds? The average size of an African male lion was around four hundred to four fifty. That would make Oberon three times that size.

His gigantic paws were like dinner plates, and each wicked claw was as long as her fingers. And his eyes... there was something wrong with his eyes. They looked like cracked ice, black and white and entirely without feeling. The only real emotion she believed he had felt throughout their confrontation was anger.

This was a dangerous predator filled with ice and fury. How was *this* man the same one that the other Daoine Sidhe loved so much?

So she was in quite a dilemma. Going to ground ranked highly in the realm of Pretty Bad Ideas. But if she was going to continue to treat him, she had to somehow win his trust and come to trust *him* enough to get close again, and that wouldn't be an easy feat.

Sprawled in a pose of apparent relaxation, the lion watched her steadily. He looked like he could wait there for years.

Finally she stirred and sighed. *I'll come down if you'll move to the other end of the hall and turn into your human form as well.*

He took his time before replying. While she waited, there was nothing in his leonine face to give her any hint of what he was thinking. He was the worst of all combinations, she thought uneasily—he had the lack of control over his animal nature that younger Wyr had, and it was coupled with an ancient, powerful, and cunning personality.

But based on their first skirmish, if he were to station himself on the other side of the hall, she should be able to shapeshift and fly out of reach before he could get to her. She was pretty sure.

Just as she was starting to get antsy, the lion rose to his feet. The lines of his immense body flowed with predatory grace. He padded unhurriedly to the windows. That end of the hall was closer to the two arched doorways as well, so his decision on where to position himself had been a strategic one. When he reached the spot that was squarely in the middle of the two doorways, he shapeshifted, and Oberon the man stood before her.

Holy cow, yes, he was bigger in person than any of the gryphons. Towering over six feet, Oberon was easily the size of Tiago, one of the former sentinels who had the Wyr form of a thunderbird, or even Dragos himself, and every inch of Oberon's proud stature said he was a monarch.

With his back to the window, his features lay in shadow. Even so, she could see enough to know that his hard expression was chilling and the strange cracked ice in his irises hadn't changed when he assumed his human form.

Crossing his arms, Oberon said, "Your turn, Doctor."

This was her idea. She had to go through with it.

Shaking out her feathers, she tipped into the short glide that would take her to the point farthest away from him. As she neared the floor, she shapeshifted in midflight. She was already walking as her feet hit the ground.

Turning, she faced the Daoine Sidhe King.

"I'm suffering from voice strain, and I had to abandon both my coat and cloak upstairs, so I need to keep this brief," she croaked. "While you've been comatose, your Power has been raging out of control. Apparently, your skills as a weather mage are phenomenal, because your own people were forced to abandon the city. Your body was the only thing that held any warmth. All the water is frozen solid. The food too. None of the fires I've built will generate any heat. I was in bed with you because it was the best way I knew to get warm. The food was with us, under the covers, so our combined body heat would thaw it enough for me to eat it."

Her throat felt dry and raw. Putting a hand over the base of her neck, she tried to generate enough saliva to swallow, with minimal results. She was too dehydrated. She had needed that water.

He cocked his head, one corner of his mouth lifting in derision. "Physician, why don't you heal yourself?"

"Because there's only so much that magical healing can do. The physical body has to do the rest." Her hoarse voice cracked, and she continued in a whisper. "All I need are rest, warmth, food, and proper hydration. Healing spells won't give me that. This cold isn't normal. You've already destroyed half your city and forced your people out. As long as you're conscious, you need to pull yourself together and get your Power back under control."

Coldly, he said, "You don't lecture me on what I need to do."

That was his only reaction to hearing how much distress he had caused his own people? She had rarely disliked someone as thoroughly as she disliked him in that moment. He had totally killed any lingering attraction she might have felt.

She snapped, "Fine, let's keep things blindingly obvious, shall we? I repeat—you're going to die unless you consent to medical treatment. I'm your best option for healing, and I've already demonstrated I can produce results. But like I said, I agreed to help you if I could—I didn't agree to put myself in danger. Either I stay and continue to work on your healing, or I give up and leave. Right now, the conditions are unlivable, so unless things change, I'm leaving. But by all means… don't take my word for things. Go take a tour of what's left of your city and see the damage you've done for yourself. It's your move, asshole. Like I said, if something doesn't change in the next two hours, I'm gone."

She paused. As unlikeable as he was, he still deserved an explanation for her earlier behavior, but right now, she was too angry to give it to him. In the meantime, she was risking hypothermia without her coat, and she wasn't going to risk damaging her vocal cords with any further conversation. She had her own physical needs to take care of.

Shapeshifting into a falcon again, she soared as high as the ceiling would let her and darted toward the nearest doorway. Her heart pounded as she neared the still, shadowed predator watching her, but he made no move to attack. Flying safely out of the hall, she made her way up to his bedroom.

Once there, she shapeshifted again. First, she shrugged into her coat, opened one of the body warmers, and tucked it underneath her sweater so it could help to bring her body temperature back up.

While it heated, she moved rapidly to collect her things—her cloak, the various items that belonged in her physician's bag, the small metal box holding her antique fire-starter kit, and the all-important emergency Mylar blanket. While she worked, she strained to hear any telltale sound that would indicate he was returning, but a deadened silence blanketed the place.

Last, she snatched up the scattered food. It had

already started to freeze again. Dammit! And she didn't even see where the tankard had landed. Tucking the nuts, cheese, butter, and dried fruit under her sweater beside the body warmer, she eased out of the bedroom and jogged down the hall.

She had given him two hours. Now she had to find a place where she felt safe enough to wait it out before she made her next move. This palace was his home. He would know it far better than she could. He probably knew all the best hiding places already.

In the end, she surrendered to instinct. There was a sundial in the rear garden that she had been using to tell the time. Slipping outdoors, she chose the largest tree she could find, a huge, ancient silver maple, that provided a good line of sight to the dial, and she climbed as high as she dared.

When she reached the place where she no longer trusted any of the higher limbs to hold her weight, she arranged herself on her perch, pulled out the Mylar blanket, and tucked it around her torso and legs to block out the bitter wind.

Oberon was so much heavier than she was, even if he climbed the tree he wouldn't be able to reach her height. She would trust her safety to physics and gravity, and when the two hours had passed, she would shapeshift and fly away.

Once she was settled as comfortably as she could manage, she wrapped one arm around the trunk to keep herself anchored and used her free hand to pull out the newly rethawed food, one item at a time.

It was a very unappetizing meal. Without water to wash it down, she had to choke down every bite, and eating the lumps of the butter felt like swallowing slime. What she really needed was fresh meat, but at least she managed to ingest enough calories to quiet the gnawing hole in her middle.

After that, there was nothing to do but wait. Pulling a flap of the Mylar blanket over her head to capture the heat from her breathing, she closed her eyes and tried to relax. Intrusive thoughts chased each other around in her head.

What was Oberon thinking? What would he decide to do next?

Very rarely, a Wyr could turn feral enough there was nothing that could be done to bring them back to their senses. Kathryn had been involved in a few cases where she'd had to diagnose a feral Wyr and recommend they be put down for the safety of everyone around them. It wasn't humane to cage them indefinitely, but each time the decision had been gut-wrenching.

Oberon wasn't feral yet, at least not quite. He might be repellant, but he still had language and the ability to engage in some kind of reasoning process. He might not reason the way she would like for him to, but he was capable of a certain amount of cold logic.

Still, she couldn't shake the sense that he was somehow fundamentally different from the impression she had received from those who loved him. Was that because she simply loathed him in real life? Or were any of her observations thus far valid for diagnostic purposes?

The scientist in her was still intrigued, but self-preservation trumped everything else, hands down. She peeked out at the sundial. Even with the heavy cloud cover, there was enough of a shadow to get a reading on the time. Only another quarter hour to go, and then she was out of here.

Danger prickled along the back of her neck. Holding her breath, she listened intently. She heard nothing but the constant wailing of the wind. And yet…

Snatching the Mylar away from her face, she looked around.

Oberon stood at the base of her tree, looking up at her. The black-and-white cracked ice in his eyes reflected the clouds overhead. There was no emotion in his wide, unblinking gaze and blank expression.

Staring down at him, she shuddered. She had seen serial killers with the same lack of expression. One of them had been injured badly in a battle with two sentinels before they had brought him down. Dragos had ordered her to heal him so the killer would be healthy enough to stand trial. He'd said the families of his victims deserved it. She had agreed, but it had still been one of the creepiest experiences she'd ever had.

"I have unanswered questions, Dr. Shaw," Oberon said.

"We all have something," she told him. After resting

for almost two hours, her voice was marginally better. "I have a full bladder, but I don't feel safe enough to pee."

Her flippant reply didn't appear to provoke any reaction. "I walked through my city. The damage here didn't happen quickly. How long was I in stasis?"

She stirred carefully. She might have indulged in some petty sarcasm, but she hadn't been lying—she had to pee very badly. "How do you want to calculate the time? On Earth, it's been two hundred years, and the social, political, and technological changes have been huge. I don't know the yearly cycle here in Lyonesse, but if you use Earth's three hundred and sixty-five days in a year, you've been in stasis here for fifteen and a half years."

Ah, now *that* provoked a reaction. His hands tightened into fists. "The scent of my old court companion threads through the city. Where is he?"

"If you're talking about Robin, I don't know." She stirred again. "After I promised to explain everything to him first before casting any spells on you, he brought me here and shadowed me for two days. Then he vanished."

His frigid gaze remained sharp and unblinking on her face. "Explain those drawings in my room."

"I drew those when I explained things to Robin. Some of my explanations became lengthy. He doesn't have a medical degree."

"Where is Isabeau?"

"Short answer: I don't know. I've never met her." She tried to consider what she should say next. How would he react if she brought up Morgan? Better not find out. "I did sit in on one conversation where your cousin said Isabeau had suffered a recent setback. Annwyn was hopeful they could defeat the Light Court, especially if we could revive you."

He reacted to that too. Features sharpening, his lips pulled back from hard white teeth as he exhaled in a near soundless hiss. "Ah, Annwyn. How is my devoted cousin?"

Growing irritated, she snapped, "She's a lot more devoted to you than I would ever be. I would have given up on you years ago, but she's the one who hired me. In fact, every member of your court that I've met is more devoted than I would be. Based on what I've seen of your charming personality, I don't get it."

"Have a care, physician," he said between his teeth. "I have chosen not to attack you again—yet."

She glanced at the sundial. "Your two hours are almost up, and I have only one more thing to say." Taking a deep breath, she reined in her temper. Despite the fact that he was an asshole and she was personally mortified about her earlier behavior, he still deserved an explanation for what had happened. "Oberon, I am truly sorry for what happened in your bedroom. It was not what it looked like, or what you thought it was. When I…" Force it out, Shaw. "…when I kissed you, I was saying goodbye. You would only allow me to work on you when I talked nonstop, and I was losing my voice. With the unlivable conditions here, I couldn't—I can't heal you without your cooperation. So I was giving up, and after having come so far I felt emotional, and I crossed a line. I promise it won't happen again."

He reacted to that as well. The dark slashes of his eyebrows drew together in a fierce frown while he laid one big, flattened hand on the trunk of the tree, as if he would physically push it away.

She stared at him, perplexed. What did that mean? He looked as if he were trying to push away her words—he didn't appear to welcome anything she said.

She muttered, "I think I'm done here. We're not making any headway, and I should go home."

"Wait," he snapped. "You may have had your say, but I am not finished yet. You demand I give my consent for you to treat me, so you owe me this interview."

Oh, for fuck's sake. Of all the times for him to come out and say something right, it had to be right as she was getting ready to shapeshift and get the hell away from this cursed place.

She glared at him. "Fine," she ground out. "What else do you want to know?"

His eyelids lowered, hiding his disturbing alien gaze. "Why did Annwyn pick you?"

The wind had picked up while they talked, and she drew the Mylar blanket tighter around her torso.

"I'm not sure," she told him finally. "You would have to ask Annwyn for her reasons, but I know my résumé would have been part of what she considered. I'm two hundred years old. I've been a trauma surgeon in the Wyr demesne in New York for over a hundred and forty years, and I've been on retainer to Dragos Cuelebre and his court for almost ninety. I specialize in combining magical and surgical techniques when I create treatment plans—"

He interrupted her, eyes narrowed. "You are the dragon's physician?"

Of course. Oberon would be well acquainted with Dragos. Sometimes that fact could work well in one's favor, and sometimes it most definitely did not.

She couldn't tell how Oberon felt about it. Swallowing what she had been about to say, she redirected. "On the rare occasion that he has needed a trauma surgeon, yes, I am. Most of my work has been on the sentinels after they've sustained injuries from battle. At first I didn't understand why Annwyn insisted I would be such a good fit for this assignment, but now that I know you've become full Wyr, her choice makes more sense."

He started to pace, his long, powerful body tight with leashed aggression. "Those are all other people's experiences and opinions. Give me one good reason I should consent to you treating me. Why should I trust you when you're working for my cousin?"

Kathryn angled her jaw as she chewed on that. Annwyn had shown her nothing but loyalty and caring about Oberon's well-being, but he didn't sound like he trusted her at all. What did that mean?

She told him a version of what she had said to

Robin. "I don't owe Annwyn any loyalty. My first loyalty lies with my patient, always. After almost fifteen years, she probably has a long, elaborate list of preconceived notions about how things are supposed to go once you're revived. None of that is any of my business. Whatever comes after you're healed is up to you. My one mission—the only job I care about—is healing."

He didn't look impressed as she spoke. Why did she even bother?

She could have let it go. Half of her was already winging home. But she knew exactly what an ancient alpha asshole like Oberon would respect hearing, so she leaned forward, met his cold gaze, and gave it to him.

"Besides," she said, her voice soft, "I could have already killed you if I'd wanted to. All I would have had to do was keep your Power acquiescent while I drove a dagger home to finish what Morgan's assassination spell had started, and we would never be having this conversation."

For the first time he smiled, a quick baring of his teeth. She caught her breath. Whatever else Oberon was, his expression of naked ferocity was breathtaking.

Then he bowed his head and held out his arms. It was only as his Power rippled out over the clearing that she realized her danger—he might very well be casting a spell so pervasive she couldn't fly away from it.

Whipping off the Mylar blanket, she stuffed it in her pack and prepared to shapeshift.

Then she realized what he had done.

He had cast his Power out in as wide and far a casting as she had ever felt, and now he clenched his fists and pulled it all back again. The draw of magic was so forceful it felt dizzying, like sensing hurricane-force winds blowing past her. Usually her sense of direction and balance were immaculate. Now she clung to her perch, afraid to take to the air until it stopped.

After a few moments, the magical hurricane died down. Oberon smiled coldly. "I have done what you requested and taken back my own Power. This winter is normal again, Doctor. I give my consent for you to treat me—at least for now. You may begin."

Excitement swelled. She could no longer remain sitting on her perch and scrambled to stand on the branch.

"Not so fast, King," she told him. "Consent might be a necessary part of treatment, but you also need to prove you're not going to hurt me before I get near you again. I don't see how you're going to do that, but I'm open to you giving it a try. Convince me you're not a sociopath... or, wait, you don't know what that terms means in a modern sense. Convince me you mean me no harm, and you won't hurt me." She glanced at the sundial. "You've got five minutes, more or less. Go."

Chapter Eight

WHILE THE WYR physician talked, she let go of the trunk and walked along her branch as casually as if she strolled along the side of a road. Her balance was immaculate.

Oberon almost laughed at her insouciance, but the long, draining years of battling the sorcerer's assassination spell had killed off any lingering sense of humor he might have had.

Besides, she had a point. He had attacked her once. Part of him still wanted to do it again, wanted to feel her blood gushing between his teeth.

The other part remembered the heat of their shared kiss—not the chaste goodbye she had spoken of so apologetically, but the other one, when he had covered her body with his and fantasized about spearing her with more than just his tongue.

Look at her, strolling so far above his head with a complete lack of fear for any potential fall, her slender form held erect. She was almost catlike in her grace. Watching her made the lion inside him twitch. Her hair looked sleek as a mink's, and her fine-boned features were chapped pink from the cold.

She was, he realized belatedly, quite beautiful in an understated way. She wasn't his type. Even before he'd been attacked, he had preferred voluptuous curves and a willing, warm personality that didn't demand much of his attention after lovemaking.

This woman would never be that kind of sexual partner. She would be spiky, intellectually challenging, and she would never consent to disappearing meekly into the woodwork after the deed was done.

Still... as frozen as he was inside, and as inappropriate as she was to his own tastes, he could appreciate the aesthetics of the view.

"Ticktock, King," she said.

He refused to let her goad him into replying before he was ready. She would wait until he said something. She had invested too much to fly off precipitously now.

What would get her out of that blasted tree, back down to earth, and treating him again?

"I want to live more than I want anything else," he said, truthfully. "I want it more than I want my kingdom, more than I want revenge against Isabeau, and more than I want to kill the damned sorcerer who did this to me—and I want all three of those things very badly."

At that she paused to give him a sober look. But she didn't leave her perch.

After a moment, he added, "It would be suicidal for me to attack and harm or kill the one person who might help me reclaim my health, and I'm not suicidal." He met her bright amber gaze. "I find you strange, and you make me angry. You and I might not like each other, and we might not see eye to eye. None of that matters. If you work on healing me, I'll do everything in my power to keep you safe while you do so. And if you free me of this infernal spell, I will lay the world at your feet."

As he spoke, she squatted, rested one elbow on an upraised knee, and smiled at him, and it was as fierce as anything he had ever seen. "I'll take that bargain."

He grinned back, and for the first time in a very long, dark time, he felt hope ignite. "Excellent. Let's begin."

She shook her head. "Not today. We'll start in the morning."

In the morning?

He snapped, "Unacceptable! You'll start immediately!"

"Unimpressed!" she snapped back. "You're not my king, and I'm not your subject. I don't take your orders. We'll start when I say we start."

As she spoke, he growled in warning. This time she went too far.

Raising one eyebrow, she laughed. "If you think you're the first Wyr to ever growl at me, think again. Tonight, for the first time since crossing over, I'm going to get my needs met. I'm going to find somewhere safe in the city to build a hot fire, melt some water, and cook a good meal, and I'm going to sleep really well for as long as I can." She pointed at him. "And if you've got any sense, you'll do the same. You're facing the fight of your life, and your body needs the fuel."

Her attitude was so infuriating, he *hated* the fact that her words made sense. Eyes narrowed, he told her, "I've never met a more insufferable woman. Why didn't you just say so in the first place?"

She did not appear to be distressed by his honest opinion. "Well, we're even. Hats off to you, Oberon— even after years of dealing with Dragos, now that I've met you I'm surprised to say I've never met a more insufferable man."

He bared his teeth at her, then burst out laughing, and that shocked him more than anything else had since he'd woken up. Her eyes widened, and she stared at him in frank astonishment.

"Go," he told her. "Get your needs met, and I will see to mine. If you're not back first thing in the morning, I'm coming to get you."

"Don't worry." She shouldered her pack. "I'll be back. I can't wait to find out what happens next." She paused to run her gaze down his form. "Have a good night. You've earned it."

Stepping back, he watched as she shapeshifted into a falcon and launched into the air.

As it happened, he couldn't wait to find out what happened next either.

Hands planted on his hips, he angled his head back to watch her fly away. He didn't like it, that she was winging out of his sphere of control. What if she changed her mind and left? Other than an apparent fascination for his case, there was nothing holding her here. As she was so determined to point out, he had no hold over her.

Assuming she didn't leave in the night, how could he *get* a hold over her? He was an accomplished magic user, but so was she. For every control spell he might throw, she could very well have one that counteracted it—and then if he tried to trap her and failed, he risked alienating her forever. If he broke the fragile trust they had managed to build between them, she would leave, and he would die.

Hmm.

Unable to take her advice and focus on food and rest, he went up to his suite to don shirt, coat, cloak, and gloves. He had no intention of sleeping. He had already been asleep for too long. Besides, Isabeau waited to haunt his nightmares.

After dressing, he headed into the dead city.

His dead city. He poked at himself, like poking at a sore tooth. He had ruined it. It was his responsibility.

It meant nothing to him. He didn't care. Presumably the man he had once been would have been saddened and horrified to have driven his people away, but the man he was right now liked the desolation, the silence, and the strange twists of ice that the howling wind and sea had wrought over the years. It felt...

It felt like it mirrored the landscape inside him.

Every member of your court that I've met is more devoted than I would be. Based on what I've seen of your charming personality, I don't get it.

Annwyn, Nik, Gawain and the others… they were devoted to the man he had once been. A man he might very well never be again. What if the doctor healed him but he stayed exactly the same? What if the Oberon that the Daoine Sidhe had known was gone forever?

If that happens, he thought, *the rest of the Daoine Sidhe will have to find somewhere else to live. Because dead or not, this city is mine.*

As he lifted his head and inhaled the chill sea air, he caught a whiff of woodsmoke and smiled. *Aha. I've found you.*

He tracked the smell of burning wood to the lower city, which baffled him. The doctor had bypassed all the grand estates that clustered around the palace on higher ground. Instead, she had chosen to go into the lower city. That area had sustained a lot more damage over the years as the sea levels had risen, and he had to pick his way through broken streets.

Finally he located her at the site of what had once been a large, popular inn at the intersection of two major roads. The main taproom had been flooded several times, he saw, when he looked in the broken doors.

But, assuming she'd found an intact store of food somewhere, there were plenty of bedrooms on the upper story that would provide decent enough shelter, and also enough fuel for a wood fire. If she were ambitious, she could even melt enough water in one of the bathtubs to take a bath.

He climbed to the roof of the abandoned shop across the street, and after a time his patience was rewarded. He caught cracks of golden light gleaming from the edges of closed storm shutters at one bedroom, and the woodsmoke took on the rich scent of cooking bacon.

A corner of his mouth notched up, and he relaxed. The doctor wasn't going anywhere. She was doing exactly what she said she would.

Still, he stayed at his post far into the night, until the scent of cooking bacon gave way to plain woodsmoke again and the last of the golden light faded from the edges of the shutters.

Only when a deep, frozen silence blanketed the city did he make his way back to the shadowed luxury of the darkened palace.

WHEN KATHRYN WOKE the next morning, she felt like a million bucks.

The night before she had eaten too much bacon, and she wasn't sorry. What's more, after eating she revived enough to hack chunks of ice from the thick layers that coated the inn's roof.

After stacking the ice in a bathtub in one of the bathrooms, she threw a simple heat spell repeatedly until the ice melted and warmed enough for a quick, shallow bath.

To top off her evening of luxurious frivolity, the fire

she'd built in one of the bedrooms actually threw off heat until the room turned deliciously toasty. The bedding she had found smelled musty, but she didn't care. After a while the room was warm, the covers were soft, her belly was full, and her hair was clean again.

After waking, she felt reluctant to leave her nest, but she had promised that blasted cat she would be with him first thing in the morning, so she rose, ate cold, leftover bacon, more cheese and mixed nuts, and dressed for the day in her last clean outfit.

Later, she would have to do something about either cleaning her clothes or foraging for new ones. She would also need to locate more food and possibly a long overdue bottle of liquor. But overall, she was in far better shape than she had been the day before.

After brushing her teeth with minty toothpaste powder from a small tin stowed in her toiletries kit, she packed up her belongings, shrugged on her backpack, and hiked to the palace.

On the return, she caught Oberon's scent almost immediately. Had he followed her to the inn? That felt creepy, but maybe he had been worried she would go back on her word and take off without telling him.

She was still chewing over how she felt about him stalking her as she rounded a corner and the palace came into view.

The lowering, malevolent presence had lifted from the city, and it was shortly after dawn. With the lifting of the unnatural cold, outside it felt like a normal winter's day. She guessed the temperature was around thirty degrees Fahrenheit. She felt quite comfortable in her winter coat, and she carried her fur-lined cloak draped over one forearm.

Brilliant early-morning sun underscored the moody clouds in the winter sky. The dawn light poured rosy beams over the pillars of the golden palace façade and the immense alabaster lion reclining on the palace steps.

Her stride hitched. The lion was magnificent. What a shame the man was so detestable.

Oberon's impenetrable, cracked-ice gaze tracked her progress as she climbed up the broad steps to him.

"Good morning," she said. "Did you sleep?"

No. Since he was in his animal form, his blunt reply was telepathic. *Your vocal cords have healed.*

"I told you all I needed was hydration and rest."

Very good. Then you are ready to begin.

"I am. Where would you like to go? I assume you don't want to be examined here on the front steps of your house."

Leisurely, the lion stood. The tiny hairs at the nape of her neck prickled, and she had to force herself not to jump back. Standing, he was as big as a horse. If he managed to land a direct blow on her, he could crush her with one of those immense paws. She had already seen for herself that he was blindingly fast for his size.

She was much smaller, much lighter, and faster. That and the fact that she could go airborne were her two major advantages. If he took her by surprise, she wouldn't stand a chance.

He paused when she did. *Is there a problem, Doctor?*

The heavy sense of his presence, like dark chocolate, poured over her. She repressed a shiver. She loved dark chocolate. "Not at all," she told him in her best crisp, professional voice. "Please lead the way."

When the lion padded ahead of her, she felt marginally better. Trailing behind by several yards, she followed him through a part of the palace she had not yet explored.

When he pushed open double doors to a large office, she looked around with interest at the large room. Windows overlooked the back gardens. Bookcases lined the walls, filled with all manner of books, interspersed with paintings coated with the patina of age.

There were a couple of sitting areas that had been created with heavy, comfortable furniture along with rich, thick rugs, a large marble fireplace at one end, and a massive desk at the other. This was Oberon's personal office.

Like most of the palace, the room had an air of neglect about it. Dust coated the furniture, and the artwork needed a good cleaning, but a new large pile of firewood had been stacked on the hearth. He had prepared for their meeting.

As the lion strolled toward the fireplace, he changed shape and became the man. Oberon wore a different outfit as well—leather pants, boots, and a white shirt underneath a dark gray jacket that had been fitted to his large, powerful frame. He looked almost urbane, until she glanced at that strange cracked-ice gaze that was so like the lion's.

He squatted in front of the fireplace and quickly, competently stacked the wood for a fire. With a flick of his fingers and a tingle of magic, he set the wood ablaze.

Then with a powerful grace that belied his size, he rose to his full height and turned. "What now, Doctor?"

She realized she had been staring, and she tore her gaze away from him to focus on one of the bookcases. "Do you have a blank journal I could use?" she asked. "I'd like to take notes."

Wordlessly, he went to his desk and pulled out a leather-bound notebook from a drawer. As she took it from him, she looked at the priceless workmanship of the tooled leather. She flipped through the empty pages. They had all been hand pressed. She passed her fingers over it lightly, savoring the quality. If she had been in New York, she would have grabbed a disposable legal pad.

"There's something wrong with it?" He frowned.

"Not at all. It's beautiful. Thank you." She looked up. "Let's start by talking for a while, shall we? We did a lot of sparring yesterday that didn't get us very far. Today I want to discuss your symptoms."

His expression tightened with impatience. "Is that really necessary? We already know we need to extract the needle from my chest. Talking isn't going to solve anything."

"That's certainly one point of view," she acknowledged. "Here's another one: you have an immensely sophisticated magic spell that you've been battling for years, yet despite your obvious magical talent, you haven't managed to defeat it."

"Neither have you, yet," he pointed out.

She decided to ignore that dig and told him quietly, "I think it's naïve to expect there haven't been consequences. So, while we certainly need to get that needle out, I want to see if we can bring you back to the man you were before you were attacked. I want to eradicate any trace of Isabeau's influence on your life. To me, that would be the real triumph. But you're the patient. What do you want to achieve?"

"Freedom," he growled. There was repressed violence in the long, taut lines of his body. He made the large, airy room feel small and closed in. "I want to be completely free of that evil bitch, and then I want to destroy her and spit on her grave."

She didn't know him well enough to predict what behavior might result from such volcanic anger. Subtly, she checked behind her to make sure she had a clear path to the open door if she needed it. "Excellent," she said. "So, let's talk, shall we?"

He expelled a sharp sigh. "Fine. We'll do it your way."

She gestured to his desk. "Do you mind if I sit at your desk?"

"Whatever, Doctor," he snapped, his icy gaze filled

with storms. He prowled the expanse of the room. "Just get started."

She didn't waste any time but slipped behind the desk. Setting her backpack on the floor, she sat in his chair and opened the journal. Damn it, she needed something to write with, and the pencils she had found a few days ago presumably still lay scattered and broken on his trashed bedroom floor.

When she cleared her throat delicately, he whirled to face her. She raised her eyebrows inquiringly and indicated his drawers. He sliced the air impatiently with one hand, which she decided to take as permission to poke around.

Quickly she found an inkwell still holding plenty of ink, a stylus, and a blotter. Being well acquainted with all three tools, she soon situated herself to her own satisfaction.

"Tell me what happened when you were attacked," she said. As he stared at her, she added, "Help me to understand how you got from there to here. I know that spans a huge amount of time and you'll need to summarize, but I want to hear anything you think is relevant—what you sensed and what you felt along the way and any physical, mental, or emotional symptoms you've had. You can clearly feel the magic working inside you, and you were able to gauge it well enough to know that you needed to put yourself into stasis. What does it feel like?"

He didn't answer at first. Instead, he paced through

the spacious office as if it were a cage, even though the door stood wide open. At first she sat poised to take notes, but after a few moments she set down the stylus, stripped off her winter coat, and sat back in his chair while she waited.

Reluctantly, pity crept through her. She might not like him very much, but chronic illness or injury were very difficult things to cope with, especially when one had previously been gifted with the abundance of long life and health that so many of the Elder Races enjoyed.

Friends and family of those afflicted didn't know how to cope either, and often those battling with adverse physical conditions also had to contend with isolation, judgment, and lack of empathy from those they had previously felt close to.

Was that what had happened between him and Annwyn?

Finally he turned to face her. "I won't bother telling you what happened. Instead, I'll show you."

She sat very straight. What did he mean? If he intended to initiate some kind of deep telepathic bond to share imagery with her, she wasn't comfortable getting that close to him.

But he made no move to approach. Instead, he unfurled one long, big hand in her direction. For a brief moment, she felt a tingle of his magic, and then a scene appeared in front of her.

It wasn't a telepathic connection that occurred inside her own head. Instead, it looked like a pale, transparent holographic image that overlaid the landscape of the office.

Instantly entranced, she rose to her feet as she stared at the scene.

A transparent image of Oberon himself stood at the edge of what looked like a dance floor. The Oberon of the past was dressed in a severe black coat, pants, and boots. His dark hair was longer and tied back in a queue, and his richly embroidered coat glittered with jet.

After taking in his appearance, her gaze swept over the rest of the scene. Snow appeared to cover the ground at his feet, and the dancers that swept by were fantastically dressed in brilliant costumes, their faces obscured by elaborate masks. Behind him, nearby bonfires blazed with light.

She had read accounts of how splendid the Daoine Sidhe King's masques had been. Even though everything in the vision was transparent, the detail was so precise she could almost hear a far-off tinkle of music and feel the roaring heat from the fires.

When the past Oberon turned to face the dance floor, her attention snapped back to him. His masculinity was so raw and overwhelming she was surprised at how elegant he managed to appear.

Smiling, he held out his hands, and snowflakes of ice, glittering with reflected gold and silver from the light of the nearby fires, fell over the scene. Dancers stopped, and everyone looked up. Silent laughter flashed over their faces, and they applauded.

She barely took it all in before staring at the vision of Oberon again. The difference between this past version of him and his present self was striking. Quickly she strode around the edge of the desk to get a closer look.

It was undeniably him. The man in the vision had the same bold, intensely masculine features with strong bones, a neatly trimmed beard, and that astonishingly sensual mouth. But the resemblance ended there.

This man's smile was keen and bright, and it lit up his face. He was enjoying himself and the people around him. His dark eyes sparkled.

His dark eyes…

She was so caught up that when he slapped a hand to his neck and spun around, she jumped.

There, not ten feet away, stood a man dressed in plain black, holding a reed. Even though he wore a black domino, she recognized him immediately. It was Morgan, of course.

The Oberon in the vision appeared to shout, and he lunged forward before crumpling to the ground. Everything in the vision whirled. Staggering from the optical illusion, she had to clutch at the edge of the desk to keep her balance. For a brief moment she saw everything as if she were lying on the ground, looking up.

Then the real Oberon clenched his hand into a fist, and the vision stopped.

Only then did she realize how rapid her breathing had become. Forcing her lungs to stop working overtime, she stared at him.

"Have you seen enough?" His tone was cold and bored.

"I certainly saw more than I expected to." Forgetting any discomfort with his proximity, she strode over until she stood toe-to-toe with him and peered up at his face.

His strange irises looked even more unsettling close up. They resembled ice and snow on black rocks—or no, more like an iced-over lake fractured with deep cracks.

His heavy, dark brows drew together. "What are you doing?"

"Oberon, what color are your eyes?"

Quick impatience flashed across his hard features. "Isn't it obvious?"

"It would be logical to assume so," she murmured. Reaching up, she touched his hard jaw and gently urged his head from side to side. Despite his ill temper, he complied, looking first at his desk and then at the fireplace. "Please humor me and answer the question."

Jerking his chin out of her grasp, he snapped, "Brown, of course."

She turned away and strode to her backpack. As she knelt to open it and rummage through the contents inside, she remarked, "I gather you haven't looked at yourself in a mirror since you woke up."

He took in a deep breath. "Doctor, kindly explain what the fuck you're going on about."

Even when he agreed to cooperate, he had to argue and fight with her at every turn. Shaking her head, she finally located what she sought and pulled out her toiletries kit. Inside, she kept a small fold-up mirror.

Opening it, she stood and held it out to him. "Look at your eyes."

Striding over, he snatched at the mirror and held it up.

As his silence stretched out, she asked, "Not what you were expecting to see?"

He clicked the mirror shut and handed it back to her. "No."

Fascinating. She almost leaped back to the desk to start taking notes. "What other symptoms have you experienced since the attack?"

Reluctance evident in every word, he replied, "I don't feel cold, but I thought that might have been from my transforming into full Wyr. The lion is a very warm animal."

Every alpha male patient she'd ever had hated to discuss symptoms, as if confessing to them meant they were admitting to some weakness.

She shook her head, writing furiously. "Maybe it's because you're Wyr now," she told him. "You'll certainly be warmer than you used to be. But maybe it isn't. Do you feel heat?"

"No," he told her. "Not without directly putting my hand into flames." As she looked at him quickly, he added dryly, "I know because I've tried it."

"Okay." She made another note. "What else?"

"Over time, as the spell got closer to my—to its target, I stopped feeling other things." He began to pace again while he recited the words as if the experience had happened to someone else. "I stopped... caring. That love and loyalty you say that members of my court have toward me—I remember feeling that for them. I remember having the emotions, but I no longer experience them. In fact, I only feel two things anymore: anger and lust."

She stopped writing, suddenly inundated with the memory of yesterday's encounter. The feeling of his mouth moving so urgently over hers as he speared her with his tongue. The delicious sense of weight as he shifted to lie on top of her, and the thick, heavy feeling of his erection pressing against her hip.

For one shocking, mindless moment it had been glorious.

His voice sounded softly in her ear, deep and dark as the ocean and rough with the lion's purr. "But I do feel anger and lust very deeply, Doctor."

She had gotten so lost in her reverie she hadn't noticed he had come around to her side of the desk, and she nearly leaped out of her skin. "For crying out loud, Oberon! Back up and give me some personal space!"

She listened to her own exclamation with deep dismay. That was supposed to have come out much more sharply than it had. Instead of sounding disapproving and offended, her voice had sounded as breathless as a gasp.

"Are you sure that's what you really want?" Callused fingers traced the line of her jaw, down the side of her neck, and lightly pressed against the very spot where he had sucked so hungrily at her pulse. She remembered. Oh, she remembered it all too well. The shadow of his body fell over hers on the desk as he bent over her, and his lips brushed against the sensitive shell of her ear as he whispered, "Or wouldn't you rather experiment with just how deep and hard my feelings can really go?"

Chapter Nine

O BERON HAD HER rattled. He knew he did.

But suddenly she laughed, and the bright, carefree sound broke the sensual spell he had begun to weave over them both. "Did you really just say that to me? My lord, that line was bad."

She wasn't funny.

And he wasn't suddenly grinning. He wouldn't allow it. Angrily, he wiped the smile off his face.

Then he noticed something else. Despite her strong-sounding words, a hint of arousal lingered in her scent.

He knew it. He knew he had gotten to her yesterday before everything had exploded on them. The predator in him took note and decided to give chase.

Leaning over even farther, he planted both hands flat on the desk on either side of her, trapping her in the chair. Her hair smelled amazing, like apricots and Kathryn, and he rubbed his face in the silken strands and inhaled deeply.

"You wanted me," he whispered. "It was only for a few moments, but I can tell your body remembers. Think of how good it can be to give in to your deepest instincts, Kathryn. There's nobody here to judge. Nobody cares. We can do anything we want, and no one will be the wiser."

He had never used her name before, and he could feel her almost imperceptible jolt as she heard her name on his lips.

"Stop it," she whispered. "I never get involved with my patients."

"That wasn't what your mouth was saying yesterday when I was kissing you." He angled his head so he could nip at her delectable neck with his teeth. Everything dominant in him wanted to pin her to the floor and cover her body with his. What would his spiky doctor think of that?

She pressed a fist against the bridge of his nose and pushed hard. Her voice was stronger when she spoke, hard and cold. "Back up, Oberon. Yesterday I promised I wouldn't cross that line again, and I meant it."

"Forget what happened yesterday," he growled, brushing her hand away. "Today is a new beginning. I can tell you want me, and I know you can tell that I want you too. Give in to it. I can bring you more pleasure than you've ever known before."

She coughed out a shaky laugh. "Those are some mighty ambitious words, King. I've had some amazing, considerate lovers. I doubt you can compare, especially since you have no empathy right now."

"Empathy is overrated." Sliding one hand underneath her jaw, he tilted her head back and held her against his shoulder. The long, exaggerated line of her slender throat aroused him more than he had expected. A hot spike of desire stabbed him.

"Oberon, I mean it—I'm telling you no," she said. "Let me go."

It would've been so easy to ignore her. It would've been so easy to push her body down on the desk and pin her from behind. But suddenly he realized that he no longer scented her arousal.

She smelled different now, like stress and anger, and her body felt strung tight as a bow.

He whispered in her ear, "I don't want to let go."

She whispered back, "Is that what you would have done, before?"

If she had reacted any other way... But she didn't give aggression for aggression, not this time, and her riposte had unerring accuracy.

And the man he once had been would have picked up on her signals and stopped a long time ago.

The realization made him drop his hold on her, as if she had suddenly become scalding hot and he had developed the ability to feel heat again.

"I don't force women," he said between his teeth.

"No, of course you don't." Carefully she straightened her clothes. "You just needed to be reminded of who you really are." Standing, she turned to face him. Her amber eyes were dilated, the lines of her face tight. "Let me be clear so we don't have any misunderstandings. Forget about what you may think you perceive in my scent. I am never going to choose an inappropriate liaison with a patient. I would not betray your trust that way, and I wouldn't betray myself either. So I would appreciate it if you would keep your distance when I'm not examining or treating you. Neither one of us needs that kind of distraction right now."

She meant it, he realized. He stared at her in fascination. "Darling, if you think what could happen between us would be a mere distraction, your considerate lovers were not as excellent as you think they were."

Her lips parted. He sensed the tiny sound of her indrawn breath as clearly as if he had felt it against his bare skin.

"We need to take a break for lunch," she announced. She bolted out of the room before he could decide if he was going to argue further.

Fine. Lunch it was. Maybe by the time it was over he could get his unruly erection to subside. He strode out of the office as well and headed in the opposite direction. He might no longer feel the cold, but he could damn well use some fresh air anyway.

If he hadn't been so determined to keep from compromising the man he used to be, he might have done something they both would have regretted and given in to his baser instincts. But he had promised her—if she worked on healing him, he would do everything in his power to keep her safe while she did so.

Not even his own promises carried much meaning anymore. He only adhered to them out of a stubbornness born from that inexhaustible well of anger he carried deep inside. It was hard to come to grips with how much of his former self he had lost. The man he had been would have loathed what he had become.

And he couldn't feel it. He couldn't feel any of it.

Outside, he shapeshifted into his animal form and raced out of the city. It was another thing he could feel. He reveled in the lion's effortless speed and strength, and in the wind blowing through his thick mane.

He ran for a long time along the nearby cliffs that bordered the city. When he was sure he had put enough distance between himself and the palace, he stopped and roared his fury at the open water. The impervious waves crashed and foamed at the broken rocks below.

Finally he returned. As he entered the palace, he shifted into the man again and made his way back to his office.

He half expected Kathryn to have gone missing, but she was in the room, slouching in an armchair near the fire, her booted heels propped on an embroidered footrest. An open bottle of brandy sat on the table near her elbow. She balanced a snifter on her flat stomach.

Pausing, he took note of a second snifter sitting beside the brandy bottle. It appeared she had brought him a peace offering from his own cellars.

Striding over to the empty armchair opposite hers, he sat. "I apologize for my earlier behavior."

She gave him a sidelong grin. "You're not really sorry."

He gave that due thought. Carefully he said, "I am regretful that I am not sorry. Does that count?"

She laughed. "Fair enough."

He studied her profile, then poured himself some brandy. "You're unlike any court physician I've ever met. You're not at all what I would have expected. When I came back to the palace, I honestly thought you would be long gone."

"What would you expect me to be like?" She took a mouthful of her brandy with evident appreciation.

"I don't know." He settled back into the armchair with a sigh. "From your animal form, I would have guessed some sort of soldier… something that would satisfy the predator in you."

She shook her head. "My predator is very satisfied. You see, *you* are my prey—or at least your affliction is. You think recovering from illness or injury isn't a fight? Sometimes it's the hardest, dirtiest fight of all, and a battlefield is a piece of cake in comparison. Battles are over in hours, or maybe days, if they're really bad. Recovering from traumatic injury can go on for years. It can last a lifetime. I've seen an avian Wyr… I saw her struggle to find a way to live every day for a month. The whole time she never knew whether her animal form would have healed enough to allow her to fly again."

"That must have been catastrophic."

She nodded and swallowed another mouthful of brandy before continuing. "She had been so badly injured, for a while I thought I would have to amputate her wings, and avian Wyr typically don't survive that kind of injury. I had forbidden her to shapeshift for the month. I was afraid she would give in to temptation and try to fly before she was ready, and then she would undo all the good we had tried to do for her. But her mate stayed by her side, day and night, and somehow with his help she stuck it out."

When she fell silent, he waited. Finally, he asked, "Did she fly again?"

"Yes, as it happens, she did. But it could have very easily gone the other way, and then her fight would have been endless. Every day she would have been searching for a reason to get out of bed and find the goodness in life. And her mate couldn't have lived without her." She gave him a twisted smile. "Enough about that. Let's get back to you, shall we? If you don't mind, I'd like to scan you to check the needle's position."

"By all means." He swallowed golden fire and relished the brandy sliding down his throat. "Come and get it."

"You're never going to make things easy, are you?" she muttered as she set her glass aside and pulled her footstool over him.

"Probably not, Kathryn." He enjoyed saying her name. He watched as she settled on the stool beside him.

Holding up her hand, she wiggled her fingers at him. "All you'll feel is a tingle of magic. Are we good?"

"All good." Half closing his eyes, he watched as she laid her hand lightly on his chest. It would not take very much for her to change trajectories, reach up and stroke his face.

Her intelligent gaze narrowed, and he felt the tingle of her magic. Her Power was a subtle presence, but it ran very deep.

He knew what she was going to find, and he watched her closely, but her expression never flickered. She was really good at hiding reactions when she wanted.

Giving him a brisk pat, she sat back. "Okay, so it's shifted closer again," she said. "That's not really a surprise. We knew it was going to happen at some point. Now we have to plan what we're going to do next."

He drank brandy. "If we do nothing, how long do you think I would have?"

"Boy, I don't know." She blew out a sigh. "Maybe another week?"

"That's what I would guess too." He set aside his glass. "What now, Doctor?"

Resting her elbows on her knees, she ran her fingers through her hair. "You're not going to like it."

He laughed. "Tell me something new."

The glance she gave him was wry. "There are really only two choices, Oberon. Theoretically, I could give you daily treatments to work on wiggling that needle out the long, slow way, but it's a really smart spell. It was built to act like a virus and mutate according to changes in its host. I think you made a brilliant choice when you focused on shapeshifting into your Wyr form. That's why you're still alive. But it has adapted now, and it has only one purpose—to shut you down."

"It's already shutting pieces of me down," he muttered. "My emotions are all but gone, and it's becoming a struggle to keep in touch with my higher reasoning."

"Yes," she said. She laced her fingers together. "And we don't know how it might adapt to the daily treatments. It might get more aggressive. That path would be a long, slow struggle, and if you're looking at the goal of full recovery, I think it's a dangerous one. I don't know what kind of long-term damage it might do to you."

"And the second choice?" He watched her closely. Her facial expressions and thought processes were fascinating.

She met his gaze with a calm, clear look. "Surgery to remove the needle. Ideally, I would want you back in New York, so I could have the full support of my surgery team. There are techniques we could use to try a less invasive approach. I could go in to the site from under your arm, but again, given that we don't know how the magic will react, we would have to be prepared to crack open your sternum and go in the hard way."

"Let's assume you would get it out," he said. "What would be the recovery time?"

"Since you've now acquired the healing capabilities of a full Wyr, I'd say four weeks before you'd be battle ready again. With healing spells and a sensible approach to your recovery, you'll be on your feet pretty quickly. As far as regaining the abilities you've lost…" Her shoulders lifted in a regretful shrug. "I don't know what the recovery time for that would be."

Obeying an impulse he didn't stop to define, he leaned forward, took both her hands in his, and turned them over to examine them. They were slender, feminine, and strong, the fingernails kept neat and short. They would look beautiful adorned with rings and bracelets, but she didn't wear any jewelry.

"I might never recover them," he said. "I might never again be the man I used to be."

Her fingers tightened on his. "No, you might not. But you might become a new man that you like and respect very much. The essential thing is, you would win back your freedom from Isabeau's influence, and that's what you said you wanted more than anything. And you'd be alive. Many people don't get a second chance at life. If we achieve that, we will have achieved everything."

His old paranoia tried to rear its ugly head. It whispered to him of treachery, but he quashed it ruthlessly, because Kathryn had spoken the truth when she'd said if she had wanted him dead, he would already be dead.

"It's been two hundred years since I set foot on Earth," he mused. "After seeing the strange things like your metallic blanket and your clothes, I'm curious to see what else there is to see."

Her gaze lit with a smile. "It's going to be

overwhelming," she told him. "There are horseless carriages and machines that fly in the sky and can take you from London to New York in a matter of hours with no obligation to a Djinn. And I'm pretty sure you're going to love modern guns. You have so many reasons to fight and beat this thing."

"It sounds wonderful, Kathryn." Releasing his hold on her, he relaxed back in his chair. "But you are going to perform the surgery in Lyonesse."

"What!" She stared at him incredulously. "You can't be serious."

The hard planes of his face settled into determined lines. "I've made up my mind. You'll perform the surgery here before Annwyn and the others arrive." She sputtered, clearly searching for a rebuttal, but he spoke again before she could. "Don't tell me you didn't think of this when I was in stasis, because I'm beginning to understand how you think, and I know you did."

OBERON WASN'T AS bad as Dragos. He was much worse. At least Dragos had a grasp on many modern medical and scientific principles.

She glared at Oberon. He relaxed back in his chair, looking every inch the king that he was. She bit out, "Yes, of course I considered it—for all of three moments. For one thing, I never would have performed surgery without consent from your next of kin."

"Do you always wait for permission to act?" He

raised one eyebrow. "That must be quite a hindrance in your profession."

"No, of course I don't!" she shot back. "When there's an emergency there's no time, but there are ethics that govern my actions, and you were stable. Besides, you would barely let me scan you. I can't imagine how you would have reacted if I had started to cut into you. Surgery wasn't a viable option."

"Well, it is now." His expression settled into hard lines.

Gods, how she hated to see that look on one of her patients, because it usually meant they intended to act in a way that flew in the face of all her best advice.

Her lips tightened. "I won't do it."

He shot forward, and before she could leap away, his big hands closed on her biceps. She tensed, but he only grasped her firmly.

"Listen to me," he said, his voice low and intense. "If I don't make it, I want to die here, in my home—not in some hospital in a foreign country. And I want you to do it before Annwyn and the others arrive, because I don't want to have to face their emotional reactions and pretend like I care. And I don't want to hurt them any more than I already have, by changing so much over the years and by being gone for so long. I don't want to die, but if I do… This is the best way I can go in peace." The tension in his body radiated through his hands. "I understand you don't want to do it this way, and you have your reasons. I'm asking you to do it anyway."

"Goddammit," she muttered. "*Goddammit*. Fine. We'll do it your way. But you're going to write out and sign an advance directive that states what you want done while you're unconscious. You're also going to write a letter to Annwyn and the others explaining yourself, so they will understand what happened, and why I did what I did." She glared at him. "Those two things are nonnegotiable."

He gave her a nasty smile. "Aren't you going to ask for more money?"

"That too," she snapped. "Standard rates for open-heart surgery apply." Technically it wouldn't be open-heart surgery as she shouldn't have to cut into his heart, but she was damned if she was going to start splitting hairs right now.

He relaxed. "Good. Then we have a deal."

Her eyes dampened, and she blinked the moisture away rapidly. She hated that he was adding more risk to what would already be a risky surgery. And she hated that his reasons had made her change her mind, especially since he would never let her back out now.

"I'll do the surgery three days from now," she told him, shrugging out of his hold.

His brows snapped together in a fierce frown. "Why wait so long?"

"We're not going to be waiting," she told him. "We're going to do all those things a surgical team and hospital staff do when preparing for surgery. I need a well-lit operating theater with a table at the correct height, and the right utensils for the job, and it all has to be sterilized. And I need a variety of spells cast into high-quality gems—I prefer diamonds—so I have them readily at hand when I get to work. We've got a lot to do. I suggest you get me those diamonds now."

He barked out a laugh. It did not sound amused. "I'll get you those damn diamonds," he said. "But first I'm going to show you where you'll be operating."

"Fine," she snarled.

"Oh, cheer up," he told her as he stood. "At least I didn't pick your first choice of treatments. You can't be regretting that."

She stood when he did and moved to put some distance between them. "At the moment, I regret having ever set foot in Lyonesse, so don't talk to me about regrets."

"You'll get over it," he said unsympathetically. "You wouldn't be where you are today if you didn't thrive on challenge."

He was right, but she didn't have to give him the satisfaction of acknowledging it. She kept silent as he led the way out of his office and picked a path through the palace that led to another unfamiliar wing.

Passing by several closed doors, they reached an old stone archway with a wide set of worn stone steps that went downward. As they descended, Oberon lit the witchlight globes set at intervals along the walls.

She was too fascinated to get worried about the strangeness and isolation as they continued to descend deeper. Just being alone with Oberon in the ruined city was already filled with strangeness and isolation. They were merely changing the scenery.

Finally, when they had gone down at least sixty feet, they came to a set of ancient iron-bound doors.

The doors were latched, not locked. He opened one and pushed it wide to reveal a deeply shadowed interior. Then he stepped inside, and as she followed, he flicked out a magical spark.

This time when witchlights flared, the entire area blazed with light. At first it blinded her, and she threw up a hand to shield her eyes. Then as she adjusted, she stared around in awe.

They weren't standing in a room. They were standing in a large cave—a crystal cave, and the crystals picked up the light from the witchlights and reflected back both light and magic until it seemed like they stood in the middle of the sun itself.

She walked slowly across the floor, soaking in the scene. At some point the floor had been leveled, and a large oblong slab sat in the middle of the expanse. It looked like it had been carved from a single creamy white stone. On the wall opposite the doors a trickle of water poured into a large, carved stone basin.

As she reached the slab, she laid a hand on the surface. The echo of long-ago magic vibrated through her senses.

She breathed, "What is this stone?"

"It's a form of agate found exclusively here in

Lyonesse." Oberon walked to the opposite side of the slab and laid his hands along the top as well. His expression turned inward. "It absorbs magic better than most other gems. As you can see, the crystal walls and ceiling provide plenty of illumination. They can be spelled to hold light for as long as a full day... three times as long as normal witchlights. Here is your operating theater, Kathryn. Healing sessions and surgeries have been conducted here for many centuries. This stone will maintain any spell you need for it to, for as long as you need it."

"It's amazing," she whispered.

She ran a finger along the edge, trying to pick up details from the echoes of the magic that had been cast into it. She could almost, but not quite, catch images, but the last magic had been cast too long ago for her to get more than fleeting impressions.

Overwhelmingly, however, she got the sense that the slab had been used for pain control and anesthesia, and she dared to relax a tiny bit. Those were her two major concerns about doing surgery on Oberon by herself.

With his cooperation, she was certain she could put him under, but she didn't know if she could keep him unconscious if the magic she used or the magic the needle emitted disturbed him in any way. And his waking up in the middle of such an invasive surgery would be nightmarish for the both of them.

"What do you think about the height?" He watched her closely.

"Hmm?" She frowned down at the slab as she considered. "Oh—it's a little tall for me, but not enough to be a problem. I can always get a flat piece of wood to stand on. I think this space will work amazingly well once it's been disinfected from top to bottom."

"Good." He turned to leave, then paused. "How many diamonds do you want?"

"As many as you can lay your hands on," she told him absently. "Say, fifty or sixty magic-quality gems."

"You want sixty diamonds?" He snorted. "That should be no problem to find in an evacuated city."

It took a moment for her to pull out of her preoccupation and realize he was being sarcastic. "Surely you've got some treasure stuck in secret closets somewhere," she said. "And while I realize that gems are very portable, there's still the chance that not everybody took everything with them. When people evacuate, they aren't always thinking clearly, and they always act in the hope that they'll be able to return home soon. I need fifty or sixty magic-quality gems—preferably diamonds, or even good-sized chunks of this type of agate, if it holds spells as well as you say."

He rubbed the back of his neck. "Fine. When do you need it by?"

"As soon as you can get it. By tomorrow morning if you can." She eyed him thoughtfully. "Do you know how to cast healing spells?"

"If you mean simple spells to heal injuries, yes."

"Good. That will help. Do you also know how to

make healing potions or how to set spells into gems?"

His eyes narrowed. She could tell he was catching on to her trajectory. "Yes."

"Even better. When you find fifty or sixty gems, you can start casting healing spells into them. It typically takes about thirty-five to forty-five minutes to cast one healing spell into a gem, so as you can see, you've got your work cut out for you. Ticktock, King."

"What will you be doing while I work on this?"

Spreading out her hands, she told him, "I'll be doing everything else."

Chapter Ten

D AY SIX.

Kathryn was too busy to remember to write the number down.

By morning, Oberon had found forty-two decent-sized, high-quality diamonds. When he showed them to her, she said, "That's not enough."

"That's what I found," he said flatly. "There's plenty of treasure still in the treasury, but it is not made up of magic-quality gems."

"Fifty or sixty," she told him. "Or I don't do the surgery."

His gaze flashed with ire. "Do you realize what a pain in the ass you are?"

"*Me* a pain in the ass?" She laughed in sheer outrage. "Do you know how many people I would have on my surgery team as backup in New York? Six. Six people, all very skilled medical professionals and all magic users. And do you realize how many things could go wrong with this surgery?"

"I'll get them," he growled. Scooping up the bag, he stalked away.

She located a ladder, and by the end of the day she had the entire crystal cave scrubbed and disinfected. She also had a cleansing spell cast into a piece of agate and ready to add to the water fountain on the day of the surgery.

She didn't see Oberon at all during the day. In the evening, when she sat down to supper in the palace kitchen—she had cooked a big pot of porridge, chock-full of nuts, cranberries, and honey, and had fried more bacon—Oberon prowled into the room and threw a velvet bag onto the table in front of her.

"How many?" she asked around a mouthful of food.

"Fifty-eight. I'll start casting the healing spells after I eat some supper." He stalked over to the fireplace where the porridge hung near the flames, peered into the pot, and made a face.

She sighed. There went her peaceful dinner. The palace kitchen was cavernous, but with Oberon filling it with his oversized presence, it seemed to shrink to a fraction of its previous space.

He helped himself to porridge without asking, scooped up a couple of pieces of bacon, and returned to the table to sit across from her and eat with quick economy. Halfway through, he studied her with his strange gaze.

"You look different. You're not wearing your odd clothes."

She scraped her bowl. "All my clothes are dirty, and I decided my time was better spent on preparing for the surgery rather than doing laundry. I've been raiding closets."

"Good. You should take what you need. None of it matters."

She nodded. That's what she'd figured too. "I need eight of those for other spells."

Without asking which spells she intended to cast, he shook out eight and tossed them across the table toward her. She watched them skitter across the hard, age-worn wood.

He had changed since the day before. He was still rude and argumentative, but other than that he was behaving himself. The sensuality... it wasn't gone, because it was an inherent part of him, but it had been set on the back burner. He was lit with purpose and focused on their end goal.

That was exactly how he should be, exactly how she needed him to be. She wouldn't have welcomed anything else.

So it was entirely on her when his scent reached her and she thought of dark chocolate with more than a hint of rebel longing. She watched his mouth fit around spoonfuls of food and couldn't remember the last time she had seen anything so sexy.

Slapping down her own spoon, she dug the heels of both hands into her eyes. She couldn't go there. She didn't want to have sex with someone she disliked as much as she disliked him. She never crossed the line with a patient, and she didn't want to cut into someone she was having sex with.

Was that why she and Bayne had never managed to get past the friend zone?

Why did she have to find the most inappropriate man she had ever met to discover he was also the sexiest man she had ever met? What was *wrong* with her?

"What's wrong?"

Oberon's question echoed her own too closely for her own comfort. When she peered around one hand at him, she found that he had fixed an all too discerning gaze on her.

"Nothing," she ground out. "I've just got a headache. It's nothing that a good night's sleep won't cure."

"Go, get your rest," he told her. "I'm going to be up all night working on healing spells."

She hesitated. "We can put off the surgery another day or so until you get them done."

"We're not putting off the surgery," he said flatly, pushing his dishes away. "I'll stay up both nights if that's what it takes to get them done. You're the one who needs her rest. I'll sleep enough when I'm dead."

She didn't try to argue with him. Macabre though it was, he had a point. She also didn't bother leaving the palace to find somewhere else to sleep. It wasted too much time and effort, and she trusted him enough to put his needs first. If he did nothing else, he would stay focused until they discovered what life after surgery would be like.

Going upstairs, she went into the rooms she had picked for herself, washed desultorily, and fell into bed. She had a big day planned for tomorrow. She needed to scour the city for physicians' offices and residences so she could scavenge for operating tools and equipment.

She had the basics with her as well as enough sutures that would work well enough for stitching him up afterward, but since she would be operating without the tools and techniques she could have employed in New York, she would have to crack open his chest wall. That meant she needed to find something she could use as a sternum saw. And the gods only knew what she was going to use for clamps.

The thought made her gut clench, but while she needed to make sure she had every possible tool available at hand, more than likely the real battle against Morgan's needle was going to be magical in nature and not surgical at all.

When she doused her witchlight and crawled into bed, she stared at the dark ceiling for most of the night. After she finally fell asleep, she dreamed that a white lion chased her through Manhattan.

On day seven, Robin returned.

AFTER WORKING THROUGH the night, Oberon needed exercise and food, so he left the palace, changed into the lion, and went hunting for fresh meat.

Now that he had taken control of his Power again,

the weather had started to warm. This morning felt like early spring, and the bizarre mountains and swirls of ice that dominated the city had begun to melt.

It would take a while for the land to recover from what he had done to it—from what Isabeau's attack had caused him to do—but at least the process had begun. Still, he knew he was going to miss the icy, desolate wasteland the city had become.

He found a sturdy wild goat that gave him quite a chase, but the warm, fresh meal it provided was much needed. He ate everything except the bigger bones and the hooves, and when he returned to the palace, he went to his office and got straight back to work.

At one point, he heard Kathryn's quick footsteps in a nearby hall. A few moments later an outside door creaked. She hadn't come to check in on him, and he was just as glad she didn't. She was a distraction he couldn't afford right now. He focused everything on survival.

Grimly, he kept at the grueling task at hand. Setting healing spells into over fifty stones was mind-numbing, but with each one he reminded himself that it might be the spell to make the difference between life and death.

Sometime after lunch rapid footsteps sounded in the hall again, and he realized they were too heavy to be Kathryn's. He had just finished casting a spell, so he set aside the new gem and strode toward the door.

Just as he reached the open doorway, Robin appeared. The puck looked as if he had blown in on the spring wind, his thin cheeks high with color and his nut-brown hair tossed wildly.

"Sire!" Robin exclaimed, gladness ringing in his voice. He rushed forward as if he would throw thin arms around Oberon.

Rage flared. When the puck came within an arm's length, Oberon grabbed him by the throat, spun, and slammed him into the wall.

"Where have you been?" he hissed. "How dare you bring a stranger into my home and then leave her alone with me while I am unconscious? *She was not Daoine Sidhe.*"

Robin did not try to defend himself. His arms hung lax at his sides. He choked out, "I stayed by her side constantly until I was sure you would be safe in her care. I didn't abandon you—I would never abandon you!"

"Oberon!" Kathryn exclaimed. She had entered the palace without him noticing. Racing forward, she grabbed his arm and yanked hard. "What are you doing? Let go of him!"

"I told him to watch this place," he roared, resisting her. His fingers tightened around Robin's neck.

If you don't let him go this instant, I'll knock you unconscious, Kathryn snapped telepathically. *You have no idea what he's done or what he's been through because of you. He's on your side, dammit, and his world revolves around you!*

He barely heard her words. All he could remember was the shock of waking to a stranger in his room.

She forced herself bodily between them, and with her back against Robin, she pushed hard against his chest. He resisted until she tried to knee him in the balls. Instinct caused him to twist to one side. Her knee grazed the inside of his thigh. As soon as he was off-balance, she knocked his hand away from Robin's throat.

When she had freed the puck, she turned to face him. Robin doubled over, coughing hard.

"Let me see," she said gently, bending over him.

She's not his doctor, she's mine. Oberon's fury hadn't subsided. It merely latched on to the next thought. "Get away from him!" he snapped. "This doesn't concern you!"

When she whirled, she looked angrier than he had ever seen before. In a hard voice, she told him, "You are out of control. This is one of your people who mourned for you. He fought for you—he went through unimaginable shit for you. We may not know why he left, but I do know that much." Telepathically, she added, *Stop what you're doing and think. You don't want to do anything to destroy the future of the man you want to become, otherwise there's no point to doing any of this.*

She was right again. Gods damn it, he hated it when she was right. He growled at her wordlessly and spun away as he struggled to get under control.

"His eyes," Robin croaked. "What happened to him?"

"He was that way when he woke up," Kathryn said. "Robin, he's not himself. We can't trust anything that he says or does right now—don't hold it against him."

Oberon had almost gotten ahold of himself, but that

sent his fury exploding again. He roared, "Don't speak for me, woman!"

"Fine!" she roared back, throwing up her hands. "Go ahead and destroy your own fucking life, and then Isabeau wins!"

Aagghh! It was the one thing she could have said that would make any difference, and of course she used it. Stalking away, he slammed his fist into the wall repeatedly until the glossy wood panel cracked and fell to the floor in splinters.

Only when the skin had split across his knuckles and blood began to spray with each piston-like blow did he stop.

When he finally looked around, he was breathing hard. Robin and Kathryn had backed away. Kathryn still stood in front of the puck, an arm outstretched to keep him behind her. Robin gripped her shoulder with one hand. Their expressions were identical—they watched him with a sober wariness.

"Kathryn is right," Oberon said to Robin. He shook out his aching hand and used his shirt to blot the blood from the split knuckles. "I am not myself. Please forgive me."

He said the words without emotion or sincerity. He didn't give a shit whether the puck forgave him or not. He looked away as Robin's expression lightened.

"There is nothing to forgive, sire. Only, please tell me how I can now be of service."

Oberon's eyes narrowed. "First, where have you

been these last few days?"

Eagerly, Robin stepped out from behind Kathryn. "After I had determined the doctor held only good intentions toward you, I decided I should go back to shadow Annwyn's party. If I could overhear their conversations, I could determine what their true purpose was. For the past several years, I have not been party to decisions and choices made by the Dark Court... for reasons. I judged they would talk more freely if they believed I was not around. And I was right."

As he listened, Oberon strode back into his office, gesturing for the others to follow him. After a hesitation, they did, but he noted how they still kept their distance from him. He had caused quite a setback in relations with both of them.

He walked over to the sitting area by the fireplace where the brandy, now much reduced, still sat. Uncorking it, he took a large swallow directly from the bottle.

"What did you overhear?"

The puck glanced at the doctor before he continued. "Annwyn, Gawain, and Rowan talked quite a bit about what their next steps might be, depending on they found when they reached the city. Of course, they couldn't know what I had done with the doctor—all they knew was that I had taken her, and we had both disappeared. Rowan said I might have brought her directly to you, and the others acknowledged that might be true. They also speculated on whether I had killed her or caused her to be so lost, it would take some time to discover her whereabouts."

Kathryn spoke up. "Those outcomes don't sound very logical. Why would they think you would do that?"

Scorn flashed in Robin's gaze. "Most in the Dark Court don't understand what drives me. They are reluctant to believe that I feel only loyalty toward my liege, or to think anything good about me whatsoever." He bowed toward her. "However, they did all express deep concern for your well-being."

She shrugged and gave him a wry smile. "They promised Dragos I would be returned home in good condition."

The puck nodded. "That was also mentioned." His gaze shot to Oberon. "But, by far, their conversations centered on what to do with you, sire."

And here it comes, he thought. He took another mouthful of brandy. "Spit it out."

"Gawain urged Annwyn to consider what must be done should you be deemed unsalvageable." Having recovered his equilibrium entirely, Robin strolled around the office, touching items here and there as if reacquainting himself with them. "He said it was time to acknowledge that the needs of the many might outweigh the needs of the individual. The Daoine Sidhe should not be displaced from their homeland just because their unconscious lord's Power rampaged out of control. If, after fifteen years, they have not managed to heal you in all that time, Annwyn should face the terrible reality that you cannot be saved. She should call on the knights of the Dark Court to do what must be done for the good of the people."

While he listened, a cold, hard knot settled in the pit of his stomach. He shifted position to watch Kathryn. As she listened to the puck's tale, her expression darkened, and she rubbed her eyes, but she did not look surprised.

He asked, "And what must be done for the good of the people, Robin? Did they say?"

Robin shook his head. "They alluded and hinted, but no one said it outright."

Oberon turned his attention to Kathryn. "When they hired you, did they ask you to make that kind of assessment for them?"

She made a face, sighed, and then said with a remarkable calmness, "No, they didn't, but I was expecting to have a conversation along those lines at some point with Annwyn, probably on the way here. And that could very well be what she'd intended, but with Robin's actions we never got the chance."

He ran his fingers along the bottom of the bottle. "What would you have said, had she asked?"

"I would have told her what I thought after examining you. Ultimately, any decision about your care would have been up to her. She would have been free to take my advice or disregard it as she saw fit." Kathryn's steady gaze met his. "I'll save you the trouble of asking, shall I? If she were here after I had examined you, and she had asked me if you were salvageable, then I would have said yes. I would have every hope that you would be—but we would only know after the needle was removed."

"And what if who I am doesn't change?" he asked in a soft voice. "Would I still be salvageable then?"

She shook her head, her mouth twisting in a wry smile. "We'll see what we're facing then. I appreciate how disturbing it is to know your people have been discussing how they might need to move forward without you. But remember, some of them have had fifteen years to cope with this, and still others were trapped on Earth where two hundred years have passed. The conversation they had is a perfectly rational, understandable dilemma that your very loyal people have had to grapple with, at least hypothetically, for a long time. That doesn't mean they're disloyal or going to war against you, and it doesn't mean you're not salvageable. It's the same hideously difficult conversation any family would have about a patient who has been comatose for a very long time."

She was dancing around the subject, and by Robin's sudden scowl, the puck felt the same dissatisfaction he did.

Oberon had heard tales of Wyr who had gone so feral they had to be put down. Had Kathryn been involved in making assessments on feral Wyr?

He heard himself ask, "How many Wyr have you been involved in putting down?"

She sighed and looked disappointed. "Five."

Disappointed in him? His grip tightened on the brandy bottle. Fuck that. He pushed for more. "How many Wyr have you personally euthanized?"

"Three." Her steady gaze never wavered.

He drank more brandy. "And how did it make you feel, *Doctor*?"

Something dark overshadowed her fine features. "I felt heartsick," she whispered. "And sick to my stomach. I wasn't able to eat for days. There's nothing worse than knowing you can't do anything to help someone—that you've tried everything, but nothing has worked. If that happens, it's a mercy when their bodies give out. But if their bodies are strong and their minds are terrible... Cages for the long-lived Wyr are crueler than anything. But it is the hardest thing I have ever done, to help make a strong heart stop beating. I wasn't alone when I did it. In the New York demesne, several medical professionals are required to act together when putting down a feral Wyr. The law is designed to help us cope afterward, but each time I felt like I had done it by myself."

She hadn't flinched away from any of his questions, he would give her that. But her eyes shone with an extra glitter as if she held back tears.

There were only a few swallows of brandy left. He upended the bottle and drank the amber liquid down. "We're wasting time," he said. "And I have more healing spells to cast."

Robin cocked his head. "Healing spells?"

He told the puck, "I have awakened, but the assassin's spell is still trapped in my body. Kathryn will perform surgery tomorrow morning to take it out. After you've eaten and rested, I want you to do whatever she needs to get ready. Is that clear?"

Dismay filled the puck's expression, and his narrow shoulders bowed. He whispered, "Yes, my lord."

Oberon threw the bottle into the fireplace where it shattered. "Get out," he said. "I don't want to see either of you until tomorrow morning."

Neither one of them argued. As they slipped out, Kathryn shut the door.

Oberon stood looking around. The empty room was full of ghosts from happier memories of a different man. He hated it in here.

After brooding, he got back to work.

Time passed, and the room darkened as the sun set outside. He lit witchlights and continued throwing spell after spell. After a while, he grew irritable about fighting so hard to save his own life when others might soon judge it needed to be taken away.

A knock sounded at the door, and the all-too-easy rage flared to life again. He roared, "What did I say earlier about leaving me alone?"

The door opened, and Kathryn walked in carrying a tray full of food. Not speaking or looking at him, she set the tray down on the desk and walked out again.

He looked at the contents. Grilled fish and potatoes, a tankard of beer, and a piece of paper lay folded underneath a knife and fork. Shaking off the utensils, he unfolded the paper. It contained a list of things to cover in an advance directive.

Gods damn it. Fine. Rapidly he wrote out the advance directive and signed it, and then he worked on a terse letter to Annwyn, labeled at the top with: In the Event of My Death, and it was all so fucking tedious when he would much rather get drunk out of his mind.

What do you say to someone who had been more loyal than you had any right to expect, and you just didn't care?

In the end, he let the ghost of the man he had once been speak for him.

Annwyn,

This damn spell has turned me into a monster, so I have decided to take what actions I can while I can still take them. I insisted Dr. Shaw perform the surgery. By the time you get here we will know if it worked or not.

Kathryn tried to talk me out of this course of action. She would much prefer to do the surgery in New York, but I wanted her to do it here in Lyonesse. The responsibility for what happens next is all mine.

If you're reading this, the surgery didn't work and I'm dead. I wanted it this way. I wanted to die at home.

You should know, I remember the many years of service and devotion you have given me. And I remember the love and very high esteem I have always held you in. You will make a splendid queen for the Daoine Sidhe.

Kill Isabeau for me. I wanted to do it myself, but you would be my next choice.

My best felicitations for a bright future.

Yours,
Oberon

After the ink had dried, he folded the letter, dripped melted wax over it, then fixed the wax with his seal and set it to one side with the advance directive. Then he ate every scrap of food and got back to work. He finished casting the final healing spell just before dawn.

Leaving the office, he went to wash and shave. After he had dressed in a clean linen shirt and black pants, he walked to the Garden Hall and stood in front of the windows, watching the sunrise. It was spectacular. Every conceivable dawn color streaked the sky in a rainbow kaleidoscope that spanned hundreds of miles.

He didn't have to open a window to know that the temperature was already above freezing outside. The day was going to be warm and brilliant, as if nature herself wanted to demonstrate all the damn pleasures he would be missing if he didn't wake up again.

One corner of his mouth notched up in a grim smile. "Yeah," he whispered, "fuck you too."

The atmosphere in the hall shifted, a subtle but unmistakable change. Even though Kathryn made no noise, a gentle current of air brought her fresh scent to him.

Turning his head, he met her gaze. She wore a

hunter's colors, browns and blacks, and her shining hair was pulled back in a tight braid. She had found a quilted, sleeveless jacket from somewhere, and it fit her slim frame well. He looked down at her hands, lax at her sides. They were steady as a rock.

She walked over to stand beside him and looked out the window.

"I left your advance directive on my desk," he told her.

"I saw it." She sighed. "You can always change your mind. You know Robin would carry us to the crossover passageway. In very little time we could be on our way to New York."

"I'm not going to change my mind." He captured one of her hands and toyed with her fingers, and she let him. "I'm putting my life in your hands. If you can't save me, don't bother waking me up."

She whispered, "Don't put that on me."

"You don't like it, tough," he growled, tightening his hold on her hand. "I would trade places with you in a heartbeat. If you can't save me, *don't wake me up*."

"Goddamn you, Oberon!"

That was when he realized she was holding on to him as tightly as he was holding on to her. "Where's Robin?"

Even as he spoke footsteps sounded in the hallway, and the puck answered, "Here, sire."

"Good." Releasing Kathryn, Oberon turned away from the dawn. He was tired of talking. "Let's get this done."

Chapter Eleven

EVERYTHING WAS READY. She had gone over it all multiple times, checking and rechecking to make sure she hadn't forgotten anything. She had even sewn two surgical masks and made a mountain of bandages from strips of fine cotton that she had cut, boiled, and sterilized.

Then, with Robin shadowing her that evening, she went over everything again and explained it to him. She didn't trust Oberon's volatile temper—for some reason, the puck set him off—so she coaxed Robin into spending the night in her rooms by sketching out the various ways the surgery might go. Ostensibly the sketches were for him, but she found it was useful for her, too, to plot out various courses of action in her head.

By the time she had finished the impromptu lecture, it was past midnight, and Robin looked more than a little spooked and wilder than ever.

"You've got to hold it together," she said. "I need you functional, Robin."

He braided his too-long fingers together and

muttered, "If only I had returned a day later."

"You're going to be fine," she told him with a conviction she didn't feel. "If you find the sight of the surgery disturbing, you don't have to watch. If you want, you can sit on the ground and wait. You're going to have one job—your only job. After I put Oberon to sleep, you can't let him wake up. No matter what happens. If the spells I set in the agate slab fail, you must keep him unconscious. If he wakes up in the middle of surgery and tries to do something to stop it, it could be fatal to all of us. Do you understand?"

His finger braiding grew tighter, and his feral gaze slid away. "You don't ask for much, do you?"

"I know you're stressed." She squeezed his tense shoulders. "But it is really very simple. I spent hours casting the spells into the operating stone. They should hold him, but if they don't, you'll need to cast the spell on him again, just like I taught it to you... And keep casting it until I tell you to stop. I'll give you plenty of warning and tell you what to do and when you need to do it. Okay?"

"I think I might throw up," he told her plaintively. Then he proceeded to do so.

She managed to grab a vase that she had been using as a wastebasket and shoved his head down over it before he hurled. When he had finished, they regarded each other gravely.

She waited for him to say something, but when he didn't, she handed the vase to him. "Go wash that out and keep it close in case you need it again."

She half expected him to bolt and disappear, but instead he did as he was told. If this had been about anybody but Oberon, he might have fled. But just as the puck seemed to set off the worst in Oberon, Oberon seemed to bring out the best in Robin. Hopefully that would continue until the surgery was over.

At last she took the bed, and Robin stretched out on a chaise in one corner. Despite his earlier distress, he fell asleep almost immediately. Kathryn knew, because she spent most of the night staring at the ceiling and listening to him snore.

It was unlike her. Normally she could sleep anywhere, through almost anything, but not that night. Scenarios for what might go wrong kept running through her mind until it was a relief to finally get out of bed, wash, and get ready for the day.

Finding Oberon ready and waiting was even more of a relief. They headed down to the crystal cave. On the way down, her senses tightened until so much energy thrummed in her body she had to keep from racing down the stairs ahead of the other two.

Outside the doors, she stopped them both. "Oberon, I want you to go directly to the slab, take off your shirt, and lie down. Robin, you stay with me—and don't touch anything."

Robin's eyes were huge in his pinched face. "Yes, Doctor."

Oberon didn't wait for her to repeat herself, and he

didn't need encouragement. Instead, he prowled into the cave, went directly to the slab, and lay down on it.

As soon as he was fully reclined, she walked over to him and laid one hand on his forearm. "Last chance to back out."

He gave her another fierce grin. "Not on your life."

Leaning over, she smiled at him. "Even though I don't agree with it, I respect your decision," she told him. "In your shoes, I might have done the same."

His cracked-ice gaze lingered on her mouth. His voice deepened as he said, "Come down here and give me a good-night kiss."

She jerked back and repeated his own words back to him. "Not on your life!"

"Coward," he said softly. The grin still played around the edges of his sensual lips.

He was devastating now. How much more devastating would he be if he regained all his emotions?

She refused to let herself be intimidated by the idea and snapped, "Principled."

Then his voice entered her head as he switched to telepathy. *I'm going to wake up, and you will have removed Morgan's infernal spell,* he told her. *Then I will no longer be your patient, Kathryn. So stick a pin in this conversation. We'll be finishing it later.*

Stop talking to me! She glared at him. She felt as ruffled as if he had rubbed all her feathers the wrong way.

He laughed softly and ran his fingers down her arm, igniting a trail of invisible fire.

I'm activating the spell now. In three, two, one…

Touching the slab, she activated the spell that lay dormant inside the stone. It flared, and Oberon's eyelids closed. The fierce sensuality in his features relaxed.

"Oberon?" she asked. "Can you hear me?"

No response. She grabbed a scalpel from the nearby tray, and with the point she tested the pads of his fingers. There was no reflex response. He was deeply unconscious. Thank the gods. Setting the scalpel back on the tray, she braced her palms on the agate slab beside his torso and let herself sag.

"Is everything all right?" Robin's question sounded shrill with fear.

She lifted her head. "Yes," she told him with a reassuring smile. "He's just… very difficult to deal with sometimes, and I need to focus all my attention on the surgery now."

The puck paced around the cave, his arms wrapped around his torso. "How long is this going to take? I really don't like being underground. I hate feeling confined."

She sagged again and had to force herself to sound calm as she replied, "This surgery might very well take twenty hours or more. That's why I'm counting on you to back me up in case the spell in the agate fails. Can you do it? Because if you can't, you need to get the hell out— and stay out. I have to focus on his problems, not yours."

His face twisted. He whispered, "I'll do it."

She studied him. She had rarely seen such an

agonized expression on anyone, and she hadn't even started yet. "Get out," she told him. "It will be safer if I manage this on my own."

His eyes filled with tears. Suddenly he looked breakable and very old. "I can't fail again."

"You can't fail in here *period*," she snapped. He flinched as if she had physically struck him, and she caught herself. Then an idea occurred to her. "Here's what we're going to do. Go wait at the head of the stairs. There's plenty of light and fresh air up there. You *stay* there until the surgery is over. If I need you, I'll shout. You'll be able to hear me from up there, so if I call, you get your ass down here as fast as you can. Got it?"

He wiped his face, already looking steadier. "Got it."

Having him gone would be a relief. Despite his willingness to help, he was too unpredictable. She smiled at him. "Go on now."

He started to leave, then paused to give his lord one last, lingering look. "He likes you," Robin said unexpectedly. "Even with the sorcerer's spell warping his soul, he still likes you."

Immensely surprised, she barked out a laugh. "You are sadly mistaken. He detests me, and I can't stand him. We've done nothing but fight since he's woken up."

Robin stared at her. In that moment, his gaze had never seemed so strange. "And yet," the puck whispered, "he is willing to let you crack open his chest and dig into the deepest part of his body. And he has trusted you enough to ask you to let him die."

Her amusement faded. He shouldn't have read Oberon's advance directive without permission, but maybe it was just as well that he had.

Turning brisk, she fitted one of the surgical masks over her lower face, strode to the water fountain, threw in the stone that carried the disinfecting spell, and began to scrub up. Even with all her precautions, the cave wasn't going to be nearly as sterile as an operating theater in New York would be—but with Oberon's hardy Wyr constitution, that shouldn't matter.

"Hopefully it won't come to that," she said over her shoulder. "Close the door on your way out."

By the time she had finished and turned around, Robin was gone.

She had arranged her array of sterilized surgical tools on trays set on a table she and Robin had dragged down yesterday, as well as the stacks of bandages. Earlier, when she had found that Oberon had finished the healing spells and left his office, she had brought down the spelled stones as well. She had put his fifty spelled stones in a bigger bowl, and her eight in a smaller one, set closer to hand.

Now she whisked away the sterilized cloth covering the tools. This next bit was going to suck so badly.

She used the last of her small vial of disinfectant to swab down Oberon's chest. Afterward, she took the first of her eight stones, set it in the hollow of his throat and triggered the spell.

For humans, brain damage begins within thirty

seconds to two minutes after the heart is stopped. For the Wyr, brain damage begins a hundred and ten seconds to four minutes after the heart is stopped. For that reason, medical freeze spells were constructed to be of short duration.

The two spells in the agate slab produced unconsciousness and blocked pain. She had eight freeze spells at her disposal, each carefully calibrated to be a hundred seconds long. And she was going to need every single second.

As soon as the first spell activated, she cut him open and clamped the layers of flesh back until the hard bone of his sternum was exposed. Then she took a small chisel and mallet, leaped on top of the slab to straddle Oberon's waist, and broke through the edges of the long, flat bone.

While she worked, she kept her magical awareness buried deep inside him to monitor Morgan's magic needle. So far, it remained acquiescent, just as Morgan had promised it would, and she breathed a sigh of relief.

His spell didn't care if its host was being operated on—incisions would be like any other injury and only aid in its efforts to kill him. No, the spell would only react if it was disturbed... and that would be coming soon enough.

When the first freeze spell wore off, she quickly checked everywhere to make sure she had the bleed points clamped well enough. After she had given his brain a couple of minutes to recover, she took another freeze spell and activated it.

That set the pattern for her way in.

Activate, cut, clamp. Pack with sterilized cloth, check for bleeding, clamp again.

Then again: Activate, cut, clamp. Pack with sterilized cloth, check for bleeding, clamp again.

Every time she froze him, she moved as fast as she could. And every time afterward, she gave him as long to recover as she dared.

She was sweating by the time she had reached the last sinewy layer of tissue that lay between his heart and the open air. With the back of one forearm, she mopped her brow. Morgan's needle lay just on the other side of that layer.

It was not the best time to let memory sneak into her thoughts.

"To be honest, I'm surprised he has survived for as long as he has," Morgan had remarked when she had met with him. "Surgery techniques were not nearly as advanced when I created that spell. So I thought the greater likelihood was that someone would try to use magic to remove it. The spell is meant to adapt to anything its host tries to dislodge or remove it, so if you use a direct magical attack, it will pulse out a detonation in response—and that detonation should kill him."

"So the last thing I want to do is attack it," she said.

"Exactly. You want to find a way to ease it away. Use finesse. The greater the force used, the more it should react." He paused, then added helpfully, "Think of it like an action movie. The clock is running out, and you've got fifteen seconds blinking at the audience in bright red LED numbers... but the heroine doesn't dare jostle the bomb. Instead, she's got to defuse it."

She rolled her eyes. "Thanks, that's *so* helpful."

"You're welcome." He patted her shoulder. "You're going to do great."

Yeah well, Morgan, she thought as she stared down at Oberon's opened chest cavity. At the moment, I don't feel so great.

Pausing as she remembered that conversation had been a very bad idea. It gave her too much time to think. Stress tried to take control and make her hands shake. Gritting her teeth, she forced them to steady again.

Finesse the needle, huh? Just wiggle it out, like a really bad splinter.

If she cut through that last layer, it might activate the needle. But what if she tried using telekinesis instead to bring it out? After all, that was how she had managed to make it move back two millimeters.

The spell wasn't a live creature, but she had grown to think of it like one. Could she "surprise" it by wiggling it through the thin layer of flesh that now separated it from the outside? The problem was, with Oberon cut open, she couldn't take as long as she had before to edge the needle back.

One of the instruments she always carried in her portable physician's bag was a steel pair of tweezers. Grasping them now, she slowed her breathing, focused on the needle, and applied firm, steady telekinetic pressure on it.

The spell activated and applied firm, steady pressure in resistance.

"Remember, it's not just one spell," Morgan had told her. Her imagination constructed a ghost of the sorcerer standing behind her, whispering instructions into her ear. "It's many layered spells sewn together, and one of them is a mirror incantation. The mirror will do what you do, only in opposite. That's why you need to finesse it."

Now, as she eased back on the pressure, she gritted her teeth and muttered, "Morgan, you're diabolical."

She could almost imagine his bright smile in response.

How could she finesse this bloody fucking spell?

All it "wanted"—its sole purpose—was to drive through Oberon's heart and kill him. How could she fool it into thinking it had completed its directive?

Or could she fool it into thinking his heart was somewhere else?

Surgery technique wasn't the only thing to advance in the medical profession since Morgan had cast his spell. Magical technique had advanced too.

Kathryn knew how to use her own two hands as focal points combined with a shock spell to create a defibrillator. She also knew how to telekinetically massage a heart back into rhythm without ever having to make a single incision.

And in the previous year, a bright doctor in the

Kentucky witches demesne had patented a spell based on sympathetic magic. The spell was cast into a small figurine that would simulate critical bodily processes for a short amount of time.

The spelled figurines cost a fortune, and they only had a single-use application. They also had an extremely limited shelf life of roughly thirteen months before the spell decayed. She had recently read in a medical journal that the doctor was looking for ways to broaden its uses and lengthen its shelf life, but for now the figurines were only useful in extreme emergencies.

With a drop of the patient's blood and the right whispered incantation, the figurine could take over the work of a collapsed lung, an area of a brain impaired by an embolism, or a heart that had stopped beating—but only for ten or fifteen minutes at most.

In an operating room, ten or fifteen minutes gave a surgical team time to implement other lifesaving procedures, but in many other circumstances that wasn't enough time for someone to get help for a victim.

Kathryn owned a figurine, but she hadn't even pulled it out of her physician's bag. She had thought it wouldn't be of any use in this situation.

But what if there *was* a use for it?

What if it could take over the functions of Oberon's heart for a few critical minutes? Sympathetic magic simulated a person's own body functions. Would the figurine's magic fool Morgan's spell long enough for Kathryn to trap the needle and get it out?

She would have to fool both Morgan's spell *and* the spell in the figurine for this to work.

Moving quickly now, she stripped off her bloody gloves and dug around in her bag that sat open on the floor near the utensil table. After a moment of searching, she found the small box filled with the precious contents.

She opened the container. The interior was lined with magic-sensitive silver, and the tiny figurine was made of the same material.

Pulling it out, she ran to the washbasin and washed it with disinfected water. Then she donned another pair of disposable gloves and ran back to Oberon's still figure. Taking one of her freeze spells, she placed it directly on Oberon's heart.

Then she activated the figurine by touching it with his blood and whispering the incantation that would bring it to life. Cutting a small incision in that final layer of tissue, she tucked the figurine gently into his chest cavity, as far away from his real heart as she could get. It was only a few inches away, but in this situation a few inches was as good as a mile.

"One spell, two spell, three spell, four," she whispered to the cadence of an old nursery rhyme.

The needle still lay much too close to its end goal. Meanwhile, Oberon's real heart lay inert, and the spell mimicking his heart functions kicked in. His blood began pumping through his body.

Now, here came the fourth spell. Grasping the

needle telekinetically, she yanked it *hard* away from where the tiny figurine lay.

The needle yanked *hard* in the opposite direction—toward the figurine.

Holy gods. Her magical house of cards was holding.

She kept yanking on the needle as hard as she could. With a surge of magic, it fought back. Yanking like a fish at the end of a line, it wriggled toward the figurine. Bending over as she teased the needle into working harder than ever, she used her scalpel where the figurine was tucked to hold the small incision open and gripped her tweezers tight.

Goddammit, the hole she had cut was so tight. She needed somebody to blot that small upwelling of blood so she could see better….

But then she saw the tiniest of silver flashes in the healthy pink flesh.

There you are, you bastard.

She didn't hesitate long enough to second-guess herself. With the lightning-fast reflexes that peregrine falcons were known for, she snapped her tweezers over that tiny silver protrusion and pulled it out.

Even as she lifted it high into the air, the assassination spell detonated soundlessly. The malicious magic numbed her fingers. If it had still been anywhere near Oberon's heart, it would have killed him instantly.

Cursing, she flung the tweezers and needle aside and shook out her hands, then rubbed her fingers together. She still couldn't feel them. Thankfully, she didn't have to do any more cutting in tight spaces.

Now she worked backward to exit the surgery. First, she pulled out the figurine and released the freeze spell that had held Oberon's heart still. Then she started using the pile of fifty healing spells as she unclamped areas and pinched the places she had cut together. Bit by careful bit, she worked to get his flesh sealed over.

One of the most critical places to get accurate was the repositioning of his broken sternum and ribs. She spent quite a bit of time picking out bone fragments and splinters, and then she made absolutely certain everything was well in alignment before she activated several healing spells to fuse the bones together.

She was shaking for real when she finally released the upper layers of his epidermis, smoothed the edges together over his sternum, and laid the last diamonds along the surface of his chest. With one final activation, the healing spells set to work and she was done.

"That's it," she whispered to him. "You're finally free. What you do with the rest of your life is up to you."

If he wasn't damaged emotionally beyond repair. They would only discover that over time.

She tried to raise her voice, but it came out in a croak. "Robin."

A body hurtled down the stairs. Moments later, Robin crashed through the doors. As she saw the crisis in his expression, she realized belatedly how terrible everything looked. She was covered in blood, and so was Oberon's body, the slab of agate he lay on, and the multiple surgery tools. The cave floor was sticky underneath her boots.

"No, no," she said quickly, waving her numb hands. "I'm done. It's out. Careful, the needle is on the floor somewhere. It might carry some residual magic."

"And he's alive?"

Damn, she usually did much better at post-op meetings. "Yes, he's alive, and he's absorbed all the healing spells his body can take right now. If you are *very* careful, you can move him upstairs." If she didn't drink some water, she was going to fall down and die. She went over to the water fountain and sucked greedily at the fresh flow before she asked, "What time is it?"

"The sun set some time ago," Robin told her. "You have been down here for at least eighteen hours."

She almost wiped her face but then realized she was still wearing her second pair of bloody gloves. Stripping them off, she held her hands under the running water. She still couldn't feel anything in her fingers, not even when her palms grew cold.

"I'm used up," she told him. "I don't have an ounce of magic left, and I can't feel my hands. He's going to be in pain if he wakes up too soon. If you don't know how to help ease it, you're going to have to tell him to suck it up. Tell him no physical exertion until I can examine him again to see how his body has responded to the healing spells. Understood?"

"Understood, Doctor." The puck gathered Oberon's lax body into his arms. It looked odd to see his thin, almost delicate-seeming frame holding Oberon's long, powerful body with apparent ease. Robin met her gaze. "Thank you for everything."

"You're welcome," she said. "He's welcome."

She watched him gently carry his king away.

When she was alone, she wiped tears from her cheeks. Then she climbed onto the bloody agate slab, curled up on her side, and fell asleep.

"GODS, I'M STARVING," Oberon heard himself say before he was fully awake.

"I have food and drink for you," someone nearby assured him.

He forced heavy eyelids open. He was in bed and stripped to the skin. Clean linens and richly embroidered bedding covered him, and his head and shoulders rested on a mountain of soft pillows.

It wasn't his room.

Oh yes, he had demolished his room when he had chased after an intruder bird. This was the room that had originally been intended for his queen, whenever he might find and marry her, which had never happened.

The nearby someone was Robin. The puck bent over him, his face wreathed with a bright smile. His hand hovered near Oberon's head, as if he would stroke the hair back from his forehead, but he didn't follow through with the gesture.

Robin said, "The surgery was a success, sire. The

doctor removed the needle, and she expressly forbade you to move until she could examine you again. Are you in pain?"

Was he in pain? He didn't know. Then he took a deep breath and winced. "Yes."

Magic tingled along his nerve endings, and the pain smoothed away.

"Better?"

"Yes—thank you." Robin's joy was so intense Oberon could hardly look at it. He could scarcely take in the enormity of waking when he had been more than half-convinced he wouldn't. It didn't feel real. He needed to see the confirmation in Kathryn's expression. "Where is she, dammit?"

"She said she was used up," Robin told him. "No doubt she went to bed."

The damned assassination spell that had dictated the course of his life for so many years was gone. It wasn't right that she wasn't here to tell him herself. She should be here to celebrate with him. To tell him how he was supposed to feel now.

"Well, go wake her up," he ordered. "How long was I out?"

"She didn't complete the operation until late last night." Robin went to the nearest dresser to collect a full, covered tray that he placed on the bed near to hand. "It's past dawn now."

"I want her here," he repeated.

"I'll fetch her right away," Robin promised.

As he turned to go, Oberon said, "Robin."

"Yes?"

The puck still wore a wide grin, and Oberon smiled to see it. "Thank you for everything."

"You provided a home for so many of us who'd never had one before, not until you said, 'It doesn't matter who or what race you are or if you are a mixture of many races. Come and pledge your loyalty to me. I will build a home for us and dedicate my life to protecting it.'" Ducking his head, Robin touched his arm quickly. "That happened many centuries ago, but I remember those words as if you had spoken them yesterday. It has always been my pleasure to serve you."

As the puck left, Oberon lifted the cover off the plate of food to discover savory rabbit stew cooked with vegetables and pan-fried bread. Suddenly ravenous to the point of pain, he inhaled everything.

When he was finished, he closed his eyes and only opened them again when Robin walked in, carrying Kathryn, who lay lax in his arms.

Ignoring the warning twinges in his chest, he surged to a sitting position and barked, "What's wrong with her?"

"I found her in the crystal cave," Robin said softly. Without waiting for orders, he deposited her on one side of the bed alongside Oberon. "She had curled up on the agate stone. She appears to be uninjured, but she's sleeping so soundly I can't wake her."

Carefully rolling onto his side, Oberon touched two

fingers to the hollow underneath her slender jaw. When he felt her pulse beating strongly against his fingertips, he relaxed. Laying one hand on her slim chest, he scanned her.

Normally her magical Power was both subtle and bright, a steady flame held in control by a sure hand. Now he could barely feel a flicker of it.

He frowned. "She's not just exhausted. She's completely depleted."

Robin cocked his head. "It appears that, like you, the only thing that will help her now is rest."

Oberon's frown deepened. She was still dressed in the clothes she wore the day before, and she was covered in dried blood. It looked lurid against her pale skin. "We can at least make her more comfortable. Bring warm water and a washcloth."

"Yes, sire." Robin returned shortly, carrying what Oberon had requested.

Together they worked to wash Kathryn's face and hands, and to strip off her outer layers of clothing so at least she was no longer covered in Oberon's blood. They left her long-sleeved silk undershirt and underwear alone.

By the time they had finished, Oberon's hands were shaking, and he felt weak as a kitten.

Robin asked, "Shall I take her to her room?"

Oberon frowned. He didn't want her that far away in case there really was something wrong with her.

"No," he said. "She can stay here with me, on the bedcovers. Just bring more bedding to keep her warm, and then you may leave us alone. I can't keep my head upright any longer."

Robin covered Kathryn's sleeping form with blankets. "Your long fight is over," he whispered to Oberon. "Rest well."

He didn't have any choice. He set one hand on Kathryn's forearm, and when he let his body relax, darkness surged up to swallow him whole.

Chapter Twelve

WHEN AWARENESS RETURNED, it did so on quiet cat feet. A sense of well-being came first, followed by something strange and warm. He came awake trying to puzzle it out.

Comfort.

It was comfort, something he had lost so long ago he had stopped looking for it. He had, in fact, stopped wanting it. Now it enveloped him in the form of a slender woman curled against his side. Her head rested on his shoulder, and he held her in his arms.

All he had to do was turn his head slightly and he could bury his face in her tousled hair and inhale her scent. The sensation was indescribable.

In the past, he would never sleep with any of his lovers. The act of sex was one thing, but sleeping with another person created an entirely different level of intimacy.

It created this exact situation, where his skin had already grown to know her skin, his hands acquainted with the elegant realm of her body. His body knew her scent, and his Wyr form, the lion, began to identify being with her as *home*.

What would it be like to roll her onto her back and delve into her mouth with a deep kiss? Plunging into her would be like diving into a deep lake. He wanted to wake her as she had awakened him and steal those first unguarded moments when she would respond to him, before she began to remember why she should not.

Recalling their first kiss caused heat to flash over his skin. It sizzled like lightning, and his cock swelled in response. As he lay there in increasing agony, he wondered how in all the hells she could sleep through something so cataclysmic.

But clearly it was only cataclysmic for him.

Finally he couldn't take the exquisite torture any longer. After he had checked her again to make sure she was sleeping peacefully, he eased away and stalked to his own rooms to wash and dress. Aside from a heavy, aching dullness that radiated through most of his chest, he felt tired but otherwise fine.

In the King's apartment, he found that Robin had made himself busy. The debris from the ruined furniture and broken witchlights had been removed. New witchlight globes now adorned the walls, and other furniture had been moved in. The bed was a little smaller than his own had been, but otherwise one would never know that he and Kathryn had demolished the room completely just a few days ago.

Then, of course, he had been utterly enraged, but now, as he thought of the anger sparking in the falcon's eyes and the way she had deliberately scratched him on the nose, he had to chuckle. She had quite a temper.

He strode down to the kitchens. He didn't see the puck anywhere, but he did locate more of the pan-fried bread and rabbit stew. Both biscuits and stew were cold, but he wasn't in the mood to be picky. After separating out a generous portion for Kathryn and setting it aside, he ate all of what remained.

As soon as she gave him the all-clear to hunt, he would do his part to provide fresh meat for their meals. The lion was looking forward to it, but the man knew he wasn't ready.

Then, propelled by the need to feel fresh air against his face, he strode outside.

Along with the surrounding estates of those most senior in his government, the palace sat on higher ground from the rest of the city. Standing on the wide front steps, he looked out over his destroyed municipality.

From where he stood, the view was more apocalyptic than when he had walked down the hill before, mostly because he could see farther. The damage from nearly fifteen years of magic-fueled storms struck him like a sword to the gut.

This was his ruined kingdom. It had been ruined because he had been too selfish to let go, and his people had loved him too much to rebel against him. Isabeau might have damaged him, but *he* had done *this*.

How many lives had he disrupted? How many had

he killed? Like a feral Wyr, he should have been put down, and Annwyn should have assumed the throne. If he had transferred power responsibly all those years ago *like he should have*, he would be looking out at a thriving populace, not a wasteland.

Feeling something other than rage or lust was shocking after so long. Grief and guilt hit him like twin tidal waves and bowled him over. He could never give back to his people what he had taken from them. He didn't even know how to begin trying.

Slender arms came around him. A strong, slim body braced against his hip and side to bear his weight. "What's wrong?" Kathryn asked sharply. "Where are you hurt?"

"Everywhere," he whispered as he went down on one knee. "I hurt everywhere."

He had fought so hard to be free of Morgan's icy trap, he hadn't given proper thought to what might be waiting for him on the other side with his freedom. He had forgotten what a burden emotions could be.

She held his head against her torso. "I told Robin not to let you exert yourself until I could examine you again." She sounded angry and worried. "What did you do?"

"I saw my country on its knees and realized it was my fault." Putting his arms around her waist, he turned his face into her silken shirt.

She held still and stroked his hair. After a few moments, she told him in a calm voice, "You're not responsible for any decisions you made while under the influence of that spell. Things look bad from up here, but there's nothing wrong with this city that can't be rebuilt, and you have people who are ready and willing to do that. Life never leaves us unscathed, Oberon. You need to count your blessings, not your losses."

Count your blessings. Yes, that was a good way to begin. Breathing deeply, he tightened his hold on her, then he straightened to his full height.

She had washed her face and slipped on a pair of pants, but her tousled hair was pulled back hastily, and a web of fine lines creased one fine-boned cheek where she had buried her face in her pillow.

In his pillow.

Smiling, he touched her creased cheek. "You slept hard."

"And apparently in your bed," she replied, her tone acerbic.

"You wouldn't wake up. I was worried about you, so I kept you close." He raised one eyebrow. "Do you have a problem with that?"

She raised an eyebrow in return, mirroring his expression almost exactly. "If I did, it's a little too late now, isn't it?"

"Indeed, it is." A demon of mischief slipped inside his skin. He let his hand drift to her narrow chin and tilted her face up to his. Bending his head so that his lips almost... almost... touched hers, he whispered, "I had such fantasies when I woke up. I would kiss you awake, like you had kissed me. And for a moment, before you remembered how much you dislike me, you would kiss me back. Your arms would wind around my neck, and you would open to me. That first time you let out a sexy, surprised little moan when I covered your body with mine. Do you remember?"

"Dear heavens, no," she murmured faintly. "Did I?"

"You're so intelligent, assured, and strong-minded." He let his lips brush hers lightly, not so much as to frighten her away, but enough to remind her of what they had shared. "The more I think of that noise you made, the more aroused it makes me. It was so uncontrolled, Kathryn. So honest. What I wouldn't give to make you sound like that again."

She had put a hand on his wrist. At first he thought she meant to push him away, but instead she gripped him tight, as if she had forgotten how to let go. "You need to stop." Her lips shaped the words, but they were soundless. "This is inappropriate."

He let his lips part and touched ever so gently at the opening of her mouth with his tongue. "The surgery is over—which means you are no longer my doctor."

She was melting against him. *He was sure of it.* The heat they generated together was blinding.

But when he spoke his last ill-advised words, she stiffened and jerked away. "Not true, King," she said. She sounded so tantalizingly breathless. "I haven't conducted your post-op exam yet."

"Really?" He laughed, half-angry and half-amused. "Then by all means, Doctor… let's go conduct your post-op exam so you can stop holding on to this pretense of an ethical line that lies between us."

"It's not a pretense." She stared up at him with a gaze that widened. Quickly she slapped both hands to his cheeks, angling his head down and tugging at the same time. "Come here—closer!"

"What?" Mystified by her behavior, he complied.

After studying him closely, a smile broke over her face. "Your eyes are changing. They're no longer black and white."

"What do they look like?" He touched his own cheekbone. His eyes didn't feel any different. "Anything like the dark brown they were before?"

"I never saw what they were like before, but they're not exactly dark brown. They're more gold and black."

He frowned. "I'm not sure I like my body changing without my awareness or consent."

"Don't be ridiculous," she replied robustly. "You should be relieved. Your body already changed without your consent when you were carrying Morgan's assassination spell. Now it's healing from that. I'm inclined to look at any difference as a good one." She grabbed his hand. "Come on. Where's the nearest mirror?"

He liked it when she touched him voluntarily. He liked it very much. Curling his fingers around hers, he replied, "Come with me."

Willingly, she fell into step beside him as he led the way to a spacious dance hall. The frescoed ceiling needed repair, he noticed as he eyed it with a critical gaze, but Kathryn let out a deep sigh of pleasure as she looked around.

Tall mirrors lined the walls, interspersed with windows of the same height, so that the immediate impression when one stepped into the hall was one of openness and light.

But he wasn't interested in aesthetics right now. Releasing her hand, he strode to look at his reflection in the nearest mirror.

His eyes... He frowned. They were definitely different than they had been before. The cracks in the irises were still present. They seemed as if the damned sorcerer's magic had cracked him open from within.

But Kathryn had been right too—instead of the white between the jagged black lines, some color had bled back. It was a lighter brown than it had been before, but even though it was different, it was far better than the alienating white.

He touched the mirror with the tips of his fingers. Somehow, seeing the physical change brought home the fact that the surgery had really worked.

He had won his freedom, and Morgan's spell was finally eradicated forever. Whoever he managed to be from this point on—and whatever choices he would make, mistakes or otherwise—would all be on him.

✧   ✧   ✧

KATHRYN HAD WOKEN up alone in the unfamiliar bed,

but even so she had known immediately that she had slept with Oberon. His scent was all over the sheets and on the pillow where she rubbed her face. On her body.

He had held her in her sleep. She didn't remember it, but the evidence told her it must be true—and she was sorry she didn't remember it. Rattled by the realization, she splashed her face, dressed, and went downstairs.

As she ran lightly down the stairs, she was very aware that she carried his scent along with her. She should have taken more time to wash properly. Would he notice? He was Wyr. How could he not notice?

But when she found him bent over on the palace steps and in such evident anguish, her preoccupation with the intimacy they had shared fled, and she leaped to see how she could help.

Now in the beautiful dance hall, she drew close to his elbow as he stared at his reflection. His hard face was impassive. There was no way to gauge what he was thinking.

His reflection regarded her. "It's not the same as before."

"It's just pigmentation," she said reassuringly. "At least I think it is. I'll know better when I scan you properly. Where do you want to do the examination— your office?"

"Go to the kitchen and eat something first," he ordered. "Whatever changes I might be undergoing, they aren't creating a medical crisis. You need to get your own needs met, Kathryn. You were very depleted last night."

"I know." She frowned. It wasn't like her to have to be told by someone else to look after her own needs. Years of working as a doctor had taught her that already, and she had started out on this journey with all her barriers fully intact. What was happening to her? "You're right. I need to eat."

He gave her a short nod. "I'll be in my office when you're ready."

Then he turned and walked away, and she was left staring after him in bewilderment. Where was the heated, sensual man who had whispered so tantalizingly against her hypersensitive lips just a few minutes ago? And why did she care so much that he had vanished?

It made no sense. After all, she was the one who had pushed him away. She had awakened with too many uncertainties and questions this morning.

Focus, Shaw! she admonished herself severely. As soon as you finish your job, you're going home… and you're really close to finishing your job.

The admonishment seemed to echo in the empty hall. Shaking her head at her own unruly thoughts and emotions, she went in search of breakfast. What she wouldn't give for a hot cup of coffee, but coffee was apparently one of those Earth commodities that Lyonesse didn't have. She had to content herself with a hot cup of herbal tea, the leftover stew, and the pan bread.

Robin was nowhere to be found. He must have had an entire, rich life here, she thought, with a home that probably now lay in ruins, and he would have to contend with his own memories of a happier time from long ago. She wished him well, but he wasn't her patient, so when she had finished she went to Oberon's office.

She found him feeding his letter to Annwyn along with the advance directive to the flames of a newly started fire. With a flicker of expression, he acknowledged her presence and walked over to a nearby armchair. "I assume your examination will be magical?"

"Yes," she said, walking closer. "I wish you had stayed in bed for another day or two for a proper rest."

There—there was that heated, sensual man from before. He wasn't gone at all. He had merely retreated momentarily.

"We can always go back to bed, if you like," he drawled. "You're still looking tired yourself."

For some reason her heart began to pound. She told it that it was an idiot.

"We're not talking about me." She kept her voice steady as she walked toward him. "We're talking about *you*, the man who had major surgery yesterday and lost a lot of blood. I just had a long day at work. There's nothing wrong with me that good food and a lighter schedule for a few days won't fix."

He let his eyelids fall and watched her approach with a hooded gaze. "If that is the case, you must be looking forward to a hot bath and perhaps a bottle of wine."

Oh, wine. Gods, yes.

Something must have shown in her expression

because his smile widened, and she could tell he knew he had scored a hit. "I could wash your back," he said gently. "I have rare wines in my cellars that are over a thousand years old. We should open one of those bottles to celebrate."

The atmosphere around him was electric. Why hadn't she given even a thought to who he would be after the surgery and how he would behave? This was not the abrasive, off-putting asshole she had been wrestling with over the past few days.

This man—she didn't know who this man was. She couldn't predict what he would do, and she didn't dislike him, which made him far more dangerous than he had been before.

Warily, she hooked a foot around one leg of the ottoman and dragged it close to his chair. "Let's just pay attention to the task at hand, shall we?"

"As you wish, Doctor."

He sat back in his chair, the very picture of indolent relaxation, but the air around him felt more charged than ever, as if the watchful lion merely waited for its moment to pounce.

Before yesterday, that feeling would have made her look for the closest exit. Now, honesty forced her to acknowledge it made him sexier than ever. There was nothing sexier than a man who knew how to be patient.

Leaning close, she held a hand over his chest for a moment before she allowed herself to touch him. "Light tingle of magic," she reminded him.

Nodding, he rested one hand over hers. No other patient had ever done such a thing, and it almost knocked her out of her concentration. Frowning, she pulled herself together and sent her awareness into his chest.

She took her time and inspected every angle of every place she had made an incision. He was healing very well, and he could, in fact, hold a few more healing spells now that he'd had a little time to recover.

He was also in more pain than his demeanor had showed. She poured healing energy into him along with a spell for pain relief. When he sighed and his powerful body relaxed, she could tell that the pain relief had taken effect.

"I did a damn good job," she said, pleased.

"How did you finally remove it?"

"Morgan's needle wasn't just one spell. It was a combination of spells, and I had to use a combination to trick it into thinking your heart was someplace else. As soon as it moved away from your real heart, I grabbed it." She told him the four different spells she had used to leverage the needle out and grinned as he laughed. "Hold still, let me check your eyes."

He allowed her to place a hand over his eyes and waited patiently while she scanned there too. The last thing she scanned was his Power. Now that he had called his magic back to himself, he carried it like a thundercloud wrapped around his body, but there was an essential shift in that too. It felt like the other Wyr males she knew, dangerous but at rest, and no longer malevolent.

Finally she sat back and smiled. "You're textbook perfect," she told him. "You're exactly where you should be a day after major surgery. Now listen to me, because I am deadly serious. If you don't want to suffer a setback, you'll make sure you do no heavy lifting for a week and no extraordinary exertion for two weeks."

"Define extraordinary exertion," he murmured as he captured her hand.

She couldn't help but laugh even as she snatched her hand away. "I mean, no matter how you might be tempted *by anybody,* don't resume sparring or physical training of any kind. I know you're eager to go after Isabeau, and I get it—I really do—but the bones in your chest need to finish knitting together. If you don't want them to be shattered by one of your knights bashing you with a sword, you will follow my instructions to the letter."

"What about after two weeks?" He had lost his playfulness when she'd mentioned Isabeau.

"Then you can resume training, as long as you listen to your body. Normally you're very healthy and extraordinarily gifted with strength and stamina, so when you get achy—and you will—your first instinct will be to push through it. Don't do that for the first four weeks. You've got to ignore that voice in your head. After four weeks, you should be fine without any further repercussions. You can push and train and fight all you need to. Four weeks is your magic number. Okay?"

"Very well, I understand."

"As far as mentally and emotionally, only time will tell you who you are now." She gave him a crooked smile. "So you've got to give it time. Have faith that you'll figure it out. And don't beat yourself up for what happened when you were under the influence of Morgan's spell. Those actions weren't an authentic representation of who you really are."

"That's harder to do than one might think," he muttered, looking away.

"I know." Resting her elbows on her knees, she laced her hands together and looked down at them. "I think you should tell yourself it's going to take a good year before you fully shake off the effects of such a long magical battle." She looked up at him. "I just made that up, but as a mental exercise it would do you good to remember there's no such thing as an instant full recovery—not even when you have the self-healing capabilities of the full Wyr."

His gaze narrowed. "What symptoms should I look for?"

"Honestly, I have no idea." She shrugged. "Maybe six months from now you're going to be frustrated because you need an hour's nap in the afternoons when you never needed to nap before—I just made that up too, but I've seen similar things happen to other patients who've been through something catastrophic like this. Maybe you'll end up feeling like you're *too* emotional for a while. That might be a reasonable effect after having been numbed for so long. Whatever it is, be patient with yourself. It should all even out over time."

"I see." He studied her. "Is there anything else?"

"Aside from my bill for the surgery, no." She almost smiled. He had no idea how much inflation had changed economies over the years, and she could guarantee the amount she was going to charge him would shock him to his boots. Then her impulse to smile died. "I've done everything I can for you, and now I need to go home."

While he appeared to make no physical move, the atmosphere around them tightened. She took a deep breath. Perhaps she should be looking for the nearest exit now.

In a soft, biting voice, he asked, "Is it your habit to abandon your patients right after major surgery?"

She pursed her lips. "Actually, yes. After an initial checkup after surgery, long-term follow-up or care is usually transferred over to another physician."

"At present, there *is* no other physician here."

That point was indisputable, but… Agitated, she thrust to her feet and paced. "Of course, but as long as you adhere to my instructions, you don't really need the follow-up care at this point."

"How do you know that for certain?"

"How do you think I know?" she retorted. "I'm the doctor. You weren't in a messy accident that mangled your limbs—you were in a carefully controlled operating room where every incision I made was to maximize your healing afterward."

As she came to the end of the room and swung around to pace back the other way, she discovered he had risen to prowl after her. He was so light on his feet she hadn't heard a thing. Realizing it sent a shiver down her spine.

"I don't accept your assessment," he told her. "I think you're trying to run away."

"Don't be ridiculous," she snapped, backing away. "Run away from what?"

"Not from what—from whom," he replied as he came after her. "From me, and you, and that second kiss we have not yet shared."

"Oberon…" She backed up against the edge of the desk. "Nothing is going to happen between us. Don't you understand? It's the definition of impossible."

"I don't buy that," he growled.

"It is! Even if I were to stay and provide follow-along care until one of your own physicians arrives, you would be my patient—and that's a line I told you I won't cross."

A bladelike smile creased his hard features. "There it is again—that pretense of an ethical line you're trying to hide behind. But I can see you just fine."

What did he mean by that?

She found that her breathing had quickened and tried to force it to slow the hell down. The effort made her words unsteady. "As soon as you're not my patient, I need to go. For every day I spend here, approximately thirteen days pass on Earth. Today is my ninth day in Lyonesse. That means a hundred and seventeen days have passed on the other side of the passageway. Even as we stand here and argue, my life back in New York is slipping away."

"You knew that when you left, and you accepted it." He advanced until his thighs brushed hers, and his expression turned ruthless. "You made arrangements. That's no excuse for running now."

He was too close, too hard, too big. His scent invaded her senses, and his Power wrapped around her like a thundercloud. Everything about him was taut with aggression.

She loved flying in thunderstorms.

She knew without trying that if she slapped a hand on his chest to keep him at bay, he wouldn't force her. And she considered it. She really considered it.

Gripping the edge of the desk with both hands, she bared her teeth. "I don't run away from anything."

He laughed and stroked a light finger down the side of her neck. The sensation ricocheted through her body. "Then you'll stay."

Pushing his hand away, she lifted her chin. "I'll stay, but just until another physician arrives. Annwyn and her troops should be here in five or six days if Robin doesn't decide to go help them. Two weeks was what I had planned for my trip to Lyonesse, and two weeks is what you're going to get. *That's all.*"

He whispered, "We'll see, Kathryn."

Chapter Thirteen

ROBIN'S LIGHT, QUICK footsteps sounded just outside the office, breaking the nearly intolerable tension that had built up between them.

Unhurriedly, Oberon turned away. As the sensation of his thighs pressing against hers lifted, she felt the stiffness in her spine dissolve until she felt as shaky as a newborn colt. *Good gods, what had she just agreed to?*

When the puck appeared in the open doorway, he looked from one to the other inquiringly. "Is everything well?"

"I just conducted Oberon's post-op exam, and everything is great," Kathryn told him, straightening her shirt unnecessarily. Oberon had barely touched her, but she still felt disheveled everywhere. "How are you?"

"Well indeed. I have just returned from hunting, and a bounty awaits us in the kitchens. The sun is shining, and the ice is melting." Robin laughed, a fey, wild sound. "Everything is coming into alignment as it should, and that is all because of you, beautiful mistress."

Oberon's expression darkened. "It's going to take a long time before everything is as it should be, Robin. We have a lot of rebuilding to do. In the meantime, I need to begin the process by assessing the weather conditions so I can make any adjustments if needed. The last thing we need are damaging storms because the temperatures are warming too quickly." He glanced at Kathryn. "Unless that falls into the category of extraordinary exertion."

He'd made the shift away from their intimate quarrel with apparent ease, but mentally she struggled to regroup. "No, not at all. My warning was for physical exertion. Just don't overextend yourself by doing too much magic. Your mind, body, and Power are all one unified biological system, and every part of you needs recovery time."

"Understood," he said. The expression in his gaze stroked her like a caress. "We'll finish this conversation later."

"As far as I'm concerned," she muttered, "we finished it just now."

His soft laugh was insidious as it wound around her senses. "You can tell yourself that if you need to."

She watched him stride out purposefully. Then she turned her attention to Robin. "I need to go downstairs to hunt for that needle. Will you come with me?"

Revulsion twisted his narrow features. "Must I?"

"Well… no," she admitted. "But it would give me a chance to talk to you."

"We are talking right now," he pointed out, spreading out long, thin hands.

"So we are." Smiling, she chose not to push against

his claustrophobia and aversion to the crystal cave. More soberly, she said, "Robin, I'm going to ask you to go back for Annwyn and her troops."

The puck's cheerful demeanor vanished. He gave her a glare that reminded her just how many teeth he had. "Why should I do such a thing? They make noise and insinuations. It is peaceful here without them. I am happy here with you and my liege."

She sighed. "I understand there are unresolved issues between you and the rest of the Dark Court, but despite how you feel about the others, Oberon needs them. While the surgery was successful, his recovery has only just begun. He needs his people here."

Robin's scowl deepened. "He has me. And he has you to guide him to the future."

She set her jaw as she considered his rebellious demeanor. "Keep in mind what's really at stake. Every delay you cause here in Lyonesse gives Isabeau more time for *her* recovery and to make her next moves."

He grew so still she knew she had hit her target. At last, he muttered, "I will consider your counsel seriously."

"Do that." Judging she had pushed him hard enough, she touched his shoulder as she passed by. "Thank you for hunting for us. After I search the cave and clean up, I'll take a turn at cooking."

He inclined his head in acknowledgment but watched her go without replying. His feral gaze had gone opaque. She didn't know him well enough to be able to guess at his thoughts, but he appeared a lot less friendly than he had when he'd first arrived.

Just as she couldn't fix him, she also couldn't make him do anything he didn't want to do. She only hoped her argument about Isabeau was persuasive enough to get him to act, because everything she had said was true. Oberon *did* need to reunite with his people.

And also, when another physician arrived, it would let her off the hook. And she really didn't know how she felt about that.

Thrusting the puzzle of her mixed emotions aside for the time being, she headed down into the cave, but no matter how long or carefully she searched, she never did find Morgan's needle.

✧　✧　✧

THE PALACE COULD hold hundreds of people comfortably, but after Oberon's consultation with Kathryn, the indoors felt stifling and closed in.

When he strode outside, the bright, cloudless sky was so immaculate it highlighted the destruction in the city below. He strangled the impulse to shapeshift into the lion and go hunting. They didn't need the food, and despite his restlessness, he was determined to follow Kathryn's instructions to the letter.

He had to recover fully, and as quickly as possible. Too many people had sacrificed so that he could. They had given everything in the hope that this might happen. It didn't matter how long it had taken or what doubts they might have had along their paths. They were still counting on him, or they would have killed him by now.

And he owed them for it.

Where were his troops? Where were the city civilians? Had they evacuated to the farmlands, or out of Lyonesse altogether? Annwyn and the others would have answers to his questions. If it weren't for Kathryn's admonishments to avoid expending himself physically, he would even now be heading out to meet them.

What he could do instead was help everyone in other ways. Going around to the back of the palace, he walked the neglected paths of the gardens until he found a section of ground that captured a patch of sunlight and was dry enough for his purposes.

Settling cross-legged on the ground, he closed his eyes and went into a meditation that allowed him to astral journey from his body.

Joining the warm air current flowing high overhead, he spun and eddied with the flow and traveled hundreds of miles inland, casting weather spells as needed.

Certain areas had been dry for far too long. Other locales had been deluged with mountains of snow and were now flooding with the onslaught of warmer weather.

He couldn't do anything about the floods. Many weather conditions couldn't be changed quickly, and those floods had already been set in motion over the years with abnormally heavy snows. But he could divert other disasters that were in the making, and by the time he had finished working, he knew the next weeks would bring a much calmer spring.

And that would lead to a decent growing season and what he suspected would be a much-needed good harvest.

When his awareness returned to his body, the day had advanced significantly, and he was shaking as he pushed to his feet. There had been a time when he could do weather working for days. Now he could barely handle working a few light spells for a few damn hours.

Stifling a surge of frustration at his own weakness, he went inside. Kathryn had been right. He had to give himself time. His stamina would soon return. For now, though, his belly signaled there was a rapidly approaching crisis and he needed to put food in it immediately.

As he stepped into the cavernous kitchen, he found it warm and full of light and good food smells. His empty stomach growled.

Kathryn stood at the table nearest the main oven. She had changed into a fresh outfit, a deep forest green dress with clean, simple lines that suited her perfectly. She had pinned her hair into a twist at the top of her head, and a few escaping tendrils emphasized the graceful line of her neck.

He had once thought her beauty was understated, but now it shone like a luminous beacon against the mundane backdrop of her surroundings. The sleek, racy lines of her body and classic femininity were deeply appealing.

On the table, golden brown pastries had been piled high on platters. Grabbing one, he took a huge bite. It was filled with seasoned chunks of venison and rich gravy that complemented the pastry perfectly, and it was indescribably delicious.

"You can cook," he said around his mouthful.

She burst out laughing. "You sound so outraged."

Rapidly he devoured the rest of his pie and picked up another one. "Not outraged. Surprised. You're a master-class physician and magician. Is there anything you can't do?"

She appeared to give that serious attention. "I can't ski," she told him. "I've tried, but I just don't have the patience. I would much rather shapeshift and fly. My sword work is only passable. When I was younger, I learned what I needed to keep my father from fussing at me. Can't paint worth a damn. Not interested in driving… one of those horseless carriages I told you about. Again, I'd rather shapeshift and fly. I don't sew or quilt. My singing is enthusiastic but lamentable. So you see, there's a lot of things I can't do. You just happened to stumble upon the two things I do well—surgery and cooking." She watched him devour a second pastry and then a third, and her expression turned wise. "You pushed yourself too hard today, didn't you?"

He glowered at her and reached for a pastry from a different platter. That one was rabbit, and it was heavenly. After swallowing, he muttered, "I didn't mean to. I was weather working, which leaves me somewhat detached from my body."

"Do you need me to check you over?"

He considered. "No, I don't think so. The food is helping. Where is Robin?"

"I don't know." Her gaze narrowed. "I've been wondering that myself. I have a few questions I want to ask him." She focused on him suddenly. "Have you by any chance gone down into the cave?"

"Not since the surgery. Why?"

She rubbed her chin with the back of one flour-coated hand. It left a powdery trail of white on her creamy skin. "I went down earlier to look for Morgan's needle. When I had pulled it out, it released some sort of magical detonation that numbed my hands, so at the time I just flung it over my shoulder." Her troubled gaze met his. "Oberon, I've been over every inch of that cave today, and I can't find it anywhere. I found my tweezers just fine, but not the needle. Would Robin take something like that?"

"I'll be sure to ask when I next see him," he replied, frowning. "I don't like it disappearing. It could still be dangerous. What does it look like?"

"It's just a thin sliver of magic-sensitive silver. I agree with you—I don't like it disappearing either, and I didn't get a chance to assess it properly. At the time, you were my only concern."

He took one of her hands and turned it over. She let him gently manipulate the fingers and rotate her wrist.

He couldn't sense any lingering magic on her, only her own light, steady Power. His frown deepened. "You should have said something earlier. You could have been seriously hurt."

"But I wasn't," she told him. "All is well. When I woke up this morning, all sensation had returned. Do you want another pie?" She pointed to the third platter. "I made those with dried figs and cherries, so they're sweet, not savory."

"They sound fabulous." He smiled at her. He had gone for so long without feeling. Now he felt awash in a symphony of emotion.

The rage was still present. It might not die down for decades. Certainly not before Isabeau was dead.

But most prominent among all of it now was desire, and that was a much lighter thing than the cold animal lust he had experienced when he had been trapped by Morgan's spell—warmer, more complex. It was both deeply familiar and totally new, because now it was wholly focused on the woman in front of him.

Another tendril of silken hair had escaped the knot high on her head. Using it as an excuse to touch her, he tucked it behind her ear. She gave him a wary glance but didn't pull away.

"I promised you a thousand-year-old bottle of wine," he said.

"Now that you mention it, yes, you did." She smiled. "If I'd known you had that kind of treasure tucked away in your cellars, I might not have been satisfied with the first bottle of brandy I came across."

He grinned. "I'll be back shortly."

Other emotions welled up as he made his way to the lower levels of the palace. On impulse, he took a detour to look in the crystal cave where his life had wholly depended on a single woman and her medical skills and ingenuity.

When he ignited the witchlights in the cave, his eyebrows rose slowly as he stared at the scene. It looked like there had been a massacre. There was blood everywhere. It had dripped down the sides of the agate slab, and there were pools of dried blood on the floor with footprints walking through it. The bloody footprints tracked all over the cave. Surgical tools lay where she had dropped them, either on the table or on the floor.

If he were to guess, he would say that normally she was a tidy person and her surroundings would be a reflection of the ordered discipline in her mind. This mess told another story. It provided an echo of the kind of intense difficulty she had endured throughout the long day. Gratitude washed over him. He shouldn't have lived so long, let alone survived this kind of surgery.

Opening his senses wide, he scanned for the slightest residue of Morgan's magic but found nothing. The crystal cave had magically returned to its neutral state. If it weren't for the physical evidence, he would never know that his life had been on the line.

He was quite sure Kathryn would have already

searched for the needle with her own highly developed magical sense, but as he had grown well acquainted with Morgan's magic over the years, he'd hoped he might detect something she had missed.

Was it possible the needle had expelled all its magic, and there wasn't any residue left to sense? If anyone had that kind of skill with their magic, it would be Morgan.

But Oberon tended to think that the spell had been too powerful and complex to dissipate completely upon detonation. However slight, there should have been a lingering trace of Power...

If the needle was indeed still lying somewhere in the cave.

So it was gone, and there were only three scents in the cave—his, Kathryn's, and Robin's. No random thief had crept into the palace undetected.

While he was sure Kathryn would be adept at dancing around truthsense if she felt the need, she hadn't lied once since he had met her. Besides, she was the one who had brought up the needle's absence, so there was only one inescapable conclusion to be drawn.

Why had Robin taken the needle? For safekeeping, or for some agenda of his own?

Thoughtfully, he headed back up the stairs and over to the wine cellar, located in a separate area. There, more emotion welled up in the form of pleasure and nostalgia. He made his way back to the dusty room that held his rare, older wines.

After inspecting them, he was torn between choosing

one of Lyonesse's oldest vintages, because he thought Kathryn would enjoy the history of it, and a precious bottle of golden salveri wine from Ys.

Combining food and magic were an integral part in all the Other lands, for healing properties, for food storage, and for pleasure, but nobody mixed food and magic together quite like the kingdoms in the Other land of Ys. Their crops were unique and their skills unparalleled.

In the end, he decided against picking one bottle over the other and took both upstairs.

As soon as he stepped into the kitchen, he could tell Kathryn's mood had changed. Large pieces of roasted venison had joined the platters of pies on the center table. The cavernous space had warmed from her cooking, and she had propped open the back door to let in the fresh afternoon air.

She stood leaning against the door looking out, her expression closed and remote. He studied her profile as he approached. As he drew close, she gave him a preoccupied smile.

"What's wrong?" he asked as he set the wine on the table.

She shook her head without answering and turned to watch as he opened both bottles. "Two bottles? Very extravagant."

"I think waking up from a years-long stasis spell and surviving a high-risk surgery entitles me to a little extravagance." He held up one bottle with his left hand.

"This wine is made from the very first harvest here in Lyonesse after we had created our demesne. And this one…" He held up the second bottle with his right hand. "…this is a bottle of golden salveri wine, from Karre in Ys."

Her eyes widened. "I've heard of salveri wine, but I've never gotten the chance to taste it before."

"You are in for a treat. It's indescribable. The finest champagne I have ever drunk tasted like raw vinegar in comparison to salveri wine." He smiled. "After this, I will have only five bottles left."

"Isn't it illegal to export salveri from Karre?" She watched him locate two plain glass goblets, which he set on the table beside the bottles.

"It was when I put myself into stasis," he replied. "So I imagine it still is, but I'd acquired my dozen bottles before that law went into effect… That was a very, very long time ago."

Fascination had taken over her expression, but she made no move to leave her spot by the door. "What about the hallucinations?"

"As long as you don't drink several bottles at once, they are beautiful and harmless. In Karre, the visions are considered sacred, a gift from their Exalted—their ruler who is both a mystical leader and head of their nation. They drink salveri during several religious ceremonies and at their Festival of Rebirth every spring. They believe the visions that come during the festival are a foretelling of what will come into their lives over the next year."

"Is there any truth to that?" she asked curiously.

"Possibly. I've never attended their Festival of Rebirth, so I don't really know." Carefully he poured a portion of the luminous liquid into each goblet and picked up both glasses to join her at the door. Fragrance from the wine had bloomed when he poured it, and her expression changed as she caught the scent.

She breathed deeply. "That is heavenly… I can't decide if it's floral or fruity. I just know I've never smelled anything like it before."

"And you never will again. Salveri is unique. I've heard stories of thieves who've attempted to steal cuttings from the vineyards, but no one has ever managed to grow salveri vines away from Karre soil. Between their salveri and their magic-infused oils and spices, Karre is one of the wealthiest countries, either on Earth or in any Other land." With a smile, he offered her one of the goblets. When she accepted it, he touched the rim of his goblet to hers. "Thank you for my life, Kathryn."

"You are most welcome, Oberon." Closing her eyes, she held her goblet close to her nose and inhaled deeply again. "How impaired will we be?"

She was cautious about the unknown and considered everything before she took action. He told her, "You're full Wyr, so I don't think very impaired. It's not the same experience as drinking other alcohol. If we decide to finish this bottle and the bottle of Lyonesse wine in one sitting, we will feel exceedingly pleasant but nothing more. I give you my word, you will be quite safe from any ill effects."

"Okay." Giving him a grin, she took a careful sip, and her expression changed again, this time with sheer delight. "Dear gods."

Her wonder pleased him so very much.

"That's how I remember it," he said with satisfaction. Now that he'd had a chance to enjoy her reaction, he took his own first sip. Bright, exquisite flavor flowed over his tongue.

He held it in his mouth to experience the full complexity of notes. When he swallowed, warmth and light filled his midsection, and he felt embraced with a sense of incredible well-being.

Beside him, Kathryn made a quiet, inarticulate sound. Her expression had become transfixed, her gaze filled with awe. She whispered, "What am I looking at?"

"I don't know. It's different each time for everybody. The first time I drank salveri, I felt like I was surrounded by people I could barely see who loved me immensely." He smiled at the memory. "I knew right then I was going to take home as many bottles as I could transport. Karreans call the experience the 'song of souls.'"

"How wonderful." She sighed. "I'm not seeing people... I'm seeing something like translucent flames, like I'm totally immersed in this bright golden light. I can still see everything around me just fine, but it's all veiled with the shining light."

"Very nice."

"It is so lovely."

Then his own vision overtook him. He heard himself whisper, "Ah, damn."

"What is it?" Her attention sharpened.

"Nothing." He turned away to stare at the ruined vegetable gardens outside. "Everything is fine."

"But what happened?" She laid a hand on his arm. "What are you seeing?"

He had to work to get words out. "Orchards full of fruit, a clear jade sea, and fields of ripe wheat rippling in the wind. I'm seeing Lyonesse the way she used to be— the way she should be."

Her fingers tightened gently. "She will be that way again."

"If I have anything to say about it, she will. I just need to hunt down Isabeau to make sure she can't hurt us ever again."

Kathryn studied his expression. "I don't think I ever heard how the whole conflict with Isabeau started. What happened?"

He barked out a bitter laugh. "She's always been bigoted and xenophobic, and she used to hunt us for sport. It was one of the reasons we banded together to create Lyonesse, but the fact that an entire demesne of mixed-race people exists is an affront to her world view. According to her, we are freaks of nature, and we need to be eradicated. She hates those with Light Fae blood the most. We have become her obsession. She won't stop until we make her stop."

"Four weeks," she told him.

"What?" Jolted out of his preoccupation, he frowned at her.

"You can go to war in four weeks." She shrugged. "Technically, since your surgery was yesterday, you can go in three weeks and six days."

The Daoine Sidhe couldn't wait that long. The time slippage between Lyonesse and almost everywhere else was too great. Four more weeks would give Isabeau far too much time to plan and execute her next attack.

But he didn't tell Kathryn that. Instead, he pressed her fingers where they rested on his bicep. Then he went to retrieve the bottle and poured them more wine.

More to change the subject than for any other reason, he said, "I took longer to get the wine than I had expected. I took a detour down to the crystal cave."

She made a face. "It's a mess down there."

"Not important. I'll get someone to clean it up." He savored another swallow of the salveri. "I wanted to see if I could catch any hint of magical residue from Morgan's needle, but there was nothing. I think Robin took it."

Her gaze flashed to his, then away again. "I do too. I just don't understand why he would, yet not tell us about it." She set her goblet on the table, and her mood changed again. Wearing the same closed, remote expression from when he had returned with the wine, she told him, "I also think I know why he disappeared again."

Raising his eyebrows, he set aside his goblet too. Savoring the salveri wine seemed too fine a pastime for where this conversation appeared to be headed. "Very well, then—why?"

She swung back around and gave him a level look. "Because I asked him to bring Annwyn and the others here as fast as he could."

Chapter Fourteen

K ATHRYN HAD NO real idea how Oberon was going to respond to what she had said, so she braced herself for anything. Maybe her heart rate increased a bit, but she'd had quite a few years' experience in Dragos's court, and she knew how to hide her feelings when she needed to.

But all he did was give her one of his long, inscrutable looks. She was not the only one who knew how to hide things. He was far too skilled at hiding his own thoughts.

"What?" she said finally, rotating one hand to prompt him to get on with it. Whatever it was going to be.

"As you might imagine, the Lyonesse wine is much earthier than the salveri," he told her. Despite his size, he moved with the grace of a dancer as he wound around the table to retrieve two more goblets from a cupboard.

He would be shockingly fast in battle. She knew because she had seen it firsthand.

And his lack of reaction was confusing. As she watched him pour a rich, ruby red wine into the two fresh goblets, she asked, "That's all you're going to say?"

The Oberon before the surgery would have snapped and snarled. He would have accused her of trying to run away, or of interfering somehow, but she had no idea how to cope with this apparent... Indifference? Aplomb?

"What would you have me say?" he asked. "I must admit your own attitude puzzles me. You're acting almost as if you expect an argument, but I have no intention of engaging in any kind of behavior that prevents me from enjoying these truly spectacular vintages." Holding out one of the goblets of red wine, he gave her a smile. "Remember, Kathryn. We're celebrating."

"Of course we are." Warily, she took the glass. She couldn't shake the sense he was outmaneuvering her in some fashion. If only she could figure out what he was up to. "About Robin."

"Try the wine first," he suggested softly. "I remember when they brought the grapes in from the fields. We were tremendously excited. We were building villages and towns, and this place, as fast as we could. This wine, to me, has always tasted like hope."

He did it. He succeeded in pulling her away from talking about Robin. Smiling, she replied, "Then it must taste delicious."

"It does," he told her. "It's one of my very favorites. I'm glad to get the chance to share it with you."

How could one try to start an argument after that

gracious statement? "Thank you, you're very generous." As he watched, she took a sip.

"There are no visions with this one, I'm afraid." With a look of deep pleasure, he drank from his own glass. "This is a mundane wine, not a magical one."

"It's lovely!" she exclaimed. "So rich, but not sweet. And the color is gorgeous."

"Better than rubies," he said, returning her smile. "Thank you for talking to Robin about getting the others. I hope that's what he's done. They should be here."

"That's what I said too," she muttered.

But the sooner they arrived, the sooner she could leave. Should leave. Was she the only one bothered by that? Rattled, she buried her nose in her glass and drank more of the beautiful wine. This wine tasting was a rare experience, and she should concentrate on appreciating it as much as she could.

His expression sobered. "You alluded to Robin having a terrible time. I meant to ask about that. What happened to him?"

"I only know what I was told, and that wasn't much." Walking over to the table, she picked one of the sweet pastries and bit into it. She had eaten her fill of the meat earlier but found she was in the mood for dessert. "Isabeau captured him and apparently tortured him for some time. My friend Sophie—you'll meet her one day—is the one who rescued him. She told me she didn't think he'd had a chance to heal from what happened.

She loves him, but she warned his thinking and decisions might be off, even dangerous." She glanced at him uneasily. "I feel funny telling you this. I don't want to create problems for him. Like everyone else in Lyonesse, he deserves to be welcomed back home and given help when he needs it."

"You're not creating problems," he replied. "I needed to know this. I'll treat him with extra care when he shows up again."

"I think that's a good idea." Damn, she liked this post-op Oberon so much. He was charming to talk to, sophisticated, and strategic in his thinking. She finished her pastry and licked the sugar off her fingers.

She caught him watching her with a slight smile. He finished his glass of wine and set the goblet aside. "Now, let's talk about *why* you wanted to talk Robin into getting the others."

She froze. "I thought we were done talking about that."

"Noooo," he murmured on a long, low purr. "No, we're not done with that. I just didn't want to fight with you. But we are definitely going to discuss it."

"There's nothing to discuss," she exclaimed. "Have you had one of these sweet pastries yet? You haven't, have you? They turned out really well, and they pair wonderfully with this red wine. In fact, I think I'm going to have another one."

"Please do," he said as he maneuvered around the end of the table and came up behind her. "Watching you lick the sugar off your fingers was one of the most delightful things I've seen in years."

"That bar is mighty low—you haven't seen anything in years." She grabbed another pastry and crammed a huge, inelegant bite into her mouth. "Whatever it is you're doing," she said around her mouthful, "you can stop it right now."

"I have no intention of stopping." He ran light fingers along the neckline of her dress at the back, and a convulsive shiver rippled down her spine. "This dress looks beautiful on you, by the way. Deep green is definitely one of your colors."

"Thank you." She swallowed hard. Without craning her neck to look at him, she pointed behind herself in his general direction. "Patient." Then she pointed at herself. "Doctor."

He captured her hand, pulled her around to face him, then lifted her sugary fingers to his mouth. First, he sucked on her forefinger, massaging her skin with his tongue. She felt the caress all over her body.

He purred, "Delicious."

Just as he was about to take her second finger in his mouth, she yanked her hand away. "You stop that," she snapped. Or tried to snap.

Somehow it came out quite differently than she had intended, in a breathless sigh.

"Kathryn darling, I'm just getting started," he assured her. Taking her by the hips, he walked her backward until she bumped into the table.

He was literally purring. Unlike some Wyr cats she had known who had light, almost effeminate purrs, Oberon's purr was deep and rough. The sound vibrated all over her skin. Aw, damn it. It was both sexy and adorable.

"Not okay, King." Her half-eaten pastry slipped from nerveless fingers.

"Don't care, Doctor." Settling both hands at her waist, he looked at her deeply. His golden and black eyes caught the late-afternoon light. "Why did you try to persuade Robin to get the others?"

His torso had come flush against hers. Longer, broader, and more muscled than she, he dominated the space. All she had to do was push him away, but her hands seem to have acquired minds of their own. Starting at his thick, powerful wrists, they worked their way up his arms to grasp at his wide shoulders.

"Because you need them," she said.

"What a very proper doctorly response." He stroked the fine hairs at her temple back and nuzzled her.

"It's the truth," she gasped.

"I know," he replied. "I heard it in your voice. Is that the only reason?"

"Of course it is!" *Dammit, Shaw!* If she could hear the lie in her own voice, he could too.

Laughing quietly, he caressed the thin, delicate skin along her hairline with his sensual lips. "If Robin brought them back, you would be free to leave sooner than you had planned, wouldn't you? You were trying to wiggle out of your commitment for a fortnight."

"Most of the two weeks are gone anyway. What... what day is it again?" She couldn't seem to think properly, and her head felt too heavy to hold up. She drooped closer and closer to his chest.

"It's day nine," he reminded her, caressing the nape of her neck. "You have five more days unless Annwyn and the others arrive before then. And if they do, you can go home. If Robin really did go to get them, this might be our last evening alone." Angling his head, he put his lips against her ear to whisper, "You don't want to waste it, do you?"

Feeling his lips against the sensitive shell of her ear, his warm breath moving over her skin, sent a convulsive shiver through her.

Doctor. Patient.

She had hoped if she said it enough that it might help reinforce a barrier between them, but it didn't. She'd just gotten tired of saying it. She wasn't really his doctor anymore. No matter what he had argued earlier, he didn't need her for that. She had known that even as she had given in to his demand to stay.

She should have left the first time she could, but she hadn't, and now...

Now she was tired of feeling at war with herself, and he was right. She didn't want to waste what might be their last evening alone together. So she did what she really wanted to do—what she'd been wanting to do ever since he had woken up from surgery.

Lifting her head, she kissed him.

It was every bit as electric as she remembered from the first time. It was also just as wrong, and more foolish than anything she had ever done. He was recovering. He was the definition of a bad bet in every conceivable way, and yet she couldn't stop herself.

His big body went still. She had surprised him. But he didn't stay frozen for long. Coming to life just like he had the first time, he wound his arms around her, tilted her back, and kissed her with such intense need it stole the breath from her body.

All that easygoing attitude. Here, drink some cool, magical wine, it's so special, aren't we having a wonderful time? He had played her like a fiddle.

He was a master-class manipulator, right up there with the very best she had known and worked with over the past several decades, because the whole time he had been circling around her, easing up slowly, de-escalating her impulse to argue and coaxing her to relax, distracting her with pleasantries and snippets of wine history while he waited for his moment to make a move.

She would have laughed if she could have. Instead, her knees felt so unsteady she wound her arms around his neck and hung on.

And man, did this guy know how to kiss. Their first kiss had been strange, brief, and very nearly disastrous. This one had just gotten started, but already he ranked in the top five kissers she'd experienced in her two hundred years of life.

No, whoops, he just leaped into the top three. And then he did something extraordinary with his tongue and bypassed the other two completely....

Gods have mercy, she thought hazily. This is *the best kiss I've ever had.*

And she didn't want it to stop.

Then every thought and list she tried to hold on to disintegrated as he angled his head, cupped the back of hers with one big hand, and ravished her mouth more deeply. He thrust a knee between her legs so that his hard thigh came up against her sensitive, intimate flesh. As he fucked her mouth with his tongue, he pressed upward with his leg.

Arousal bolted through her entire body. He couldn't have ignited her more completely if he'd set a match to her. Arching against his long, tough body, she clamped his thigh between hers and kissed him back as wildly as he kissed her.

Never lifting away from her mouth, he palmed her breast. His hand felt big and hot through the material of the dress. His fingers were shaking.

They weren't shaking any more than hers were. There were too many layers of clothes between them. Her skin felt like it was on fire, and she needed to feel him closer against her.

She wasn't the only one. His body poured off heat, every heavy muscle tense. This was moving too fast. Tearing her mouth away from his, she gasped, "We have to stop."

"No," he growled. "We don't."

"You don't know what you're doing. You just had your surgery—"

"Stop trying to manage me," he growled. "I know exactly what I'm doing. I wanted you before when all my emotions were suppressed—and I want you even more now." Freezing, she met his gaze. He looked harder and more determined than ever. "Trust me, Kathryn. I've known myself for a very long time. It's all flooding back, and it's everything I knew I was missing before. I'm not becoming someone new—I'm returning to the man I've always been."

"You're asking for a lot of trust," she whispered.

"I know." His gaze was clear and rock steady. "And I'm worth it."

It crumbled the last of her resistance. She yanked at his shirt, widening the opening so she could run greedy fingers along the crisp black hair that sprinkled his massive chest.

Diving in for another kiss, he bent her farther, urging her to lie back as he began to sweep everything on the table aside.

A single semblance of sanity remained. Pulling away from his mouth again, she gasped, "Don't! I spent hours cooking that food, and there's no takeout here."

His chest heaved as he sucked in a breath. The skin along his hard cheekbones was flushed dark. "Gods, your mouth is amazing. I have no idea what takeout is."

"Doesn't matter," she gasped, glancing behind her.

"Don't knock the food on the floor. Oh—and there's still more wine." For some people, the value in the amount of wine that was left equaled a mortgage payment.

"Fine, dammit," he muttered.

But when he bent farther and made as if he would pick her up, real sanity intruded just in time. She struggled against his hold. "Oberon, you can't. Remember, no heavy lifting for a week."

Growling, he held her tight around the waist as he sank to his knees, bringing her down with him. "How the hells did you remember that? I'm burning up."

"I am too," she whispered. Sitting on his angled thighs, she yanked the ends of his shirt out of his trousers, and he released her long enough to help, the broad muscles of his torso and arms flexing as he pulled it off over his head.

Seeing him half-naked only fueled her urgency. Wiggling the dress up over her hips, she pulled it off. Underneath, she only wore the underpants she had washed clean, as well as silk stockings from the unknown Daoine Sidhe woman whose wardrobe she had raided. Her bras were still drying, so she hadn't bothered wearing anything else.

As she bared her breasts, he let out a low, urgent groan that went to her head with more potency than the wine. Staring down at them, he cupped the soft globes and rubbed the tips of her nipples with his thumbs. She didn't have very large breasts—she was built too slightly for that—but they were very sensitive, and more sensation jolted down her body as he played with them.

He noticed, and his caresses slowed. Watching her face now, he rolled the stiffened, dusky peaks between thumbs and forefingers, flicked and scratched lightly at the tips with his fingernails. As he teased her, the urgency in her body localized into an urgent, empty ache at the juncture between her legs. It rapidly grew into a serious sense of pain.

Hunger for him was driving her wild. She couldn't touch him enough, taste him enough. As he played with her body, she ran her shaking lips down the side of his neck and along the broad, strong curve of his collarbone.

She'd never understood recreational drugs until that moment, but his taste was more addictive than crack. She couldn't get enough of his scent, his warmth. He was sexy enough all on his own, but added to that, now she could scent his arousal. She needed to rub herself all over him.

Part of her was disturbed at how fast and completely this had exploded between them. But that was a dying part as the rest of her became consumed with taking him any way she could get him.

Laying one hand over the bulge in his trousers, she rubbed him until he hissed. With fast, violent movements, he yanked open the fastening and his large erection spilled out.

He was beautiful everywhere, the skin like velvet over the thick, hard cock, with a tracery of veins. His large, round testicles had drawn up tight underneath with his arousal.

She needed him inside her body. She needed to take this crazy ride they were both on to completion, because she didn't think she could take it if they stopped now.

Reaching between her legs, he fingered her, and this time they both groaned as the wetness of her own arousal coated his fingers. She twisted to take hold of his cock so that she could work him while he worked her, but after a few moments he hissed and pulled out of her hand.

"Not yet," he gasped. "I don't want to spill until I'm inside you."

"Then come inside me!" She lifted herself up and angled her pelvis to help him gain entry.

His eyes were alight, golden and feral, the pupils dilated, but for some reason he paused. His uneven breathing shuddered between his teeth, and a light sheen of sweat glistened on his forehead. "I usually have more finesse than to take a woman on the kitchen floor."

What was that in his voice? Concern? Opening her eyes very wide, she exclaimed, "Why are you still talking?"

With that, whatever the emotion was, it vanished. What was left behind was total focus, total animal. *And that was exactly as it should be. It was exactly what she needed.*

He took hold of his erection and rubbed the head against her folds. Digging her nails into his arms, she widened her legs farther, inviting him in. Hissing between his teeth, he pushed until the broad head of his cock was inside her.

He was big. Really big, and it had been a while since she'd had a lover. He stretched her inner muscles to the point of pain. Face twisting, she stroked his taut cheek. "Easy now," she gasped. "Let me get used to you."

"No worries," he whispered. "I'll get you there. Lean your weight back on your hands."

With her sitting on his spread thighs, that would arch her torso up and put her on display to him. She liked that idea, very much.

Easing back, she leaned her weight on her hands. His reaction was immediate. Face tightening, he growled, "That might have been a mistake."

Licking her lips, she asked, "Why?"

"My control is… very precarious right now." He touched her breast, stroked down her flat belly to the soft brown curl of hair between her legs. Then he forked his fingers and rubbed her on either side of his cock. "I want to eat you up," he told her roughly. "I want to suck on you until you scream, but I won't put you on that cold stone floor to do it. It's going to have to wait until we can get into a bed."

Her eyelids fell half-closed as he caressed her. "I want that too. Mostly, though, I just want you to come deeper inside."

"Are you ready for more?"

When she nodded, he pushed in, then rocked back. Slowly, he pumped back in, going deeper and stretching her farther before pulling back out again. His expression was taut to the point of pain.

She understood that pain. She felt it too. The inner need had built to a crescendo. Pushing into his next thrust, she impaled herself all the way on him. As she did, her small, stiffened clitoris rubbed against his root, and the flare of climax that swept over her was like a lightning bolt spearing through her core.

As she shook and gasped, he gathered her up in his arms and rocked gently against her. "There you are," he whispered as he stroked her back. "You're exquisite in every way."

As her climax ebbed, she flung her head back, tightened her inner muscles on him, and gasped, "I'm not done. I need more."

And it was her turn to set a match to him as her words ignited him.

Where he had cradled her against him before, now he gripped her body with selfish greed. Where he had stroked so gently along her nerve endings, now he went roughly, thrusting into her with a hard rhythm that increased as she catapulted precipitously into another climax.

She cried out as it took her over, and she flung out a hand, questing blindly for something solid to hold on to. The most solid, most real thing around was him, and she held the back of his neck as he drove into her.

He arched and gasped, and she was stretched so tightly around him she could feel him pulsing as he came. She rocked gently until he had finished, and afterward she threw her arms around him in a hug.

She still wanted more, but what they had shared was gorgeous, glorious. More could come soon enough, she told her urgent body, trying to bring herself down from the frenzy.

But then he grasped her by the hips and growled, "I'm not finished."

That was important. She should take a moment to consider why. But as his deep voice vibrated over her skin, she lost control of all thought. Raking her nails down his back, she hissed, "Give me all you've got."

HE HAD NEVER been so far outside his own control before. That was the single coherent realization he had. The rest was all animal, all rut, and every detail about her fueled the frenzy.

The graceful bones of her rib cage, rippling under her supple torso as she flexed and arched, meeting every one of his rough thrusts as he drove into her.

The reddened areas on her fine skin where he had rubbed her with his short beard.

The lambent light in her fierce eyes as the afternoon sun slanted over them, so unlike any other woman he had ever been with before.

When her hair knot slipped and came undone, the soft brown length spilled over her shoulders. Strands stuck to her hot damp skin. He loved all of it. He loved watching his intelligent, sarcastic physician lose control.

He had to bite her, and he wasn't careful about it. As his teeth sank into the juncture where her neck met her shoulder, she growled and pressed the back of his head, urging him on.

He came, and he came, again. And again. It wasn't enough. He could never get enough, couldn't get deep enough inside. He would never tire of taking her in as many ways as he could. He thought she climaxed again too, but he couldn't be sure—he wasn't paying attention to what she needed any longer.

He was taking what he needed and trusting her to do the same. Her teeth flashed, and she bit him too. She scratched him as well, and each tiny pain flared as punctuation to the extreme ecstasy. Some deep instinctual part of him knew she wasn't fighting him. She was fighting with him to get to the heart of this blinding-hot reality they generated between them.

He had never expected the act of sex to be transcendent. Sex was sex, enjoyable and even necessary at times, but a transient pleasure at best. He had always believed when he found the right woman, the emotions they shared would become the transcendent experience.

But with Kathryn it was all one and the same. That beautiful body of hers housed a strong, bright spirit, and he needed to get inside her as deep as he could, to watch her peak, spirit and flesh, her parted lips shaking as yet another climax rippled through her. He was inarticulate in the face of such joy. All he could do was strain toward more, until the accumulation of multiple releases finally brought them back down to earth.

When at last they came to a halt, the light was fading outside. They were both breathing hard as if they had just completed a marathon, and she had her legs wrapped around his hips. He had long since given up trying to spare her the cold flagstones, and they lay sprawled together on the floor. It was awkward and not at all comfortable.

Slowly he came to realize he had his arms clenched tight around her. He should loosen his hold, or she would think he was even more of a madman than she must already.

But she wasn't complaining. She held him just as tightly.

He noticed a marking on her skin in the distinctive shape of his fingers, and finally the capacity to speak returned. Stroking her hair back from her face, he murmured, "You're bruised everywhere. I knew we should have gone to the nearest bed." But the flagstone floor hadn't made those marks. His own feral satisfaction at seeing how he had marked her shocked him. "Are you all right?"

She nodded and traced a finger lightly down a scratch on his arm. Her quiet voice was hoarse. "You took some damage too."

He wanted to smile, but he still couldn't gauge how she was feeling. "I don't mind if you don't."

"Not in the slightest." She pressed her lips to the

scratch she had just stroked, and the light touch of her healing magic flowed like golden salveri through him.

Disappointed, he drew in a breath to protest, but by then it was too late. The marks she had made, both scratches and suck-bites, smoothed over and healed completely. Quietly, he said, "You didn't need to do that. I would have healed soon enough anyway."

He would have healed too soon either way. He would have liked to wear her marks on his body for as long as he could.

"It was the least I could do after everything you've just done for me." Lifting her head, she gave him a smile.

But it was a preoccupied smile, he noticed, and that darkened his own mood. His cock hadn't even softened enough to slip out of her, and she was already withdrawing emotionally from the incredible experience they had just shared.

"What is it?" As he spoke, since she had already healed him, he returned the favor—magical healing was not one of his strengths, but he could do that much. He watched as the redness and marks on her skin smoothed away. If he had not still held her in his arms, she would have looked untouched.

In reply, she kissed him. It wasn't a deep kiss but a lingering one, and when she finally pulled away, she met his gaze. "That was truly amazing and beautiful, but Oberon, we can't do it again."

Chapter Fifteen

H E WASN'T QUITE sure he had heard her correctly. "What do you mean, we can't do it again?" he growled. "Of course we can. We can do whatever the fuck we want."

"Well, what I *want* to do is go upstairs to my rooms and clean up. I'm starting to get cold, and I don't want to talk to you like this." She pressed a kiss against his shoulder.

The caress didn't make him feel better. Instinct told him not to let go of her, but he couldn't see any rational way to hold on. "All right," he said finally. "I could certainly stand to wash up too, so let's go upstairs together."

"I need time by myself," she told him.

Goddamn it, why was she wearing her doctor face? His eyes narrowed. "Why?"

"*Why?* I just do, that's all!" She caught herself up visibly, then said in a more measured tone, "Let's meet down here soon. We can eat supper and drink some more of those amazing wines you have so kindly shared with me. I'll be ready to talk then."

After a few moments, he could unclench his teeth enough to say, "Fine, let's do that."

"Good. See you soon." She kissed him again, swiftly, and peeled away from his embrace. Gathering up her clothes, she strode out the kitchen.

He watched her go. She was a source of constant surprise. With the kind of swift retreat she had just executed, he had expected her to show some evidence of body shame or embarrassment—something that would have explained her behavior.

But there was none of that. Her speed was derived from purpose. She held her clothes in a careless wad in one fist, and her sleek, nude body moved across the open room like exquisite poetry flowing off the tongue. She was completely at home in her own body and not embarrassed in the slightest to be seen nude by someone else.

No, her retreat had nothing to do with her. It had something to do with him.

The only way he was going to find out what was going on inside her head was by getting to the next part as fast as he could. Grabbing up his own clothes, he stalked through the silent palace to his own apartment. Once there, he went into the spacious, richly appointed bath and opened the flue to let water flow into the tub that was so capacious it was really a small swimming pool.

Nearly everyone in Lyonesse with magical capability knew how to heat water. It was one of the first workings of magic they learned as a child, and one of the most useful. After the water had filled the tub sufficiently, he cast a warming spell into it and dove in.

Soaking underwater had the welcome effect of clearing his head.

What he and Kathryn had shared... He had never experienced anything like it before. He had never before been capable of maintaining an erection after having ejaculated, nor had he ever experienced multiple climaxes before, just like every other male he had ever known... except the Wyr.

Had their lovemaking been just as spectacular for Kathryn?

When the Wyr mated, they went through an extraordinary process. While he was fuzzy on details, he had heard it described as a frenzy of insatiable desire.

Yes. That was exactly what it had been like.

And when the Wyr mated, they mated for life.

When the thought occurred to him, he stopped breathing, transfixed. It opened up a whole new vista for him to consider. *And he loved every bit of it.*

Was *that* what Kathryn had wanted to discuss... but only after a suitable time had passed and she'd had a chance to get some privacy, so she could erect all her barriers again?

Hurt spread through him like a bruise, but he deliberately shoved it away and reached for anger instead... Anger, his old companion, only this time it wasn't cold in the slightest. It was volcanic, blazing hot.

Wrestling himself under control, he finished washing and dressed again in plain, unrelieved black—pants, shirt, boots, jacket. The severe clothing suited his mood. Kathryn hadn't yet appeared, he found when he returned downstairs to the kitchen.

Pouring himself another goblet of the Lyonesse wine, he strode to the main front doors of the palace and opened them wide to the oncoming sunset. Outside, a flamboyant kaleidoscope of celestial colors greeted him.

Nature did not reflect his mood in the slightest. Scowling, he drank his wine and considered turning into the lion for the foreseeable future. He was very tempted to sink deep into the lion's animal, predatory nature.

Kathryn could do her damned reasonable talking to the cat for all he cared. The cat wouldn't give a shit about whatever words came out of her mouth and would focus on doing whatever it wanted anyway.

A flicker of movement in the distance caught his attention. At the lower edge of the city, down along the water line, someone—several someones—were picking their way carefully across a broken causeway.

Quickly he tossed back the rest of the wine, set the goblet on the step, and headed for the causeway. He was running by the time he reached the lower city. Just a few more blocks along the high street, then over another two would bring him to the docks.

When he raced past the last of the warehouses and into the open, the group of people had finished crossing the causeway. They must have heard his approach, because several of them lifted their heads as he appeared.

One of the nearest was a tall, older male who was a mixture of Demonkind and Dark Fae, with long white hair tied back from wicked, saturnine features. When he looked at Oberon, his expression filled with incredulous joy. "Sire?"

It was Owen, the castellan of the palace, and one of his oldest friends. This time when emotion welled up, it threatened to split him in two. "Owen," he said deeply, striding forward. "Gods, it is so good to see you, old friend."

Owen sprang to meet him. They didn't so much hug as collide together. Dull pain bloomed in Oberon's chest, but it was only a warning. He hadn't done any real damage, so he ignored it.

"Your majesty," Owen whispered, tears standing in his eyes. His pupils were slitted like a goat's. "For so long I had hoped for a day like this…."

"What are you doing here?" Letting the other man go at last, Oberon looked around at the rest of the group. There were almost seventy people now standing around him in a great circle. "Elias—*Edrid*… Brielle and Zara. And Alden, Isla… Elliana…"

Beaming and wiping tears from their cheeks, they greeted him as well with multiple hugs, shouts of delighted laughter, and exclamations. The others of the group who were not in his inner circle bowed deeply or curtsied.

"Where have you been?" he asked Owen. "And how

did you know to come back?"

"Some of us stayed with family and friends, scattered across various farms, but most of us had evacuated to a new settlement at Raven's Craig," Owen told him. "The flooding had gotten very bad, and Raven's Craig is some of the highest land in Lyonesse. When the weather changed, we knew something important had happened."

Raven's Craig was also much closer to the city than the crossover passageway where Annwyn and her group were traveling from, so of course Owen's group had arrived first. If Oberon hadn't been so focused on himself, he might have considered that as a possibility.

Before the surgery, he... hadn't cared. And afterward he had been totally consumed with Kathryn.

He clasped Owen's shoulder. "You knew I had either died or gotten better."

A shadow passed over Owen's expression. "Yes, your majesty. A group of us gathered together, and we decided to hike back to the city to discover what had happened. Seeing you looking so robust and well—it's everything we had dreamed of, and more. How did you recover?"

"I had some much-needed help from a wise physician," Oberon told him in a loud enough voice that it carried to the others in the group. "Without her intervention, there's no doubt in my mind I would have been lost. She's at the palace now, so you'll get a chance to meet her. Her name is Dr. Kathryn Shaw, and I think quite highly of her. I'm sure you will too."

"The physician is here?" Owen turned to indicate one of the women, whom Oberon realized was leaning heavily on the male who stood beside her. "Isla took a bad fall and needs medical attention."

"We will get her help." Everyone in the group looked tired. They had clearly pushed to get here as quickly as they could. He almost stepped forward to offer to pick the woman up and carry her, but at the last moment he remembered Kathryn's sternly worded instructions.

So instead he hooked an arm around Owen's shoulders and turned with him in the direction of the palace, and the others fell in line behind them.

As they walked, he said quietly, "I can't tell you how good it is to see you and to hear your voice."

"It is the same for me, your majesty. The same for all of us, but most especially me." Owen's expression fell as they walked through the city streets. "The damage is quite extensive. I had not realized how much."

"It's just damage. Nothing more." He let his conviction sound strongly in his voice. "We are going to rebuild and repair everything, and Lyonesse is going to be better than it has ever been. That's my promise to all of you."

And he felt that promise. He felt every word. It would be a joy and a privilege to see that it came to fruition.

As they climbed the hill to the palace, he asked Owen some quiet questions about various individuals. A few had died. Still others had emigrated to England and other countries.

But many of his people, by far most of them, would be flocking to the city as word spread of his recovery. Some of the males in this group were part of the palace and city guard, but he wouldn't get a true reckoning of the state of his army until he talked to either Annwyn or another senior officer.

As anxious as he was to hear what Annwyn would have to say, that reunion would be coming soon enough, so for now he focused on the people who were right in front of him.

The sun finished setting during the short walk back, and true night set in. Kathryn had made herself busy, he saw, as she had lit all the outside witchlights that were still whole around the palace. When they neared, he saw her slim, straight figure standing in the open doorways of the palace's main front entrance.

She looked refreshed and composed, smart and beautiful, with her shining hair pulled back in a simple braid. She wore trousers and a warm, cream-colored tunic.

Hunger and anger surged at the same time as he looked at her, and both feelings were so similar to how he had felt before the surgery it jolted him. She looked from him to Owen and back again, smiling.

"You found some of your people," she said. "I'm so happy for you."

"Thank you. This is Owen Margeld, the castellan of

the palace. Owen, this is the physician who saved my life, Dr. Shaw." He waited until they had greeted each other, and then he added, "Kathryn, they have an injured woman. I assured them you would help her."

Her expression changed. "Of course I will!"

The male who had been assisting Isla had carried her up the hill. As they stepped forward, Kathryn greeted them and then turned her attention to Isla.

Oberon knew what it was like to be the sole subject of her considerable focus and attention. After a few questions, a quick scan, and a smile of reassurance, Isla and the male both visibly relaxed, and all three turned to go inside.

Oberon touched Kathryn's arm as she passed. When she looked at him in inquiry, he told her, "Feel free to use my office."

Her expression brightened. "Thank you."

"You're welcome." He couldn't bring himself to return her smile, and hers faded as he turned away.

They would still have that damn talk, but for now he had other things to do. He told Owen, "There's some food already prepared in the kitchen, but it's not going to be nearly enough to feed everyone."

Owen replied in a low voice, "Food would be good, but my main concern is where everybody is going to sleep for the night. Many of those buildings we passed didn't look safe, and I don't think inspecting them in the dark would be wise."

"Nobody is going anywhere." He looked around at

all the exhausted faces. "There's enough room here to house everyone safely. Brielle, you know where the palace kitchen and pantries are. I want you and a team of others to go and prepare a meal for everyone. Owen, you and Edric need to decide which rooms would be suitable to use for the night. The past couple of days have been warming up, but it gets cold after dark. Be sure there are fireplaces in the rooms you choose and check to see that the weather hasn't damaged the chimneys. I know you've all had a long day, but Alden, you and some of the others need to bring in plenty of firewood for each room." He smiled. "You have just a bit more work to do, and then you can eat and rest."

"It's glad work, and we will have a good night ahead of us!" Owen said. "Thank you, sire!"

As people divided into their work groups, he felt the impulse to join Alden and the other strong bodies who would be carrying in the firewood, and frustration surged once more as he remembered he couldn't.

Again, Kathryn's words came back to him. She had known what kind of frustration he would be facing. She must have seen the same thing in dozens of patients before, but that didn't make it any easier.

Finally he chose to go with Owen to help inspect rooms. When there was a break in activity, he said quietly to the older man, "Tomorrow after everyone is well rested, take a cleaning crew down to the crystal cave. Don't be alarmed by what you find down there. Kathryn had to perform surgery to remove the bastard's assassination spell."

Owen gripped his forearm and switched to telepathy. *But you are well?*

Rest assured, I am well, he assured the older man. *Frustrated because I can't lift anything right now, and I have to be mindful of a few other restrictions for four weeks, but I'm very well.*

Owen relaxed. His Demonkind features could be frightening to those who didn't know him, but for centuries Oberon had seen nothing in his expression but love and kindness. *Then nothing else matters.*

He forced himself to kick thoughts of Kathryn into the background and smiled. *You're right, nothing else does.*

AT FIRST WHEN she realized Oberon had left the palace, Kathryn had been worried. He'd been baffled and angry at her earlier, and with good reason. She had coupled with him like a wildcat, only to withdraw so completely afterward it gave her whiplash. He had to be feeling it too.

It was far outside her own normal behavior, and it wasn't fair to him. But when Wyr entered the state they had slipped in to, they tended to be unpredictable and sometimes dangerous. Not knowing what else to do, she had activated the witchlights outside, watched, and waited.

Now, with the arrival of the group, everything had changed as she had always known it would.

A male named Jorrend carried Isla as he followed her

to Oberon's office. They both looked around in awe, and with a rueful, inward smile, she realized how quickly the palace had become familiar surroundings over the past several days.

Following her instructions, Jorrend set Isla carefully into one of the armchairs, and Kathryn eased the injured woman's leg onto the footstool.

After deeper examination, she told Isla, "You didn't just hurt your leg, you hurt your back. But the good news is, you don't need surgery."

Isla blanched. "I might have needed surgery?"

Jorrend exclaimed, "You're lucky to be alive!" Turning to Kathryn, he said, "She hit her head and lost consciousness."

"I saw that," she replied, keeping her tone calm and reassuring. "But there's no lasting damage. Isla, you have deep bruising at the back of your head, and you may have headaches for a few days, but there's no skull fracture and no concussion. You have torn ligaments in your knee, but I think the most painful thing right now must be what happened to your back. You have what is called spondylolysis, which is a stress fracture at your vertebral arch." Turning, she pointed to her own back to give them an idea of the area she was talking about. "I'm going to treat you with healing spells to address the fracture and the torn ligaments. You might feel achy for the next few weeks, which is to be expected. I don't think you'll need a brace after the healing spells, but you mustn't do any heavy lifting until all the pain and achiness is gone. Understand?"

Isla nodded. "Thank you, Doctor."

"You're welcome." She cast the spells in rapid succession until Isla's body wouldn't take any more. Then she finished with a deep pain-relieving spell that should last well into the next day. When that was completed, she sat back on her heels and grinned. "You're going to feel really good until that wears off... Don't let it fool you into thinking you can do more than you should."

"I won't, I promise." Isla smiled. "When his majesty said he thought very highly of you, I knew everything was going to be all right."

"He said that?" A welcome warmth stole through her. Perhaps what he thought of her shouldn't matter so much, but it did, especially since they appeared to be at odds again. And she really didn't want to feel estranged from him. There was a hollow place in her middle where a warm glow had resided earlier. She murmured, "That's good to know."

Since she was done helping Isla, she went to look for Oberon, but there were people everywhere, and he had disappeared somewhere with his castellan. Not knowing what else to do, she made her way to the kitchen to help with the cooking.

Brielle, the woman in charge of the cooking crew, greeted Kathryn warmly. "Your food is set aside over in the corner, love. Nice job on those pies!" Leaning closer, she whispered, "Both bottles of wine are over there too.

Goodness, that must have been a treat."

She laughed. "It was. And that's everybody's food now. Please add the roasts and pies to what you're feeding people."

Brielle nodded, looking pleased. "With your permission, I'd like to cut up that venison roast and throw it in the stewpots."

"I'll cut it up for you." Rolling up her tunic sleeves, she got to work.

Tired people cycled in to be fed, and Brielle cooked hot oatcakes to stretch what they had for dinner and help fill hungry bellies. Kathryn created a quick syrup to pour over the oatcakes, made with honey, dried apples, spices, and pecans. Even though she made a large pot, the syrup was gone within minutes.

"Well, I misjudged that," she said with a laugh.

"You'll have to make more in the morning." Brielle licked her spoon with an expression of bliss. "That was sublime."

"I would be happy to," Kathryn told her. She frowned. "I haven't seen Oberon in a while, have you?"

The other woman shook her head. "I would have noticed if his majesty had come in for some supper. We all would have."

Of course they would have. To Kathryn, he was just Oberon, but to them he was their king. She wondered how often he would have entered the kitchen before. Probably not very often.

"I'm going to look for him. He needs to eat too."

Grabbing two of the last pies, she wrapped them up in a cloth and set them on a tray with a bowl of stew. After adding the partial bottle of salveri, she headed out.

This time she found him easily enough in the first place she checked. He had gone to his office and was sitting close to the fireplace, contemplating the flames. He didn't look around when she entered.

"There you are," she said. "I've been looking for you."

"Not now, Kathryn," he replied.

She didn't budge. "You didn't show up in the kitchen, so I brought you some supper."

He still didn't look at her. "Leave it and get out."

This was very bad. His anger toward her was a palpable thing. Pursing her lips, she closed the door behind her and, after a moment's consideration, turned the lock. No doubt in the normal course of things, his palace staff was very protective of his privacy, but these were not normal times, and exhaustion and excitement were running high for everyone. Right now, people were more likely to do something they might regret.

That thought echoed back at her, and she knew very well that it applied to her too, but it wasn't going to stop her from acting. Feeling regret was often in line with asking for forgiveness, and she would far rather ask for forgiveness than for permission.

She deposited the tray on his desk, then walked toward him. "We should have that talk now."

"For fuck's sake, what did I just say to you?" His

growl shook the floor as he sprang from the armchair and rounded on her with an enraged expression.

She felt herself flinch as it whipped across her face. As angry as he had been with her in the past, he had never sworn at her before. "I heard what you said," she replied quietly. "But you're going to get busier now that your people are beginning to arrive. We should finish what we—there are things I should tell you...."

"You mean you want to lecture me about the Wyr birds and the bees." After his first growl, he spoke just as quietly but with a vicious bite in each word. He advanced on her, aggression in each tight muscle. "I'll save you the trouble. There only one reason you think we shouldn't make love again—we've begun to mate. Because there's only one reason I should suddenly gain the ability to climax multiple times... and I know you were right there with me the entire time. Weren't you, Kathryn?"

Even though she'd known he was clever, she hadn't foreseen that he would have figured everything out on his own. Shaken by his words and attitude, she backed away as he came closer, until her calves collided with something hard.

Thrown off-balance, she began to fall backward. He lunged to catch her by the shoulders, but instead of helping her regain her footing, he yanked her against his chest. She clutched at his waist as she collided into him, looking back for what had tripped her. He had moved the footstool away from the armchairs and she hadn't noticed.

Then, as she felt his body against hers and smelled his scent, the visceral memory of what they had done together stabbed her low in the gut. Her traitorous body flared with renewed hunger, clashing with her more sensible instincts.

He shook her, a single, quick jolt that snapped her gaze up to his fierce expression. "Tell me I'm wrong."

"You're not wrong!" she gasped. Gods, what he had done to her with that outrageously sensual mouth. What she wanted him to do to her again. What she wanted him to do that they hadn't yet explored together. "Wyr who have started to mate can stop in time if they recognize the symptoms early enough…"

He let go of her suddenly as if she had burned him. "If they recognize the symptoms early enough," he spat out. "Well, I'm sorry you find the prospect of mating with me comparable to a disease."

"*I don't!*" she snapped as she ran shaking fingers through her hair. This had gone wrong so badly, so fast, she struggled to think of a way to bring them back onto a kinder, more reasonable course. "Oberon, we had to stop. *We had to.* You deserved to know what was happening to you—what nearly every other Wyr learns about before they ever hit puberty, because mating with someone is irrevocable. Do you hear me? It's a life sentence. There's no greater tragedy than when a Wyr has mated badly, because it can *kill* them. And your emotions have been numbed for so long, and as for me…" For a moment her voice failed her. "I never expected anything like this to happen."

"No," he agreed bitterly. "And as you've said before, you have a full life waiting for you back in New York. Friends. Lovers. You've made it quite clear from the beginning that your biggest goal was finishing here and going home."

"I don't know anybody in Lyonesse," she whispered. "I know you, and Robin, and I've had two conversations with Annwyn. I've seen the bones of a ruined city, and that's *it*. And this has hit us with lightning speed—you and I have known each other for less than a week. This is so far outside anything normal or comfortable for me, I don't know who I am anymore."

He was silent for long moments, big hands resting on his hips. He had angled his face away while she spoke, his long body taut with rejection.

"I agree with you. This is happening far too fast, and the timing could be better—but it's still happening. And while I appreciate you were trying to look out for me, I figured things out on my own. I can look after myself and make my own choices. I don't need you to make them for me." He paused, then asked, "You know that bedroom you woke up in, the morning after the surgery?"

He had switched gears on her again. She felt as if something fragile inside her was grinding as it worked to switch focus with him. "Yes. It wasn't your normal room."

"No, that was the queen's suite."

Queen? He had been married before? An insane beast of jealousy roared up inside her, and her hands tightened into fists as an avalanche of questions hit her. She felt her talons come out. The tips punctured her palms.

Who—when—*who?* Nobody had said anything about a queen. Had he loved her? Had she died? Was she still alive, *and were they still married?*

Chapter Sixteen

THE BARRAGE OF questions hit with lightning speed and left her shaking. Turning her back to him, she opened her hands and stared at the bleeding punctures. "I didn't know you had a queen."

"I don't. When we built this place, I wanted to create a space that my future queen would enjoy, should I be so lucky to find the right woman. I never did." He sighed. "But I thought about her quite a bit, and I prepared for her, in case. I would have welcomed her if she had come along. I would still welcome her, but..." His voice sharpened. "Do I smell blood?"

"Yes."

He was beside her before she realized it and snatched at her wrists. "What did you do?"

"I balled my hands into fists, and my talons came out. Don't worry—the punctures have already healed." She tried to pull away, but he wouldn't let her go.

The lion's eyes looked out at her from the man's face. "Why did your talons come out, Kathryn? It happened just now, didn't it—when I mentioned the queen's suite?"

Again, she tried to tug her wrists free, and when she couldn't, the fragile something snapped inside. She cried, "Do you think this is easy for me?"

If anything, he grew even more inhuman-looking. "I don't think that now," he purred. "Listen to me. I want you more with every breath I take, and I have no intention of backing away from this—bad timing, lightning speed, and all. But I also heard what you said. I see your struggle, so I will give you this much and no more. If you need to, walk away. I won't stop you, and I won't come after you. But that's all you'll get from me, and you'd better leave now."

More agitated than she could ever remember being, she wiped her hands on the thighs of her leggings. "You don't have a doctor here."

"We'll get by until one comes. Likely enough, Annwyn's group will be here by tomorrow night." That steady gaze of his was pitiless, and he didn't blink once. "What are you waiting for? How many times do I have to tell you to get out?"

"I-I don't know." She lifted her shoulders and held out her hands in a helpless shrug. Her boots seemed to have fused to the floor. "Maybe a lot."

If she left now and went back to New York, she wouldn't see him again for years. He would embroil himself in hunting down Isabeau—and they lived so far apart it was more than likely that she would never see him again.

They would never argue again. They would never

stare deeply into each other eyes, as they were doing now. He would never make her angry. She would never roll over in bed and discover what it was like to wake up peacefully with him beside her.

She would never have him inside her. Never again. And he would be completely free to fill his queen's apartment with anybody else that he chose.

She felt like her broken pieces were tearing her in two.

"You're out of luck," he whispered. "Because I'm done talking. What are you going to do?"

"I'm leaving!" she shouted. "Don't think I'm not!" She launched at him.

When she smacked into his chest, he staggered and grunted, "Seven hells, woman. You're heavier than you look."

"Why are you still talking?" she hissed.

A savage smile lit his face, and he didn't bother to answer. Muscled arms the size of tree trunks snapped around her, and he sank a fist into the hair at the back of her head. It was confining and so barbaric it took her breath away.

How could he think that was acceptable? That she would—that she would have a total meltdown at his rough dominance and practically orgasm over the fact that he *yanked* her *hair*...

...even though she did....

She tore at his shirt. Material ripped. He tugged her down with him as he went to his knees and shredded her tunic. Next he jerked down her leggings. She tried to struggle free of them, but they had forgotten her boots. Even as she swore and tried to yank her leggings back up to take care of the boot problem, he bodily flipped her around and pushed her forward until she was on her hands and knees, leaning over the footstool.

"Wait," she gasped. "Was that heavy lifting?" Through the urgent haze of need clouding her mind, she tried to calculate.

"Who's talking too much now?" he growled. "Shut the fuck up."

"You didn't go *up* with my body weight, so much as *around*..." Holy shit. He came over her from behind and covered her. Her legs were trapped. The weight of her torso rested on the footstool, so her arms were free, but she couldn't reach him.

Meanwhile, his heavy weight settled on her. She could feel the crisp hair on his chest rubbing along the sensitive curve of her spine. He grabbed her hair again—this was so not like her—and he pushed her head down and held her there.

"You stay down, do you hear?" he hissed into her ear.

"Oberon!"

He paused. His breathing was rough and loud as his lungs worked overtime. Gently, he whispered, "Is this okay?"

He hadn't gathered all her hair into his fist. The rest fell around her face, the ends trailing on the floor. She had no idea what to do with her hands. Her talons had sprung back out. She dug them into the thick, rich carpet and hung on while she snarled, "If you stop now, I might murder you."

"We can't have that, can we?" he purred.

His teeth came down on the nape of her neck, and he held her pinned that way, with his body, his fist and teeth, while he palmed one breast and pinched the tip of her nipple, stroking and exploring wherever he wanted. However he wanted.

When he reached around her hip to stroke her, she started swearing. Then he found her clit and rubbed, and the resulting shock wave of pleasure was so intense she almost levitated the both of them off the stool as she bucked and squirmed.

It was like fighting, and he easily overpowered her as he held her in place and stroked and stroked. All the while she could feel his huge, gorgeous erection pressing against her ass. It was just lying there, wasting away.... She wanted to touch it, suck on it, and pull it into her body where the ache was sharp and knifelike.

Her next climax crested like a rolling wave, so hard she heard herself cry out hoarsely. His fist left her hair, and he clamped his hand over her mouth. All the while he massaged her with a relentless rhythm, until the climaxes crashed and crashed, and the waves tossed her head over heels.

She cried out harder. His fingers on her cheek tightened, the sound blocked by his broad palm. "Not everyone is in bed yet," he whispered hoarsely. "But scream all you like. I'll muffle it."

Goddammit! Goddammit! There was only one way she could make noise, and that was by yelling telepathically at him. She reached behind her to yank at his short hair and claw at the back of his neck. *Why aren't you fucking me?*

You have the patience of a gnat, he told her.

Gnats don't have patience! she snapped, then scowled as she realized that was what he had meant.

Another climax was coming…. Sweet gods, she couldn't take it…. This one was like a tsunami, and it flattened everything in its wake. Tears sprang to her eyes, and she sobbed as she convulsed with it.

He rocked with her, mimicking the act of sex without penetration, stroking, stroking. Then his teeth eased from her neck as he muttered, "I can't wait any longer."

Nobody asked you to! she exclaimed.

He gasped out a laugh. "Do you always tell your partners off when you're having sex?"

Nobody has made me feel the way you do.

She trembled on the edge of saying the words, but she already felt so bared, so overextended, she swallowed them down and kept them to herself.

✧   ✧   ✧

I'M LEAVING! DON'T think I'm not!

The words wormed through the back of his mind, leaving a dark shadow like rot even as he made love to her and brought her to climax over and over.

She was leaving him, and her arousal drenched his fingers. She was leaving even as she egged him on. Even as her body shook with the pleasure he gave her.

He couldn't fathom it. There was so much he needed to do before she left. It stripped away niceties and left nothing polite behind.

Finally he couldn't take it any longer. He had turned into a hot spike of need. Rubbing the thick head of his cock against her entrance, he thrust all the way home in one long, aggressive push. By then she was so ready for him his entry was a slick, tight slide in. He strained to get in farther, tighter, but he was already in at the root. There was nothing left to do but pull out and slam back in again.

She clenched around him, tight as a fist, and started swearing telepathically again. He would have laughed if he'd had the room to do so. She had a filthy mouth. He never would have guessed from her educated composure.

After three hard thrusts, he came. It felt glorious and hollow at once.

It wasn't enough, and he strained to another one. And then another one. All of it felt hollow. The synergistic blend of spirit and flesh was marred, and the shadow of that fucking worm had stolen something essential away. Something he hadn't realized he needed until it was gone.

His arms shook as he finally finished emptying

himself. Lying heavily on her back, he rested his forehead on the slender blade of her shoulder as he fought to get his breathing under control. She cupped the side of his head and stroked his hair, and he let the hand that had been muffling her mouth fall away.

He couldn't say the frenzy had died down. In the face of their exhaustion, it merely retreated enough so they could resume other functions. How he was going to live with this when she left, he didn't know. He might have survived all this time only to have his healer kill him after all.

"Can you move?" she murmured. She sounded hoarse.

He stirred. "You must be tired of my weight."

A ghost of a chuckle shivered through her torso. "Your weight is fine. I just want to get my boots off."

He laughed as he pulled away. Laughter pushed the rot away, at least for now. As she rolled off the footstool and into a sitting position, he helped her get the leggings untangled and her strange boots—*hiking boots*, she called them—unlaced. They were both unsteady in the aftermath, and her hands trembled as much as his.

Another urgent need made itself known. He lifted his head. "You said you brought supper."

She tried to finger comb the tangles out of her hair. "I did." She sounded more than tired. She was exhausted. "I didn't mean to stay, so I only brought enough for one. You're going to have to share it."

"Of course." He had never taken the time to strip off

his pants. Tucking himself back together, he fastened them and went to retrieve the tray.

As he returned to the area in front of the fire, she slipped into his shirt. She had ripped it, but he had totally destroyed her tunic. His shirt was far too big on her. She had to roll up the sleeves, and then she tied the long trailing ends into a knot at her waist.

He liked her wearing his clothes. He liked the fact that this time she didn't think to heal the marks on either of them, nor had she managed to get her tangled hair sorted out.

And he hated that being with him was such a struggle for her, because for him, being with her was simple. It felt easy. It didn't matter that the timing was all wrong, that he was recovering from major surgery, or that they went too fast. Life was full of accidents, opportunities, and surprises, and one made of them what one could.

She was everything he had ever hoped to find in a partner—she was strong, analytical, caring, and ethical, and deeply feminine and sexy. She surprised him and made him laugh. She made him rock hard with desire.

She was someone to rely on when you had to face the worst challenges of your life. She was someone to trust when you had to place your life in her hands.

There you are, he wanted to say. I've been looking for you all my life.

The mating frenzy only heightened what was already true, but bitterly, he realized she probably wouldn't welcome those words, or believe him if he did say them. She was too mired in her struggle and her doubt.

He kept what he was thinking from showing in his expression. As he set the tray on the footstool and sat on the floor beside her, she yawned and murmured, "This day has gone on forever."

"It's been an epic one," he agreed. Half the salveri was left in the bottle, and she hadn't bothered to grab any goblets. He offered the bottle to her. She accepted it, drank, and handed it back. As he drank, she murmured a quiet sound of pleasure. "What are you seeing?"

"I don't know how to describe it," she told him. "It's like someone just wrapped a beautiful red silk cloak around me. It's warm and comforting, and it feels like your Lyonesse wine tastes. Like hope."

"Very nice."

"I'm curious—did you name Lyonesse because your Wyr form is a lion?"

"There are several of us who have a Wyr feline in our ancestry—Annwyn, Nikolas, and others," he told her. "Lyonesse means 'city of lions.' When we founded this demesne, we thought it was a strong name, and something we could be proud of."

Just then his own vision unfurled. He took in a quiet breath.

"What do you see this time?" She sidled closer, gaze bright with curiosity in her tired face.

"I see a peregrine falcon in flight." His mouth twisted into a crooked smile. "She's quite beautiful, a little empress of the sky."

"Did you know," she said with a sly, sideways look, "that when we're diving, we're the fastest creatures on earth? Faster than gryphons, harpies, or dragons."

"That's because they're huge and built like my lion is, full of bone and muscle, whereas your bird is built like a bullet when she goes after prey." He broke apart one pie and offered her a piece. "Have you ever recorded your fastest speed?"

She ate the pie. "Bayne and Graydon recorded me in a diving stoop once at two hundred and forty miles per hour. I remember that flight clearly—I was hungry and straining hard to catch a starling that had just tried to outmaneuver me, and I was pushing with everything I had so if their recording is accurate, that's got to be my fastest speed."

He had enjoyed falconry many times over the centuries, and he could just imagine the flight she described. In the air, she would be perfectly deadly. She could have taken that deadliness into any profession and done anything that required superlative grace and speed.

"You would have made one hell of an assassin," he said, smiling. "Or a hell of a swordswoman. Instead, you chose medicine."

"I did, and I love it, although these days I just take on extreme cases." With a crooked smile, she pushed her elbow against his upraised knee. It was an open, relaxed, and affectionate gesture.

"That reminds me," he told her. "Be sure to add

Isla's treatment to my bill."

"No, Oberon. You don't need to pay me anything. She wasn't hurt that badly, and I was glad to help, especially when they were both so tired and frightened."

"As long as you're sure."

"I am. It's all right."

He didn't want this night to end, but the fire was dying down, and the rest of the palace had quietened some time ago as the newcomers had fallen asleep.

And morning hurtled inexorably toward them, bringing change.

"Past time for bed," he told her.

He watched her eyes darken, but she didn't disagree. "Yes, it is."

He touched her hand. She would turn him down and execute one of her strategic retreats. He was certain of it, but he still had to ask while he could. "Come sleep with me."

She hesitated. Then her beautiful eyes smiled first, and the rest of her expression followed suit. "I would love to."

He felt himself lighten so much the inner rot almost disappeared.

Almost.

Lacing his fingers through hers, he kissed the back of her hand. Then they stood and made their way quietly upstairs through the darkened hallways. As he pushed the doors open to his apartment and ignited the witchlights, he began to apologize for the mess but stopped in midsentence.

Someone had come in to tidy. They had made the bed and taken away the dirty clothes. Warmth spread through him as he looked at the waiting empty brandy glass and decanter on the nearby dresser.

He touched the edge of the tray. "This was Owen's doing. It's a nighttime ritual from years ago."

"It's obvious how much he loves you," she replied. "How much they all do."

"No more than I love them." He smiled as he said it.

He did love them, and he didn't just remember the feeling—he felt it. The words had become true again.

"From what I've seen, they are pretty loveable," she told him, yawning. "Is your amazing plumbing working now that everything has thawed out?"

"Yes, it is."

When they went into the bathroom, he found the tub had been drained and clean towels had been stacked on a bench near the sink along with a sharpened razor, a robe and slippers, and bowls of soft cedar-and-citrus-scented soap.

"I've had fantasies about using your incredible bathtub, but I'm too tired tonight." Her words came out slowly.

"Use it in the morning," he told her. "It will still be here."

"True enough."

She left briefly and came back with her pack and a pile of clothes thrown over one arm. Together they went through their evening toilettes, almost as if they were in fact married and mated.

He let her have the sink first and noticed every small thing, how she cleaned her teeth with the odd-looking toothbrush and minty-smelling powder, how she washed at the sink with an experienced economy of motion that hinted at many other times of exhaustion and using minimal effort to achieve maximum benefit. After dragging a hairbrush through her hair a few times, she kissed his shoulder on her way out.

He followed soon enough. He thought she was already asleep when he slid between the bedcovers, but she turned over to curl around him. They were both nude, and the last of the tension between his shoulders left him on a deep sigh. Being skin to skin with her was everything he had imagined, and so much more necessary than he had realized.

As he wrapped his arms around her, she settled her head in the hollow of his shoulder.

They could do this every night, sleep together in complete peace and comfort, if only she wouldn't leave.

He almost said it. But the worm rot was still there, quietly residing underneath all the good they had created that evening, and he didn't want to give strength to it by airing it out loud. She would either leave or she wouldn't, and she wouldn't do either of those things because of what he said. She had already shown that she was far too strong-minded for that.

So he sank his awareness deep into his lion, because

the cat only knew and cared about the present.

The future had not yet occurred, and the past was gone. *Now* was all they had—it was all they ever had. Contenting himself with that and with the knowledge that his mate was lying with him for the very first time, the cat kept his secrets private and purred himself to sleep.

A formless time later, he was inside her before he had fully woken up to know what he was doing. He came alert in a surge of adrenaline. She was sitting on him, riding him. The sky outside the windows carried a hint of predawn gray, leaving the room in near total darkness, but he could still see perfectly well.

She had tilted her head back, and her expression was almost dreamy. When he grasped her by the hips, she looked down at him with a shadowed smile. He lost a little more of himself to her in that moment.

"Come down here," he whispered huskily, stroking her lightly.

Pulling her hair to one side, she did, and met his kiss with parted lips. They made love fiercely, in near total silence, and afterward they lay entwined together and did not pull apart.

No future, he told himself. No past. Hold on to *this* now.

She fell back asleep, but he didn't. He was too busy soaking in this reality.

That meant he was awake when, sometime later, the door to his bedroom opened silently. Owen poked his head in, and his eyes widened when he saw Kathryn in Oberon's bed.

Oberon put a finger to his lips. Owen nodded and eased the door shut again.

How odd, to lie in bed and listen to the distant sounds of the palace coming to life again after all these years. People hurried down the hall several times, talking together in quiet voices. They were very respectful. He only heard them because his senses had become so acute.

Good morning, sire, Owen said telepathically several minutes later. *I have set a breakfast tray with tea for you and the doctor here, next door in your sitting room. Alden is at guard at your door should you require anything else.*

He smiled. They had known for many years that the position of Oberon's bed meant Owen could telepathize to him from the sitting room if need be. *Thank you, Owen. There's no need to post a guard at my door, not while everyone is still tired from their journey and there's so much to do.*

Sir, I beg to differ, Owen said. An uncharacteristic steel thread had entered his mental voice. He almost never contradicted Oberon. *You are the one still recovering from an assassination attempt that happened years ago. There's every need for a guard on your door at all times, along with regular guard duty everywhere as soon as we can manage it.*

I stand corrected, he said. *You're right, of course. Thank you. It is entirely my pleasure, your majesty.*

Silence fell, and peace stole over him. The tea and breakfast that Owen had so thoughtfully provided would go cold, because he intended to lie quietly and hold Kathryn for as long as she would sleep. Then when she awakened, he had other plans in mind.

Outside, someone shouted in the distance. At first, he thought it was all part of the group growing more active after having broken their fast. Then someone else shouted, closer to the palace, and he heard people running.

He lifted his head. He wouldn't have been able to hear any of it if he hadn't been full Wyr. He was sorely tempted to pretend he didn't hear it now.

But then came the distinct, rhythmic sound of horse hooves on cobblestones—several horses. It could very well have been another party, but he knew in his bones that Annwyn and her troops had arrived.

Carefully he eased away from Kathryn and out of bed. She stirred and mumbled, "What is it?"

"Never mind," he whispered, bending over to smooth the hair back from her face. She was indescribably beautiful in the morning, her fine-boned face vulnerable and open. She hadn't yet assumed any of the formidable shields she had learned from her profession. He kissed her forehead. "You stay in bed and sleep. Breakfast is in the other room whenever you want it."

"Mmm." When he would have straightened, she sought his hand and held it, only reluctantly letting go after a moment.

She might be leaving, but at least it wouldn't be easy

on her. He took dark, selfish satisfaction in that. Dressing quickly, he headed out the door.

"Good morning, sire," Alden greeted him.

Sometime in the early hours of the morning, Owen had unearthed uniforms for the palace guard. He would have smiled, but there seemed to be an urgency to the sounds of the new arrivals outside.

"Come with me," he ordered.

Alden followed as he strode down the hall. He picked up his pace and was running by the time he reached the main staircase. Together they sprinted down to the main floor.

Several of the newcomers from the night before were gathered at the open front doors, looking out. They fell back to let him and Alden pass.

Below in the spacious courtyard, a party of soldiers had arrived—and it was much larger than what Kathryn had described. They were mud-splattered and grim, and several looked as if they had seen battle. He could smell the iron scent of old blood.

Annwyn was in the middle of a swirl of activity along with Gawain, Rowan, and Robin, who looked drawn with exhaustion.

Some sixth sense made Annwyn turn as he ran down the steps. Her tight expression transformed into relief and incandescent joy. Launching at him, she threw her arms around him in a tight embrace as he snatched her close.

"*Gods, Oberon!* When Robin told us the news, I didn't

dare believe it." She buried her face in his neck, and he felt the wetness of her tears against his skin. "Kathryn did it—she brought you back to us."

They were cousins, but they had been raised as if they were siblings. As a boy he had played with her, fought with her, and trained with her. They had gone on some of their first hunting trips together, and she had been the first to talk with him about his dream for creating Lyonesse.

That he had ever entertained the possibility Annwyn might betray him would forever stand out in his memory as the most severe symptom of how badly he had been affected by Morgan's spell.

At first he couldn't let her go. He kept one arm hooked around her neck as he roped Gawain in for a hug, then Rowan. While Robin stood back several paces and watched, Oberon motioned him over to pull him into a tight hug too.

The puck's slim arms tightened around him briefly before letting go. After that there were others to greet and hug as they crowded close around him, loyal, hardworking soldiers he had known and led for so many centuries.

They were, all of them, closer than friends. They were his family.

Deep inside, the worm rot spread, burrowing into his bones and stealing his joy. Connections like these were irreplaceable. How could he hope that Kathryn might leave behind everyone she knew and loved as well as the life she had worked for so long to build for herself?

He couldn't. She had been right and honest about that all along.

Pain spiked through his middle as if someone had driven a sword through his body. He pushed it away. Now was not the time to give in to despair over what he could not change.

"There's so much to talk about," he said to Annwyn. "And so much I want to hear from you, but first—what is the news?"

With that, the lightness in everyone's expressions turned stark and grim again.

Annwyn's clear gaze held a hollow look of horror as she replied, "I'm afraid it's inconceivably bad. I don't know how it's possible, but Isabeau has invaded. Oberon, she's here in Lyonesse."

Chapter Seventeen

W HEN OBERON LEFT, Kathryn scooted over to the big area in the bed where he had slept. The sheets were still warm and carried his scent, and it was almost as delicious as actually sharing the bed with him.

She had spent most of the night lying sleepless as everything that had happened ran through her mind in an endless loop. *Trust me,* he had said, and just like that, she had flung every other consideration aside and done just that. That kind of impetuous decision was not at all how she normally behaved.

Normally she thought through every conceivable consequence before she acted, and that deliberation had stood her in good stead in her practice. But with Oberon, she was impetuous and impulsive, and she crossed lines previously she would never have considered crossing. He had barely had his surgery before she had caved in and kissed him again, let alone leaping to have sex with him at the drop of a hat.

But he had said *trust me,* and she did. She really did, already, so soon, right now. He *had* known himself, for far longer than she had been alive, and as he revived from the spell it must have felt like coming home. She loved fiercely the fact that he was coming into his own.

Things were getting dangerous. She should have packed her gear last night and left.

But what if she didn't? What if she chose to stay instead? At that, a cacophony of conflicting emotions surged up. All her broken pieces were rioting.

It was too overwhelming. She shoved it aside, reaching for a few more stolen moments. Her body pretended to ignore the rest of the world as she wallowed in the spot and soaked up his warmth, but her mind had switched on, and it wasn't buying the ploy.

She heard his exchange with Alden in the hall. She also heard the noise outside, and even though he had urged her to take her time, she threw back the covers, tore into her clothes, and ran after them.

Oberon was out of sight by the time she reached the group that stood crowding the open doors. She elbowed her way through without apology and made her way outside in time to hear what Annwyn said.

Isabeau was here, in Lyonesse?

Nooooo.

Kathryn's brain refused to take in the information. It ran contrary to everything she had been told. The last she had heard, the Light Fae Queen had been badly injured and was in hiding, her society thrown into disarray, and her army fractured. Even her famous, deadly Hounds had abandoned her, and the Daoine Sidhe—Annwyn herself—had been optimistic about taking her down sometime soon.

She fixed her gaze on Oberon, who stood very still upon hearing the news. Then a murderous smile creased his features.

"She has finally gotten up enough courage to break into my house," he growled. "That will make it easier to find and kill her, so we can be done with her spite once and for all." Looking around, he told the soldiers, "Get your needs met. See to your horses, seek medical attention if you need, and eat and rest as much as you can. Those who can need to be ready to ride at a moment's notice. Robin, that goes especially for you."

"Aye, sire," the puck replied. "I swear on my life, I will be ready." As exhausted as he looked, there was a feverish tension vibrating through his slender frame. It hurt to look at him.

But it hurt even more to look at Oberon. He was on fire, burning with purpose.

This was beyond disastrous. Every one of the Daoine Sidhe, she saw, were looking to him for strength, purpose, and guidance. They were soaking in his presence like dying plants receiving a much-needed rain. Even the most exhausted of the soldiers were visibly reviving in the face of Oberon's burnished vitality.

None of them knew what she knew. The fool was supposed to avoid outright war for three and a half more weeks—and he wasn't going to do it. And war would lead to battle... and she knew without having to be told that he was not the kind of ruler to lead from behind.

After everything she had done to save his life, he was going to run off and get himself killed.

She clenched and unclenched her fists while her mind raced.

Focus, Shaw. This isn't your country. It isn't your fight. You're supposed to be going home, remember? And he's been an adult for far longer than you've been alive—he knows how to take instruction or not, as he chooses. You were clear in every one of your warnings, and he was very clear when he urged you to trust him.

What are you waiting for? How many times do I have to tell you to get out?

She glanced over her shoulder. Brielle stood at the forefront of the group at the door, but when she saw Kathryn looking at her, the worried expression smoothed from her face and Brielle gave her a warm, reassuring smile.

Down in the courtyard, several people had gathered together—Oberon, Annwyn, Gawain, Rowan, Owen, and three other harsh-faced soldiers Kathryn didn't know—while the rest of the party burst into activity, some leading horses away while others raced forward to hug members of the first arrivals.

Oberon, Kathryn said, a sense of urgency tightening her telepathic voice. *We need to talk.*

He stilled, as he had when he absorbed the news of Isabeau's invasion. His gaze met hers over Annwyn's head. They stared at each other, the only two who didn't move, while purpose drove everyone else around them.

Something in his expression and posture looked terribly final. *I'm sorry, Kathryn,* he replied gently. *There's nothing I would love more than to talk with you, but now is not the time. I understand you intend to leave. When you're ready, let Owen know and he will see that you get an escort to the nearest safe crossover passageway.*

I'm still your physician! she snapped.

He shook his head. *That agreement ended the moment Annwyn and her troops arrived. Be sure to leave your bill in my office before you go.*

The pieces of her that had broken hadn't fused back together in the night. Conflict, hurt, and anger compressed them into grinding pain.

That was it? After everything they had shared, *leave your bill in my office* was all he had to say? Oh, she wasn't going to get over that in a hurry. She was going to make him pay for it in a thousand different ways.

He strode past her, surrounded by the core group of senior officers. In that moment he looked every inch the Daoine Sidhe King. Annwyn had moved to the edge of the group and was talking to Owen.

When Kathryn grabbed Annwyn's arm, the other woman started and looked around. Her tight expression warmed into a brief smile. "Dr. Shaw, it is so good to see you safe and well. We were worried when Robin absconded with you. You have the entire demesne's gratitude for the service you have rendered to us. I wish I had time to thank you properly for everything you've done—"

Kathryn interrupted her telepathically, *Forgive me, Annwyn, I understand how urgent matters are right now, but you have to make the time. Oberon is not as robust as he seems.* As the general paused, her eyes narrowing, Kathryn added angrily, *He doesn't want to listen to what I have to say—he's trying to brush me off, but somebody needs to hear it...*

Kathryn, he just discovered we've been invaded and we're at war, Annwyn replied, although her frown deepened, and she didn't move.

Her fingers tightened on Annwyn's arm. *I know things are bad!*

Do you? You've been here for all of a week—I don't think you can possibly realize just how bad they are.

From the palace doors, Oberon said, "Annwyn, I need you right now along with the others."

Annwyn's attention snapped to him. "Yes sir, of course."

Kathryn stood clenched with rage, grief, and deepening fear. Just when she was convinced she had lost Annwyn's attention for good, Annwyn grabbed her wrist and pulled her along as she strode forward.

Stay with me, Annwyn ordered. *And keep your mouth shut.*

If that's what it took to be included and heard by someone in power, she would comply, at least for now. She fell in step with Annwyn's rapid pace as they followed the King's group to yet another area she hadn't explored, a room down the hall from Oberon's office that was large enough to hold up to sixteen people comfortably around a large round table.

Kathryn took in everything at a glance. A large fireplace dominated one end, and paintings of maps hung on the paneled walls. Along another wall, tall cases with cubbyholes stood filled with scrolled parchments. Owen hadn't yet had time to turn his attention to this room. It felt chill and damp, and thick dust covered everything.

Owen stepped back into the hall, past Annwyn and Kathryn as they entered, and he issued a rapid set of orders to various people who had trailed behind. Three leaped into the room. One hurried to check the fireplace, then ran out to return quickly with firewood and light a fire, while the other two hastily wiped everything down with cloths before slipping away again.

Neither Oberon nor the seven council members paid any attention to the servants' ministrations. They gathered around the table while Oberon yanked out a large scroll from one of the cubbyholes to slam it down and spread it out over the table's surface.

From a sideboard, Rowan grabbed iron weights shaped like lions and set them at each of the corners. The scent of adrenaline was strong in the room, and no one sat.

"Report," Oberon said.

While she didn't know everyone in the room, and she didn't know the ones she was acquainted with very well, the scene felt completely familiar. She was no sentinel, but she had witnessed and participated in many council meetings like this before. She took a stand beside Annwyn.

Everyone else hesitated. A few glanced at Kathryn and looked uncomfortable. Others, like Gawain and Rowan, appeared at a loss. Well, they were just going to have to get over that. Crossing her arms, she planted her feet in a sturdy I'm-not-going-anywhere posture.

Annwyn said to the group, "Remember, fifteen years have gone by here, and he doesn't know anything." She looked at Oberon. "Here are the broad strokes. Since you went into stasis, the war has not gone in our favor. By now you must have an inkling of the damage and challenges we've faced here, but it was far worse than floods and bad weather. Remember what happened in that battle by Westmarch, off Old Friar's Lane?"

Oberon rubbed his mouth. "All too well."

"That was just a precursor for what came next. After you went into stasis, Morgan either broke or hid the rest of our crossover passageways under a web of concealment spells so strong we couldn't break through them. We were completely cut off from Earth. Our people in England were hunted and killed until only a few survived. Your puck disappeared—for a long time we thought he had run off, but we found out later that he had been captured by the Light Fae Queen."

"I heard something of what happened to him," Oberon replied. His dark head was bent over the large map on the table. He hadn't yet noticed Kathryn was present. "So, we have lost control over most of our passageways?"

Gawain spoke up. "No, sire. We had lost *all* access to crossover passageways, but the recent summer in England brought about a huge change in our fortune. First, we found a way to use the broken passageway near Westmarch. Then Morgan reopened all the other crossover passageways, and we regained control of them."

Oberon looked up quickly, eyes narrowed. "Why would he do that—give us back control of our own passageways?"

"It turned out the sorcerer had been trapped in a geas for the whole of this war," Gawain told him. "He had never voluntarily worked in the Queen's service. Every act he had committed in her name had been as her slave. A few months ago—at least in England it was a few months ago—we discovered he broke free from the spell. Isabeau was injured severely in some kind of battle. Morgan killed Modred, destroyed one of Isabeau's cities, and either scattered or destroyed most of her Hounds and took the rest with him."

Annwyn took up the rest of the story. "We thought her back was broken. She was hurt and in hiding and had lost much of her fighting force. Her people were scattered and in disarray. We thought it was only a matter of time before we found and killed her." Her expression twisted with bitter self-recrimination. "And I made some of the worst decisions I could have possibly made. I divided our own forces even further—I stationed some to guard each of the four crossover passageways. There are more troops at Raven's Craig as well as quite a few of the evacuees, and I sent out several parties to hunt for Isabeau...."

During the briefing, Kathryn's gaze had never left Oberon. She saw the exact moment he glanced at Annwyn and realized Kathryn was in the group. Something raw whipped across his features like an open wound.

It quickly transformed to anger. He leaned forward and planted both hands on the table as he growled, "What are you still doing here? I already fired you."

"Did you? I have news for you, King." She leaned forward as well, meeting his aggression with a hard stare of her own. "I don't care if you think you've fired me or not, because I don't work for you—Annwyn is the one who hired me, and she wants me here."

"Gods damn it, Kathryn!" he shouted, slamming one fist down so hard the ancient, heavy table cracked. "This is none of your business!"

"It is too my business!" she shouted back. Then she broke another one of the cardinal tenets of her profession without the slightest twinge of regret. "And it's going to be the business of every person in this room when they find out you're not as healed as you look!"

If he had ever been angry at her before—and he had—it was nothing compared to his incandescent fury at that. "My personal medical information is not yours to tell!" he snarled. He strode around the table. "How dare you!"

She decided not to stand meekly and watch him come, so she leaped onto the table, kicked aside the map and weights, and positioned herself in the middle of it. He could reach her if he lunged for her ankle, but she hoped to see him coming in time so that she could leap back to the table's edge from every angle.

"You don't have a clue what I might dare!" He lunged, one arm snaking out, and she hopped back just in time with an angry laugh. "Oh, do you think this is the first time I've ever been in a shouting match? You think Dragos and I have never gone head-to-head before?"

His eyes glowed golden and hot. "I think it's a testament to that dragon's patience that he's never strangled you!"

"He's threatened to." She leaped back again as he made another lunge for her.

Everyone else had jumped back from the table and stared at the confrontation with varying degrees of alarm and consternation.

"What's going on?" Rowan asked quietly.

The unknown soldier beside him whispered, "Ssh."

"What is it going to take to get you out of my life?" Oberon said savagely.

"*Now* you want me gone!" She danced out of his reach again. "You weren't talking that way last night."

"You said you were leaving!" His roar shook the room and cracked the windows. *"How long do you want to stand there and watch me bleed?"*

She stopped dancing out of his reach and whispered, "Oberon, I'm bleeding too."

One of his hard hands clamped around her ankle. His fierce lion's gaze never left her face, as he said, "Everybody, out. We need a few minutes."

Rarely had she seen a room empty so fast. Only Rowan dragged his feet so that he was the last one to exit. When the door shut behind him, Oberon pulled her forward. She didn't fight him. Instead, she let the strength in her legs go and sat down hard on the table's edge.

Once she was down, he didn't attempt to touch her again. Instead, he stood with his hands on his hips, looking down at her silently. A muscle in his jaw jumped spasmodically. Otherwise there was no expression on his hard, set face.

"What you just did was totally inappropriate," he bit out.

"I know." She nodded. Her cheek tickled. When she raised her hand to it, she realized her face was wet. She wiped it with the back of her hand. "I'm not sorry. More of your people have come, and they *all* need you.... Their need is a palpable, physical thing. And events have gotten shockingly shitty—and I see you too, you know. You're ramping up. You're pushing me away, and you intend to be everything they think they need from you. And you have every right to hate Isabeau so much—but you can't engage in combat for three and a half more weeks, or it will very likely kill you."

His lips turned white. "That's none of your business."

"It is!" she shouted. "Because *nobody* needs you more than I do!"

He took in a tight, harsh breath and stepped close enough to grip the table's edge and press his forehead to hers. "You can't need me like that and go home, Kathryn."

"I know." Her throat closed.

It felt like her skin turned inside out, and all her broken pieces were laid bare. A part of her took a step back and watched her shake and cry noiselessly. She couldn't remember the last time she had felt such devastation—not even when she had learned her father had been killed. The grief had been terrible, but it hadn't threatened to destroy her like this did.

His broad shoulders sagged. "You can't tear yourself up like this, love," he whispered. "I wish you didn't have to make such a hard choice, but you do. You have to either stay or go, because I'm not leaving—not even for you, not even for my life, my heart. They gave *everything* for years and years because of their faith in me, and now they have nothing left. If I could walk away from that, I wouldn't be me."

"I know." Her face twisted. "Tell me what want."

"I want you to leave," he said between his teeth. "I want to become a fond memory in your mind of an adventure you'd always wanted to take and you're glad that you had. I want you to go back to New York, recover from this, and thrive for many long years to come." She could hear the lie in every word, but then what he said next rang with truth. "I don't want you to be in danger. I don't want you to be embroiled in this hellish war, or to deal with the kind of struggle we're facing to survive and rebuild. I want you safe so much more than I want you with me, because if you are with me and die, I will never recover from it. It will kill me too."

Pitching forward, she leaned against his chest, pressing her cheek to the bare skin at the opening of his shirt. "Sounds like you have a hard choice too."

Finally, his arms came around her, and the relief was so deep she almost cried again. "Not like yours. Before the surgery I was worried about the man I would become, but I'm not anymore. Morgan's spell numbed me—it didn't change who I was fundamentally. I know who I am and what I have to do. Would I have preferred meeting you during peacetime, so we could have all the time in the world to explore each other and our own feelings? Of course, but you know, kings rarely get the luxury of having all the time in the world."

"Thank you," she told him. "You told me just what I needed to hear."

He stroked her hair. "What was that?"

"You *are* an adventure I've always wanted to take— and I'm so glad I have. But adventures have consequences…. You know, I'm not sure they would be adventures if they didn't. I'm not leaving you," she told him. Inside, she felt the disparate pieces come together again. They weren't aligned the way they had been before, and she no longer felt broken. "Nobody is more surprised about that than me. If the consequence of my adventure means I have to walk away from my old life and build a new one, well then. That will be another adventure, won't it?"

He gripped her by the back of the neck. As she spoke, every line of his big body had gone rigid. "You're staying. You're mine. You're going to be my mate. You can't take that back, Kathryn. I gave you a fair chance to walk away—hell, I practically shoved you away…."

"No hurt feelings here over that," she muttered. "Yes, that was sarcasm."

"What the hell else was I supposed to do?" he snapped.

"I–I don't know, Oberon." She walked her fingers across his chest. "You were trying to be generous and selfless… I think… and I'm sure it wasn't easy for you…"

"*Easy!*" he exploded. "Fuck me, I should think not!"

She loved it when he swore. "…but *be sure to leave your bill in my office before you go?* Really? Why didn't you just kick me in the teeth and be done with it?"

He jerked her head back and stared down at her, jaw locked. His lion's gaze was glowing again. "Is that where you want to go? Let's talk about all the kicks in the teeth you've given me, shall we?"

Lifting both shoulders, she angled her chin and gave him a sidelong smile. "Why don't we get back to talking about how I'm going to stay instead?"

His gaze heated, and he lowered his head. "I've got a better idea," he said against her mouth. "Why don't we stop talking for a few minutes?"

Suddenly her eyelids were too heavy to hold up. "Sounds like an excellent idea to me."

Then he kissed her so hard and deeply she lost all ability to think, much less speak of anything.

✧   ✧   ✧

HE WAS DOING everything wrong. He knew it.

He shouldn't let her stay and get embroiled in the hell that was coming next. That decision was more selfish than anything he had done while under the influence of that damned assassination spell.

By accepting her decision to stay, he was putting her life at risk—and as they continued to deepen their mating bond, by extension, he was adding greater risk to his own.

All that paled in comparison to the fact that she had just chosen to give up her life in New York and stay.

Mine. Mine. Mine. The possessive word beat in his mind to the rhythm of his pulse. He wanted nothing more in that moment than to mark her. His hands shook as he framed her face.

She was giving up more than just her former life—as if that wasn't enough. She was giving up privacy and the freedom to act as an individual without taking the needs of an entire demesne into consideration. She was going to make a fierce, splendid queen.

He muttered against her mouth, "You're never sleeping in the Queen's apartment. Not without me anyway."

An unsteady laugh shook through her. "As crazy as this has been, we're going to have a long time to figure everything out. I do like the idea of having my own space, and I'm not going to give up practicing medicine somehow, but there are more urgent things to think about right now—like how many people are waiting impatiently on the other side of that door for us to get our act together so they can plan a war."

"I know." With an immense effort, he managed to let her go. *Now* had turned into a shining certainty that killed off the hollow rot, but as soon as they opened the door they would let in all other kinds of uncertainties and risks. He told her, "I'm putting a guard on you at all times."

She heaved a sigh but for a wonder didn't argue. "Fine."

He needed to move forward and tackle this fresh hell that Isabeau brought, but he lingered long enough to touch her lips with a finger as he promised, "No matter what else happens, we'll sleep together again tonight."

Her gaze lit. "Yes," she agreed. "No matter what."

It was everything he wanted—the only thing he wanted—and it was far more than he thought he would ever get from her. "Okay then?"

Squaring her shoulders, she gave him a nod.

With that, he strode over to open the door and let the rest of the world back in.

In the hall, the others stood in small clusters, talking in low voices. They turned to face him, and he gestured them in. As they entered, they glanced between him and Kathryn warily. Annwyn and Rowan picked up the map and scattered weights and set them back on the table. This time everyone took a seat except Oberon.

He put a hand on Kathryn's shoulder and stood behind her. How should he begin this? "We have a lot to cover," he said. "Nobody knows that more than I do, but first we should address what just happened. Everybody in this room knows that I successfully transitioned to full Wyr before I had to go into stasis, correct?"

"Yes, sir." This time Malin, one of his generals, answered.

"There are… repercussions to living life as a full Wyr," he told him. "Some of those you may not have considered before now. Kathryn and I have begun to mate, and the Wyr mate for life—but if they are aware of what's happening early enough in the process, they can choose to end it. We've been struggling with that choice, and we've just decided to go ahead and see what we can make of our new lives together. That means Kathryn would be my Queen, but many of you don't know her, or at least don't know her well. So I have to present this to you. Will you accept her? If you won't, I need to abdicate right away so Annwyn can step into place as the rightful ruler of Lyonesse as quickly as possible."

He felt Kathryn stiffen with surprise as he talked. She tried to turn to look at him, but he tightened his fingers, silently urging her to stay put.

Annwyn snorted. "If you think I'm going to step into your shoes after everything I did to get you back, you'd better think again. Your argument was certainly disruptive and uncouth, but other than that, Kathryn is a lovely surprise." She looked at Kathryn. "I don't know whether to offer you congratulations or condolences."

"Hey—Ann," Oberon growled. "I'm standing right here."

"Personally, I'm crushed," Rowan muttered. He winked at Kathryn.

Smiling, Owen spoke up. "While I haven't known you long, I've seen only generosity and kindness from you. I've also been down into the crystal cave, so I have an inkling of how hard you fought to save his majesty's life. And clearly you are strong-minded enough to stand up to him should you find it necessary. We would be blessed to have you come live with us."

"Thank you, Owen," Kathryn murmured. "That means a lot."

"We just got you back," Gawain said to Oberon. "We're not letting you go again. You wouldn't bring anybody into our lives that we can't accept. If you love them, we're going to love them too." His rough expression was severely at odds with his words. "So right now, I think we need to move on to discuss other things. Dr. Shaw, you need to explain just exactly what you meant when you said Oberon is not as healed as he looks."

Chapter Eighteen

"Y OU'RE ABSOLUTELY RIGHT," Kathryn replied. "His health is much more important than whether or not people like me, although…" Covering Oberon's hand on her shoulder, she squeezed his fingers and told him, "…I appreciate everything that's been said. Oberon had to undergo major surgery for me to successfully remove Morgan's needle. That's what Owen was alluding to. He can't do any heavy lifting for one week—four more days. He can resume training *carefully* in two weeks, but he can't go into physical combat for three and a half more weeks. If he takes a hard enough blow to the chest right now, it will very likely kill him."

Dismayed silence greeted her words.

Then Annwyn said heavily, "Then we have to make certain he doesn't take a hard blow to the chest."

"Exactly," Kathryn said. "Thank you. I didn't trust him to tell you, which is why I went against every ethic in my profession and broke doctor-patient confidentiality."

Anger resurged. He snapped, "That was not acceptable, Kathryn."

"I'm not sorry, so there's no point in yelling at me

for it," she told him. She rubbed her face. "But I promise I won't do it again."

"There are other ways to fight than the physical," Oberon reminded their onlookers. "Moving on—our troops are scattered, with some stationed in various places here in Lyonesse and some on assignment in Other lands. And Lyonesse hasn't seen a decent harvest in years. Should I assume food stores are low?"

"You should," Annwyn said grimly. "We've begun to rectify that by transporting in grains and other supplies, but there's more than one problem—some shipments have reached Raven's Craig, but not nearly enough. Then there's the problem of what to do for food here in the city. We're going to get more and more refugees pouring in, and Owen was just telling me that the granaries in the lower city were flooded. The stores there are ruined."

Gawain pinched the bridge of his nose. "Hopefully those flocking here will bring some supplies with them, but how much that might be will be anybody's guess. And it won't be enough, not for anything long term."

Oberon watched Annwyn. "How are we doing on funds?"

"We have investments in England that have done very well recently," she told him. "But, unfortunately, the capital has gotten depleted, especially with a few recent major transactions."

"Don't worry about money right now," Kathryn spoke up unexpectedly. "I have some. There's quite a bit in the family fortune, which I have almost never touched, and I've made a good amount on my own. I own my apartment in Manhattan, which is worth a couple million dollars. I also own another flat in London that's worth at least that much."

Silence fell in the room, and everyone regarded her gravely. Deeply moved by their expressions, Oberon squeezed her shoulder again.

Gawain said softly, "That is extraordinarily generous of you, Doctor."

She shook her head. "I made the choice to stay, and I'm not going to do it halfway. I'm all in with you now."

"And we will be the better for it," Owen told her.

He's right, Oberon told her telepathically. *I couldn't have chosen better if I had sat down and written out a list of requirements for what I would have liked in a mate and a Queen.*

She looked up at him with a gleaming smile.

He cleared his throat. "So—our fighting force is depleted and overextended, we have a population that's already been uprooted and is about to become more so, and the housing here is damaged and inadequate. We have some food, but not enough, and it's in all the wrong places."

Rowan added, "And we only have one puck, who doesn't have the best track record for showing up and following through with tasks."

Oberon nodded. "Now, let's talk about Isabeau." It was growing difficult to discuss the challenges they faced without engaging in physical activity. He let his hand drop from Kathryn's shoulder and prowled around the room. "Annwyn, you said her army was scattered and depleted as well."

"It is. The problem is, she's not here with her army." Annwyn rubbed her face. "Gracelyn, show them what you've got."

One of Oberon's senior captains, Gracelyn stood. Mostly Light Fae, she had a streak of troll in her ancestry, which gave her a height that nearly matched Oberon's, along with gray, heavy features, and a wide, powerful build.

For the first time he noticed she had been gripping a rolled cloth throughout the meeting. She shook it out and threw it on the table. It was a banner from an Elder Races demesne he didn't recognize. He stared at the red-and-black castle. Underneath, the word ARKADIA had been stitched.

"Does anyone know who this is?"

Silence around the table until Kathryn said tentatively, "I think I might. Arkadia is a Light Fae demesne out of Russia." She twisted around in her seat to face Oberon. "I didn't want to tell you some things while you were under Morgan's spell, and I certainly don't want to tell you like this, but I met with Morgan several times in New York before coming here."

"You *what?*" He could barely believe what he was hearing.

She winced. "I knew you wouldn't take it well, not until you'd had a chance to absorb the fact that he had been Isabeau's slave. He was never a willing participant in the things she made him do, but he was part of the focus of your hatred for so long…." She let her voice trail away.

He stared at Annwyn. "Did you know about this?"

With a sour tilt to her mouth, she nodded. "I initiated the meeting. I still want to kill him, but I'm willing to concede that desire may be irrational at this point."

His gaze snapped back to Kathryn. For a terrible moment the old paranoia came back. How could he mate with someone who could withhold such vital information from him? And Morgan's spells were so sophisticated. How could he trust that the sorcerer hadn't unduly influenced Kathryn in some diabolical fashion?

She saw his instinctive withdrawal, and she didn't flinch away from it. "You may have to take a while to digest this information, and that's perfectly okay and normal." The expression in her steady gaze was calm and accepting. "Just don't let your reaction keep you from hearing the rest, okay?"

After a moment's inward struggle, he bit out, "Fine. What else?"

Kathryn continued. "Morgan and a perfectly wonderful musician named Sidonie met when Sidonie was kidnapped and taken to Isabeau as a gift of tribute. They fell in love and started working together to break the geas. Robin was there too, but they didn't tell me much about his role in things. While they were searching for a way to free themselves, there was a Light Fae nobleman named Valentin at Isabeau's court. He was visiting from another demesne called Arkadia and courting Isabeau's hand in marriage. Sidonie ended up killing him when he threatened her with rape. Then Isabeau tried to force Morgan into betraying who had done it." She took a deep breath. "It was clearly a very painful subject for them, so I'm a little sketchy on the details of what happened next, but that crisis created an opportunity for Morgan to break free from the geas."

"Why did they tell you this?"

"Since I had already agreed to come, I think he was trying to warn me about the various players that might be in action in your conflict," she said thoughtfully. "He said he always wondered what would happen when Arkadia discovered one of their own had been killed. He's been hoping it wouldn't bring more trouble for Sidonie—they have a small band of Hounds with them, and the group has been living at high alert since breaking free from Isabeau's control."

"So somehow Isabeau persuaded Arkadia to go to war with her?" Rowan swore. "Why in hells would they do that? We can't catch a fucking break here."

Oberon let out a sigh that turned into a low growl of frustration. "Maybe we'll find out what motivated them, but at this point the whys don't matter. They're here now, and we've got to figure out how to get rid of them. Gracelyn—how did you capture that banner?"

She compressed her lips while unshed tears glittered

in her small eyes. "I was in command of a hundred troops and charged with defending the Tellemaire crossover passageway. We were pretty confident we could hold it. You know what defending a passageway is like."

He did. Crossover passageways were a specific kind of land magic that created narrow pathways from one land to another. To use one successfully, one had to enter at one end and follow the correct path of magic. Walking at a diagonal line *across* a crossover passageway didn't work. You had to walk through it.

In many ways, protecting a passageway was like defending a narrow mountain pass, just without the high physical walls. It took relatively few soldiers to defend a passageway against an invading force.

"Go on," he said.

"They took out the troops I'd stationed on the other side of the passageway, in Wales, but we caught them before they got all the way through, and for a while we did well at holding them back." Gawain gripped her shoulder when her gravelly voice broke. After a moment, she continued, "But it didn't matter how many Arkadians we killed—they kept coming and coming, and the dead kept piling up…. After a while we were fighting on a hill of bodies. Most of my hundred troops died in that passageway. When I realized we weren't going to be able to hold them, I sent riders to Raven's Craig and the other passageways. The last of us held on as long as we could to make sure they got away with the news. The six I brought with me are the last troops from Tellemaire."

Grief and anger—it always came back to those when dealing with Isabeau, he thought. The room was heavy with it when she finished.

After a moment, he cleared his throat. "Were you able to get any idea of how many Arkadian troops they have?"

"There must be thousands," she whispered. "Maybe five thousand? Seven? We were too busy running to get an accurate count."

"Dear gods!" Owen's face blanched.

"She really means to exterminate us this time," Malin said bitterly. "Because there's no way we can hope to hold against an army of that size, not as broken as we've become."

"That's enough," Oberon snapped. "I don't want to hear any of you talking like that again." He stared around the table. Every one of them had arrived exhausted and spent. With calm deliberation, he told them, "You have fought against impossible odds for too long, and it's a major triumph that we can all sit here together again. I'm incredibly grateful that I now get the chance to look you in the eye and tell you how proud I am of what you've accomplished. You are miraculous and heroic, and I'm honored to call you my friends."

Annwyn wiped her face. She was so fierce and strong-minded, he had not seen her tears since they were children. Not until today.

He paused to let his words sink in. Then he said,

"Now, I'm going to order you to do the same thing as the others—go eat and rest. Get your needs met and be prepared to ride at a moment's notice. I'll let you know what my plans are soon enough, so you'd better get at it."

Everyone except Kathryn rose to their feet and obeyed. When the last one left, Oberon closed the door again, leaving him alone with Kathryn.

Leaning back against the door, he smiled at her. She didn't return it. She sat with her chair at an angle from the table, her legs crossed and chin resting on the heel of one hand as she regarded him with that steady, intelligent gaze.

Admiration stirred. She had a spine made of steel. Crossing his arms, he told her, "You can always change your mind again and leave. I guarantee no one would blame you if you did, not even me."

Her eyebrows rose, and a spark of anger snapped across her face. "Fuck. You."

He laughed quietly. His cat was a little confused that he was mating with a bird, but other than that, it was deliriously happy. Living in the now.

She studied him as if he were a strange biological specimen she'd never seen before. "I've never heard a briefing so grim," she remarked. "It was already clear before that Lyonesse is broken. There's no way you can stand against an army of that size."

"No, we can't," he agreed. "Right now, we can't even muster a decent enough guard to protect this city.

Thankfully, the Tellemaire passageway is far enough to the west that we have some time before the Arkadian forces can reach here."

Rubbing her forehead, she studied the map spread on the table. "That gives us… what, maybe three weeks' time to figure something out before they get here?"

"If we wait that long before we take action, they'll be spread all over Lyonesse like a terminal disease," he replied wryly. "I can't let that happen. Besides, three weeks isn't going to give us enough time to fix what's broken here. If I stretch your restrictions…"

She snapped, "I said three and a half weeks, and with good reason. I never said three or less."

He raised one eyebrow at her interruption, but now was not the time to get sidetracked into another argument. "…I said *if,* Kathryn. Then I might theoretically be able to go into battle, but I would still have no army to march against them, so this conflict can't be won by physical means. Are you with me?"

She scowled at him, but said, "Fine. Yes, I am."

"We have only one thing in our favor that Isabeau can't know."

"What's that?"

His teeth felt a little too sharp as his smile widened. "If she has heard anything about my condition, she must believe I'm in a coma, but I'm not. I'm alive, and I'm awake. Arkadian army notwithstanding, I don't believe she would invade if she thought otherwise. She wouldn't dare."

Launching from her chair, she headed around the table and stalked toward him. She said, "You already have a plan."

"Oh, no." He shook head. "I don't have anything nearly as put together, optimistic, or functional as a plan. But I do know what I'm going to do next."

"Which is?"

As she came to stand in front of him, he rubbed her arms. "Something long overdue—I'm going to go talk to my puck."

✧   ✧   ✧

AFTER THOROUGHLY KISSING Kathryn, he made his way out of the palace, and as he heard people nearby he cloaked his presence, so they couldn't distract him from his mission.

Outside the city, he walked along a very old, overgrown path. At one point it seemed to run right over the edge of a cliff. Only when one stood at the very edge of land was it possible to see a series of narrow protrusions—by no means could anyone have called it a *path*—that might allow someone with the grace, nerves, and balance of a mountain goat to climb down to the sea-drenched rocks below.

Oberon had climbed down the cliff with some difficulty before. This time it was easier, now that he had his cat form to assist him. When he had very nearly reached where the sea crashed and foamed against the rocks, what had appeared to be a dark fissure in the side of the cliff became the narrow opening of a damp, brine-scented cave.

He made his way inside. It grew dark, then light again as the fissure delved deep into the land and widened after some distance. The morning sun slanted through dense, tangled vegetation overhead to light the narrow, rocky area below. Mosses, lichen, and stray tufts of grass grew along the sides of the fissure, and a thin trickle of fresh water ran along the floor.

It was a very private place. The only sounds were the distant wind, the echo of surf, the stream's quiet trickle, and the occasional birdcall. To the best of Oberon's knowledge, he and Robin were the only two individuals who knew it existed.

Up ahead, a narrow figure in a coat and blue scarf crouched beside the stream. Oberon felt a tingle of the puck's wild magic. As Oberon picked his way across the uneven ground, Robin looked over his shoulder. For a moment he looked as feral and dangerous as Oberon had ever seen.

Then with a blink, his tense posture softened, and he slipped something into his pocket.

Unhurriedly, Oberon finished the journey and sat on the flat surface of the rock beside him. Looking around, he remarked, "It's been quite some time since you and I have been here together."

"That it has," Robin agreed. His voice was hushed. "Too long."

"I agree." He knew how strong those thin shoulders

were, but now there was a distinct fragility in the way Robin held himself that made his chest ache. Carefully he flattened one hand on Robin's back. "I should have made a point to talk to you before now. I apologize."

"You were busy fighting for your life." Robin's gaze cut to his, then skittered away. "And before the surgery, you weren't very nice about it."

He chuckled with a distinct lack of humor. "No, I wasn't, was I? That needle—it was making me grow numb and cold as it killed me. I could remember having emotions, but I didn't feel them."

Robin looked at him again. "You're different now, warmer. You're like *him* again. Your old self."

He nodded. "Yes. Anyway, I'm sorry I was such an ass when you arrived. I'm glad Kathryn was there to step between us, but mostly I just wish I could take it back. Will you forgive me?"

Robin gave him a quick smile and leaned toward him, not quite enough to come in contact with his body, but enough to let him know there were no hard feelings. "There's nothing to forgive, sire."

Oberon let silence fall. As they sat together, he listened to the calming trickle of water and the distinct *caw caw caw* of a crow flying overhead. Then, very quietly, he said, "While I don't know any details, I heard she hurt you."

Robin made no reply. He looked down at his long, thin fingers, rubbing them together as if they ached.

The puck was no child. He was as ancient as

Oberon, if not more. But sometimes even the oldest and wildest of creatures still needed to be touched and held.

Moving as gently as he knew how, Oberon gathered Robin into his arms. As he did, a hoarse keening sound broke out of Robin. It was the sound of an animal that had been injured beyond its endurance or understanding.

He pulled the puck onto his lap and held him as he sobbed uncontrollably. "If I could take that from you— if I could take it instead of you, I would. I don't want you to ever hurt like that again, and I will do everything in my power to see that you get to live wild and free again, the way you are meant to be."

"The cage is still around me!" Robin wailed. "No matter what I do, it surrounds me wherever I go. *I cannot bear it!*"

He wanted to savage something. The wilder creatures of Lyonesse were some of the things he loved the most.

Holding Robin tighter, he said softly, "It won't always be that way. I swear on my life it won't. We can get help for you if you will only trust me enough to explore the options." Kathryn was familiar with advances in modern medicines. He felt certain she would be able to recommend something. "Can you hang on a while longer? It must have taken incredible strength, but you've gone this far—go with me a little farther, and I'll see that you get home. Maybe you're like I was. Maybe you can't feel it yet, but can you *remember* what home feels like?"

The silence stretched on for too long. Then Robin

gave a tentative nod.

He felt his own eyes grow wet, and he kissed the puck's forehead. "Good job. If you ever feel that memory slipping away, I want you to find me, and I'll remind you of it. All right?"

Robin nodded again. His body felt light and boneless against Oberon's, as if his magic was almost spent.

Oberon could not allow that. Gathering his own Power, he poured it into the puck. It was not quite a healing spell but more like a transference of energy. He had to give quite a bit before he sensed Robin couldn't absorb any more.

When he was done, he told Robin, "I'm so proud of you for surviving everything. I'm proud of how hard you fought…"

"I made so many mistakes," Robin muttered.

He continued without missing a beat. "And I'm proud of all the mistakes you've made because you cared enough to try. You are important to me, and I value you now more than ever. If you feel like you can't do more, I will understand and support you. I want you to know it is all right, Robin, and I will love you just the same." He took a deep breath. "But if you can do a bit more, I need your help."

"Aye." Robin sighed. "I expected there would be more to do. How many troops do you need me to transport?"

"There won't be any troops," Oberon said.

The puck pushed out of his lap to whirl and crouch

at his knees, staring up at him wide-eyed. "What do you mean?"

Oberon told him what he had said to Kathryn. "We can't win in a physical battle against the army Isabeau has brought with her, so we will have to win with a magical one. Robin, the only person I want you to transport is me. Will you carry me to Isabeau and her army, so we can drive them out of Lyonesse if we possibly can?"

A smile broke over Robin's narrow face, as bright and keen as his earlier pain had been black and bleak. Oberon recognized the expression. It was the look of a hungry predator who had been forced to wait for far too long to taste his prey.

"It has always been my highest honor to carry you," Robin said, "I will always take you wherever you need to go."

"Excellent," he said fiercely. "We're not going to make an announcement. That would open the door for people to argue and create delays." He paused, thinking. "I do have to tell Kathryn, but other than that, we're simply going to leave. Meet me in the palace gardens in an hour. And for the gods' sake, eat something before you get there. You're nothing but skin and bones, and you've got a long road ahead."

"Aye, sir," Robin said with a vicious, anticipatory smile. "That I do."

Oberon clapped him on the shoulder and stood. As he made his way out of the cave, he started thinking about how to have an extremely difficult talk with

Kathryn.

He knew in his bones she was going to resist everything he had to say—and he wouldn't blame her, especially after what they'd just committed to. If she ever tried to come to him with this kind of plan, he would lose control.

It was only when he was almost back to the palace that he realized he had forgotten to ask Robin about Morgan's thrice-damned needle.

Chapter Nineteen

THE SOUNDS OF conversation and cutlery against dishes came from the dining hall as Kathryn made her way to the kitchen.

She thought to grab something to eat quietly in the rooms she had appropriated for herself, but once in the kitchen, she realized it had become a major hub of activity. It was filled with the roar of heat, the scent of cooking food, and a crew of busy people working on a variety of tasks. She looked around for Brielle but didn't see her.

"Dr. Shaw!" Isla rushed up, beaming.

"How are you doing, Isla?" She took the other woman's outstretched hands for a brief squeeze.

"Very well, and it's all because of you. I have some aches, but they're easy to manage now that I know they aren't an injury that would get worse if I ignored it. Thank you for everything you did."

"You are quite welcome." She backed out of the way as a male pushed by carrying a large tray of filled dishes. "I just came to grab a quick bite of something—I don't mean to get in the way."

Isla wiped her hands on a cloth. "Go find a seat in the dining hall. I'll bring you a nice hot plate of food."

"If you're sure you don't mind…."

The other woman snorted. "It's the least I can do! Go on with you now."

"Thank you." With an inward shrug, she went with the change in plan and walked into the dining hall.

As soon as she stepped inside, Brielle and Owen, who were sitting together and talking over empty plates, saw her. Immediately they stood. At first she thought they meant to walk over or to make some other welcoming gesture.

Instead, they began to clap. Kathryn watched a wave wash over the hall as other people turned, noticed what was happening, and stood to join in with their own applause.

Well, goodness. That wasn't awkward or embarrassing at all. Stopping in her tracks, she felt an uncharacteristic blush heat her face.

Brielle hurried over. "Your grace, if you would be so kind, would you care to sit with Owen and me?"

Your grace? Word had begun to spread of her and Oberon's decision. That wasn't awkward either, was it?

"Thank you," Kathryn told her. "That would be delightful. Only, please stop clapping at me."

"We are all so grateful for what you've accomplished," Brielle told her. "You saved his majesty's life. We owe you everything." She lowered her voice. "And I went with Owen into that cave. It's cleaned up now, but we saw what was down there. You must allow us our excess of sentimentality on this subject."

She exhaled a quiet laugh. "Put like that, I suppose I'll survive."

"Do you need breakfast?"

"Isla's bringing me something."

"Very good."

Sitting with Owen and Brielle, she visited with them as if imminent doom wasn't hanging over all their heads. Isla brought her a cup of hot tea, a bowl of porridge, and a plate with cheese and dried fruit.

She would have much preferred meat or fish, but what with the impending food crisis, she wasn't sure she would be getting any without hunting for it herself. By far, most of a peregrine falcon's prey was made up of other birds, but she could also eat other small prey like reptiles and mice.

She could hunt rabbit and squirrel, but they were a little large for her and weren't her preferred prey, and none of those would go very far to helping stretch the kitchen's resources. The most powerful way she could help was by buying food to transport in... and that would take precious time they didn't have. Stifling an inward sigh, she thanked the other woman and dug in.

Soon Owen and Brielle left to resume their work, and she enjoyed a few moments of solitude while she drank her tea.

Then Rowan slid onto the bench opposite her, leaned one elbow on the table, put his chin in his hand,

and smiled at her. As immune as she was to his charms, getting hit point-blank with those wicked eyes and that smile was quite an experience.

"Tell me," he said, "what's it like to fall in love so quickly?"

She shook her head. "That's a common misconception about Wyr mating. We don't have to fall in love to mate, and we can fall in love without mating. They are two separate things—although when we're very lucky, we can sometimes get the complete package. Not every Wyr who mates gets that."

He frowned. "All right…. What is it like to mate so quickly?"

She shrugged, at a loss. After a moment of searching for the right words, she replied, "It's meeting a stranger and then getting shocked by how quickly you can grow to need someone you barely know and don't know if you can trust. Oberon and I are discovering that we need each other in our lives. We need each other sexually. It's a driving, overwhelming force that is possessive, intensely uncomfortable, irrational, and quite often dangerous."

Her frank reply had shocked him, she saw, as his eyes widened. Quietly, he asked, "Should we be worried about him?"

She had to pause again as she considered how to answer that. "You should adjust your expectations of him," she said finally. "At some point I will become more important to him than Lyonesse. He may hate it, and he may struggle against it, and it may poison him with resentment toward me if we're not careful—but if we don't change our minds and break things off, it's still going to happen."

In that moment, even though Rowan's expression never flickered, a sudden flash of intuition told her she was in danger. She knew that behind his charming, handsome façade, he was weighing the potential advantages to killing her.

She could see the reasoning perfectly. The opportunity to mate was a rare, precious thing, and it would be the cruelest thing he could ever do to Oberon, but from his point of view it might possibly be the best thing he could do for Lyonesse.

Killing her would also destroy a centuries-long relationship that must matter to him very much, and she had no doubt it would cost him his life.

She admired that. It took a special kind of dedication to his country to face all that unflinchingly. Rowan had a lot more going for him than a pair of sinful rock-star eyes.

Pushing her empty teacup to one side, she leaned her elbows on the table. *Thankfully,* she said telepathically, *I have no intention of doing anything that would poison my relationship with my new mate. Mates are unbelievable treasures to the Wyr. Not everyone gets the chance to have such a blessing— which is why I've chosen to give up a full, enjoyable life in New York to stay here and why I'm risking my own life to do so, because you guys are in really bad shape right now. Luckily for you, I have a lot of money and some useful skills to bring to the table.*

Slowly he replied, *You have courage too, I'll give you that.* He gave her a sudden grin. *Have you and Dragos really gone head-to-head?*

With that, she knew the danger had passed. Throwing up her hands, she exclaimed out loud, "*YES!* He makes me crazy!"

Rowan's face creased with vivid amusement.

In that moment, she sensed Oberon striding into the hall and turned to look for him. He didn't bother trying to thread his way toward her. Instead, he held up a hand. "Kathryn, I need a word with you."

"Of course." She double-tapped the table in front of Rowan as she stood. "Good talk."

"Catch you later." He gave her a warm smile.

In the ninety or so seconds it took her to cross the hall, five people approached Oberon. She watched as he dealt with each of them patiently, and it was so unlike the cold asshole she had met she had to smile to herself.

"Ah, there you are," he said as she joined him. He curled a hand under her elbow and told the others, "You must excuse us now. Talk to Owen or Annwyn if you need anything."

Turning, he strode rapidly down the halls. His stride was much longer than hers, so she had to trot to keep up. She didn't mind—it got them to a private space quicker.

He took her outside and along a garden path to a

good-sized clearing, out of sight from any of the palace windows. Then he turned to face her. His face was set.

Uh-oh, she thought. She braced herself.

"I want your word that you will keep this confidential until it doesn't matter anymore," he said.

"Ouch," she muttered with a wince. "But I deserve that. You have my word."

He relaxed slightly. "Thank you."

"You've made a decision about what to do, haven't you?" Even as she said it, she realized she didn't know how to brace herself for what came next. Nothing short of drastic measures was going to turn the tide of that invading army.

"I have. Robin and I will be leaving in a few minutes." He took a breath. "We're going by ourselves. I plan on departing without talking to any of the others, but I wouldn't do that to you. I had to tell you."

For a moment she couldn't believe what she had heard. Then the detonation that went off inside was so nuclear she was surprised it didn't flatten everything in the clearing.

There wasn't anything she could say, shout, or scream that would properly communicate the immensity of that internal explosion. Shaking her head, she said in a flat voice, "No."

Then it was Oberon's turn to look like he couldn't quite believe what he had just heard. Cocking his head, he repeated incredulously, "*No?* Are you trying to *forbid* me?"

"Correct," she bit out. "I assume you have some sort of plan or intention. It doesn't matter. I forbid you to do this."

He barked out an angry laugh. "I never gave you that right. Nobody has the right to forbid me anything."

"Well, you selfish bastard, I never gave you the right to make unilateral decisions while you're mating with me," she whispered. "I'm giving up *everything* for you. *Everything.* I did not ask you to do the same, and I did not do it, just so I could watch you ride off on some lone, heroic mission without decent backup. At the very least you should be taking Annwyn, Rowan, and Gawain with you. And there is *no way in hell* you're doing it without me."

He sliced a hand through the air. "They're all exhausted, damn it! If I asked them to go, they would—of course they would—but more likely than not they would get themselves killed. And Robin is exhausted too! The less he has to transport, the faster and farther he can go."

The major muscles in her thighs tightened as she remembered the wild ride that was faster than she could fly. Tapping a foot, she raised her eyebrows and pointed at herself. "I'm not exhausted, and I'm standing right here."

"Kathryn." Striding over rapidly, he grabbed her shoulders. *"No."*

"Why not?" she snapped, knocking his hands away. "Do you think you get to have it all your way? You don't want to have to give anything up—and you're the one who gets to take all the risks?" She watched his face tighten as if he was holding in his own inner explosion. She forced out the next words. "If that's who you really are, I am not your kind of mate. You gave me an ultimatum. I had to stay or go, because you weren't going to leave here. Fine, but now here's *your* ultimatum—you adapt right now and accept me as your full fucking partner in every fucking thing, or I'm leaving without a second look back. Don't think I won't this time, and I promise you it won't even be hard."

It would, of course. It would be wrenching and awful, and many other kinds of hell, but she knew she could do it, because she couldn't live with the alternative, and she made sure he could see that in her hard stare.

"*Goddammit*," he swore, running his hands through his hair. "You have so many gifts, but you are not suited for this battle!"

"Don't give me that bullshit," she snapped. "As a trauma surgeon, I am *uniquely* suited for this or any other kind of battle situation. I'm also fast, small, capable of attaining great heights, and I have exceptional vision. My hearing is pretty awesome too, by the way. Need an aerial scout? You're looking at one. You're just resisting because you don't want me to go. You want me waiting here in safety until you get back. That is a reality *I will not accept, do you hear me? I cannot do it—I cannot watch you go off and know that you might get yourself killed without me. That's never going to be livable. I'm never going agree to that kind of mate, and I WILL NEVER FORGIVE YOU IF YOU GO WITHOUT ME ANYWAY."*

By the time she reached the end of her rant, she was screaming at him. A part of her stood back and watched in astonishment. She had never lost her shit so badly before. She sounded like a crazy woman.

His face had whitened, his eyes stark. "Stop. Kathryn, stop." When he tried to reach for her again, she slapped his hands away, but then he snatched at her anyway and wrapped her in a tight clench. "I'm sorry. I'm sorry."

"You can go fuck yourself with all your sorries," she snarled. She was shaking again as badly as she had in the council room.

"All right, damn it," he said, gripping her by the back of the neck. He stared down into her eyes, fierce gaze golden hot. "I'll adapt. Do you hear me? I'll hate it passionately, but I will still do it."

"There's no room for misunderstanding right now." Digging the heels of her hands into her eyes, she gritted, "I need to you spell it out."

He swore again, then said more quietly, "I will never willingly take on a risk without either your presence or your approval. I promise you, this will be a complete and full partnership in every way. I don't know how to do that—I've been a ruler for a long time, but I've never had a life partner, and neither of us have had any time to adjust to this—so I'm going to make mistakes, and I'm sure you will too. But I promise you it will happen. All right?"

She looked down and to one side as she listened. Nodding, she whispered, "I'm sorry I screamed at you like that." Then she paused to think about that. "That's not true. I'm not sorry I screamed at you. I'm just shocked I did. I've been in some righteous shouting matches before, but I've never lost it so completely."

His arms tightened. "I apologize for pushing you to it. Kathryn, I do not want you to come with us. I really, really don't. I ask most urgently that you reconsider and stay home."

She took in a shaky breath. "Complaining is acceptable."

"You're still coming, aren't you?"

"Do you still want me for your mate?"

"Yes." His eyes burned. There wasn't a hint of hesitation.

She told him, "Then from here on out, if you ever feel the need to ask that question again, you can henceforth answer it yourself with *oh hell yeah*."

"Henceforth?" His expression was bleak with resignation, but at that he raised one eyebrow.

"Yes." She tried to remember when henceforth was in common use, but her mind was still a little fried from her meltdown. "Did I use that word correctly?"

He burst out laughing. "Who cares?"

She watched him laugh. She couldn't bring herself to smile yet. "We're both paying a steep personal price for this, you know."

He framed her face in his hands. The lion looked out of his eyes. "I've seen a strength and a fineness in you that sets you apart from any other woman I've ever known. You are worth any price. You are worth more than my kingdom or my pride. You are worth my life."

So what she had described to Rowan had already happened. Closing her eyes, she felt something deep and essential settle into place. It felt good, like coming home.

Like that red silk cloak settling around her, bringing softness, comfort, and warmth.

She told him, "You are worth my life too. When do we leave?"

"Any moment now. As soon as Robin arrives."

"Then I'd better hurry." She pulled out of his arms.

"What are you doing?"

"I'm going to grab my physician's kit." She met his gaze. "Hopefully we won't need it, but I don't make travel plans like this based on hope. I'll be right back."

He nodded. "I'll wait here."

She hesitated. For one awful moment she wondered, will he still be in the garden when I return?

He saw it, and his expression gentled. "I made you a promise, and I will always keep it. I will be here when you get back. Or would you feel better if I came with you?"

She could hear the truth in his voice, and that helped. She gave him a small smile. "No, it's okay."

Leaving him, she slipped inside and jogged through the palace. Decades of working in a large hospital had taught her the fine art of moving through a place filled with a lot of inhabitants. If she bolted, others would assume there was an emergency and follow. If she walked too slowly, people would try to talk to her. But a brisk, steady jog not only meant business. It also kept everybody else at arm's length.

Back in the room, she tore through her pack of essentials. She discarded most of the clothes, only keeping a clean set of underwear and her toiletries kit. She needed lightness for speed, but this suicidal mission, scouting expedition, magical showdown, last-ditch stand, whatever you wanted to call this... whatever it ended up being... might take days.

Physician's kit. Underwear. Toothbrush and tooth powder. What else?

The last things she grabbed were the bag of nuts and the bag of dried fruit she had stashed in her room for late-night snacks. Personally, if she never saw another pecan or dried peach slice again, it would be too soon for her, but in an emergency, calories were calories.

Her pack was much lighter and smaller by the time she was through. She slung it onto her back, then took off jogging through the palace again. Slipping out the first door she found, she wound her way around to the clearing.

Oberon stood talking to Robin. The puck's nut-brown hair spiked even more than ever, as if he had run his many fingers through it repeatedly, and the adoration in his body language was palpable as he looked up at

Oberon's much larger frame.

Oberon clearly meant the world to him. How would Robin accept her, now that she and Oberon were mating?

She found out a moment later when they noticed her arrival. Robin gave her a sweet smile, his feral gaze lighting with welcome. She asked gravely, "Robin, will you agree to carry me again?"

A surge of wild magic filled the clearing as Robin changed and expanded rapidly until the massive black stallion appeared.

Stamping one giant hoof, the puck nodded. Lightning flashed in his large dark eyes as he replied, "I consent."

He was so beautiful. She reached out to touch his soft nose, and he allowed it. "Thank you."

"We must go." Oberon started to hold out his hands.

He meant to offer to help her mount, but with a leap, she landed astride on the stallion's broad back. The trick was much easier to do when she wasn't wearing layers of winter clothing.

He raised an eyebrow, and she laughed down at him silently. Yes, she was showing off, but she was also making a point.

Full partners.

He sprang from a standstill and landed on the stallion's back behind her. Okay, that was much more impressive than her own leap. He was over twice her body weight. She laughed harder as he hooked an arm around her waist and settled her firmly back against him, and she remembered to gather a couple of handfuls of the stallion's mane just in time.

"Go," Oberon said.

The stallion's broad, powerful body bunched. He sprang forward, and the rest of the world fell away.

FOR OBERON, RIDING Robin again felt like another homecoming.

He savored the wild rush of wind, Robin's ability to reach amazing speeds, and the incredible sense of freedom in leaving the city where he had been trapped for so long.

But mostly he savored Kathryn's lithe body flexing with the rhythm of the stallion's stride and held her back against him as they rode.

They moved too fast for intelligible speech. She exclaimed telepathically, *I love this as much as I did the first time! Riding Robin is the only time I haven't gotten impatient with being on horseback!*

Laughing, he tightened his arm in acknowledgment. He might have known they would have that in common.

As the rolling hills and plains scrolled by, impossibly fast, he began to do some calculations. In a march, cavalry could go roughly thirty to thirty-five miles a day, but infantry could only go for twenty to twenty-five miles, and those estimates were in ideal conditions. After a days-long battle at Tellemaire, they had probably camped just inside the passageway for at least a day to recover.

Gracelyn and her soldiers had met up with Annwyn and her party on their way to the city. Roughly, that would have taken Gracelyn's party three days of hard riding from Tellemaire. Then Robin had transported them the rest of the way.

That meant Isabeau and the Arkadians had been in Lyonesse for about four days. Give them a day for recovery and for possibly sending their injured back through the passageway, and that whittled their time down to three days, which meant they could be anywhere from sixty to a hundred miles from the Tellemaire passageway, but in which direction?

They would have stationed troops to guard Tellemaire so they would retain control of the passageway. Lyonesse had dozens of townships, settlements, and smaller cities, forests, lakes, and mountains, and an abundance of lush farmland and prairie, but they had only one city of any great size. And Isabeau wasn't known for great stretches of imagination.

She believed he was in a coma. From her spy network, she probably knew he was not yet dead. Finishing the job and killing Oberon once and for all would absolutely be her first priority. She would want the satisfaction of crushing the city once and for all, and then she could take her time destroying the rest of the demesne.

Sire, where do you want to go? Robin asked.

Head straight for Tellemaire, Oberon told him. *We're going to run right into them.*

The rest of the day melted away. Late in the evening, they stopped to drink at a quick-moving stream that was swollen from the mountain runoff. The icy water was refreshing. When they first stopped, Robin was blowing hard, his gleaming black flanks flecked with white foam. He had to walk awhile before he was able to drink.

When the puck finally joined Kathryn and Oberon at the stream, Oberon laid a hand on his burly shoulder and gave him more strength. The stallion's dark gaze rolled to him in brief thanks. While they waited for Robin to refresh himself, Kathryn pulled out bags of nuts and fruit and offered them to Oberon.

Oberon ate two handfuls quickly. She didn't eat any, he noticed, but she offered handfuls of the food to Robin, who inhaled everything she stuck under his nose. She looked at Oberon with a frown.

"What do you think about camping for the night?" she suggested. "We could move on in the morning after we've slept?"

"No." Oberon and Robin spoke at once.

They looked at each other. Oberon could see that the puck was in complete accord with him. Stopping for the night would certainly be the rational thing to do but knowing Isabeau was in his land was simply intolerable.

"We'll press on," Oberon said. "Once we've had a chance to scout their army and gather some intelligence, we'll decide what to do then." A thought struck him.

"Unless you need to stop?"

"Nope. I'm good for days of this," Kathryn said with a grin. She crooned at the stallion, "I would let you take me just about anywhere, you beautiful thing."

The stallion's eyes went very wide. Then he snorted, and with a toss of his mane, he nudged Kathryn so hard he almost knocked her to the ground. Laughing, she recovered her balance and kissed his nose. It was very good to see them being playful with each other.

You were right, Oberon said to her telepathically. When she turned to look at him inquiringly, he told her, *He is still very hurt. We need to find ways to help him.*

She looked saddened but unsurprised. *He's probably suffering from something called post-traumatic stress disorder. It's when someone has difficulty recovering from a traumatic event, or series of events. It can cause terrible problems for the victim.*

He said he's still in the cage.

Her gaze darkened with compassion. *His captivity ended only a short time ago. Surgery is my forte, but I know quite a bit about dealing with other forms of trauma since they often go together. With your permission, I'd like to try talking to him.*

His concern eased somewhat. *I was hoping you might have some idea on how we can help.*

She nodded and gave him an encouraging smile as she leaned against Robin's shoulder and stroked his mane. Lipping at the trailing ties of her hiking boots, the puck allowed the petting. She told Oberon, *I'll know better what we can do after I've had a chance to evaluate him.*

Listen to them, planning for a normal life as if the

three of them confronting an army of thousands wasn't the height of insanity.

He gave them a hard, quick grin. "Ready to move on?"

"Absolutely," Kathryn said.

Mounting, they continued their breakneck ride.

In the early hours of the morning, when the air had turned damp and chill and the moon lay wreathed in a film of white, Oberon caught the scent of horses, Fae, and campfires, and he signaled for Robin to slow.

He knew this area very well, and he could picture exactly where the Arkadian army had camped. They were in a wide, shallow basin of land, taking advantage of a river that ribboned through it. The basin was bordered on the north and east by higher ground.

He nudged the stallion to the north, and without further instruction, Robin carried them up a steep incline to a broad bluff. Once there, Oberon dismounted, and Kathryn followed suit. With a moonlit shimmer, the stallion disappeared, and Robin's human form took its place.

Moving very quietly, Oberon led the way to the bluff's edge. When he came close, he crouched down, and the other two followed and did the same.

From that vantage point, they looked out over the lower land. The Arkadian army spread out in front of them, filling the entire basin.

Now what? Kathryn asked telepathically.

Now we need to find where Isabeau is in all that, Oberon

told her. *Along with whoever their commander is.*

She cocked her head. In the moon's shadowed glow, her eyes looked bright and as alert as they had that morning. *I think this might be where I come in.*

He clenched his fists. *I hate you getting involved in this. Absolutely fucking hate it.*

But it must also be said, even if it was only to himself, that he loved having her with him.

Duly noted and complaint accepted. She touched his hand. *Relax a little.*

Kathryn, there is no relaxing, he snapped. *She's an accomplished sorceress in her own right. The Light Fae's hearing is very acute, and who knows how many other magic users they have in camp—possibly its commander is one as well.*

Well, she replied, *just as they don't know that you're awake, they also don't know about me, and there's nothing more natural-feeling than a Wyr in her animal form.*

He put an arm around her shoulders and pulled her close so that he could kiss her forehead. *Your Power is light and strong, like tempered steel, and feels nothing like a mundane peregrine falcon.*

I'll cloak myself, she assured him. *Dragos has always insisted the avian Wyr in his court learn how to cloak themselves well. It will be all right.*

Gritting his teeth, he said the hardest single word he had ever said in his life. *Okay.*

Shrugging off her pack, she handed it to Robin and whispered, "Don't lose track of that. My physician's kit is in there."

Oberon noticed for the first time that Robin looked pale and a little sick. Swallowing hard, Robin whispered back, "I won't."

Giving them a grin, Kathryn shapeshifted, and a sleek falcon perched on the ground in front of them. Then with a beat of her wings, she lifted into the air and arrowed overhead.

She was completely fearless. She didn't have nerves of steel, Oberon decided. She didn't have any nerves at all.

Thoughtfully he noticed that talons had sprung out on both his hands.

Robin noticed and touched his arm. Then, with a simple economy that Oberon wished he could emulate, the puck curled into a tight ball around Kathryn's pack on the ground at his feet and fell fast asleep.

Left to watch out for Kathryn on his own, Oberon settled down for what would be an undefined period of time filled with the blackest kind of hell.

Chapter Twenty

F OR SEVERAL MINUTES, Kathryn cloaked her Power and flew for the sheer joy of it. She let the falcon's instincts take over and simply did what a falcon wanted to do. For one thing, she was hungry, so she hunted for something like a prairie mouse for supper.

For another thing, by acting out what was in her nature she would appear entirely natural to any sharp-eyed Arkadian guard who might happen to notice her. After catching and eating a light meal, she took a few passes over the army to study the formation of their camp.

If she were an army with its very own queen-in-residence, she would want that queen right in the middle of all the fighters for maximum protection…. There.

She found a couple of tents that were much more spacious than those around them. They also had extra guards and campfires, and when you saw the configuration from the air, it couldn't be more obvious than if a giant X had been painted on the tent tops.

She opened her talons, mimicking the act of letting go of a bomb. *Boom.* That's how easy it would be if they were doing this on Earth, where technology worked.

But they weren't on Earth. They had to do this the Lyonesse way.

Using her long-range eyesight to her best advantage, she took another pass over the army from a great height and made note of every guard and campfire. Not all the guards were stationed by campfires, and not all the guards were in the bulk of the army camp—there were perimeter sentries at watch in silent darkness in various positions outside the camp.

Sensible of their commander, and good to know.

Was that enough information to start with, or did she dare try to get closer? She ran a quick risk-assessment calculation. It was the early hours of the morning, well before dawn. This was the time when most of them would be asleep.

Plus, the Arkadian army had completely crushed Gracelyn's force. They believed they had no immediate threats to be concerned with. More likely than not, Isabeau and other commanding officers were asleep, so there wouldn't be much gain to weigh against any possible risk of discovery.

Right now, there wasn't any point in doing any more reconnaissance, so she flew back to Oberon and Robin on the bluff. Swooping down, she landed and shapeshifted a few feet from Oberon's crouching figure.

He snatched at her, gripping her so tightly against his tense body she grunted against the pressure. He snarled, *What took you so long?!*

Ease up, she coughed. *You wanted me to do a thorough job, didn't you?*

Gods damn, woman! I just aged a thousand years. He sucked in a harsh breath.

They had awakened Robin, who pushed to a sitting position and rubbed the sleep out of his eyes. He started to whisper, "Has so—"

They had not been discovered yet, but they had been lucky—some of those sentries were stationed closer than they had realized. Kathryn touched Robin's lips with her forefinger, and he stopped.

Telepathy was an intimate form of one-on-one communication, but it turned awkward when there were more than two people who needed to be in on the conversation. She told first Oberon and then Robin about the location of the perimeter sentries closest to them.

Robin's gaze flashed to Oberon, and Oberon nodded. She didn't need to hear what they said to each other to understand that exchange. Moving soundlessly, Robin handed her pack back to her and melted into the shadows.

Oberon told Kathryn, *He'll be back when he's finished.*

A shiver ran down her spine. She had been a predator all her life, but some things were just creepy. Quickly she told Oberon the rest of what she had discovered—the layout of the camp, the large tents positioned in the middle, and where the other perimeter sentries were located.

After finding a sharp, oblong stone, she used it to sketch a rough map on a rocky patch of dirt, trusting Oberon's own catlike vision to see it in the dim moonlight. If she had pencil and paper, she could get more detailed, but she hadn't thought to grab those when she had weeded out the nonessentials in her pack.

After she told him the exact number of sentries that appeared to be active around the various campfires and she began to describe exactly where each campfire was, he started to shudder. She realized he was laughing quietly.

What? she asked, blinking at him in confusion.

I've never been given such a thorough and detailed report from an advance scout before, he told her. *Thank you. This is very useful.*

She felt disgruntled, as if he had rubbed her feathers the wrong way, but she replied, *You're welcome. I wanted to get closer, but I didn't think it was worth it until we had a chance to talk things over. Now what?*

Now we wait for Robin to return, he said. *I want to know we have a clear stretch around us for some distance so we don't face a surprise attack too quickly.* He rubbed her back. *How are you doing?*

She bit back a smile. She'd been enjoying herself so far, but she had no doubt that was going to change. *I'm good,* she told him. *I caught a small bite for supper.*

I saw your dive. It was pure poetry. She heard his smile in his telepathic voice. *I can't wait to see you hunt during the day.*

She couldn't wait to see him either. His animal form

was as big as a horse—he would be utterly mesmerizing and terrifying. Leaning against his side, she told him, *We'll have to go camping as soon as we can.*

Yes. Putting an arm around her, he rested his lips against the side of her head, and they fell silent as they waited for Robin's return.

Relaxing into his warmth, she let herself doze and woke only when he tightened his arm. Shaking herself alert, she looked around for Robin.

Movement low to the ground caught her eye. A king cobra snake was sliding out of the nearby underbrush. A single bite from a king cobra wouldn't kill any of the larger Wyr, but several bites would—and a single bite would probably kill her. She had no doubt it would also be quite lethal to the Light Fae.

Her heart kicked hard even as she realized Oberon's body remained relaxed. Meanwhile, the snake kept coming and coming…. It had to be at least eighteen feet in length, and she couldn't relax until the cobra transformed into Robin.

"Holy crap," she whispered. Her heart was still pounding. "I just realized I don't know anything about the poisonous creatures native to Lyonesse."

"We will have to teach you many things." Robin didn't bother to lower his voice as he came close to squat in front of them. "They're gone."

"Well done." Oberon stood, and she did as well. "Did you find a suitable shelter nearby?"

Robin nodded. Turning, he pointed east where the

land rose from the basin in sharp, jagged spikes of rock. "There is a cave over to the right of that white oak tree, hidden under a granite ledge. It's very shallow—at most it's four and half feet deep and perhaps three and a half high, but that should be enough."

"And the granite ledge is solid?" Oberon asked.

Before she could query why that was important, Robin replied, "Yes, sire."

"Excellent." Oberon swung around to stand in front of her. His face was in deep shadow, but what she could see of his features set her heart to pounding again in long, hard strokes. Laying a palm to her cheek, he said, "I really, really wish you had stayed back in the city."

Complaining was one thing, but now he was beginning to scare her. She gripped his wrist. "Why? What happens now?"

"Dawn is still an hour away. They're confident and relaxed, and there's no better time to attack. Very shortly, it's going to get too dangerous for you to be out in the open. You need to take shelter in the cave Robin found. As soon as you can fly again, I need you to scout for Isabeau's exact location. It would also be very helpful if you can identify and locate the Arkadian commander, but *Isabeau* is the one who has nursed an obsession with destroying the Daoine Sidhe for centuries—she's the one we really need to eliminate. If we cut off the head of that snake, the rest of it will die eventually."

Then Robin added with an almost languid smile, "Remember, no matter what you see, Doctor, take very great care now. Even if we kill the Light Fae Queen, don't relax your guard—severed snake heads can bite up to an hour after decapitation."

Great Scott, that was creepier than ever. She shuddered as her mind raced over everything. It was clear Robin and Oberon knew exactly what they intended to do. She wanted to protest every fucking thing about it, without even knowing what was going to happen next. She wanted to ask, Why can't I stay with you?

But Oberon had already made that clear. While he hadn't wanted her here, now that she was, he needed her to find Isabeau while he and Robin concentrated on their fight.

And full partners had to learn when to let go and trust the other to do their part.

"Okay," she said when she was sure she could keep her voice steady. "You got it."

He hauled her against his chest and gave her a searing kiss. Before she had time to wind her arms around his neck, he shoved her away again. "Go. *Hurry.*"

From the ruthless set of his features, she saw they had reached a point of no return. As she retreated a few steps, Robin shapeshifted into the stallion again, and Oberon swung onto his back.

Standing a few feet away, she saw them together for the first time, and she realized how the stallion's massive size was a perfect match for Oberon's broad, muscular frame. In profile, they looked seamless and ancient in the moon's subtle light, and her skin prickled with the sense of an oncoming storm.

No wonder Isabeau had been so intent on capturing the Daoine Sidhe King's mount and breaking them apart...

Oberon had already told her to hurry. Whirling, she shapeshifted into the falcon and flew to the granite ledge by the white oak tree. But instead of crawling into the shallow cave, she perched on the ledge to watch what happened next.

Oberon and Robin hadn't moved. They stood like a statue carved from obsidian. When would they start the attack?

In sharp contrast to what had been a comfortably mild night, a cold wind blew. The gust grew stronger, and the filmy, pale moonlight darkened. Looking up, she saw a towering bank of black clouds rolling over the wide bowl of the sky.

Frowning, she fluffed out her feathers for added warmth. It would be the height of inconvenience if she had left her winter coat behind only to find she needed it after all.

Within minutes, the cloud bank had taken over most of the stars, and the wind increased to a howl. As the first driving pellets of rain fell, she felt a tingle of Oberon's distinctive magic, and, feeling rather foolish, she realized his attack had already begun.

Lightning tore the sky apart, followed almost immediately by a crash of thunder so huge she felt it reverberate in her body. With a sizzling pop, more lightning struck the ground…

…and another.

Only this strike hit in the army encampment sprawled below.

And then another strike hit. Holy shit. After a few moments, she couldn't distinguish between the peals of thunder. It was all one rolling drumbeat of cosmic destruction.

She was too far away to hear screaming, but she could see the flare-up of fires just fine. Multiple lightning strikes kept hitting the basin—they lit the scene so that it almost looked as bright as noon—and the rain turned into driving pellets of deadly hail.

The panorama was so bloody apocalyptic she found herself shivering. All *this* came from the man who had devastated an entire land while trapped in a vegetative state. She finally began to understand why the Daoine Sidhe King had gained such a deadly reputation, and also why Oberon believed Isabeau would never have dared invade Lyonesse if she'd known he was alive and awake.

She should have internalized that already. Invariably, the most ancient of the nation-builders in the Elder Races were ambitious visionaries with enough Power to hold and protect what they claimed.

Another streak of light sizzled, only this was a different beast from the white-hot lightning. This light was yellow, and it streaked through the air on a horizontal trajectory—toward the motionless man on the stallion.

She recognized it. The bolt was a battle spell called a morningstar.

The Light Fae had located Oberon and Robin, and they had begun to fight back.

As the morningstar streaked toward them, the black stallion reared and trumpeted out a scream of hate and defiance. Sparks flew as his hooves struck the ground. He tore away in a gallop, moving so fast he became a blur. A fraction of a moment later, the morningstar exploded where they had been standing.

More morningstars exploded, thrown from multiple locations. The Arkadians had several proficient magic users. The blast of hail died down, and Oberon's lightning strikes grew more infrequent. He and Robin had to move desperately fast to keep from getting hit.

Now that the advantage of surprise had waned, the battle was getting scarier. Oberon's lighting had already done extensive damage to the camp, but the Arkadian army was massive.

As Robin had pointed out, it was one big damn snake, and they still didn't know where its two heads were.

Now that most of the sizzle and pop had a horizontal trajectory, maybe it was safe enough to fly. She shook out her wings and had started eyeing the clouds overhead when there came a sound like a distant train.

She froze. For crying out loud, now what?

Lyonesse didn't have any trains….

Rapidly the sound grew into a roar. Craning her neck, she tried to locate the source. When she saw the vertical funnel that reached from the black cloud bank in the sky to the ground, recognition slammed into her.

Dear fucking gods. It was a fucking *tornado.* Oberon's attack hadn't slowed in the slightest. It had ratcheted up to the next stage.

Tornadoes could move as fast as three hundred miles an hour, much faster than she could fly. Diving for the cave, she shapeshifted and scrambled to the back and pressed her shoulder blades hard against the uneven stone wall while the world outside turned into a whirling, screaming hell.

Something else scrambled into the small cave. She caught only a glimpse of rain-wet brown fur, but she could identify it by its scent. It was some kind of badger.

In North America, badgers were aggressive. She had no reason to think this one was otherwise, but right now she and the badger had more urgent things to consider than a battle over territory. It made no move to attack, and she left it alone.

Be okay, she said mentally to Oberon, even though she knew he was much too far away to hear her. *Be okay, be okay.*

The roar of the train noise grew so loud her ears popped. A giant *crack* sounded nearby. That sounded like it might have been the oak tree. Then, just as rapidly as it had grown, the noise moved into the distance. It left behind an intense silence like another roar. Her ears popped again as the air pressure changed.

Scrambling out, she changed into the falcon and flew up to the ledge again. Nearby, the oak tree lay torn from its roots, and the Arkadian army... They were the invaders, the enemy, but even so, her gut twisted.

The tornado had touched down in the basin. At least half the encampment had simply vanished, and the rest was flattened. They'd had only tents, after all. They'd literally had no protection and nowhere to hide. Fires still burned in places. Oberon's scorched-earth strategy had been exceedingly effective.

Where were Oberon and Robin? She looked around but didn't see them, and the vertical lightning strikes had stopped.

Gods, she thought as she launched into the air. I hope he didn't get killed by his own weapon of mass destruction.

She couldn't take the time to look for them. She had her own job to do.

This time her risk assessment underwent a radical shift. The Arkadian survivors weren't paying any attention to one small raptor overhead. She glided low, her quick, sharp gaze traveling over the terrain and organizing details of the frantic soldiers below.

It was utter chaos on the ground. Male. Male. Female. Male. Female. Female. Male. I don't know what that one is. Male. Male... The two largest tents had been flattened along with the rest, and a significant number of

the army's horses had panicked or run off altogether….
She saw soldiers deserting in the distance.

She had no idea what Isabeau looked like. She didn't
know who she was looking for. She could have just
passed over the Light Fae Queen and the Arkadian
commander in her head count, and she would never
know it. Any commander worth his salt would never
desert his own troops, but…

These weren't Isabeau's own troops, and now she
knew beyond a doubt that Oberon was awake and alert
and able to fight for Lyonesse just fine.

On a sudden hunch, Kathryn wheeled and flew hard
after the deserters that poured through a light scatter of
trees like fleas abandoning a drowning beast. Yes—up
ahead, there was a party of twelve Light Fae on
horseback. That was too coordinated and intentional for
most of the deserters. People didn't band together like
that when they panicked. They just ran randomly
wherever they could go.

Now that she had expanded her search area, she saw
a great white lion and a tall black stallion standing about
two miles away due west.

Then she comprehended everything as if it had been
laid out as clearly as the map in the council room.

Oberon had been several steps ahead of everybody.
He knew the terrain, and he'd planned it out. The
tornado had come in from the northeast and cut
diagonally southwest across the basin where the army
had camped.

He had known people would run instinctively, and it would be natural for them to run away from the tornado.

He had known Isabeau would make a run for the crossover passageway, and even though he was weaponless, he had decided to make a stand.

Kathryn had been wrong.

That diving stoop to catch the starling, when Bayne and Graydon had recorded her speed, wasn't the fastest she could fly.

THE MORNINGSTAR BOLT, when it hit, had been an act of inspired genius that came right before the tornado hit.

Some archers were like that. They could see not where a target *was*, but where a target *would be* when they fired a shot. It would seem an unknown Arkadian magic user had the same talent.

If Robin had not seen the morningstar out of the corner of his eye and dodged, it would have hit them squarely and killed one or both of them. As it was, the puck caught the edge of the bolt on one haunch and screamed in agony. Somehow, he managed to keep from tumbling end over end. At the speed they were going, that was a miracle all on its own.

But he still stumbled hard enough that Oberon lost his seat and pitched over his shoulder. The lion's reflexes kept him from slamming into the ground—he was pretty certain Kathryn would regard that as a *hard enough blow to the chest*—so even as he flew through the air, he arched his body and shapeshifted fast enough to land on all four of the great cat's feet, which spread out some of the impact.

Luckily, they weren't in the tornado's path, because as he limped over to the stallion, he saw right away that Robin wouldn't be racing anywhere anytime soon. The stallion's hind leg was broken and burned badly. The scent of sizzled flesh hung in the air.

"All right," he said gently. "I've got you." He caught the stallion by the nose and did a quick scan.

There was nothing good about a disaster, but at least the break was a clean one. Ignoring the fading roar as the tornado passed, he cast a few healing spells targeted to the area low in Robin's leg where the break was, and then along the haunch to seal over the raw, burned flesh.

The puck sagged in relief as the worst of his pain lifted, but even though Oberon knew Robin could use more healing, his own tiredness forced him to stop.

Weather working took a lot of strength. He had almost used the last of his magic, and in any case, all the healing spells in the world wouldn't recover Robin's ability to move at great speeds. Only time and rest would do that. They were spent, and they knew it.

And they still had yet to come face-to-face with Isabeau. He supposed it was too much to hope that the tornado had killed her. When Robin could walk, he turned, and they headed together to a natural dip in the land between two hills. As the hilltops were broken and craggy, it was the most logical path to anyone who wanted to travel due west.

If she was going to bolt, it would be right through this grove of trees.

At some point dawn had come. In the aftermath of the storm, the early morning was weak and uncertain. The pallid light made everything look gray and black.

As they waited, Oberon said, "I want you to find Kathryn and make sure she's okay."

"No," Robin replied, peaceably enough. "You know she's okay."

They didn't speak again. It was good to stand beside his friend.

The rhythmic beat of horse hooves drummed the ground. Several riders approached. Here we go, he thought.

Then he saw them, winding through the trees.

Twelve Light Fae on horses slowed as they grew closer. Oberon smelled Isabeau before he located her. They had not come face-to-face in centuries, but he had never forgotten her scent. His hackles rose.

She rode between two guards. Her beautiful face was stark with the knowledge of her own defeat, and it was everything he had needed to see before one of them died. Her expression turned to loathing as she looked at Robin.

"What are you doing here, dog?" she spat. "And why aren't you with your master?"

Robin growled, a steady, nearly inaudible sound that sounded bizarre coming from the stallion.

Oberon watched coldly as the Light Fae began to spread out. Isabeau turned her attention to him. She gave him a pretty smile that didn't quite mask the worried wariness in her eyes. Things weren't adding up for her.

"I had no idea there were any Wyr in Lyonesse, much less one of your stature," she told him. "My disputes are solely with Oberon and his abominations—I have no quarrel with you, sir. All we want is to leave this land, so let us pass and we'll go in peace."

His lips pulled back in a snarl. Telepathically, he growled, *Isabeau, as the gods are my witness, you're not leaving this place alive.*

She blanched. "*You!* How can you be alive after all this time—how can you be full Wyr?" She screamed at the other Light Fae, "This is Oberon, you fools! *Kill him! KILL HIM! KILL THEM BOTH!*"

Looking as stark as their mistress, the Light Fae drew weapons. Some began to mutter spells. He noted each one. Light began to glow between Isabeau's gloved hands as she concentrated on creating a morningstar.

I'm sorry, Kathryn, he thought. I'm not able to avoid physical combat after all.

With that, he unleashed his control, and the lion roared. Years of outrage and hate poured out of him. It shook the ground. Enough of the man remained to raise the last of his own magic as the lion lunged to engage the nearest soldier who rushed him.

With a sweep of one giant paw, he snatched the male off his horse, sank his fangs into his torso, and broke his back. Spitting the dying man to one side, he leaped to the next. Robin reared, kicked, and lunged to fight with teeth and hooves. The black stallion had grown fangs.

Oberon killed the next warrior, and the next. They died quickly, screaming in terror. His vision narrowed to a single focus—he needed to get to Isabeau before she loosed her morningstar. She was still too far away for him to stop.

He had to try anyway.

He crouched, readying for a massive spring, but then the most perfectly shaped, deadly feathered bullet plummeted out of the sky, talons outstretched.

The peregrine falcon did the oddest thing. She tapped the top of Isabeau's head with both talons. He felt a brief, bright spark of her magic, and then she swooped away.

Isabeau's morningstar spell fell apart as her body stiffened. She toppled gracelessly off her horse.

Oberon had no fucking clue what had just happened, but he *loved* it. He *loved* that murderous little falcon. *He loved her.* Letting loose another roar, this time in delight, he and Robin tore through the other Light Fae. A morningstar burned along the side of his neck and shoulder.

It hurt like a son of a bitch, but as he whirled to contend with the magic user who had cast the spell, the falcon tore out of the sky with lightning speed and executed her perplexing maneuver again. The magic user toppled just as Isabeau had.

By the time they had killed the rest of the Light Fae, Oberon was laboring hard. His torso felt like one gigantic bruise. It was hard to breathe without pain, which was localized in the front of his chest. The falcon landed and turned into Kathryn. She looked sharp with worry.

With a massive effort, he shapeshifted back into a man and stood wheezing, one hand flattened on his chest.

She sprang at him, raging. "*I told you not to—*"

"Oh darling, hush," he said tiredly.

Her scolding stopped as abruptly as if he had stuck a cork in her mouth. She threw her arms around him and scanned him. He hugged her—he was covered in blood, but she didn't seem to mind.

"No more fighting," she whispered. "I mean it. You've strained the fresh connections in your bones."

"I know. I can feel it." He looked around. "What you did—did you kill them?"

She had gotten blood on her face, and she wiped it off as she shook her head. "No, I used a medical procedure called a defibrillator spell. It's an electrical current that's meant to restart someone's heart if it stops beating, but their hearts were already beating fine, so their bodies seized up and they lost consciousness. That's going to wear off soon."

Well, in that case. He strode over to the magic user and unceremoniously broke the male's neck. Then he turned to Isabeau, which was when he noticed Robin.

The puck had also shapeshifted back into his most humanlike form. He sat cross-legged on the ground and had put Isabeau's head in his lap. Stroking her golden hair, he contemplated her lovely, still face.

"Robin...," Oberon began, but he stopped when he realized he didn't know what to say.

He wanted nothing more than to keep Isabeau alive, so he could put her on trial in front of everyone that she had wronged in Lyonesse. But she was much too dangerous to keep captive, not while the three of them were either injured or overextended in some way and with Arkadian soldiers sprinkled like poison throughout the area.

He exchanged a troubled glance with Kathryn. Threading her fingers through his, she said quietly in his head, *Maybe he needs this more than you do.*

Maybe, he admitted. It was difficult to let go, but so much easier, he knew, than what Robin must have endured.

They watched as the puck sat with Isabeau until she began to stir.

When her perfect, cornflower blue eyes opened, Robin gave her a smile filled with too many sharp teeth.

"Hello, darling." He showed her a slender, shining silver needle that he held pinched between thumb and forefinger. Oberon felt a flash of the puck's magic. "I have a present for you."

Isabeau's gaze widened. She opened her mouth to scream as her hands flew up. Tired as he had to be,

Robin still struck before she could defend herself. With a king cobra's swiftness, he drove the silver needle through the soft flesh of her temple, deep into her brain.

Kathryn covered her mouth as the Light Fae Queen convulsed. None of them moved or looked away until she finished dying.

Chapter Twenty-One

A S FAR AS Oberon was concerned, the most important part of the battle was finished, but it still wasn't over.

"Corral mounts for yourselves," he said to Kathryn and Robin. "And check their saddlebags—we need whatever provisions they have, and we have to get out of here fast."

Kathryn got straight to work. Robin stirred as well, but as Oberon's gaze lingered on him, he saw the puck take a knife to slice out the dead Queen's tongue. With a violence that spoke of some dark, untold history, Robin flung it aside. Then he cut off Isabeau's golden hair at the nape and stuffed the length into one of his coat pockets.

Oberon might never learn the full story of what had happened to Robin while Isabeau had kept him in captivity, so it wasn't his place to judge. If Robin needed something physical from Isabeau to convince himself she was truly dead, Oberon hoped her hair brought him some peace.

Turning away, he found that Kathryn had already caught two of the horses. The Light Fae horses were experienced battle mounts, and none of them had wandered far. Even though they were uneasy with Oberon's scent, it was relatively easy work to capture several more.

Robin joined them. Rapidly they collected weapons and rummaged through the packs. There was plenty to harvest: knives, small iron cooking pots, dried jerky, pouches of salt, flint and strikers for fire starting, and stores of hard biscuits that were the staple food of many armies on a march. Kathryn called it *hardtack*. Each mount also had a bag of grain for horse feed as well as a cloak and blanket tied in a roll behind the saddles.

"Isabeau and her party were remarkably well prepared," he said. "They must have kept ready in case they needed to desert the Arkadians for any reason."

"Yes, I can see that they did," an unknown male said in a cold, clipped voice.

Fuck. They weren't the only ones who knew how to cloak their presence. He hadn't heard anything, and obviously neither had Kathryn or Robin.

Oberon spun to face the new threat while Robin snarled, and Kathryn shapeshifted and flew to the top of the tallest tree. The part of him that remained constantly aware of her presence took note and passionately approved of her decision. She knew how to use her strengths to everyone's best advantage. It also got her out of arm's reach of the twenty Light Fae cavalry that stood facing Oberon and Robin.

To a person, their expressions were white and drawn. Like Isabeau, they must have come believing they would enjoy a resounding victory.

One Light Fae male's horse stood a few feet yards in front of the others. That, along with a strong aura of Power and an air of command, told Oberon this was the leader of the Arkadian army.

"Whoever you are, you have excellent cloaking skills, I'll give you that," Oberon said grimly. Maybe if they hadn't been so exhausted and focused on their tasks, one of them would have sensed the Light Fae's approach, but he couldn't guarantee it.

"I am Asheroth, Lord of Arkadia," the Light Fae male told him. "And you must be the infamous King of the Daoine Sidhe." His hard gaze glittered like blue diamonds set in stone. He didn't glance at Isabeau's body. "According to the reports received by the Queen's council, you were unconscious and dying."

He spread out his hands. "As you can see, their reports were mistaken. Asheroth, you are trespassing on my land. Have you accepted how drastic a mistake that was, or do you need more evidence?"

Standing relaxed and confident and drenched in Light Fae blood, he threw everything he had into the bluff. He had fresh injuries and the surgery to contend with, and he'd used nearly all his available Power. Robin had driven himself to exhaustion and was too injured to run. Of the three of them, Kathryn was the best off, but she was only one person.

If this came to another battle, it wouldn't go in their favor.

But most people didn't realize weather magic couldn't produce instant results. The majority of weather events had to be built over time. Lyonesse's weather had been disrupted for years and had not yet settled into a more stable pattern. That was one of the reasons why Oberon had been able to create such a massive and powerful storm so quickly—that, along with the fact that many preexisting conditions for spring storms had already been present.

But maybe this foreign lord wouldn't know anything about weather magic either.

"You destroyed more than half my army," Asheroth said in a clipped voice through whitened lips. "Over three thousand souls. Their bodies are scattered everywhere."

"And you sacrificed all of them for a woman who deserted you the first chance she got," Oberon said. "Was the price Arkadia paid worth it?"

"I did not come here for her," Asheroth bit out. His horse danced uneasily, and he hauled it under control. "I came because the Daoine Sidhe are responsible for my brother's death! *He was my only heir.*"

Robin laughed wildly. "Is that the story *she* fed you? You fool, nobody in Lyonesse had anything to do with your brother's death—they don't even know who he was! She manipulated you into going to war! She used you to get what she wanted, just as she used everyone else and everything around her. She probably wept pretty tears over Valentin's body as she spun the story without ever stating a real lie... She kept me in a cage for years, and I watched her do it over and over again."

The puck's voice rang with a truth so sharp and bitter Oberon could almost taste it.

"I never mentioned my brother's name," Asheroth said slowly as he stared at Robin.

"You didn't have to. I was in Avalon. Everyone knew who Valentin was. He tried to rape someone, and she killed him for it." Robin showed his teeth. "And before you try to insist, no, I won't tell you who killed him. Was it the cook in Isabeau's castle, or maybe one of the housemaids? Valentin must have raped so many women. But I'm guessing you already know about that. It's hard to keep a habitual crime like rape hidden for so many centuries."

The Arkadian lord drew back sharply, and for a long, tense moment, Oberon thought he was going to attack.

Digging deep inside, Oberon raised what Power he could so that the Light Fae could feel it amassing like a warning thundercloud. He drawled, "It appears she misled you over just about everything."

"Yes," Asheroth said between his teeth. "It appears she did." He nudged his horse forward, deliberately walking over Isabeau's body, and dismounted. Meeting Oberon's gaze, on the same level as equals, he said, "Just as my dead are scattered all over your countryside, so are the living. Despite the blow you have struck against Arkadia today, I offer a truce, so I can collect my people and take them home."

"*Despite* the blow I struck?" Oberon gave him a hard stare. "Let's be clear about this. You and I will never be anything other than enemies. You invaded my home and slaughtered my people without verified evidence to justify your need for war. I took your three thousand souls as payment for the hundred you took of mine without asking. You have four days to collect what's left of your army and leave Lyonesse. Any Arkadian I find after that will be slaughtered without mercy—and I will be looking for them."

Now hatred blazed from Asheroth's eyes. He said bitterly, "We will be gone by the end of your fourth day. Sooner, if I can manage it. I never want to lay eyes on you or your cursed land again."

THE ARKADIAN LORD mounted and issued a command in a harsh-sounding language, and he and his party rode off.

After watching how Oberon had bluffed his way through that parley, Kathryn's wings felt strengthless and watery. She felt relieved that all she had to do was coast down to the ground and shapeshift.

As soon as she appeared, Oberon said to her and Robin, "Mount up. He may change his mind, and even if he doesn't, it's going to take a while for his commands to spread over the countryside to all his troops. We've got to put distance between us and this place."

Her body ached with exhaustion. All she wanted was to be done, to have a hot bath and good meal, and to go to bed. But if she felt that way, Robin and Oberon must feel ten times worse. Robin couldn't walk without limping, and he moved as if every bone in his slim body hurt. And Oberon had a long raw streak down his neck and shoulder that she hadn't had time to attend to yet.

She would be damned if she complained before either of them did.

Mounting, they rode in an odd zigzag pattern up hillsides. It had to be uncomfortable for their new mounts, but the horses were much better rested than the three of them were and took the challenging terrain steadily.

In the air, her sense of direction was almost as impeccable as her balance and coordination. On the ground and surrounded by trees, and enveloped in a growing haze of exhaustion, she quickly grew lost. But Oberon moved like he knew where he was going, so all she really need to do was stay on her horse and doze if she could.

At dusk he called a halt by a narrow stream of fresh running water, so they could set a fireless camp. By then they all moved as if every bone in their bodies hurt, but the horses needed attending to first. They needed to be fed a measure of the grain and given water and then hobbled so they could graze.

Only then did Kathryn turn her attention to Oberon and Robin. "Which one of you is worse off?"

"Robin," Oberon said.

At the same time, Robin said, "Oberon."

She snorted. "Never mind, I'll check for myself."

As bloody as Oberon was, she was surprised to find that Robin was worse off. He had taken deep tissue damage from a morningstar that impaired muscle and ligaments, and she found the break in his leg that had barely been patched together. Remembering how viciously the stallion had fought, she was surprised he hadn't shattered the leg again.

She started by numbing the pain, and then she poured every kind of healing technique she had into him, repairing ligaments, urging muscle regeneration in strategic places and strengthening the bone, until his body couldn't absorb any more magic. By the time she finished, he had long since fallen into a deep sleep. She tucked a cloak and blanket around him.

Oberon had washed at the stream and sat quietly, watching her work.

"He needs to sleep until he wakes on his own, if we can let him, and then he needs to keep doing that until he's better," she told Oberon as she moved to kneel beside him. She could feel the pain radiating from his body as soon as she laid her hands on him. It made her wince. "The same goes for you, by the way."

"If we can," he agreed. His voice was rough with

exhaustion. He held steady while she worked on him.

As soon as she had completed her work, he pulled her to him, and she settled against his body. After all the stress and fear she had endured, she meant to only soak in the comfort of a hug before she washed and ate something, but the heavy, muscled weight of his arms acted faster than any drug. They fell asleep stretched out on the rocky ground near Robin.

The next morning, Kathryn woke first. She didn't want to, but her neglected bodily needs were making themselves known. Easing away from Oberon's long, lax form, she gnawed on jerky and hardtack until her empty stomach stopped hurting, and then she washed at the stream and took care of other personal functions away from the camp.

Afterward, she shapeshifted to scout around. As soon as she discovered there were no Arkadians in the area, she went hunting. After catching three good-sized rabbits, she hauled them to the camp one by one. Working briskly, she soon had them skinned, cut up, and cooking in their three small pots, along with salt, chickweed, and dandelion that she found growing all around.

While that cooked, she went hunting for herself. The land was rich with wildlife, so she caught enough for a satisfying breakfast easily enough.

The chores gave her plenty of time to think. After the stew was done cooking, she set the pots around the edge of the fire to keep them warm. When Oberon finally stirred and sat, his sharp gaze flew immediately to the fire.

She smiled. "We're safe. I scouted before I started it. There's nobody around for miles. Are you ready for breakfast?"

Relaxing, he told her, "You're a goddamn miracle."

"I know." She accepted his kiss with a murmur of pleasure. As he took one of the pots and inhaled appreciatively, she told him, "The chickweed is good for muscle and joint pain, and the dandelion is good for the blood. Remember that—both you and Robin need it, so I want you to eat lots while I'm gone."

A fierce frown darkened his features. "What do you mean—while you're gone?"

"I've been thinking, and no other option makes sense," she replied. "Robin can't transport us right now, and you and he both need to take things easy. In the meantime, we left everyone back in the city without a word of explanation and panicked about the Arkadian invasion." She paused, remembering Annwyn's severe composure. "Or if not panicked, severely worried."

Oberon ate too as he listened. "You were right the first time. Most of them will be in a panic, just some will hide it better than others."

"You and Robin need to take your time," she pointed out. "But I'm not injured. I've slept well, and I've eaten, and I'm the fastest messenger we've got."

"Put like that, it *is* rather obvious," he said dryly. "I don't suppose I need to ask if you can find your way back to the city."

"If you like asking the kind of questions where you already know the answers, by all means, be my guest." Her eyes laughed at him.

His gaze narrowed. "Your sarcasm can be very sexy, you know. Very irritating, but very sexy."

As they stared intently at each other, heat thrummed through her body.

Robin sat, roused by their voices. His hair stood up in tufts around his thin face. She handed him one of the cookpots by way of greeting, and he gave her a look of surprised gratitude before bolting the contents down, crunching through bones and all.

"So, we're agreed I should go?" she asked Oberon.

"We're agreed." He played with her fingers and switched to telepathy. *I don't like it.*

I don't either.

She hadn't expected him to say anything else, but it was still remarkably difficult to tear herself away. She knew they were in no imminent danger, and now that they'd had some healing and a chance to rest, they could take care of themselves.

No, this difficulty was all about the mating. She put off moving, rubbing the ball of her thumb along his strong, broad palm.

"Be sure to tell them we're directly east of the Tellemaire passageway and headed for the Plajette caravan route. They'll understand what that means."

"Okay."

Suddenly he muttered, "I can't fucking stand this."

"Me neither," she whispered.

Before she lost all ability to move, she shapeshifted and bolted skyward.

She thought it would get easier the more distance she put behind her, but it didn't. With each passing mile, she felt like she was trailing something vital like entrails behind her.

What a bloody thought. It didn't augur well for what she intended to do next.

They had been correct about the state of tightly controlled panic back in the city. Over the short time they had been gone, even more people had poured in. All the troops from Raven's Craig had arrived, and every broken barracks and building was strained to overcapacity.

The members of Oberon's inner counsel were both angry and relieved to see her. Annwyn was incandescently furious and threatened to throw her in jail for her part in facilitating Oberon's crackbrained plan, but her rage quickly shifted to fierce exultation on hearing the news of Isabeau's death.

In short order, Annwyn herself, Rowan, and a party of a hundred and fifty troops rode out to meet Oberon and Robin. Some would provide a safe escort back while the majority would scour the landscape for any sign of a lingering Arkadian presence.

When they departed, Kathryn let herself into Oberon's office, sat at his desk, and wrote a series of letters. She used his own wax and seal to seal them and left one on the clean surface of his desk while she took the rest.

She could neither rest nor settle, and she certainly couldn't face eating anything, so she left directly afterward. Flying hard for the crossover passageway that would lead her back to the old manor house in England, she only stopped once, briefly, when she absolutely had to rest. Then she pushed onward.

The troops stationed at the passageway were overjoyed with her news. Keeping her report concise over a quick cup of hot sweet tea, she told them everything that the public back in the city knew, and then she insisted on crossing over.

With every mile, every decision, every minute, she was leaving pieces of herself behind.

When she emerged from the passageway into a cold, rainy English night, a guard escorted her over to Sophie and Nik's cottage. The guard knocked on the door, and it only took a few moments before it was yanked open by a bare-chested, dangerous-looking Nik while a sleepy Sophie peered around his shoulder.

"Oberon is awake and healed, and Isabeau is dead," Kathryn told them. By then her voice had turned hoarse with exhaustion. She had to pause while they reacted to the news. After they whooped jubilantly and hugged each other, she went on. "They need food badly, and a lot of it. The time slippage is a serious problem right now—we've got to get supplies back over that passageway as quickly as we can." She looked at Nik. "The city has sustained serious damage, and the stores in the granaries are ruined. I don't suppose you know any Djinn who owe you any favors?"

"Not a single one," he said. "We've been buying food as fast as we can afford it."

"Don't worry about money," she told him. "I'm contributing to the cause…."

Her voice trailed away as she looked around. They still stood on the doorstep, and spring flowers decorated the stoop.

Time slippage was the worst kind of jet lag ever.

Of course. It was no longer autumn in England. It was now spring. Months had passed since she had been gone. She had known this would happen from the beginning. She swayed.

"Come inside now, Kathryn," Sophie said encouragingly. "You've clearly been through a lot, and you can barely stand upright."

"I can't!" Kathryn exclaimed. "I've got to get back." She turned to go.

Sophie sprang forward and put her arms around her while Nik said, "No, you don't." His voice was patient. "Dr. Shaw, all the urgency is in Lyonesse. On this side, you've got a lot more time to figure things out…."

"You don't understand!" she shouted, shaking. "I've come too far!"

Their expressions went blank with surprise. Sophie asked cautiously, "Honey, what do you mean?"

Belatedly, she realized how irrational she was acting—she hadn't even finished what she had come so far to do, and she was already trying to get back. Gripping the doorpost, she forced her mind to work.

Deep inside, she knew there would never be another time to reevaluate all the choices she had made over the last week and a half.

She could still choose to go back to New York. Back to the life she knew so well, her friends, her medical practice. But it would be the worst kind of betrayal to Oberon. Her talons came out and she dug into the wood as she fought with her animal side to hold still so she could grapple with herself.

He would hate her forever, and she wouldn't blame him. And they wouldn't get a second chance. Wyr mating was not just based on sex—it was based on timing and personality as well as other life events.

But she had spoken the truth when she had said he was worth her life. The man who had surged out of the spell's influence was strong, caring, clever and honest. He was honorable. No, he wasn't perfect, but neither was she. They had a lot to learn about each other, and maybe their mating hadn't turned to love yet, but there was every hope that it could.

And the glimpse of the future she could have in Lyonesse was alluring as anything else. Mating with Oberon might be intensely personal, but it was also a mission, and she needed a mission in her life. There was so much to do there, so much she could help with.

He was the most complete package she could ever hope to find. And despite how scary everything felt right now, she wanted that future. She truly wanted it. She truly wanted *him*.

Pulling the tatters of her self-control together, she told them as calmly as she could, "I'm mating with Oberon, and I've gone too far away from him. I'm only here to tell you how important it is to get as much food to us as quickly as you can and to give you access to my bank accounts, so you can pay for it." Then she remembered and dug into her shirt to pull out the packet of signed and sealed letters she had brought with her. "These are for people back in New York. Will you deliver them for me?"

"Yes, of course!" Sophie said quickly.

"You still need to step inside for a few more minutes, Kathryn." Nik backed up and held the door open wider. "How do you want us to access your accounts? Do you want to make an online transfer?"

Reluctantly, she stepped inside. "I don't know how much to allocate for this, so I'm going to just give you the account information, and you can draw on it as you need."

Sophie gave her a sober look. "That's a lot of trust in us."

Kathryn managed a twisted smile. "We've been in quite a scramble. In a couple of weeks or so—in Lyonesse—I should be able to come up with some more solid plans, but in the meanwhile, I know you'll make the right decisions."

Pressing a hand to her forearm, he gave her a grave smile. "You've done so much for us. Thank you for all your service, and welcome to the family."

"It hasn't really sunk in," Sophie murmured. She and Nik looked at each other. She told him, "Now that Isabeau's dead, we can finally make that trip to Lyonesse for you, like we always said we would."

"Yes," he said, his voice tight with emotion. "I need to see Oberon for myself, and I would love to see home again."

"That settles it—we're going," Sophie said to Kathryn, "We'll bring the first shipment of food over ourselves, and I'm going to see if we can find a Djinn who will bargain with us for a favor we can live with, so we get it transported to the city quickly."

"That would be simply amazing." Kathryn sighed. A little bit of the tension between her shoulders eased. "I've met many wonderful people in Lyonesse and I know I'm going to love them, but they are all so new to me. It will be really good to have you there, for as long as you want to visit."

Nik and Sophie looked at each other again and laughed. Sophie confessed to Kathryn, "It may not be just for a visit. We've talked about not coming back."

"One step at a time," Nik said. "For now, let me take down your account information." He wrote down what she told him, then asked, "Do you want me to do anything else?"

Belatedly, she remembered from Sophie's stories that Nik was a financial wizard. "Buy a lot of food, and don't skimp. Make sure there's a good, healthy variety for a lot of people, for several months. A spring thaw has begun, but we've got to get through the growing season. Get the first shipment to the city fast, and don't worry about the cost—I expect it to be quite expensive. That should do for now."

"Excellent," he said, fierce satisfaction evident in every line of his body.

His kind of intensity was sexy, Kathryn realized, but she saw it from a long emotional distance, as if admiring a beautiful painting. Then Oberon's lion gaze flashed through her mind. It was followed by a hollow physical ache so bad she almost sank to the floor to curl in a ball.

But she had come this far. She just had to get through the rest of it.

When they had finished, she felt fifty pounds lighter. "I've got to go," she told them again.

"Are you sure you won't stay for a quick shower and a bite to eat?" Sophie asked.

That would be the rational, healthy thing to do, but...

"I'm sorry, I just can't."

"We'll walk you back to the passageway." Nik shrugged into a sweater while Sophie pulled a wrap over her short nightdress.

This was agonizing. Kathryn shifted from foot to foot until they walked out the door, and then she couldn't merely walk anymore. She started running, and they kept pace with her, all the way through the jigsaw puzzle manor house.

When they reached the oubliette, she paused only for a moment. Smiling, Sophie said, "Go—go on! We will see you soon!"

"Goodbye! Hurry!" She bolted down the passageway tunnel and emerged into Lyonesse's pristine air. No exhaust. No electric lights. No fuselage trails or satellites overhead. Thank the gods.

By that point, she was in a frenzy. What to do, what to do? How could she get back to him as quickly as possible? The sun had set once or twice... hadn't it? It had to have set at least once. She remembered dozing in darkness with her eyes slit.

Should she head directly to where she had last left Oberon and Robin and track them from there? Or should she head back to the city first?

She had just completed a marathon, and now she needed to fly another, but she didn't know how to calculate everything she had just done. The long hours and distance soul-searching and tasks and time slippage blurred together into one big, confused heartache.

She had no idea how to estimate where they might be. How far could they travel in the amount of time she had been gone?

Feeling crazed, she flung herself into the air and flew madly toward the city. Exhaustion bore her down. Raging at her own weakness, she found a place to roost and fell into a black pit. Then with a start, her eyes popped open and she launched into another mad flight.

What was he thinking? Had their time apart given him a chance to reconsider too? What if *he changed his mind?* Doubts like acid melted away logic and common sense.

Because it was like meeting a stranger and then being shocked by how quickly you can grow to need someone you barely know and don't know if you can trust.

The only way you could keep reassuring yourself was with constant proximity.

Touching the other person often.

Making love, turning it into a mating frenzy.

Witnessing the truth in their own mating frenzy.

Talking together for hours about how to handle the overwhelming, life-changing experience you were both going through.

The precious newborn cord between her and Oberon felt broken, but it couldn't be, could it?

Finally, the city came into view. Several minutes later, she landed in the courtyard in front of the palace and shapeshifted. The world spun, and her legs buckled.

Exclamations came from nearby. She turned her head toward them, working to focus her eyes, and the world spun again. Well, fuck. That was inconvenient.

Someone bent over her, blocking out the sun. "Oh, dear lady, are you hurt?" A woman's voice.

"I should've showered and eaten," she said. Her tongue felt too thick, and the words kept slurring.

Frustrated, she tried them again. "Should have. Should. Have. Goddammit."

Then strong arms came around her. Picking her up, Owen said, "Welcome back, your grace. I'm so sorry you're feeling poorly." He raised his voice in a shout. "Get his majesty!"

That made her lift her head. "He's here?"

"Yes, your grace," Owen told her as he carried her rapidly up the palace steps. "He and Robin arrived a few hours ago—"

A boiling hurricane exploded out of the palace front doors. Oberon roared, "What did you do?—*Kathryn!*"

She cringed from the noise. Suddenly he loomed right beside them, and with tense, gentle care he took her from Owen.

"You're heavy lifting," she reminded him.

"The. Fuck. I. Am." His quietly spoken words came out with the force of bullets. "We haven't seen each other for a few fucking days—how the *fuck* did you drop so much weight?"

"I should've–sh-should have showered and eaten," she told him. "But I couldn't stop. When I crossed over to Earth, I got too far away from you. There was this crazy animal in my head, clawing to get back. I couldn't stop to eat. I just had to get back as fast as I could."

"You flew all that way—*twice*—without eating? I don't even want to talk to you right now." His growl sounded low and vicious even as he cradled her close and ran up the stairs.

Someone kept pace with him. Owen was still with them. Oberon rattled off orders for food and fresh clothes, and Owen swung away and disappeared.

As Oberon approached the doors to the King's apartment, the waiting guard opened them, Oberon strode inside, and they shut again discreetly. "You *crossed over to Earth* without telling or asking me—"

The world was beginning to stop spinning. "That's not true—I wrote you a letter. I'm so thirsty." Her nose wrinkled. "And gods, I stink."

"You really do," he said. "And you look like shit. You're not making a whole lot of sense either."

In his bathing room, he set her on the fancy carved bench beside the clean towels, and he went to open the flue to let water gush in. Now there were two clean robes on the bench instead of one, she noticed, and soaps that smelled pleasantly like jasmine and lavender had been placed beside the cedar-and-citrus soap.

She struggled to get out of her clothes. Her arms felt like rubber. After a moment he knelt in front of her to help. His face was tight. He was so furious.

Once she had her clothes off, she went to the sink and turned the lever. It wasn't like the sinks she was used to. The lever pulled up a metal slide, and water from an open pipe gushed in.

She stuck her head all the way under it, and the shock of cold helped to clear the last of the dizziness and confusion. Drinking until she couldn't hold any more, she came up gasping for air.

He had kept one hand on her bare hip the whole time, presumably to keep her from collapsing again. When she finished, he was waiting with a towel and wrapped it around her, tucking the ends into her hands so she could hold it herself.

She met the lion's hot golden-black gaze. Paradoxically, she felt better than she had in days. "Spit it out."

He laughed, and that was really a growl too. Then his hard hands clamped on her shoulders, and he hissed, *"You went to Earth without me!"*

"Well, yes…" She blinked and frowned. Maybe she was still more confused than she realized. "And now I'm back again?" Without her conscious volition, her voice trailed upward, turning it into a question. "Could you sense when I was gone?"

If anything, that fanned the flames of his rage higher.

"NO!" he shouted. She could feel each of his fingers separately as they dug into the soft flesh of her upper arms. "I just found out a few hours ago when we returned! We met Annwyn's party, and then Robin and I pushed as hard as we could to get back—I pushed him to transport me the last of the way here, and even though he wasn't ready to, he did. And you weren't even here. You left me a fucking letter and went to fucking Earth, where anything could have happened to you. And if it had, I wouldn't have known. You could have disappeared. And I wouldn't. Have. Known."

Ah. She began to get an inkling of why he was so

angry.

"How long were you there?" he demanded. Possessive jealousy burned hot in his eyes.

Her cold, wet head was starting to make her shiver. Just as she became aware of it, he flung a warming spell at the gigantic bathing tub and gave her a rough nudge toward it. She complied, dropping the towel and letting herself topple in.

Blissful, blissful warmth. The water closed over her head, and then she bobbed to the surface. She told him, "I'm not sure. Maybe I was there a half an hour? They wanted me to slow down, shower, and eat something—they said, and rightly so, that I had all the time in the world on that side of the passageway, but Oberon, a part of me was in this perpetual panic." She waved the fingers of both hands at her head. "I had all these crazy thoughts running through my head—I'd traveled too far away from you, and you were going to change your mind about us, I just knew it."

He stripped off his own clothes with angry movements as he listened, and once he was nude, he grabbed a couple of bowls of the scented soap to set at the side of the tub. Every part of him was beautiful. His masculine frame was long and broad enough that they carried the heavy muscles with what looked like weightless, catlike grace.

Then he dove in and joined her.

"I'm glad it was so hard for you," he said flatly, swiping his wet black hair back from his face.

"Now you're just being mean." Swimming over to him, she cuddled against his torso, and they both groaned as they came skin to skin.

"I feel mean." Hooking an arm around her neck, he glared into her eyes. "Did *you* pause to reconsider?"

"I'm never going to lie to you." She met his gaze steadily. "I did some quick soul-searching. I think that's part of why I felt so panicked afterward." His breath shook out, as if she had physically struck him. As gently as she knew how, she added, "I'm not sorry, and I didn't do it because of anything you did—I did it for my sake. This is the most extreme life decision I've ever faced, and I didn't want to be second-guessing myself later when it would be too late to do anything about it. And as hard as it must be for you to hear, I'm not sorry about telling you now. I want you to know you can rely on me for having made my choice."

She watched as he closed his eyes and absorbed the blow. Then he growled, "You will never, ever do that again. You will never make such a drastic trip without *talking to me first*. You never use a crossover passageway without me. You never go someplace where I don't know where you are, or if you're safe or in danger—or if you're even alive."

Gently she rested her fingers against his mouth.

He stopped, looked at her again, and said with a quiet edge, "You should not look so peaceful when I'm yelling at you."

"You can yell at me all you need," she told him. "I

didn't know the trip was going to hit me that hard. When I started out it was a simple, easy plan—I was going to cross over to tell them we needed large shipments of food as quickly as they could get it to us. I would make sure they had the money to cover it, and then I would be back. It didn't make sense to wait for you when Robin had to recover and so many people were arriving and there was a food shortage happening right now. So this was something I thought I could do for everyone. I didn't make the trip so I could reconsider everything, and I didn't know I was going to panic. All that just happened."

"You're not going to disarm me with your naivete and altruistic motives," he growled. "There's no room for misunderstanding right now. I need you to spell everything out."

The beginnings of a smile trembled at the corners of her lips. "You know how to nurse a grudge, don't you?"

"I really do," said the King of the Daoine Sidhe. "And I know how to keep a war going for years on end. Give me what I want, Kathryn."

Opening her eyes, she gave him a direct look. "Don't ever let yourself doubt me. I am really, truly wholeheartedly here—because I want to be. I will never make a decision like that again without talking things over with you first. I'm never going to use a crossover passageway without you again. I'm never going to disappear so that you have no clue whether I'm safe or in danger or if I'm even alive."

"And you will eat regular meals, gods damn it," he said. "This weight loss is for shit. You will let me keep you safe."

"I will let you keep me safe," she agreed. Twisting so that she came face-to-face with him, she wrapped her legs around his waist and hugged him with her whole body. "And you will let me keep you safe too. You are still my chosen mate, Oberon, and I really missed you."

At that, the last of his anger bled away. Cradling her close, he kissed her.

That was setting a lit match to tinder that had been dry for days. They ate at each other, tongues dueling as they desperately worked to deepen the kiss. He was so damn slippery and hot. Every tight, rock-hard muscle she rubbed against made her hunger spiral higher. She sucked at his earlobe, his neck, while his hard hands roamed everywhere.

It wasn't comfortable. Maybe someday they would achieve the easy, comfortable kind of lovemaking that could happen on a lazy winter afternoon, but right now they were far from that. This was too elemental.

He lifted her to the water's edge and pushed her back, so he could come between her legs to lick and explore every part of her. He knew just what to do with that clitoris of hers, and it was so extremely pleasurable she nearly leaped out of her skin with every jolt.

She wanted to relax, but she was too wound up and couldn't take it. Pushing him away, she slid underwater and down to caress and lick his cock, one hand braced against his thigh.

Grasping her by the hair, he pumped into her mouth, short, shallow jabs that indicated his own urgency, but it wasn't a position either of them could hold for long. After a moment he pulled out and urged her to the surface.

"No," he said. "Not like that, not this time."

"Then how?" she asked, stroking his cheek.

"Face-to-face," he whispered. "I want to look into your eyes when I come."

"I want that too."

In response, he picked her up in his arms and used the steps to walk out of the bathing tub. He carried her so easily, this time she didn't even bother to bitch at him about the heavy lifting.

When he reached the great bed, he let her legs slide to the floor as he yanked back the bedcovers and tumbled down with her, and their urgency shifted into coupling. Using two fingers, he eased into her passage, stroking out the evidence of her arousal and preparing her for him.

She twisted under his attentions, burning up as if she had a fever. She loved it when he worked her. With little nips along his bicep and pectoral, she took his erection in her hand and pumped it.

She wasn't the only one who felt feverish. Heat poured off his tight body. He pushed his hips to the rhythm she made with her head, until finally, with a muttered curse, he pulled away and spread her legs wide to enter her. From that point on, they shot even further out of control. The animal that lived in her, the one that had panicked so badly when she had gotten too far away from him, clawed and cried out to him.

And his animal answered, pinning her down, thrusting harder and deeper until he pistoned with such a relentless, driving force that when she climaxed, it shot through her with the force of a bullet. More climaxes came, each one higher than the one before, until they were almost unendurable.

The extreme ecstasy would have been a terrible, lonely thing to experience on her own, but he was right there with her—his back arching with each spurting gush. She adored watching him lose control. They pushed each other on until they simply couldn't go any further, coconspirators to the end.

Afterward, they lay entwined. The sheets were damp. She thought about suggesting they move into the Queen's bedroom, where the bed would be dry. A giant yawn cracked her jaw. Maybe she would in a little bit.

Oberon shifted to rest his head on her shoulder. With an exhausted sigh, he pressed his lips to her shoulder and muttered, "God, I'm finally home."

He'd already been back at the palace all day.

Warmth spread through her as she realized he meant her. Then she realized something else. Even at his angriest, even when she had hurt him the most, he had taken such great care with her. Holding her, paying attention to every detail, seeing to her needs. He knew exactly how strong he was and how to rein that in and control it when it mattered.

They wouldn't always get it right. They had each made some pretty big mistakes already, but that was the moment she knew everything was going to work out beyond anything she could have hoped for.

He had a heart as big as it was wide, her lion. As big as Lyonesse. No wonder his people adored him.

No wonder she did.

She would always remember this exact moment, when she lay warm and easy and close to sleep as she fell in love weightlessly with her mate.

Epilogue

Three months later.

THE LION LOUNGED in the sun at the top of the cliff, soaking in the afternoon warmth as he looked out over his city. The rebuilding was going very well. They still had a lot of work to do before winter came again, but he was confident now that they would manage to finish the most urgent repairs before the first frost.

Most importantly, they had a plentiful supply of food until they could generate enough on their own. After he had cast daily spells to make adjustments to the weather where they were needed, conditions had stabilized, and healthy crops grew in the farmers' fields throughout Lyonesse.

For almost everybody in his demesne, the worst of the crisis was over.

He was very aware of the woman who climbed the path toward him. Anticipation thrummed through his body, light and golden like salveri wine.

As Kathryn grew near, she said with a smile, "You look comfortable."

I am. He blinked at her lazily. *How was your session?*

She assumed her doctorly give-nothing-away expression. "It was fine." He growled so softly it was nearly inaudible, and she tapped him on the nose. "Stop that. No matter how many times you ask, I'm not going to talk about it."

Suppressing a sigh, he replied, *I do understand, but all I ever want to know is if I should be concerned about him and do something to help.*

Amber eyes narrowed as she looked out over the water, she paused a little too long for his liking. Then she told him carefully, "It's only been a few months, but I don't think so. I will tell you this much—Robin's no longer giving me the silent treatment. He has started talking, and even though it's difficult for him, that's a very good sign. He's trusting me, and he's no longer keeping everything bottled up inside—he's letting the poison out."

He relaxed again. *I'm glad to hear it. Thank you.*

"You're welcome." She threw herself down beside him and burrowed into his mane. "Mmm, you're all yummy and warm. Why did you want to meet up here?"

The temptation was too much to resist, and as he shapeshifted, he slipped his arms around her. "Because you and I never get enough time to ourselves. I had the kitchen pack a picnic. It's waiting in the shade behind us."

"What a thoughtful idea—thank you," she said. "I'm famished."

"So am I." He kissed her swiftly and then stood to

pull her to her feet. "Come on."

As he led her to the picnic, he watched her face light with pleasure as she took in the charming scene. He had spread out a large blanket, and a basket full of food waited for them along with a bottle of wine that rested in a bucket filled with ice from the palace's underground store.

Settling on the blanket, they unpacked hard-boiled eggs, ribs cooked in a delicious sweet and smoky tomato sauce—*barbecue sauce*, she called it—and roast chicken, slices of cheese, olives, and a small jar of caviar from Earth, with packets of salt bread.

"This is quite a feast," she said, surveying the bounty.

"We deserve it." He reached for the bottle of wine to open it. "We haven't yet had a chance to take that camping trip we talked about, but this is the next best thing."

"It's beautiful." Her eyes widened as she looked at the wine he poured into goblets. "And we get to enjoy some salveri? I thought you only had five bottles left."

"I did. After this, there will be four." Smiling, he handed her one of the goblets.

She smiled as she accepted it. "Is there a special occasion I don't know about? Are we celebrating something?"

He certainly hoped so. He told her, "I don't think we should wait for special occasions to celebrate. Being alive is something to celebrate. I don't ever want to forget how close I came to losing everything, or how grateful I am to have regained all of it—along with so much more."

Her smile widened, and she clinked his goblet gently with hers. "Hear, hear."

She let him serve her a plate of food, and she waited until he had served himself. Then they talked over various things as they ate.

Sophie and Nikolas were settling into their new home very well, close to the palace, and she and Kathryn were enjoying working together on running a free clinic for people who were relocating back to the city. After a few more months, Kathryn planned on handing the clinic over to other healers, and she would turn her attention to something new.

Annwyn was absent from court a great deal as she assembled the scattered troops and reassigned them to repairing Lyonesse's infrastructure of roads and passageway stations.

Oberon and Nikolas had the task of rebuilding the crown's finances, and they took the influx of capital from Kathryn's assets to use in a variety of investments. Even though she told him repeatedly that she didn't care, Oberon was determined to not only replenish Lyonesse's resources but to pay her back every penny she had given them.

Rowan had left with a small party to join an expedition from the States to locate Isabeau's lost library and work to stabilize the Light Fae demesne, and Gawain and Brielle were deepening a relationship that had been put on hold for far too long.

Things weren't always easy. Sometimes Kathryn disappeared for hours to take long solitary flights, once she had received her first packet of letters and packages from New York. She always told Oberon when and where she was going. As she never chose to go very far, he couldn't object, but he never quite relaxed until she was home again.

It wasn't that he didn't trust her or believe she would be safe. Lyonesse's borders were secure again, and he did trust her. Plus he knew the falcon could look after for herself very well. But he also knew she was using the solitary time to deal with the loss of everything and everyone she had loved and left behind.

"It's not that I don't love everything here," she tried to explain one night after she had returned. "I do, very much."

"Kathryn, it's all right," he told her gently. "You lived in New York for a long time, and you were settled and happy there. Even if we do visit someday, it won't ever be the same. You get to mourn giving up your old life."

Besides, he could afford to be understanding and magnanimous, because he had won. He got to keep his mate. But he would still be glad when she stopped needing to take those flights.

Now, as they finished their meal and set the plates aside, he reached into the picnic basket and pulled out a box.

He told her, "I have something for you."

"You do?" Looking pleased, she eyed the box curiously. "What is it?"

Opening the lid, he reached inside and pulled out an agate-and-diamond ring. Holding it out for her inspection, he said, "Here's the most important piece. I had it made especially for you. While I know agate isn't usually paired with diamonds, I thought you might enjoy this piece with these diamonds. It's part of the slab from the crystal cave, and the diamonds are from the ones you used when you operated on me. The ring itself is made of white gold. As soon as my favorite artisan returned to the city, I commissioned him to make it."

As he talked, her gaze widened, and she looked deeply touched. "Oberon, it's stunning."

He rolled out of his sitting position and knelt on one knee in front of her. Taking her hand, he said, "Because we rushed into everything else, I wanted to wait and take my time with this. I didn't want us to be overshadowed with a sense of emergency, and I wanted you to have a chance to feel more comfortable with being here—"

"I do feel comfortable! Remarkably so after such a short time." Catching herself up, she gave him a sheepish smile. "I'm sorry, I interrupted you."

He kissed her fingers. "It's all right. I'm glad you feel so comfortable with being here. I want you to know that you are the most amazing person I've ever met. And you are not just my beautiful, strong, capable mate. You've already become my best friend. And I fell head over heels in love with you months ago."

"You never said," she whispered.

He cocked an eyebrow at her. "You never asked. It was one of those things I wanted to tell you after we'd had a little time to lend some weight to our relationship. I didn't want you to think it was infatuation with our mating."

Leaning forward, she laid a hand to his cheek. "I fell in love with you too, the night I got back from crossing over to Earth. You were so angry with me, yet you were still so careful in almost everything you did."

"Almost?" At that, he put both eyebrows up even as he warmed with pleasure and relief at her words.

She laughed. "Well, we weren't very careful when we made love that night—or the next morning either."

"All right, I'll give you that." He grinned. "I fell in love with you before then, and I'll never forget it. It was when I watched that little falcon hurtle out of the air and tap Isabeau on the head. I had no idea what you were doing, but you were so deadly and fearless, and fast, and perfect. You were perfect, and I wanted to laugh out loud from joy except I had too many assholes to kill. Dr. Kathryn Shaw, you brought me back to life. You make me laugh. You make me crazy, and you have my back, even when I don't know that I need it. I love staying up too late talking with you. I love making love to you. I love having you as my partner and my mate. Will you do me the utmost honor of marrying me?"

She was nodding before he could finish the question.

Tears spilled over as she laughed. "Henceforth, you can always remember that I answered your question with *oh hell yeah.*"

"Henceforth, I shall." He laughed too while he slipped the ring on her finger. And then he had to take a few moments to kiss her deeply while she nestled against him and wound her arms around his neck. Holding her close, he told her, "I have other things for you. Would you like to see them?"

"I would love to."

Positioning the box close beside them, he opened the lid again and pulled out more jewelry—a diamond bracelet, and a necklace of diamonds with a gold pendant of a lion's head with diamond eyes. "The three pieces are made with the fifty-eight magic-quality diamonds from the surgery. Granted, the necklace is probably too grand for everyday wear, but I'm hoping the bracelet isn't." He paused. "I know you don't usually wear jewelry, but you could—and you could use the stones in the ring and the bracelet for healing spells, so that you could have them on hand for emergencies."

She took a slow, deep breath, her expression filling with wonder as she pored over the pieces. "What a brilliant idea. I could, and I will. Oberon, these are simply gorgeous."

"I'm so glad you like them." He kissed her forehead.

"Like them—I love them! Thank you so much. I've never been given such thoughtful and beautiful gifts before."

"Get used to it, because I've got a promise to live up to," he told her. "I told you that if you saved my life, I would lay the world at your feet. Now I've put my life in your hands twice, and I've not once regretted either decision."

She turned her shining gaze up to his. She told him fiercely, "I'll never give you cause to."

Everything that made her Kathryn was there in her eyes—her steadiness, intelligence, and determination. Everything that he loved.

"I know you won't," he said with complete certainty. "And I never will."

They were too busy kissing to notice when a small monkey slipped onto the picnic blanket to steal the caviar, the packet of salt bread, and what remained of the bottle of salveri. He climbed the nearby tree and enjoyed his loot while looking out over the sparkling water.

He probably shouldn't have eavesdropped, but he had never been any good at doing the things he probably should do.

It was a good day to be alive. As Oberon had said, that was something to celebrate.

It was good to be free. Good to be home.

Thank you!

Dear Readers,

Thank you for reading *Lionheart*, book three of my NYT bestselling Moonshadow trilogy. I truly loved Kathryn and Oberon's story, and I hope you did too. And Robin, the puck, ended up being one of my very favorite characters of all time.

Would you like to stay in touch and hear about new releases? You can:

- Sign up for my monthly email at:
  www.theaharrison.com
- Follow me on Twitter at @TheaHarrison
- Like my Facebook page at
  facebook.com/TheaHarrison

Reviews help other readers find the books they like to read. I appreciate each and every review, whether positive or negative.

Happy reading!
~Thea

Look for these titles from Thea Harrison

Peanut Goes to School
Dragos Goes to Washington
Pia Does Hollywood
Liam Takes Manhattan
The Chosen
Planet Dragos

ELDER RACES SERIES COLLECTIONS

Divine Tarot
Destiny's Tarot
The Elder Races Tarot Collection: All 4 Stories
A Dragon's Family Album
A Dragon's Family Album II
A Dragon's Family Album: Final Collection
The Elder Races: Complete Novella Bundle 2013-2018

GAME OF SHADOWS SERIES

Published by Berkley

Rising Darkness
Falling Light

ROMANCES UNDER THE NAME
AMANDA CARPENTER

E-published by Samhain Publishing
(original publication by Harlequin Mills & Boon)
*These stories are currently out of print

A Deeper Dimension
The Wall

CPSIA information can be obtained
at www.ICGtesting.com
Printed in the USA
LVHW051303270519
619132LV00024BA/1891/P